Passing THROUGH

I0587557

WALK ON
By

SARAH HEGGER

To Debbie and Emily,
because it's about damn time I dedicated a book to you girls.
For all the love and all the family feels, this one's for you.

Acknowledgments

This book stumbled into publication as we were moving out of our house in Colorado, USA, and making the trip back to our new house in Ottawa, Canada.

There were times—I tell you—*times* when this looked like it wasn't happening. But here the book is and here she stands, and I love her.

And she stands thanks, as always, to Penny Barber.

And also thanks to my bestie, Chris Kennedy. Nobody gets my weird quite like your weird does.

Format and cover design by: Deranged Doctor Design
First Electronic Edition: June 2019
ISBN-13: 978-1-7329331-7-0
ISBN: 978-1-7329331-8-7

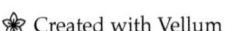 Created with Vellum

CHAPTER
One

SOME THINGS NEVER CHANGE. Unfortunately, the Bugling Elk in Twin Elks, Colorado, was one of them. Gabe had traveled as far as his passport could take him, lived away from Twin Elks for over fifteen years, and he could say, with certainty, that it remained one of the ugliest bars he'd even been in.

"Gabe Crowe. And still pretty." Maddison Watts, the Elk's owner and barkeeper, leaned her elbows on the counter. "Beer?"

"Whatever's cold and on tap." The beer there was always good and cold.

A white spangled Elvis suit with yellow armpit stains still watched over the bar. Elvis bobbleheads, allegedly the largest collection in the state, were right where they'd been when he last saw them, stacked up next to the singing carp, which he'd lay money still did an eerie version of *Take Me to the River*. A couple more pairs of panties might decorate the elk head hanging over the women's bathroom, but Gabe didn't want to get any closer to check it out.

The characters in the bar hadn't changed any either.

Ronnie Falkirk, well into her eighties and still working dispatch for Gabe's brother Ben, sidled up next to him. "Well, well, well." She waggled her shocking copper-colored head and eyed him with a sharp brown gaze nearly buried beneath layers of blue goo. "Look who's back in town."

"Hey, Ronnie." Gabe expected no less. He'd gotten out of Twin Elks for college and came back as rarely as he could get away with. "You look good."

"No, I don't. I'm older than dirt." Ronnie cackled and winked at him. "Your mom sure must be glad to have you back."

Guilt double-tapped him, and Gabe hid his wince behind a sip of beer. "Yup."

"She missed you." Ronnie layered more guilt on. "Missed all her boys, really. Other than Ben. Of course, he didn't go anywhere." She whistled and wheezed out a laugh. "Got himself a nice little family now, Ben has."

"Yup." Gabe had returned for Ben's wedding a few weeks back. At the time, he had every intention of getting back to Australia as soon as he could. Funny how life laughed when you were making plans.

Ronnie motioned Maddison over and placed her order for a pitcher of margaritas. "Girls and I still have our regular book club meeting."

Gabe followed her gaze to the far corner.

The group of seven or so octogenarians waved and hollered at him.

Maddison motioned his empty glass. "Get you another one, Gabe?"

"Sure." He had nothing else to do. Ma had bustled off to one of her meetings and Ben was tucked up with Poppy and her kids.

He liked Poppy, and after Ben's disastrous first marriage to Tara, Gabe was happy for him. Ben loved Twin Elks and had come back from his tours of duty and settled into being police chief.

Gabe didn't feel the same. Not even a little bit. Of course, Ben got on his high horse about being the only brother doing his part by Ma. Yeah, Gabe felt like shit about that. Not shit enough, however, to stick around.

The only reason he was still there was that, at this precise moment, his options were somewhat curtailed.

"Whelp!" Ronnie gathered up her pitcher. "See you around, Gabe." She stopped and waggled her painted-on eyebrows. "While you're in town, you should drop in on that nice young lady veterinarian we got now."

"Will do." He tapped the bar to get Maddison's attention. "Wanna add a Jack shooter to that beer?" He got the feeling he was going to need it.

"You got it, handsome." Maddison grinned at him.

Maddison had served him his first legal drink with a grin like that one. Like her father before her, Maddison was a Twin Elks fixture. He bet the local teens still tried to convince her they were twenty-one and fool her with their fake IDs.

Good luck with that in a town like Twin Elks where Maddison had probably attended their baptisms.

A few people he didn't recognize were playing darts in the far corner. Not that he was likely to know everyone anymore, but Ben had been having trouble with locals and newcomers recently. After an incident with Finn Williams a while back, things had died down.

"They okay?" He asked Maddison as she pulled a draft.

Maddison glanced at the group. "Oh, yeah. Mostly that lot are looking for some action." She waggled her eyebrows. "If you know what I mean."

"In Twin Elks?" The singles scene was deader than three-day-old roadkill. It wasn't even nine p.m., and the Elk was the only place open.

Maddison shook her head. "Go figure! They keep talking about this thing on that Facebook and stuff."

It was an indication of his level of boredom that he asked, "What thing?"

"Well, would you look what the cat dragged in?" Hank Styles

clapped him on the shoulder. "Gabe Crowe, right back here in Twin Elks."

"Hey, Hank." Gabe shook Hank's hand. It looked like Hank had shrunk.

"Woo hee!" Hank shook his grizzled head. "Dot must be tickled pink to you have you back."

"Yup." He wasn't staying in Twin Elks, but he didn't feel like that conversation was one he wanted to have. People in Twin Elks didn't get why anyone would want to live anywhere else.

Hank cackled and nudged him. "You clapped eyes on that pretty new lady veterinarian we got here?" He nudged Gabe again. "Wanna find yourself a sick creature and make her acquaintance. If you know what I mean?"

Gabe very much did know what Hank meant and reached for his Jack shooter. It burned the back of his throat and hit his stomach like an anvil.

Damn! He'd forgotten how rough that first one was.

Hank leaned in on a waft of cherry pipe tobacco and jerked his head at the dart players. "Wanna get your feet under the table before that lot do. Competition for the fillies is getting mighty stiff hereabouts." Hank cackled and nudged him. "Mighty stiff. Get it."

Gabe managed a wan smile.

"Well, well, well. Look who's back in town." A curvy blonde with big blue eyes took Hank's place beside him. Her mouth, almost too big for her face, broadened into a smile that promised naughty things. "And drinking already."

And, hello to you too. It took Gabe a moment to place her, and then he grinned. "Well, well, well, if it isn't Kelly Ashford." He let his gaze deliberately linger from her booted feet, over the tight fit of her jeans, up to the way she filled her flannel shirt very nicely and back to her pretty face. "And looking as tasty as ever."

"Shuddup, Gabe." Kelly nudged his shoulder. "You had trouble even remembering my name."

Busted, and he didn't even try to fake it. "It's been a long time, and we only shared a couple of classes together."

"We shared every class, Gabriel Crowe. Every single one." She raised a brow at him. "I even sat next to you for most of those."

The ball busting, Gabe remembered, and a whole lot more about Kelly. "As I recall, you only cared about Vince Greerly back then, so how would you even know if I sat next to you?"

"You were hot." Kelly shrugged and then chuckled. "Shame how you've let yourself go."

He might have taken offense if the look in her eyes hadn't said an entirely different thing. A tingle of awareness tiptoed up his spine.

An answering spark lit her blue eyes.

Kelly had always made him laugh back in school, and the way he had always noticed her sexy curves was all coming back to him. Unlike a lot of stick-insect women, Kelly was built to be explored and savored. She looked soft and silky in all the right places.

Kelly cocked her head, sending a fall of blond curls tumbling down her arm. Even her hair looked ready for a man's hands to get tangled in it. Kelly Ashford screamed forties sex siren and damned if Gabe didn't like it.

"Are you ogling me?" She raised a brow.

"Yeah." Gabe didn't bother to hide it. "Vince was a lucky guy."

Her smile faded. "Pity Vince didn't think so."

"I sense a story." Gabe didn't want to be alone anymore, so he patted the barstool next to him. Time with Kelly Ashford was just what he needed. "Tell doctor Gabe all about it."

"You're a veterinarian." Kelly perched her sweetly rounded ass on the barstool anyway and motioned Maddison. "I'll have what he's having, and he's buying." Her smile was pure evil. "Speaking of veterinarians."

"Yeah, I've heard." He gave her a hard stare. "Apparently she and I should get acquainted."

"You totally should." Kelly kept her face straight, but her blue eyes laughed at him. "Then the two of you can make sweet, animal love to each other."

More good memories bloomed, specifically how much he'd liked sharing a desk with Kelly. "There's nothing sweet about animal love, Kelly." Sexual awareness entered the two feet separating them and swirled with possibilities. Not that either of them had to act on those possibilities, but a little hot flirting might make the walk to the Elk worthwhile. "Animal love is dirty, hard, and nasty."

"I hear it's also quick." Kelly pulled a face. "Kind of over before it's worth it."

Holding her gaze, he shook his head slowly. "Nah, that's only because you haven't been doing it with the right animals."

"Gabe Crowe." Kelly fanned herself with her hand. "Look at you, turning the heat up on a girl."

"Is it working?"

She wrinkled her nose at him. "I'll let you know."

Gabe picked up his new shot of Jack. "In the meantime, why don't we drink?"

"That's a great idea." Kelly downed her shooter without a flinch. "I actually came in here for a burger, but this is a way better idea."

"A burger?" Gabe barely suppressed his shudder. "From here?"

"Times have changed." Kelly gave him a serious face. "Maddison hired a new cook a couple of years back. We don't know much about him, but he makes one helluva burger."

Ma had made him dinner, but Gabe always seemed to have room for something else. Fortunately, he had the metabolism to allow for that. "Wanna have dinner with me?"

"Are you planning to put out?" Kelly giggled.

Gabe couldn't resist smiling. "I'll let you know."

Kelly ordered their burgers before turning back to him. "You know what? Why don't we get our burgers to go and take a drive?"

"Lookout Point?" Some things you never forgot no matter how long you'd been away.

Kelly grinned. "You got it."

Despite the flirting, being with Kelly was comfortable and Gabe nodded. They waited for their burgers and then took them to Kelly's SUV.

It took about ten minutes to get to Lookout Point, plus another five for the quick stop they made for a six-pack of beer along the way.

Lookout Point was not much more than a path beside the main road leading out of Twin Elks. Over time, cars stopping there had made a small parking place.

In the daylight, it was the perfect place to see the rows of orange boulders rising out of the brush and sharing the same diagonal.

At night, it was a great place to stargaze as coyotes chuckled and bitched at each other.

Gabe waited until they were comfortable. "So, no Vince and Kelly and tiny little Vinces and Kellys."

"Nope." Her face grew serious and she stared out the windshield. "Vince and I managed to screw that up after our senior year."

"No." At Twin Elks High, Vince and Kelly had been the couple who would make it, the high school sweethearts who would beat the odds and stay together forever.

Kelly took a big bite of her burger and chewed and swallowed before she answered, "We got into some stupid fight. Actually, on prom night. I had my panties in a wad and wouldn't let Vince make it up to me." She waved a hand. "One thing led to another; three weeks later Vince hooks up with Chelsea Finster."

"Was she the one with the braces and the huge rack?"

"Yup." Kelly took another bite of her burger. "She still has the huge rack, by the way. The braces are gone, however. She also had Vince until earlier this year."

Gabe found it hard to believe. "Vince chose Chelsea over you?"

He took a bite of his burger. Kelly was right. Whoever was in Maddison's kitchen knew their way around some beef and a bun.

Kelly opened a beer bottle and handed it to him. "It got more complicated than that. Turns out Vince's one night with Chelsea had some serious repercussions. Vince, being Vince, did the right thing and married her."

"Huh." Gabe sipped his beer. He'd been too busy trying to get his ass into vet school when it had all gone down to pay it much mind. Still, going from Kelly Ashford to Chelsea Finster was a seriously boneheaded move. As he remembered it, Chelsea had been a nice enough looking girl, but with an annoying way of whining everything she said. "You said Chelsea had Vince until earlier this year?"

"They're divorced." Kelly said, and there was no missing the smug satisfaction in her voice.

A tiny pang of disappointment surprised him. "You and Vince are back together?"

"No." Kelly shook her head. "But I've spent enough of my life waiting for him."

"You made your move yet?" Gabe didn't want her to say yes.

Kelly chuckled. "I've made it clear that I'm amenable to a move," she said. "But he has to do some of the work."

"And in the meantime, you're sitting under the stars drinking beer and eating burgers with me?"

He could hear her naughty smile in her voice. "In the meantime, I am sitting under the stars, drinking beer and eating burgers with Gabe Crowe. The hottest boy in our senior year." She fist pumped. "Kelly scores!"

CHAPTER
Two

KELLY CRACKED an eye open and blinked the room into focus. Nope, that couldn't be right. She definitely didn't have a poster of vintage cars on her wall. Also, her walls were a soothing taupe that she'd spent hours picking out, and not steel blue.

Nor did she sleep in a twin bed with a man spooning her. And a man who was most definitely naked.

Maybe if she shut her eyes again the scene would right itself. Also, take the roiling stomach, parched mouth, and thumping head with it.

"Umm…" The arm around her waist tightened, and Gabe said, "So, that happened."

"Uh-huh." Words weren't happening yet.

His erection pressed against her butt but moving away from it seemed pointless. Firstly, because a twin bed didn't allow her anywhere to go, and secondly—and probably more relevantly—she'd already made friends with that part of Gabe.

More than once, if her hazy, night-before recollections were to be trusted.

"Why here?" They had not only ended up doing the dirty but had snuck into Gabe's childhood bedroom. She had vague recol-

lection of lots of giggling and shushing. Discarding of clothes
had followed, again much giggling and shushing, and then the
up close and personal part.

And, wow! She needed to take some time and dwell on those
memories, because along with his still-killer body, Gabe Crowe
had skills, of the multiple sort.

Gabe wriggled to his back. "It was the closest place."

"Okay." Which meant she was currently in Dot Crowe's
house, and she would be doing the walk of shame through Dot
Crowe's house.

Dot Crowe, mother of Gabe of the wicked skills, and also
mother of police chief, Ben Crowe. In addition, community
pillar, all round great lady, and president of the Twin Elks Prayer
Chain.

Kelly couldn't put it off any longer and wriggled around to
her other side and faced him.

Gabe's grin was unadulterated wicked, and his voice a
rough, slightly thrilling rasp as he said, "Do we need to talk
about this?"

"I really would rather not." Sweet tortoise tits, she couldn't
say how much she didn't want a rehash. But she was beginning
to get an inkling of how she'd ended up there. "Let's chalk it up
to the Jack Daniels."

"Works for me." Gabe rubbed his palms over his face. His short
dark hair stood up like someone—*ahem*—had been digging her
fingers in it. Dark morning stubble covered the sharp line of his jaw
in a perfect nature-made contour that highlighted killer cheekbones.

Don't get her started on the body, because no girl was
prepared for that. You saw this sort of pretty in magazines, sat in
darkened movie theaters and watched it flit across the screen,
binge watched Netflix in the hope of more, but you knew it
wasn't real. Men who looked like that came courtesy of phot-
oshop, body contouring, and excellent lighting.

And then Gabe Crowe kissed you at Lookout Point, you let

events take their course and your theory evaporated. Perfect was real and lay in bed next to you with a sheet artfully draped low over his hips.

It was such a pity she had nobody to high-five right then. She'd tapped that, and Kelly felt sure in the annals of girls who scored above their league, this had to rate a perfect ten.

There was also the not insignificant matter of getting out of Dot's house without anyone—specifically Dot and Ben—being any wiser.

Gabe turned and looked at her, a smile teasing his mouth. "Kelly Ashford, can I say that was a great night?"

"You may." An answering smile met his, because it had been a better than great night. "And then we will agree never to speak of it again."

"But I can think of it, right?" He tangled a hand in the hair at her nape and brought her in for a kiss. "Last night filled up the spank bank for a while."

"Ugh." She only pretended to push him away, but men who made you laugh got you every time. You laughed and laughed and then you were naked, begging God for the O and demanding they give it to you harder. "You're a pig."

"Last night was fun, Kelly." He pressed his beautiful mouth to hers. Flashes of hotter, needier kisses followed the lip to lip connection. Kisses that made her senses blaze and erased good sense.

Kelly pulled out of the kiss before she lost all hope of escaping before Dot woke up. "It was, but you're not going to get weird on me about it are you?"

"Weird?"

"You know." She edged away from him and pulled the sheet with her. "Begging me to have your babies. Locking yourself up in a monastery because you know you'll never have it that good again."

Gabe chuckled and sat up, making no effort to hide his

nakedness, exposed as he was by her hogging the bedding. "I can't make you any promises."

"Try." She unearthed her panties and spotted her jeans nearby. She shoved her panties into the back pocket. Keeping the sheet in place—because no way was she letting perfect Gabe clock the jiggly bits in daylight—she wriggled into her jeans. "I'm not even sure how I ended up here."

"Well." Gabe stood and stretched. A ridiculously beautiful snapshot of muscle, sinew, tanned skin and male lickability.

And she stood there with her bra in her hand with no idea what to do with it.

"It started with you saying how long it had been since you'd had sex." He dug up her shirt and handed it to her. "And then I confessed to a distressing dry spell as well."

Kelly got her bra on and pulled her shirt over her head. "You and the girlfriend not getting along, right?"

"Ex." He pulled his jeans on and fastened them. "She dumped my ass."

What a pity to cover all that. "You deserved it."

"You said that last night as well." He pulled a face at her. "I don't think you appreciated the finer points of our breakup."

"Nope." Kelly hauled her socks on. Before she and Gabe had got to the more fun part, they'd spent a lot of the night talking and getting to know each other. "She wants more; you don't. She said fish or cut bait. You didn't fish. She cut bait."

He flinched but disappeared inside his shirt as he pulled it over his head. "I'm sure there was more to it than that."

"Your career." Kelly pulled on her boots. Even now, and after last night, she was surprisingly comfortable with him. "You work for her father, and he's not very happy with you right now."

"Yeah, there is that." Gabe looked suddenly vulnerable.

It was him looking like that, like his world had come crashing down on him, that had led to the cuddling, the confessions about dry periods, the kissing, and then the stuff she didn't have time to dwell on, but planned to replay in detail later. "Right." She stood and faced him. "Time to get me out of here. Secretly."

Gabe snuck to the door and cracked it open. He peered into the dark hallway. "All clear. I'm sure Ma is still sleeping."

And how old were they exactly? "She better be."

Kelly crept down the hall behind him, wincing at every tiny noise they made, holding her breath.

They reached the kitchen door and Gabe opened it a crack and peeped inside. He motioned her forward with a smug smile. "All clear."

Yes! Kelly did a mental fist pump and slid into the kitchen. She'd been there countless times when she hadn't spent the night doing the nasty with one of Dot's boys. Then again, Dot had five seriously yummy boys, so she couldn't have been the first girl to sneak out.

"Well hello, Kelly." Big grin on her face, hair as always a wild gray tangle, Dot bustled into the kitchen. "Coffee?"

"Ergh!" Kelly tried to back into the hallway and smacked into a hard body.

"Steady there." Ben Crowe took her by the shoulders and shifted her to the side. "Nervous, Kelly?"

He stood beside Dot, and they both grinned at her.

Gabe groaned and threw himself against the wall. He covered his face with his hands. "Have you been waiting?"

"Not so much waiting as being available to the opportunity." Dot grinned at them and straightened her *Chief's Mom* sweatshirt. "And now that you're well and truly busted, would you like some breakfast?"

"Umm…" What she really wanted was to get the hell out of there, crawl under her bed and stay there for the next thirty years or so.

Ben poured himself a cup of coffee and leaned his hips on the kitchen counter. With dark hair and eyes, tall and broad, Ben and

Gabe carried an obvious genetic stamp. "Don't tell me you're going use my brother and discard him?"

"You dick!" Gabe, the idiot, had his hands on his knees as he continued laughing. "You may as well stay to breakfast."

"Oh God." She hung her head and willed the earth to open up and swallow her.

"Good." Dot rubbed her hands together. "Gabe, can you get me my pancake bowl?"

Kelly stopped fighting the inevitable and took a seat at the kitchen table. "This is so embarrassing."

"Really, dear?" Dot gave her a saccharine smile that put Kelly on her guard. "But probably not nearly as embarrassing as being woken up by your son and his…er…friend." She tutted and shook her head. "One of you is a screamer."

Kelly dropped her head on the table. "Please make it stop."

"Exactly what I said at about three a.m." Dot snort laughed.

Ben snickered.

And Gabe groaned, took the seat next to her, and threw her a sheepish look. "Sorry about this."

"Oh, come on." Dot threw her hands in the air. "How old are you two? It happens." She shrugged, and then her grin turned evil. "But I'm glad to hear you inherited some of your father's best qualities, Gabriel."

Ben shuddered and looked green.

Dot cackled.

Gabe looked ill.

"Now, Kelly." She banged around putting frying pans on the stove. "What month do you fancy for the wedding?"

Once she gave in to the inevitable, Kelly enjoyed breakfast with the three Crowes.

Ben had popped in on his way to work. Recently married to her best friend, Poppy, Ben Crowe was one of the good guys. He even dropped into his mother's house every day or so to make sure she was okay.

After breakfast, Gabe walked her out. Dead leaves crunched under their feet.

"Well." Kelly tugged her coat around her. "Thanks for a lovely evening."

Gabe threw his head back and laughed. It was a great look on him. "You're welcome." He tugged her closer to him. "I really did have a great time, Kelly."

"Are you getting soppy on me?" Last night had been fun, but it was over, and they both had lives to get back to. Hers included finding a way to turn back the clock on her relationship with Vince.

Vince! She should have been thinking of him, not rolling around the sheets with Gabe.

"Never." Gabe chuckled. "We good to leave things here?"

"Perfect." Kelly rose on her toes and kissed his cheek. "It was fun, but it stops here."

"Agreed." Gabe's gaze drifted to her mouth and lingered for a heart-stopping moment. He sighed. "It sure was fun."

———

Gabe walked back into the kitchen and only Ben was still there. "Ma gone?"

"To get dressed." Ben nodded and carried on reading the *Twin Elks Crier*.

Taking the seat opposite Ben, Gabe sipped his coffee. Only a year separated him and Ben, but they had never been close. Maybe because as kids they'd competed for everything. At school Gabe had been way ahead of Ben, but Ben had been better at all things sports. Now they didn't seem to have that much in common.

"The thing with Kelly." Ben kept his eyes on the paper. "It going anywhere?"

Not that it was any of Ben's business, but Gabe suppressed the childish knee jerk to say so. "No."

"She good with that?"

"Yup." It would be easier not to react like a kid if Ben didn't insist on going all big brother on him. At thirty-five and thirty-four, they were past that shit.

Ben turned the page and smoothed it down. "She and Vince have a shot."

"She said."

Glancing up, Ben raised a brow then returned to his paper.

The familiar itch started beneath Gabe's skin. Sitting in Twin Elks watching his brother read the paper was time out of his life he wasn't getting back. He needed to shower and get on with his day. "I'll see you around."

"Gabe." Ben stopped him as he got to the kitchen door. "I know I don't need to say this, but Ma doesn't need you bringing your hookups here."

No, Ben didn't need to say it, but he had anyway. "Right."

"Any idea how long you're staying in town?" Ben put his paper aside and stood.

By the set of Ben's jaw, Gabe knew to brace for it. "Nope. That will depend on what happens in the next couple of weeks."

Ben kept that heavy stare bent in his direction.

"I have a couple of feelers out about new positions. The thing in Australia is not totally dead, so I still have to hear on that."

Nodding, Ben shoved his hands in his pockets. "Ever think about staying?"

"Here?" Gabe almost laughed, but Ben's serious expression stopped him. "You asking for you or for Ma?"

"Both of us."

That rocked Gabe back.

Ben said, "You know Ma misses you. She misses all of you."

Gabe nodded. He did know that. All of them knew that. Not that Ma ever nagged about it. She was a great mother for boys, always giving you room you needed to do you. "Twin Elks is not for me." He didn't want to disparage the place Ben loved and made his life in. "And there's nothing for me to do here anyway." Gabe tried to lighten the mood. "Unless the ocean has suddenly made its way up here."

"You could do other stuff," Ben said.

He was serious, too, and Gabe was missing something. They didn't hate each other, but it wasn't like he and Ben needed to spend more time together. "I don't want to do other stuff. I like what I do."

"I get that." Ben's jaw clenched, and his eyes flashed a warning that Gabe recognized well. They were about to get into it. "But maybe what you want isn't all there is."

"Like what else?" Gabe glared right back. If Ben wanted to throw down, he would meet him there.

"Like leaving me to take care of Ma," Ben said. "Taking no responsibility."

"Are you kidding me?" Since he'd been back, Gabe had been waiting for Ben to bring that up. Ben liked to shine up his armor and dazzle you with it. "You chose to stay here. Nobody made you. Certainly not Ma."

Ben stilled and stuck his chin out. "So that makes it okay to dump this all on me?"

"Nobody's dumping anything on you. And Ma is hardly a burden. She gets on with her own shit." Fear snaked through him. "Unless there is something you're not telling me. Like Ma is sick?"

"She's fine." Ben made a dismissive gesture. "But she's lonely, and I'm worried now that I have other responsibilities that I can't give her the time she needs."

Now it made more sense. Ben's recent marriage had brought four young kids with it. Big brother heaviness aside, Ben was not being an asshole. "What about Luke? Or Mark? Mark won't play hockey forever. And sooner or later, Rafe is going to get tired of working all over the world."

Ben gave him a hard stare. Finally, he nodded. "Got ya."

"Jesus, Ben," Gabe said. "This is not where I want to be. This place stifles me."

Shrugging into his heavy jacket, Ben nodded. "I said I get it, Gabe."

Frustration boiled inside Gabe as Ben opened the back door and stepped outside. Long strides eating up the walkway, Ben got to his cruiser and climbed in. Gabe wanted to follow him and make him understand why he couldn't stay. Twin Elks had nothing to offer him. Unfortunately, if he called Luke, Mark, or Rafe they would say the same thing.

CHAPTER
Three

THANK GOD IT WAS SUNDAY, the only day of the week Kelly didn't have to open her coffee shop, Kelly's Koffee Klatch. After getting home, she had a hot shower and pulled on yoga pants and a comfy sweater. Hangover aside, Sunday was the day for getting her chores done.

Her muscles ached from her night with Gabe. It had been a spectacular end to her dry spell, but she had waited all that time for another chance with Vince, and she was going to take it.

She cleaned her condo before heading off to Grover's for her weekly groceries. Despite the big shiny Walmart on the edge of town, most people still bought their groceries at Grover's. As a small business owner herself, Kelly supported other small businesses.

Inside the door of Grover's hung a selection of large information boards, the second reason for her trip to the store. When she had first come to town and opened her coffee shop, the long hours had been out of necessity. She couldn't afford help. Now, with the coffee shop doing better than ever, she wanted someone to come in during her busy times, help out with the early mornings and give her the flexibility to extend hours.

On the Help Wanted section of the boards, she pinned her advertisement.

"Hey, Kelly." Mia Grover hung over her shoulder and peered at her ad. "Are you looking for someone?"

"Yeah." Mia would be perfect for her, but she already worked at her family's store. "Do you know anyone?"

"I'll ask around. A lot of the high school seniors are looking for something." That she remembered Mia as a senior made Kelly feel old.

Mia had blossomed into a young woman, and a pretty one. Her big brown eyes dominated her delicate features. With her braces off, she had a big, beautiful smile that drew attention. Her little girl shape had filled into womanly curves, and Kelly wished Bart luck with keeping the men at bay.

Not that there was much scope for trouble in Twin Elks. It was part of the reason so many younger people left town. Although lately, there seemed to be an influx of newcomers, like the lanky twenty-something boy currently giving Mia the chin jerk.

"Hey, Parker." Mia gave him an eyelash flutter.

Going red to his hairline, Parker tripped into Grover's.

"Friend of yours?" Kelly couldn't resist teasing Mia.

Mia shrugged. "He's home from college. His family moved here about a month ago."

"I think he likes you."

"Parker?" Mia scoffed. "He's too young for me. I'm into older men."

So Kelly had heard. According to Claire Winters, Mia had a thumping crush on Claire's man, Finn Williams. Mia was heading for disappointment that way. Not only was Finn way, way too old for her, he was also totally gone on Claire. "I wouldn't rule out younger men too fast," she said.

Chelsea Finster nee Greerly—Vince's ex-wife, still Kelly's longtime enemy—walked by pushing a shopping cart of bagged groceries.

Chelsea caught sight of her and stiffened. "Kelly."

"Chelsea."

Chelsea and Mia greeted each other.

Kelly was locked in a stare down with Chelsea, like they'd done since high school, and both of them would be damned before either backed down.

Chelsea swept past her and into the parking lot. She and her daughter loaded groceries into a top of the line SUV, which Vince must have paid for because Chelsea didn't work.

"God, I hate her," Mia whispered. "Worst baby-sitting gig I took when I was in high school."

Kelly kept her gaze locked on Chelsea's recently red hair and hot pink, bedazzled skinny jeans. "Me too."

The rest of Kelly's day passed uneventfully. She tidied her condo, did her laundry, and like an upstanding citizen, went to bed at a decent hour, the sex siren from the night before safely tucked away deep inside her.

———

Kelly jerked awake to someone banging on her door. Being woken in the middle of the night never meant anything good, and for a moment, she wondered if it was her sins of the night before coming to get her.

Scrabbling for her phone, she knocked it off the bedside table, and then lunged after it. Goddammit! It was three a.m., and she had to be up in two hours.

"Shit!" She tumbled out of bed in an inelegant heap to the hardwood floor. Crawling in the direction of the noise, she yelled, "I'm coming."

The banger didn't give a crap and kept right on pounding. "Kelly!"

"India?" Heart in her throat, and hurrying, Kelly flung open the door. "What's happened?"

India stood on her doorstep, a sleeping Jacob clutched in her arms, tears making mascara rivulets down her cheeks. "I need to come in."

"Are you okay? Is it Piers? Are you sick?" Kelly had a million questions, and they all fought to come out of her mouth at the same time. "Oh my God, is it baby boy?"

"No." India shook her head. Her cloud of silvery-blond hair looked disheveled. Even as a kid India had always had perfect hair. "Jacob's fine." India stroked her baby's back. "Is there somewhere I can put him down?"

"Yeah. In my room."

India knew the way and Kelly trailed her. Surrounding him with pillows, India laid Jacob on Kelly's bed.

Bad feeling blossoming by the passing second, Kelly waited until they were back in her open-plan living space before she turned a light on in the kitchen.

India reeled and blinked. She tried to duck out of the light but not fast enough.

"India!" Kelly cupped India's chin and turned her face to the light. A large purple bruise marred the delicate line of her cheekbone. Another one swelled India's jaw. Four finger-shaped bruises stood out against the pale, slim line of her throat. "Fuck! Fuck! Fuck!"

Tears tracked down India's cheeks. "Please don't be mad at me."

"India." That her sister would even think that hit Kelly like a truck. "I'm not mad at you. How could I be mad at you?"

"For this." Sobs made India's words garbled. "For not telling you. For all of it."

"Sweetheart." Kelly put her arm around her sister's shoulders and led her to the sofa. "What happened? Who did this?"

"It's not as bad as it looks." India winced as she sat.

Kelly wasn't having any of it, but she kept her tone gentle. "Where else?"

"Kelly, you're overreacting."

Like hell she was. India had arrived in the dead of night, with nothing but her baby and proof that somebody had been using her as a punching bag. "Who did this?"

India shivered and cried harder. At that rate, she'd make herself ill.

Holding her and rocking her, Kelly fought to keep it under control. Unadulterated rage surged through her, fighting to escape in a primal bellow. Some dead man had hurt her India, and only one name came immediately to mind. "Is it—" She wanted so much to be wrong. "Did Piers do this?"

"Kelly." India's slight form shook with the strength of her emotion. "He's changed. He's not the same man I married. He gets so angry."

Kelly breathed deep. She needed to be smart. Think things through. "I'm calling Ben."

"No." India reached for Kelly's phone. "You can't do that."

"I'm doing it, India." Kelly hit Poppy's number. India needed her to stay calm. Proof. They needed proof that Piers had assaulted India, and while the marks were still all over her body.

As a mother of four, Poppy was used to being woken, and she answered promptly. "Kelly?"

"Hey, Poppy." Her throat tightened. "I need Ben."

"Now?" Concern colored Poppy's tone. "Has something happened? Are you all right?"

"I'm fine." She was far from fine. "But India needs him."

"India?"

"Yup. My little sister."

"Just a minute." Muffled sounds came from Poppy's phone, and then she was back on the line. "We're on our way."

"Poppy, you can't—"

"Finn and Claire are here, and so is Horace. They can keep an eye on the children," Poppy said in the same voice she used to stop her son Ryan dead in his tracks and turn around whatever mission he had going on in his six-year-old head. "You're my friend, and I'm coming."

India stood blinking at her, chewing on her bottom lip. "I

wish you hadn't done that. I don't want everyone in Twin Elks talking about this."

"India." Kelly found a gentle tone. Her sister was so vulnerable, and she needed to take care of her. "You can trust Ben and Poppy. And Ben is police chief, he's going to need to know."

India paled. "Why?"

"Sweetheart." Kelly kept it calm and gentle, but the question shook her. "Nobody has the right to do this to you."

"I know that." India chewed her lip. "I do know that. It's just —the police?"

"You could be in danger," Kelly said. The raging part of her wanted Piers to arrive on her doorstep. She'd show him what happened to bastards who hurt her sister. "You and Jacob could be in danger."

Nodding, India subsided into silence. She finally calmed enough to wipe her face and blow her nose. "You're right. I need to do something about him."

"Ben won't be long." At least Kelly hoped not.

To keep herself busy, Kelly put the kettle on. What the hell, a cup of tea couldn't hurt. "Has this happened before?"

Please say no. Please say no.

India shivered and folded her arms around her torso. She'd always been slim, but she'd lost weight since Kelly had seen her last Christmas. Had it really been that long?

"Piers has always had a temper, but it's never been this bad before. And he's never gotten angry with Jacob before."

Even as she'd prayed for a different answer, Kelly wasn't naive enough to believe she would get one. "Did he hurt Jacob?"

India shook her head. She was shivering like a stray dog. "No. He got angry at him, but I...didn't let him touch my baby."

How could Kelly not have seen any of that before? Okay, Piers gave off a possessive vibe and could be controlling, but that...

Fetching a throw from the back of her couch, Kelly sifted

through the months since last Christmas. She'd spoken to India on the phone but hadn't seen her.

That meant Jacob was almost a year old now, because he'd been born last November. Kelly had shut her business for a couple of weeks over Christmas and driven up to see them in their beautiful home outside Denver.

Come to think of it, India had tried to delay her visit with excuses about how she didn't have time to give to Kelly with the new baby and all. Had Piers been behind that? Given this new development, she had to believe he had been.

Isolation. The first step in an abusive relationship. Separate the victim from anyone who could or would help them.

Kelly wrapped the throw around her sister's shivering shoulders and rubbed her back. "You're safe now, Indy. I'm going to make sure of it."

Somewhere in heaven, Gram was shaking her head. The one thing she'd asked of Kelly before she died was to look after India. Christ on a cracker, she'd done a super job of that.

A soft knock on the door ended her foray into self-flagellation. Good thing too, because that was not going to help India either.

Ben and Poppy stood in her doorway, both of them dressed in jeans and jerseys and looking like they'd not long since tumbled out of bed.

"Kelly." Ben had his police chief voice on. The one that said he was there and he had this.

Poppy provided the much-needed quick hug. Poppy had arrived in Twin Elks this past summer and she was already Kelly's closest friend. The pint-size pretty brunette was a hundred kinds of sweet and quirky and had won the entire town over.

Ben slipped past her into the condo. He approached India slowly and sat at one of the counter stools near her. "India."

India tried to hide her face again, hunching her skinny shoulders up to her ears. "Hi, Ben. Sorry to wake you up."

"That's okay." Ben gentled his tone and folded his hands on the counter. "I see Kelly put the kettle on. Maybe we can have some tea, or coffee, and chat."

Taking the hint, Kelly got with making coffee. At her coffee shop, she had all the fancy machines, but at home she used a simple French press. Her business also meant she knew how everyone took their coffee.

Her hands shook as she added grounds to the press, scattering coffee over the countertop.

Poppy nudged her out of the way. "Go and sit. I'll make the coffee."

Kelly didn't know if she could sit still, but now that Ben was there, she relaxed. Ben would know what to do, how to handle the situation.

"Piers do that?" Ben gave India's face a pointed look.

Swallowing and hunching her shoulders again, India nodded.

India had always been timid and shy, but now she seemed terrified.

Ben simply nodded. "How did you get away?"

Damn, Kelly hadn't even thought to ask that.

"He's not there." India cleared her throat. "He went on a business trip, after..." She gestured her face. "I waited until I knew his flight had taken off, and I got in my car with Jacob."

"Well done." Ben's tone conveyed his approval. "That was an incredibly brave thing to do."

India sobbed, caught the sob on a small choked noise and shook her head. "I'm not brave. I stayed there. I stayed there and let him do this to me. He almost hurt my baby because of me."

"Sweetheart." Ben loaded the endearment with so much empathy it made Kelly tear up. "That's not how these things work. If it was as simple as walking out, this would never happen to anyone."

Poppy's big brown eyes held all the anger and grief that

Kelly felt. She gave Kelly's hand a squeeze and returned to making coffee.

Kelly said, "She said he got angry with Jacob. India's baby."

Ben glanced at her and then turned all his attention back to India. "Is that true? Is that what made you leave?"

India nodded. "I couldn't let him hurt Jacob."

"You did the right thing, India," Ben said. "You saved your little boy."

Silent tears streaked down India's cheeks. "I thought it was only me. I was the only one who made him so angry all the time. I didn't think he could be angry with Jacob. He loves Jacob."

Kelly couldn't stand it anymore. She gathered India in her arms and held her. Over India's head she looked at Ben. "What do we do?"

"First, we need to document the abuse." He indicated India. "I think she'd be more comfortable if you helped her with that."

"What does that mean?" India stared at Ben in horror.

"Photographs." Kelly tightened her hold. "I need to take photos of your bruises. All of them."

Ben had his cell out. "I'm going to ring Doctor Cooper to come and examine you," he said. "Unless you want to go to a hospital?"

"No." India shook her head. "I don't want all those people to see me. Why does Coop have to come?"

"Proof," Ben said. "And we also need to be sure he hasn't done more lasting damage."

The night was like a nightmare, and she wanted to go back to sleeping off her night with Gabe. She wanted to wake up and find it was all a bad dream.

Except India needed her. She'd failed to be there for her sister. Kelly couldn't let her down again. "Let Ben call Coop, or Doc if you prefer. Then we can take it from there."

For a long moment, India stood there, still shaking and looking like she might refuse. And then she said, "All right."

Poppy handed out coffee to everyone.

Kelly helped India to her couch, rewrapped her in the throw and placed her coffee on the table in front of her.

Staring at it, India made no move to take the cup.

Kelly approached Ben and kept her voice low. "What happens now?"

"We document the abuse and get Coop to verify it," Ben said. "We don't want the son of a bitch coming back and saying it wasn't him or the pictures aren't real. It would be better if we could do this in a hospital setting, but I think she's been through enough for one night."

"Yeah." Kelly nodded.

India looked like she might crumble at any moment.

Ben sipped his coffee and gave her a level stare. "If there's one good thing about this, it's that it happened in Colorado."

"What do you mean?" Kelly didn't see any good.

"Colorado has some of the most stringent laws against domestic assault. We're a mandatory arrest state." Ben glanced at India. "All I need is probable cause to arrest that prick, and I've got it."

Savage satisfaction surged through Kelly. "India doesn't need to press charges?"

"Nope." Ben's gaze met hers, and she saw the same raw emotion in his eyes. "When I see him, I arrest him."

"Arrest him?" India paled even more. "You mean put him in jail? I'm not sure I want him arrested."

"India, it's the law." Ben kept his tone gentle, but firm. "I have no choice now but to arrest him." He crouched at her feet. "If you're scared, I also need to let you know that as of right now, a mandatory restraining order is in place. He can't come near you without risking a secondary charge."

India pushed her hair back with a shaking hand. "What if I change my mind?"

It would be a cold day in hell before Kelly let that happen.

"It doesn't matter." Ben shook his head. "Piers is going to pay for what he's done."

CHAPTER
Four

GABE HAD BARELY GOTTEN one sip of coffee in him when the door to Ma's kitchen opened. That was Twin Elk for you, and Dot's kitchen was like Twin Elks central. Thank God he was wearing pants.

When Kelly walked in, he brightened. "Hey."

"Hi." She looked stressed and…furious.

Gabe set his coffee aside. "What is it?"

Another woman walked in behind her, this one holding a young child. Ben brought up the rear. From the looks on all their faces, Gabe surmised a lot more coffee would be needed. He got another pot started. "What's going on?"

"Gabe." Ben nodded to him. "This is India, Kelly's sister. She was a few years behind us in school."

Gabe didn't remember her, but India resembled Kelly, only a more muted version. Slimmer, blonder, and more delicately featured, India gave off a fragile air to Kelly's vibrant one.

That could also have to do with the bruises on India's face and neck.

Ma bustled through from the house. "I just got off the phone with Poppy." She wrapped the young woman in a hug. "India."

Some of the tension drained out of India. Ma's hugs were like that; they took the bad thing away.

"I'm sorry to be so much trouble," India whispered.

"You're not any trouble." Ma took the baby from her. He immediately snuggled into Ma's neck. "I have your room ready for you."

Gabe sipped his coffee and waited for someone to tell him what the hell was going on. Whatever it was looked serious.

"Let's get you settled." Kelly guided her sister into the corridor outside the kitchen. The differences between them got more obvious.

India drew closer to Kelly as if sensing Kelly would protect her, and India desperately looked like she needed protecting. She reminded Gabe of a fawn, so heartbreakingly vulnerable to predators. He wanted to pick her up and tuck her away safe. From the way everyone hovered around her, India had that effect on lots of people.

He waited for the women to leave before he turned to Ben. "What's going on?"

"India needs a place to stay for a few days." Ben grabbed a mug and helped himself to coffee. He stood with his cup in his hand and scowled out the kitchen window. "I would have taken her to Winters House, but we're full up until I get our house finished."

Call him clairvoyant, but Gabe didn't think Ben was upset about his renovation project. "Are those bruises the reason she needs somewhere to stay?"

"Yup." Ben's knuckles whitened against the handle of his coffee mug.

Down the hall, women murmured to each other, the baby cried, and Ma soothed him.

"Can I ask who put those bruises on her?"

Ben shrugged. "That's not my story to tell."

Gabe had expected as much. "Then I need to know if

whoever put those bruises on her might be coming around to have another go."

"I don't know." Ben's jaw clenched. "Maybe, but being here should make her harder to find."

"And if it isn't?"

"Then she has you living right here." Ben turned on him with a scowl. "And Finn and I are up the street."

That didn't reassure him in the least. "And Ma?"

"What about her?" Ben looked impatient.

"Is she in any danger?"

Ben's anger darkened on his face. "Jesus, Gabriel. You live halfway across the world for years, and now you come back here and accuse me of putting Ma in danger."

"I'm not accusing you of anything."

Ben's self-righteous prick had escaped its cage. Sure, Ben had stayed and been there for Ma when all the rest of them had fucked off, but that didn't mean the rest of them had no say in Ma's safety.

"If whoever did that to India is around, I don't want him hurting Ma."

"And I do?" Ben dropped his mug in the sink with a clatter. "You're in or you're out, Gabe. You want a say in how we do things around here, then be around. Otherwise, shut the hell up." He stormed out, throwing over his shoulder, "Tell Ma I'll been in touch. I need to get some stuff done."

"Sure." Not being around didn't mean he didn't care about Ma. Gabe would give you even odds on Ben not wanting him around more anyway. The two of them could barely spend ten minutes together without getting into it.

Kelly came back into the kitchen. "Ben gone?"

She looked strung out and Gabe wanted to ease some of that for her.

"He said he had stuff to do but wouldn't be long." Gabe took a mug out, filled it, and gave it to her. "It's nothing like your coffee, but you look like you could use it."

"Thanks." Kelly's hand trembled around her mug as she took a seat at the kitchen table. "Ben tell you what's going on?"

Ben had been too busy being self-important.

"Nope. He said it wasn't his story to tell."

"That was good of him." Kelly sipped her coffee and grimaced. "Got any sugar and cream?"

"Sure." Gabe brought what she needed to the table and propped his hips on the counter. What was going down looked serious. Ben was doing his job, and he was good at it. Gabe needed to show his grownup and not let childish habits kick in.

Kelly fixed her coffee and took another sip. "It was her husband, Piers."

Gabe had wondered about that. "He hit her."

"Yup." Kelly's voice shook. "Apparently, it's not the first time either." A sob rippled through her.

"Hey." Gabe pulled her against him and wrapped her tight. "I'm so sorry, Kelly. This is awful for you guys."

"Ben and your mom have been so wonderful. I don't know what we'd do without them." Kelly turned her face into his shoulder and sobbed quietly.

"You won't have to do this without any of us. We've got you." Not knowing what else to do, Gabe held her until the storm passed, then settled her at the table with a box of Kleenex. The primal part of him rejected the idea of Kelly being upset. It wanted to fix the problem and make things right for her.

Ma stepped into the kitchen and took a seat opposite Kelly. "I've put them in Mark's old room. We had a travel crib from when Poppy first arrived. It was all set up anyway." She rubbed her eyes. "She's worn to the bone. I hope she can get some rest, poor thing."

"Kelly said her husband did that." Gabe jerked his head at India's bedroom door.

Ma looked like she could do with some comforting as well. "I don't understand men who do that; I really don't"

"Me neither." He put an arm around her shoulders. Ben had

been right to bring them there. That bastard wasn't getting anywhere near Gabe's women.

Kelly leaned into him. "Ben is trying to find Piers, so he can arrest him."

"Good."

Ma nodded. "Works in Denver, makes a lot of money. I met him, Gabe." She sighed. "I was at their wedding. I would never have suspected he was like this."

"Nobody ever does. Until it's too late," he said. He preferred animals. Animals didn't beat the shit out of each other just because. If they fought, they did it for a reason, and if they killed, it was to eat or to protect themselves.

Ma pressed her fingers to her eyes. "So true. She said he threatened the baby, and that's why she left."

A dangerous rage swept through Gabe. Hitting a woman as delicate and tiny as India and then going after her child was a special kind of evil. "What kind of fucking asshole is he?"

"It makes you wonder." Ma must have been upset, because she didn't touch his language. She turned her attention to Kelly. "How are you doing?"

"I'm fine." Kelly's chin wobbled, and she took a deep breath. "Nothing happened to me. Nobody did anything to me."

"Something like this touches all of us." Dot patted Kelly's hand. "You did the right thing calling Ben."

Kelly grimaced. "I'm not sure India is happy about it. She resisted the idea of Piers being arrested."

"It's too often the way." Ma sighed. "Is anybody hungry?"

"Thanks, but no. I should get to work." She glanced down the passage and sat again. "Do you think I should go? Maybe India will need me."

"We're here," he said. "And while I might be useless, Ma is the best at this sort of thing. Believe me, I know. As a kid I brought all sorts of people and creatures home to her."

A smile ghosted over Ma's face. "You certainly kept things interesting."

"I…" Kelly rubbed her face. "I keep thinking what if she needs me, and I'm not there for her. Again."

Gabe had heard enough, and he took a gentle grip on her shoulders, enough to make her look at him. "This is not on you. None of this."

"Yes, but—"

"This is about some sick bastard who makes himself feel like a man by beating on those who can't fight back."

Kelly's shoulders slumped. "Part of me knows that and accepts it, but there's this other part…"

Gabe knew that feeling well, but he shoved the thought aside. Being in Twin Elks always brought it out of hiding. "I'm here as well, and I promise to call you." He handed her his phone. "Here, put your number in and I promise you, I will call."

"Thanks." Kelly took his phone and added her number. Then she called herself. "Now I have your number as well." She gave him a small smile, a tiny flash of the Kelly he'd spent the night with. "Now I can call you to firm up our wedding details."

Ma laughed. "I always like a June wedding."

"Do that." Gabe let her take the out from all the heavy. "I'm sure Ma has a couple of color scheme ideas she'd like your input on."

Kelly bumped him with her shoulder. "I much prefer the circumstances behind my last visit to this kitchen."

"Me too." He bumped her back. "Can I walk you to work, or are you driving."

"Walking." She hesitated, and then said, "I'd tell you not to bother, but I could use the company."

He opened the door and motioned her to precede him.

The weather was lulling them with a mild day that made winter seem months away. It would probably change its mind by noon.

Kelly raised her head and took a deep breath of the clear mountain air. "I can't believe this happened."

It took some believing all right. Gabe hoped to God Ben got the fucker. "She's safe now."

"Thanks to Dot and your brother," she said. "You know what the worst part is?"

"What?" Dead leaves scattered about their feet as they walked.

Kelly bent and grabbed a fallen yellow leaf. "She says she loves him. How can you love someone who hurts you like that? And even as I say that, I know it's not that simple."

Gabe shoved his hands in his pockets. If she needed to talk, he could give her that.

"Ben also told me that so many women change their minds and try to get the charges dropped. They say they love him and don't want to send him to prison." She gave a bitter laugh. "I'd like to see them throw away the key on Piers."

"Ben will get him," he said. His own childish shit with his brother aside, he meant it. "He won't stop until he's made sure that bastard pays for this."

"Ben is going to put a call in to the Denver PD, see if they can pick him up," Kelly said.

Gabe wished he could do something, anything. "You leave Piers to Ben. You concentrate on yourself and India and her boy. The best you can do is love and support them and be there for them."

"You're right." She tore bits off her leaf and dropped them. "I know you're right, but doing nothing has never sat right with me."

He nodded, because it was another thing he could relate to.

"The logical part of me knows that if he's been isolating her, telling her that he's the only one who really cares about her, the best thing I can do is show her that he's wrong. But…"

He put an arm around her shoulders and hugged her to him. "But it doesn't feel like enough."

"Exactly." She left his arm where it was. "I'm scared I won't be able to help her."

Gabe pulled her closer. "You will be, Kelly. You're a kickass woman, and nobody could ask for a better sister."

Gabe walked her to her store, accepted a cup of coffee for his trouble, and returned home.

Ma was waiting in the kitchen staring at her coffee. "Kelly okay?"

"As good as she can be."

"It was nice of you to walk her."

"Just doing what you taught me." He kept his tone light. Despite yesterday morning, he didn't want Ma getting a head full of ideas. He liked Kelly, liked her a lot, and the sex had been incredible, but he wasn't staying. Even if he was, Kelly and Vince had a happily ever after they needed to get started. "I'm sure she'll call Vince now."

"Vince?" Ma glanced at him.

If he read that look right, she might already be brewing a half-baked notion. "They're together."

"Really?" Ma raised a brow at him. "Then why was she with you?"

Heat spread over his face. This was not the sort of conversation he wanted to have with his mother. "I mean, they're not together yet, like a thing, but she wants to pick up where they left off in high school."

"Hmm." Ma had her thinking face on. "It doesn't seem to me like she wants Vince all that much. Given the other morning."

"Ma, I think you're reading too much into that. We had a few drinks. Things went further than they should have."

"Okay." Ma shrugged, but Gabe wasn't buying it. Ma had only gone quiet for now. "Right now, I'm sure both these girls could do with all the support they can get. They've had enough man trouble for one day."

CHAPTER
Five

ABOUT MIDMORNING THE FOLLOWING DAY, Vince walked into Kelly's coffee shop and gave her his sweet smile. He'd been coming in every morning at around the same time since she opened Kelly's Koffee Klatch.

Unlike every other morning, he came up to the counter and stood there. "Morning."

"Morning." Kelly made his regular coffee. She had barely slept, and she was dragging herself through work.

Vince had gotten even better looking since high school. The slight lines around his eyes and mouth seasoned his face and made him look manlier. Unlike her, he hadn't gained a pound, or if he had, it had gone to broadening his shoulders.

He looked good. Great even, and it sometimes made her wonder if he still saw her the same way he had in high school. Did he still find her attractive?

"How are you doing today?" Vince took a seat at the counter and nodded his thanks for the coffee. "You look stressed."

Vince had always noticed stuff. It's part of what made him so special. Having him there was comforting.

"I'm okay. I—" She was lying, and she didn't need to lie to Vince. She wasn't even slightly okay, and if anyone was safe with her secrets it was this man. The boy she'd grown up with, and the man she still respected. "Actually, things really suck this morning."

Vince stopped with his mug halfway to his mouth and studied her. It was the same look he used to give her in high school. It meant he really cared to hear her answer. "Kelly? What's going on?"

She teared up, so she ducked her head and concentrated on her orders until it passed. "It's India."

Vince had been in and out of her house during high school. He had known exactly how things had stood with her family. He frowned. "Didn't she get married a couple of years back?"

"Yes. And that's the problem."

He winced. "Marriage not working out?"

"In a manner of speaking." She slammed coffee grounds into the bin. Lowering her voice so it didn't carry to the rest of the store, she said, "It seems Piers likes to make his points with his fists."

"Shit." Vince gaped. "Kelly, that's horrible. I'm really sorry to hear that."

"I didn't know." She blinked at her coffee machine and tried to get a grip. "I knew Piers was domineering, but you know India; she's always needed someone to hold her hand through crap." Kelly felt stupid for totally missing what and who Piers really was. "I didn't know until yesterday what she was going through."

"I'm so sorry, Kelly." Vince stood and walked around the counter. Taking her by the shoulders, he bent his knees so they were eye to eye. "But this isn't your fault. You get that right?"

This is why Vince and her made sense. Why there had been nobody like him in her life since they broke up. He got her. She didn't need to explain things to him. He already understood.

Like Gabe had understood yesterday at Dot's.

"Kelly?" Vince stared at her. "You've always taken responsibility for India, but that doesn't make this your fault. Hear me?"

Even though her heart wasn't really there, she nodded. "I suppose I should be glad that she's out of it."

"Is she at your place?" Vince slipped back around the counter and took his seat.

Kelly shook her head. "No, she's staying with Dot Crowe until Ben can arrest Piers."

"Dot is good people." Vince sipped his coffee. "India's in good hands."

"Yup." Not in Piers's hands either. "I called a little while ago, but she was sleeping." India had looked the sort of bone-deep weary that came from months of not getting enough rest. Kelly's imagination had been at her all morning. Had India lain in bed beside Piers night after night, too terrified to sleep? "Dot and Gabe said they would call me if she needed anything."

"Gabe?" Vince raised an eyebrow. "I saw him at Ben's wedding. Is he still here?"

Guilt took her for a quick twist. "Yup. He's staying for a while."

"How about that?" Vince leaned his elbows on the counter. "Gabe Crowe back in town. You used to think he was hot shit in high school."

Kelly's face heated, and she turned away to hide it. "Everybody thought he was hot shit in high school."

She didn't owe Vince an explanation. Even if she wanted to see if they could pick things up again, he might not feel the same. He'd been divorced for months now, and today was the closest he'd come to her physically.

A few meaningful looks and a couple of texts between them —hers of support through his divorce, and his hinting at them having missed a chance—didn't make for a whole helluva lot.

"It used to make me jealous as hell." Vince winked at her.

"It was meant to."

They smiled at each other and their gazes locked.

God, but she'd loved the shit out of him. Vince's smile always seemed to surprise him as well as everyone else, as it crept across his serious face. His hair still curled around his nape. While he kept his hair short because he hated the curl, she had always loved to wrap those silky curls around her fingers.

"Anyway, tell me how you are." Kelly got a couple of orders ready and called out to their owners.

Vince nodded. "I'm good."

"The children?"

"They're okay." He shrugged. "Adapting."

He sipped his coffee, and she made up another order and walked it to her customer.

"You still in the same house, right?" She already knew the answer, but she didn't want him knowing that. It made her seem creepy.

"Yup." He nodded. "Chelsea and I thought it best for the kids to maintain as much of their normal lives as possible."

Thank God, Jacob wouldn't remember. If Kelly had her way, divorce would be in India's near future.

"Morning, Kelly." Pete Sparks tapped on her counter. "Can I get my regular order?"

"Sure." Kelly got busy with Pete's hazelnut lattes, nonfat cappuccino and double americano. He did the morning coffee run for the small realty office across the road from her. India would hate having her problems aired to Twin Elks, so Kelly forced her normal chirpiness. "Business still looking up?"

"Totally." Pete beamed at her. "We seem to have more and more buyers interested in our part of the world." He turned to Vince. "Say, if you ever want to put your house on the market, I could get you a good price for it. You could make some money on it."

"No, thanks." Vince grimaced. "It's the kids' home. They've had enough disruption as it is."

Pete nodded and handed Kelly his reward card. "I respect that. Now that you're a free man again, you should give me a call. We can get a beer sometimes. Plus, I have a regular poker night on Thursday with the same group of guys who get together for football games."

"Yeah?" Vince looked interested.

"Unless you're not a free man anymore?" Pete winked at Kelly. "You might want to put a ring on that."

Vince flushed, which made Pete laugh all the harder.

He grabbed his order. "You're welcome to join us if you're free."

The doorbell jangled behind Pete. He crossed the road, carefully carrying his tray of coffees.

"It's good news that the real estate market is picking up," Kelly said. "This town could do with some fresh blood."

"I like it the way it is." Vince finished his coffee and pushed his cup back. "Quiet. Everybody knows everybody else."

Spoken like a man who hadn't gotten stuck in the narrow dating pool. Then again, he had a way out of that. Only he didn't seem inclined to take it. "New people bring new opportunities."

Vince pulled a face. "There is that. But you know me, Bunny, I don't like change."

"Yes, I do know you, Stretch."

And just like that they were back in high school. Bunny and Stretch, together forever and ever, amen.

Vince's eyes darkened to almost black and his gaze drifted over her mouth. She knew that look. It was the one that came before he kissed her.

She and Vince had spent hours lying on her bed, petting and kissing, both of them virgins and nervous to take that final step.

Funny thing, when they had, it had been almost anticlimactic. Distinctly not what she'd read about in the dogeared passages of books she and her buddies had passed around. But then, what eighteen-year-old boy on his first time had enough experience to rock his equally inexperienced girlfriend's world?

A little subtle prodding couldn't hurt. "So, are you going to give Pete a call? Get together with him? I mean, if you have nothing better to do."

"Maybe." Vince stood and shoved his hands in his front pockets. "I'm not really that social, and I have the kids."

Chelsea had given up primary custody in their divorce. Two children didn't work with her new lifestyle. Chelsea brought out the bitch in Kelly, but she wasn't apologizing for that.

All through high school, Chelsea had set her sights on Vince. Whenever Kelly turned up late to something, Chelsea had been there, keeping Vince company until she arrived. Every class Chelsea and Vince shared, miraculously, Chelsea had ended up sitting next to him. Finally, when Vince and Kelly had their biggest fight of all, who had stepped into the breach and soothed Vince's ego with kind words and sex? No prizes for guessing the answer.

Chelsea had played the long game, and she'd won. Vince had married her once he'd found out she was pregnant.

And Kelly?

Well, she'd dated some. Maybe even come close to falling in love a time or two, but she'd never gotten over her Stretch.

"You know, you don't have to be alone if you don't want to." Kelly was practically asking him to ask her out, for the love of God.

"I know that. See you tomorrow, Kelly." Vince squeezed her hand. "I really am sorry about India."

"Thanks." What did a girl have to do to make him ask her out?

Vince strode out the door and sauntered toward his rig. A pregnant wife meant Vince had given up his college dreams and found a job to support his wife and imminent family. A few years ago, he'd started driving long-haul trucks. He said it was for the money, but Kelly bet part of it was getting away from his toxic wife.

Damnit! She needed to get Zen with the Chelsea thing.

Chelsea was in the past. Kelly was exactly where she needed to be, when she needed to be. *Yada, yada, yada.*

Why the hell didn't Vince make a move already? Something.

Anything. He'd give her one of those melting looks and then nothing. Nada! Zip! Zilch!

Her cell rang and Piers showed on the display. Her Zen left the building like its ass was on fire.

She nearly didn't take the call, but then it should be interesting, so she answered, "Yes."

"Kelly." Piers sighed. "Thank God I've reached you. I got home and India isn't here. Neither is Jacob. Do you have any idea where they are?"

"Really?" She had to take a moment. She couldn't believe what he had said. "Give me a minute; I'm at work."

She took longer to fill the next order to get her composure back. Ben would be very interested to know Piers had gotten back from his business trip. "Why are you calling me, Piers? You already know India and Jacob aren't home, and you know why."

"Kelly?" Piers sounded confused. "What's going on?"

"As if you don't know."

"Kelly, please." Piers took a jagged breath. "I'm freaking out here. I've called all her friends, and none of them have seen her. Do I need to call the police?"

Customers were glancing her way and she lowered her voice to a whisper. "You've got a nerve calling me."

"What are you talking about?"

"Let's cut the bullshit, Piers. I'm not buying."

"Buying what?"

"I know what you did to India."

The silence on the other end of the line stretched so long, Kelly nearly hung up.

Piers finally said, "I want to know that they're safe. Please tell me they're safe. I don't understand what's happening here."

"They're safe." And she aimed to keep it that way. Piers wouldn't get close to India and Jacob. "Not like you really give a shit."

Piers didn't speak for a long while. "Kelly, I get the feeling there's something you're not telling me." He gasped. "Has India...done something?"

Oh, no, he was not going to deflect to someone else's behavior. "What kind of something would India do?"

"It doesn't matter." He sounded impatient as he asked, "But you know, for sure, that they're safe?"

"I do."

Piers heaved a sigh of relief. "Thank God. I got back from Houston, and they weren't here. I called the housekeeper, and she said they weren't here this morning when she came in, and it didn't look like their beds had been slept in."

Giving him anything, even the simple admission that India was safe, made her feel tainted. She certainly wasn't going to listen to him play the confused, worried husband another second. "I have to go now, Piers."

"Kelly." Piers's tone took on a sharper edge. "Listen to me for a minute. I'm not sure what you've heard, but India left here without her medication. And she needs it."

"Medication?"

"Yes." Piers took a deep breath. "She didn't want anyone to know, particularly not you, because she looks up to you so much. I don't know, maybe she thought you would judge her."

The son of a bitch to suggest such a thing. "India knows better than that."

"Yes, she does." Piers's tone gentled. "Normally. But Kelly, she's been battling postpartum depression, and it's been going on for a while now."

"Bullshit. She would have told me." She and India shared everything.

Except, apparently, they didn't anymore.

"I know how close you are." Piers sounded apologetic. "And you're her big sister, and she idolizes you. Maybe that's why she never told you. She didn't want you to think less of her."

"I would never think less of her." Kelly hated that Piers was getting in her head. She would never have said India kept secrets from her. Up until the moment she'd opened her door and seen India standing there with bruises on her. Bruises given to her by this motherfucker.

"I tell you who I do think less of, Piers." She took her time, hoping it'd sink in, knowing he'd deflect. "I think less of the cowardly piece of shit who puts his hands on his wife in anger. The piece of shit who leaves bruises on her body. I think someone like that is the lowest debris of human filth I can imagine."

CHAPTER
Six

GABE LEFT Ma fussing over India and Jacob and took a walk with her big rambunctious puppy. The weather had turned in the middle of the night, like it did in Twin Elks. Crazy high winds blew in the change, and he had his coat on and a hat pulled over his ears.

After about fifteen minutes of lunging and squirming, the pup settled into the occasional jerk and pull. He needed training before he got much bigger and harder to handle. He also needed a name, but Ma kept saying it was disloyal to Poppy's son Ryan to go ahead and name a dog he'd found. Apparently, Ryan and Ben had come across him cowering in a culvert. Like the days when Gabe was at home, Ma had ended up with another pet.

The dog shied at a swirling whirlwind of leaves and tried to hide behind Gabe.

With a firm yank, and a command to heel, Gabe got them walking again.

His years in Australia had turned him into a wuss for the cold. He wanted to get back there, not only to the place but to his project.

As one of two veterinarians working with a team of specialists on shark behavior and how to protect those incredible predators from the way overfishing had forced changes in their behavior, every day on the job had challenged him.

Then Belinda had hit thirty, and everything had changed.

A silver sedan stopped in the street a little ways up, and Peg's permed gray head poked out of the window. "Hello, Gabe."

The dog lunged at the car and Gabe jerked him back. "Heel." It took a moment to get the squirming, eager-to-please puppy under control.

"Hi, Peg." A great friend of his mother's and chairman of the Twin Elks prayer chain, Peg had a thumb in every pie. As boys, they'd spent hours snickering and speculating about the size of her bra. "You look well."

"And so do you." Peg eyed him, top to toe, with an appraising gleam. "Dot says you didn't get married over there in Austria."

"Australia, and no."

Peg screwed up her face in thought. "Don't they speak German?"

"They actually have four official languages in Austria, and one of those is German, but I was in Australia."

"Hmmm." Peg tapped her hand on her window ledge. "You know, the Beckers are German."

Some things you would never win. "Who are the Beckers?"

"The Beckers," Peg boomed. "Live over on Homestead. They used to own the butchery until old man Becker got too old to run it anymore. Well, that's what Charlene said, but between us, I think the butchery interfered with his time with the bottle." Peg gave him a meaningful stare.

None of it meant a thing to him. "Er…sure?"

"Anywho." Peg patted her rigid curls into place. "Their daughter, Sandra…no Stephanie, she speaks German and she's single."

"I'll give her a call."

"See that you do." Peg winked at him. "You off to anywhere specific?"

"Nope, just taking a walk."

"Hey!" Peg snapped her fingers. "You should meet our new veterinarian. She's also single, but she doesn't speak German." She frowned. "At least, I don't think she does."

"Will do, Peg."

That satisfied Peg enough to send her roaring off with a wave out the window.

Actually, he was curious about the new vet. As a boy, he'd spent his life running in and out of Dr. Roberts's office. The old man had retired before Gabe left for school. He had kind of gotten the impression Doc Roberts would have liked him to take over the practice, but that was before Dad's death, and shit hadn't been the same since.

Not that Gabe had really considered taking it over. Family pets were not where his interests lay.

No, he wanted the sort of project he'd been working on in Australia before Belinda turned thirty, and her biological clock got to ticking.

Belinda was a great girl. They had so much in common. They both liked the outdoors and anything associated with that: hiking, rock climbing, camping, skiing, diving. Their vacations had been more like adventure getaways than relaxation, but that was the way they both liked it.

He took a right on Alameda and walked two thirds of the way down to the rambling, concrete seventies block that housed the Twin Elks veterinary hospital

The building was more or less the same, except for a new bright blue on the trim and the front door. The sign was new and under the name Twin Elks Veterinary Hospital was the name Cara Addison.

The new vet, who he really should meet, and who didn't speak German. Maybe.

Sticking his cold hands in his pockets, he tried to warm them.

It had all started for him there. As a kid, he'd been drawn to animals and driven Ma nuts picking up strays and the injured. He'd brought them all to Dr. Roberts and watched in amazement as the doc put them back together.

Sometimes he couldn't, and those ones it had taken Gabe a long time to forget. It was through watching doc work that he'd decided what he wanted to do with the rest of his life.

The dog pulled at the end of the leash, eager to get going again.

The clinic door opened, and a brunette strode out, arms clasped around her torso against the cold. About his age, with tight jeans and a sweater showing her curved in all the right ways, she was the sort of woman to pique anyone's interest.

"Gabe Crowe." She gave him a broad, sunshiny smile and held out her hand. A small, strong capable hand with nails cut short, made for working. "I'm Cara Addison."

"The new veterinarian."

"You got it." She gave a husky laugh. "I keep hearing we should meet."

Gabe responded to her easy manner and her laugh. "You too, huh?"

"They're thinking we'll rip each other's clothes off over de-fleaing a dog." Cara was the sort of forthright woman he liked. A trait she shared with Kelly.

"I think their hopes were more around marriage and breeding a litter of little veterinarians."

"Right." She threw back her head and laughed, a husky sound that worked with her pinup vibe. She crouched and petted the dog. "Hey, there. You got a name?"

The dog lunged at her, tongue whipping every which way as he tried to make a new friend.

Gabe wrestled him back. "He doesn't have a name, actually. My mom keeps refusing to give him one."

"That's not right," Cara said to the dog and stood. "So,

instead of standing out here in a semi-creepy way, do you want to come in? See what I've done?"

He really had nothing better to do, and he was curious. "Sure. If you're not too busy."

Cara pulled a face. "Unfortunately, I'm not. Twin Elks is slow to trust their pets to a newbie. They still insist on driving over to Springs rather than coming to me."

"Dan Roberts was an institution around here." Gabe followed her into the clinic. He made a mental note to chat with Ma and see what she could do. There was no power greater in Twin Elks than the prayer chain.

Inside, he hung his coat by the door. The old reception desk had been replaced by a sleek wood and stone desk that ran one side of the waiting room. In neat little alcoves to keep feisty pets separated, new benches sat ready for patients.

A big fish tank looked over a neat station for coffee and tea.

"It looks great." A whole lot better than the old office. Dr. Roberts hadn't cared much for decor and settled for blue walls and a couple of faded posters of dog breeds. Gabe walked over to a state-of-the-art scale. "This will make life easier."

"It does." Cara stood by the coffee station. "Coffee?"

"Great." He really would talk to Ma. Cara had set the place up well.

The dog tried to sniff everything at once, and Gabe had a bitch of a time dissuading him and getting him back under control. He really needed more walks, more time and a goddamn name. Every time he spoke to the creature, he had to settle for you or dog or puppy.

"Black, no sugar," he responded to Cara's silent question. Now he wanted to see what she had going on behind the scenes.

"You can let him explore." Cara handed him a cup of coffee and walked through reception to the heart of the office. Four doors led off a central corridor and Cara opened the one nearest them. "I have four exam rooms."

Gabe dropped the leash and the dog got to satisfying his nose.

The setup was as great as the reception. No cold stainless-steel table stuck in the middle of the room, but a wooden work-bench and enough space to treat bigger patients from the floor. Behind the workbenches were small fridges and stocked cupboards with state-of-the-art computer systems to integrate patient care and billing.

Cara led him through a second door at the back of the exam room. "Each room leads to this central treatment space."

Gabe grew more and more impressed as he followed her into an operating room, a recovery room, and a room full of cages for patients who needed to stay longer.

A lone border collie wearing an Elizabethan collar lay in one of the cages, his head on his paws, with that infinitely stoic look dogs got.

Gabe crouched. "Hey, there. What's up with you?"

"He cut his leg on some wire." Cara crouched beside him and stuck her fingers through the wire.

The dog nosed her fingers and gave his tail a thump.

"Unfortunately for Casper here, it took his owners a day or two to spot the tear and by then he'd gotten an infection going."

"Poor Casper." Gabe let the dog sniff his hand through the wire. "I bet you're feeling better now."

Cara stood. "He goes home tomorrow."

"This is a great facility."

"Yeah." Cara looked around her. "I may have underestimated the level of distrust in the community. I also had ideas of having a VA and secretary, but it's just me. Unless you—"

"Ah, no." Gabe shook his head. "Anal glands and neutering are not my thing."

Cara crossed her arms and gave him a hard stare. "So you're one of those are you?"

"One of what?"

"The glory boys." She sniffed, and her dark eyes flashed at him. "Too good for a normal family pet clinic."

Gabe felt attacked, but then he had come across as an arrogant ass with what he'd said. "It's not that. I've been really loving what I did in Australia."

"Why aren't you still over there enjoying it then?" Cara simmered down a touch. "Miss the cold too much?"

"My girlfriend wanted to get married." He saw no reason to lie. "I didn't, and her dad ran the project."

"Ah." Cara pulled a face. "Well, that sucks. But as long as you're in town, and if you ever feel like expressing a few anal glands, come on by."

"Thanks." She really was funny and good looking, and he had nothing better to do. He could call Kelly, but she was making her move on Vince. "Got any plans for dinner?"

"When?"

He shrugged and kept it light. "Whenever you're free."

Cara cocked her head and studied him. Her scrutiny nearly made him fidget. "Nah!" She shook her head. "The gossip didn't lie. You're not too hard on the eyes, and then there's our mutual lust for de-fleaing, but you and I aren't a thing." She shook her head. "No spark."

"I'm not sure I would say that." Gabe's ego took a hit. From his side, Cara definitely had something going on.

She laughed and waved at him. "You're a guy; it doesn't take much. But I suspect you and I have too much in common." Eyes laughing at him, she leaned forward. "Also, I've heard all about your reputation with the ladies."

"What reputation?" Gabe tried to think what she might have heard. "I left here after high school."

"Folks around here have long memories." Cara tapped her temple. "They remember everything."

He couldn't believe that town sometimes. "You realize they are remembering the antics of an eighteen-year-old, and I hate to break it to you, but it wasn't nearly that exciting."

"Regardless, Gabe." She tucked her arm through his and looked up at him, eyes still laughing. "You and I are going to be friends, which is why you're going to let me buy you a beer and kick your ass at pool sometime."

Her complete lack of affectation went a long way to soothing what smart her rejection might have caused. "What makes you think you could?"

Cara snorted. "I am the undisputed champion in these parts for the last nine months."

Gabe met her challenging stare. "That's only because I haven't been around."

"Bring it." Cara held out her hand and he shook it. "Give me a call when you're ready to eat those words."

He called his mother on the way home. Her dog had improved on the leash already and wasn't pulling his arm out of the socket the entire way. "Ma, can you get that coven of yours busy?"

"Doing what?" Ma sounded suspicious. "And it's a prayer chain, not a coven."

"The new vet." The prayer chain was the power that abided in Twin Elks. "She needs some more business, or she's not going to be able to keep going."

Okay, so he exaggerated.

"Oh, dear." Ma sighed. "I'm not sure what I can do, but I can ask the prayer chain to see if they can help."

For the sake of diplomacy, Gabe suppressed a snort. Cara Addison was about to get a whole shit ton busier. "Thanks, Ma."

CHAPTER
Seven

AFTER SHE SHUT the coffee shop for the day, Kelly walked to the Crowe house. She waved to Pete, who was closing the realty office at the same time.

Two men came down the sidewalk toward her, neither of whom Kelly recognized. The taller of the two, nice looking in a regular-featured way, gave her a scintillating eye meet and grin. "Hey, there."

"Hello." Kelly sidestepped them and carried on down the sidewalk.

"We're new in town," he called after her.

"Congratulations?" Kelly waved over her shoulder and kept walking. All those new faces in town and at the Elk were disconcerting. Not to mention that weird exchange two minutes ago.

Turning into Dot's road, she passed Winters House. Finn and Claire were on the front porch, snuggled in a blanket.

"Stop canoodling," she called as she walked past. "This is a family neighborhood."

From the front yard, Poppy's son Ryan popped his head over the hedge. "What's canoodling?"

"Ask Ben," she said. No way she was touching that one with someone else's child.

Despite lingering worry about India, the walk lifted her spirits. That was why she'd come home to Twin Elks, for the sense of community and family. Sure, at times it got annoying with everybody all up in your business, but for the most part, it was nice. People gave a crap about each other.

As a young woman, she hadn't been able to wait to get the hell out. That had also had something to do with Vince and Chelsea being married and expecting their baby. She'd left Twin Elks with no intention of ever returning. But craving the peace and healing of being in a place where everybody knew your story, she'd come back.

India needed the same thing. It still felt surreal, like it couldn't be happening.

Dot really was a saint, but Kelly would need to make a more permanent arrangement for India and Jacob. They couldn't trespass on Dot's kindness forever.

"Kelly!" Dot called from her garden, looking up from filling her bird feeder. "How was the coffee shop today?"

"Good." Kelly let herself through the garden gate. "Busy. Pete from the realtor was in, and he said we're getting a real estate boom."

Dot looked smug. "How lovely." She rehung the feeder on its hook under the eaves. "I thought you'd be by, so I included you for dinner."

She really didn't want to put Dot out. Then again, Dot's cooking was awesome, and Kelly could barely heat soup. "I don't want to be a bother."

"Pfft!" Dot waved a hand in the air. "I used to feed five hungry boys and one hungry man. This is nothing."

The kitchen smelled heavenly when Kelly followed Dot in.

"I hope nobody is a vegetarian." Dot put the birdseed bag away in the laundry and washed her hands. "Because we're having beef tonight."

"Not that I know of." For all Kelly knew, it could be another thing about India she'd missed. She lowered her voice. "How has she been today?"

"Up and down." Dot made a face. "One minute she misses him, and the next, she never wants to see him again. She's scared and confused and heartbroken. It's going to take her a while to find a new normal."

It wasn't like one of India's scrapes that she could bandage, or a knotty hair snarl she could untangle. Trauma would take time and patience. And love. Lots and lots of love.

God! How had it happened? Anger surged through her anew.

As if reading her mind, Dot reached over and gave her a hug. "You're a good sister, Kelly. None of this is on you."

"My head sort of knows that." Something about Dot made you spill your guts. "But you know how Mom and Dad were, and before she passed Gram made me promise to take care of India."

"We can't protect them from everything. Nor should we." Dot cupped Kelly's face. "I'm not saying this is a good thing that happened to India. It's awful, and she is in no way responsible. But neither are you. Our children need to learn their own lessons. It would be so much easier if they could learn from ours, but they generally don't."

India was her sister, not her child, but it had been Kelly making sure she got to school with a packed lunch. Kelly had sat with India at the kitchen table doing her homework with her. And Kelly had stopped India from going to her prom with the school's biggest manwhore.

"I knew Ben shouldn't marry Tara," Dot said. "I also knew all about Tara cheating on him, but Ben had to reach his tipping point all by himself."

"It's my future bride," Gabe said from behind her.

Dot snorted and bent over her stove. "I wish."

"Just so you know, I'm expecting a big diamond. Huge." Kelly raised her eyebrow at him.

"How about I get you a drink instead?" He grinned.

"That works too."

"Wine? Beer?" Gabe's ass was pure magic in a pair of worn Levi's.

And she really needed to stop noticing. "Wine, please. How long are you staying in Twin Elks?"

The other night, they had gotten to his reasons for being home, but not for how long. Matters had gotten deflected by a light kiss under a full moon that had exploded into a hot and sweaty marathon of lips, teeth, and tongues.

Gabe opened the wine, the cork popping out of the bottle. "I'm not really sure. It will depend on what I can line up."

"Have any prospects?" She propped her hip against the counter. The thought of Gabe leaving left her feeling flat. He was good fun, and he certainly upped the town's hotness quotient.

"Not really." Gabe shrugged. "But anywhere they have great white sharks."

"Those must be some fairly limited options."

"Good news if you're a seal," he said.

Dot's large puppy sauntered into the kitchen, caught sight of Kelly and lurched into a squirming launch at her.

Gabe caught his collar and held him until he settled down. The dog stared up at Gabe with slavish devotion.

"He likes you," Kelly said.

Gabe laughed. "He'll get over it. Most who know me do."

"You!" Dot huffed. "And why couldn't you have fallen in love with wolves? Or coyotes? Something we have right here in Twin Elks?"

"I did it to spite you, Ma." Gabe put an arm around her shoulder and tugged Dot in for a kiss. "I do miss you when I'm not here."

Although she snorted, Dot succumbed to the hug.

"Kelly?" India stood in the doorway, pale and drawn and looking like a harsh word would crack her. "Are you done at the coffee shop?"

"Yup." She hugged India. "I close at five."

"Is that the time?" India glanced around, confusion on her face. "I thought it was earlier."

"You've been sleeping," Dot said and motioned India to the table. "I'm not surprised with all you've been through."

India blinked at her. "Oh. I thought I had put my head down for a few minutes."

The confusion bothered Kelly. Despite her doubts, her conversation with Piers popped into her head again. She needed to talk to India about it.

From deeper in the house, Jacob cried.

India jerked and looked startled, as if she didn't quite grasp the significance.

"I'll get him." Gabe strode for the door. "Have a seat, India, and I'll bring him to you."

India made a halfhearted attempt to follow. "He might need changing."

"If I can tag a shark, I'm sure I can find my way around a diaper." Gabe smiled at her and left, the dog at his heels.

"Sit, sweetheart." Kelly guided her sister to a chair by the table. She took the place settings from Dot and set the table. The silence felt heavy, and she wanted to dispel it. Her voice sounded too hearty as she said, "Dinner smells great, Dot. Doesn't dinner smell good, India?"

God, what an idiot. The situation was out of her lane, and she needed to do some research before she mistakenly did or said something wrong. The last thing she wanted was to send India running back to Piers.

Gabe came back carrying Jacob, clearly having solved the diaper issue. He took a bottle of baby food out of the fridge and found a feeding spoon in the cutlery drawer.

"I can do that." Kelly felt bad enough for imposing.

He waved her off. "Nah. The big guy and I are going to enjoy some—" he peered at the label—"strained peas and carrots. Yum!"

Jacob stared at him with big, serious blue eyes. He looked a lot more like Piers than he did India. Two sets of blond, blue-eyed genes had created an angelic looking mix. Irrationally, she resented Piers even that. He didn't deserve his little family, his beautiful wife and baby.

"Put him in the highchair." Dot motioned to the laundry.

Gabe's arms were full, and Kelly got up to get the chair and set it up. With confident proficiency, Gabe got Jacob into the chair and a bib around his neck.

"You're awfully good at this." Kelly tried to lighten the atmosphere. "Is there something you're not telling us?"

"Sean trained me." Gabe gave her a naughty smile. The sort of smile that could get a girl into all sorts of trouble. "Although he's now decided he wants to eat at the table with the rest of us."

"You have no room to complain." Dot waved a slotted spoon at him. "As soon as Ben ate at the table, you refused to go in the highchair." She looked at Kelly and rolled her eyes. "Everything Ben did, that one had to do."

India sat at the table, like an island in their midst. She barely glanced at them but stared out the window at the darkening night sky.

Gabe fed Jacob while Kelly helped Dot put the meal on the table.

Kelly filled everyone's wineglasses and took a seat.

"India?" Dot softened her tone. "Can I get you something to eat?"

"What?" India started. She looked at the food on the table and flushed. "Oh, no. I'm not very hungry."

India was too thin as it was, and Kelly wanted to protest.

"Okay." Dot put a piece of meat and a small spoon of veggies on a plate and put it in front of India. "I'll leave that there. If you change your mind."

"Thank you." India stared at the plate as if it repulsed her.

"Kelly?" Dot passed her the meat platter. "Help yourself."

"Thanks, Dot. It looks fantastic." Again with the overly eager and jovial. She didn't need to fill in for herself and India. Dot would understand.

Before she could make more of an idiot of herself, she picked up her knife and fork and ate her dinner.

After a while, India managed a few bites from her plate.

Gabe swapped between feeding himself and feeding Jacob. "I dropped by to see the new vet today," he said.

"Oh, yes." Dot peered over her wineglass at him. "I meant to tell you that I called a few people. She's a good girl, that Cara. It would be nice if she stayed."

"I don't really know her." Kelly dismissed the jab of jealousy because it was ridiculous. It shouldn't matter to her that Gabe and Cara Addison must have so much to talk about. Or that Cara was undeniably sexy. "I've seen her around, because this is Twin Elks, but I should get to know her better."

"You should." Gabe wiped Jacob's mouth. "She's really nice and down to earth. The sort of woman you'd like."

"Piers doesn't like animals in the house. He says they're dirty," India said.

Gabe waded into the awkward silence. "For sure they bring a lot of fur with them. You can't be too particular if you own a pet. Speaking of—" He looked at Dot. "You need to train that bear of yours."

"Oh, Gabe." Dot made a face at him. "He's a baby."

"Ma." Gabe leveled a hard stare at her. "He's a hundred-and-ten-pound baby with teeth. He needs training." He finished his dinner and freed Jacob from the chair. "It's bath time for this guy."

"I can—"

"Talk to your sister," Gabe said to her. "Why don't you guys take your wine into the lounge and have a chat?"

Kelly stood. "I'll help clear—"

"Go." Dot shooed her out, with a meaningful look in India's direction. "I think a nice quiet chat might be lovely."

Meek and listless, India followed her into the lounge and took a seat in one of the large, comfy chairs beside the fireplace.

Someone had turned it on earlier, and it warmed the lived-in room and filled it with a mellow glow.

Kelly sat on the stone step surrounding the fire, and Dot's "baby" immediately joined her. He put his huge head in her lap and treated her to soulful eyes until she petted him. It gave her a minute to order her thoughts.

"I had a call today," she said.

India stared into the fire. "Oh?"

"Yes, it was Piers."

Starting, India stared at her. "He knows I'm here, doesn't he?"

"No." She hoped Piers wasn't going to find his way to Twin Elks. "I only told him you were safe, and not where you were. I also called Ben and told him about the call. He contacted the Denver PD to pick Piers up."

India winced. "He'll be furious about the police getting involved."

"You're safe here, India. You have that restraining order, and none of us are going to let Piers near you." Now came the awkward part. "But, sweetie, he mentioned something I wanted to talk to you about."

India chewed her lip and checked behind her as if Piers might be coming through the door at any second.

"He said you suffered from postpartum depression."

Raising her chin, India gave a bitter laugh. "Of course, he did."

"It's not true then?" Kelly was reluctant to push India, since she seemed so fragile.

"I honestly don't know." India looked at her. Her eyes gleamed with emotion Kelly couldn't identify. "Piers said I wasn't myself after Jacob was born. He said I was acting differently. But I'd just had a baby, Kelly. Things change in a marriage when you have a baby."

Kelly waited for more.

"You aren't...the same. I was tired all the time, and the hormones..." She took a deep breath. Firelight created deeper shadows in her gaunt face. "Piers didn't think he was getting the...attention he deserved."

Shit, that raised a whole other hideous specter Kelly didn't want to confront. "Are you talking about sex?"

Flinching, India nodded. "We waited until the doctor said it was safe, but I didn't feel like it. I was tired all the time, and he didn't think that was right."

"India." God, Kelly didn't want to ask, but she had to. "Did he force you?"

"No!" India recoiled. "Whatever you think of Piers, he isn't that. It's more that he didn't make it easy to say no." She shrugged and stared into the fire. "You're not married, Kelly, so you don't understand. Sometimes it's easier to go along with it."

You didn't need to be married to know that was bullshit, but India's expression was shuttered. "Piers mentioned medication."

"The doctor gave me that," India said. "Piers insisted that I go and see him and tell him about my symptoms. I didn't want to, but Piers is hard to say no to."

Apparently in more ways than one. Kelly wanted to put her fist through something.

India shrugged. "It did make me feel better, which made Piers happier. For a while."

"And then what happened?"

India huffed and stood up. "I'm tired, and I don't want to talk about this."

"But—"

India left the lounge, said goodnight to whoever was in the kitchen and walked down the passage. A door shut.

Damn it! Kelly hugged Dot's dog. There was something about dogs that made the bad thing back off.

"Hey." Gabe appeared in the kitchen doorway. "Everything okay?"

"Yes." Her response came automatically, but she didn't know why she was lying. "Actually no."

Gabe cocked his head, waiting for more.

"Piers called me today."

Gabe hissed in a breath. "Is he looking for her?"

"Yup." She wrapped the dog's silky ears around her fingers. "I let Ben know already, but I'm not sure if he's going to pitch up here or not." Why wouldn't India talk to her about the medication? "Then he mentioned that India had been suffering from postpartum depression. He said he was worried about her when he came home and she wasn't there."

"Really?" Gabe snorted and propped a shoulder against the doorframe. "It sounds like someone is trying to build himself a case for the defense."

Kelly wished India would let her in. "He said she left her medication at home and she needs it."

"You believe him?"

"No." She couldn't meet Gabe's eye. "But I can't completely dismiss the idea of her having depression. India has always been…fragile. Emotionally."

He dropped his chin to his chest. "I take it you tried to talk to her about it."

"Yup." Kelly huffed out her frustration. "Now I'm more confused than ever, and she doesn't want to clear things up for me."

"Right." Gabe straightened and called over his shoulder. "Ma!"

"Yes."

"You got everything here? I'm taking Kelly for a beer."

"How nice." Dot sounded delighted. "You two run along now and don't give us a thought."

Gabe rolled his eyes and handed Kelly her coat. "She's matchmaking."

"I'm flattered, but I'm really not the marrying kind."

Gabe cocked his head. "Not even for Vince?"

"Yes. No. I really don't know." It suddenly seemed strange that she'd been pining after a man for all these years and never thought the end game through.

"Way to commit." Gabe laughed. "Anyway, I wouldn't panic yet. Ma would marry me to Hank Styles if she thought it would keep me here."

A beer with Gabe sounded like a great idea, so Kelly slid her arms into her coat. "Hank has a wonderful personality, and when he puts in the effort, he really is quite dashing."

Pulling her arm through his, Gabe chuckled. "You up for walking it?"

Things between them felt so easy. Kelly tucked herself closer to his side and leached his body heat. "Sure."

CHAPTER
Eight

A COLD, crisp night settled around them. Not a single cloud obscured the stars from view and their breath made puffy vapor clouds in the air. Their footsteps clopped along the silent street.

"You and Dot have been so kind," she said. "I'll make arrangements for India and Jacob as soon as I can."

"Don't stress it, babe." Gabe covered her hand on his arm with his. "Ma loves having someone to fuss over, and it's not like I'm doing anything much anyway."

"No luck on the job hunt?"

"I few nibbles." He nudged her. "Nibbles? Sharks? See what I did there?"

Kelly had to laugh. "Dumbass."

They walked farther, both of them enjoying the silence. The cold air and the walk cleared her head, and Kelly was grateful to Gabe for the idea.

"Do you ever think about staying?" She peered through the dark to read his expression.

Gabe didn't say anything for a while, and then he grimaced. "Nope. There's nothing for me here."

"Ouch!" She punched him. "I'm sure your mother and brother would disagree. Not to mention your friends."

"Are we friends?" Gabe's voice dropped into a velvety murmur.

"Yes." The other night aside, she liked Gabe. Actually, the other night had been spectacular. Dot's boys took care of their women. Poppy said the same of Ben.

"With benefits?" His tone warmed and she got the feeling he was thinking about that night as well.

She couldn't afford to go there, however. Not with her chance with Vince still hovering out there, in addition to India's troubles. Currently, she had all the entanglements she could handle. "Probably not a good idea."

"Probably," he said, but sounded about as convinced as she was. As in, not really.

They reached the Bugling Elk, and Gabe opened the door for her. The familiar smell of beer and woodsmoke rushed toward them in a draft of warm air.

Maddison looked up from the bar and nodded. "Hey, you two. How's it going?"

"Good." Gabe took Kelly's coat and hung it on a coat hook before shrugging out of his own and hanging it.

Kelly looked at him. "Two beers?"

Gabe nodded and took the barstool next to her.

"On it." Maddison turned and got to pouring their drinks.

The same two guys who had spoken to her on the street sat at the bar bracketing Robin Cameron and making her giggle.

Propping one elbow on the bar, Gabe turned sideways and rested his feet on the footrest of her stool. "About India," he said. "This has all just happened, and she's dealing with a lot. Maybe a lot of this doesn't even make sense to her yet."

That sounded right to her, and Kelly nodded. "Patience is not really my thing."

"I remember." Gabe gave her a naughty grin, his eyes glinting with a sensual message.

"Now, Gabe. God, please, now!"

That may have been her the other night—as in totally had

been her—begging Gabe to put out the fire he'd stoked into an inferno inside her.

"Stop that!" She jabbed a finger at him. "We agreed it was a mistake."

"Mistake?" Gabe pulled a face. "I don't know if I'd call it a mistake as such." He broke into a grin. "At least, from what I remember, it was pretty rocking."

For her too, and heat climbed her cheeks. "Fair enough. It was passable, but we agreed it couldn't happen again."

He raised an eyebrow and called her bullshit. "Passable?"

"Yes, passable." She held his gaze. "Because if I admit you rocked my world, then I might have more trouble with the not happening again part."

He grinned. "Fair enough."

Maddison put their beers in front of them, and they both took a sip.

"Speaking of reasons it can't happen again, how are things with Vince?"

Kelly turned to face him for that one. "Such a clumsy segue."

"I work with animals." He shrugged. "I don't always speak human."

It struck her that he might be able to provide a different perspective. "Actually, I don't know what the hell is going on with Vince."

He sipped his beer and waited. Gabe did that a lot, gave you a silence to fill. Of course, she loved to fill a silence.

"He's been coming to the shop since I opened it. Every day. Same cup of coffee and we chat, make each other laugh. From the day I came back and opened the Klatch, even when he was married to Chelsea." But she had thought something new would have happened by now. "And he still does. But…"

"Same old same old?"

"Right." She slapped her hand on the bar as an outlet for her irritation. "Only now, he comes up to the counter and gives me these meaningful stares. Like he wants to say something and can't. And then I find myself wondering if I'm doing the chick thing."

"Chick thing?"

"Reading into his every gesture and word as if it's all meaningful. When most of the time you guys are hearing elevator music in your heads." She finished her beer and motioned Maddison for two more.

Gabe straightened on his barstool and gave her a look of reproach. "We do not hear elevator music." He counted his points on his fingers. "First off, it's either jazz or rock we're hearing, and secondly we do that because if you knew what we were really thinking, you'd probably knee us in the balls."

He'd caught her with a mouthful of beer that nearly ended up shooting out her nose. "You're such a guy."

"I didn't hear you complaining—"

"Ah-ah." She wagged a finger at him. "We shall refer to that night, as the night of which shall not be spoken."

"Sounds like a mouthful to me." Gabe grinned around the mouth of his beer bottle. "So, Vince is dragging his feet?"

Hauling on her big girl pants, she asked the question nagging her, "Do you think he might not be interested anymore?"

"Maybe." Gabe mulled it over. "I mean, it's always a possibility, but if he's still hanging around, it's not that likely. If he really wasn't interested, he would avoid you and hope like hell you didn't push the issue now that he's free to do something about it."

"Is that what you did?" All his wisdom was pissing her off.

Gabe grimaced. "Yup. I earned a master's degree in ignoring the signals. I even managed to overlook the magazines left on the coffee table, page opened to engagement rings."

"Wow." Kelly felt for his ex. "Those are some impressive ignoring skills."

"I wasn't ready to get married." He shrugged. "I'm still not."

"Hmm." They drank in a comfortable silence. "Do you believe there is someone out there for you?" She felt silly asking, but she'd gotten this far. "I mean, like a one person for you."

He glanced at her. "The one?"

"Yes."

"I do." Gabe nodded. "Look at Ben. After Tara, I would have sworn he'd never marry again. She fucked with him in about every way a woman can screw with a man. But look at him now."

"Poppy is special." And Kelly's best friend since the day Poppy had thrown herself out of her minivan and begged to be arrested.

Gabe studied her for a moment. "So are you." He held his hands out, palm up. "No bullshit. You're a great girl, Kelly, and Vince is lucky to have you."

"Only he keeps trying to throw me back." His compliment warmed her from the inside out.

Shrugging, Gabe said, "It's not that so much as he's hesitating to take you off the hook."

"Nice." She snorted. "Can we stop with the fishing analogies now?"

Gabe chuckled. "Sure thing." He cocked his head and studied her. "If Vince is struggling to ask you, why don't you ask him?"

"Gabe." Kelly squirmed on her barstool. "Because I want him to ask me. I'm that girl."

He gave that some thought. "Yeah, and I'm that guy. I can't imagine not making my move if I'd waited as long as Vince." He sipped his beer. "Who broke up with whom way back when?"

"I broke up with him." And regretted it immediately after and for the next fifteen years. "He wanted to stay in Twin Elks, and I wanted to head for the wide blue yonder."

"Ah!" Gabe nodded as if he understood the secret to life. "That makes more sense."

"How, Yoda?"

"He needs a show of faith from you. You broke up with him, probably broke his heart, and definitely dented his ego. Now he needs to know you're on the same page before he puts himself at risk again."

Kelly let that sink in. It made a sort of sense. "Is that what you would need?"

"Nah." Gabe shook his head. "If I'd missed out on my girl for years, I'd be at that like a rat up a drainpipe."

She was glad she wasn't drinking as he said that. "Nice!"

He gave her that Gabe bad-boy grin and a wink. "But I'm an asshole. Ask Belinda."

"Is that why you didn't marry her?" A pattern was emerging, and it made her understand him better. "If she wasn't the one, and you knew it, you knew she wasn't the right one to marry."

"Yup."

"That's not wrong per se." But her girl card demanded she speak for women everywhere. "What makes you an asshole is you stuck around knowing that."

"Agreed." He pointed his beer bottle at her. "Except Belinda knew the score. Or at least she did until she didn't want to know it anymore."

He glared behind the bar and drank his beer.

Kelly took the hint; talking about Belinda was a no-fly zone. "What sort of gesture?"

"Eh?"

"You said Vince might need a show of faith from me. What would that look like?"

Gabe cocked his head. "You make the first move."

"Like seduce him?"

This time Gabe almost spat beer. "I was thinking more of you asking him out."

Kelly weighed that over. After all these years, it wasn't really the same as asking a complete stranger out. Still, it would be nice if Vince asked her. Then again, what if he didn't and they let another fifteen years slip by?

She needed to think. "I need to get going."

"Let's do it." Gabe dropped some bills on the bar for Maddison and waved her good night.

While they put their coats on, Kelly felt she needed to offer, although she didn't mean a word of it. "You can stay if you like."

"Nah." He opened the door for her, and they stepped into the night. "Ma would have my balls if I didn't walk a lady home."

It had grown colder since they'd arrived, and Kelly shivered.

Gabe dropped his arm over her shoulders and pulled her closer to him.

It seemed the most natural thing in the world to slide her arm beneath his coat and around his waist.

Her mistake didn't wait around to make itself known. Gabe smelled fantastic. Not of aftershave, but of soap and clean skin and that hormone incinerating male musk. He felt even better. Under her arm, his waist was trim, and through his shirt, his back muscles flexed with each step.

Knowing that he looked as good as casual contact suggested exacerbated her problem and sent it soaring into dirty dreams territory. All she had to do was close her eyes, and it was right there waiting to give her a replay.

Dammit. It replayed behind open eyes as well.

Gabe slid his hand into the hair at her nape and cupped her neck. His hand was warm and calloused against her skin.

Hands that had petted and stroked her into a frenzy of desire. Hands that knew where all those secret sweet spots on her body were.

Her belly dipped and swooped, and her skin heated. Her nerve endings tingled and demanded she press her body closer to his.

They were both breathing hard, and the notion that she affected him like he affected her made her girl parts scream at her. Her nipples hardened and pressed against her bra, and it had nothing to do with the cold. She wasn't feeling any cold right that moment.

Their steps matched perfectly, their bodies finding a natural rhythm. Just like they had the other night.

She had to stop thinking about it.

Vince! She owed it to herself to see where things with Vince could go. There might never be another time.

They stopped in her parking lot, with Kelly not really registering the time between the bar and there.

"Kelly." Gabe faced her. His breath misted into hers on the cold night air. His gaze asked the question.

Stamping on her clamoring libido, she whispered, "We shouldn't."

"You're right." He dipped his head and pressed his mouth to hers, softly, coaxing.

There was only so much a girl could take, and Kelly opened her lips to the slight touch of his tongue.

Groaning, Gabe gripped her skull and took her mouth. The kiss leaped from a tentative query to a mind-numbing, ovary-blasting assault on her senses.

Ending it was not an option, and Kelly threw herself into the kiss. Tongues tangled, teeth clashed, lips mashed as she pressed her body to his.

A light blinked on in a condo opposite hers.

Kelly grabbed what few wits she could locate and ended the kiss. "We can't."

Running a hand through his hair, Gabe chuckled. "I think we've established that we can. The issue is more if we should."

"No." She didn't have enough words to gather. "We shouldn't."

He stepped away and shoved his hands in his pockets. "You're right." He jerked his head at her condo. "But for fuck's sake, get in your condo, Kelly. I'm hanging on by a thread here."

CHAPTER
Nine

KELLY GAVE herself a good talking to as she opened the Koffee Klatch the next morning. Kissing Gabe last night had been a reaction to the conversation about Vince, a confidence booster to help her make the first move with Vince.

She still didn't want to be the one leaping first, but somebody had to, and after fifteen years of circling each other, the worst case was letting another fifteen slip past before one of them did anything.

If they kept that up, Vince would be shuffling into her coffee shop on his walker and she'd be turning up her hearing aid to get the orders right.

She could ask him out. She was a strong, assertive, independent woman. No biggie. Women did it all the time. The days of Rapunzel waiting in her tower were over. Rapunzel was rappelling the hell outta that tower and finding her man.

There! She got ready for the day, turning on the coffee machines, filling the shelves with cups, setting out the pastries the bakery had delivered.

She opened the door, and her customers drifted in, mostly regulars but a few new faces as well.

A ginger-haired man with a slight paunch and a Star Wars T-shirt stood at the counter and leered at her. "Hi. What's your name?"

"Says it right here." Kelly pointed to her badge. "What can I get you?"

He grinned and eyed her boobs. "Well, Kelly—"

"Coffee." She didn't need a psychology degree to see where ginger ninja was heading. "What can I get for you coffee-wise?"

"Oh." He blinked and colored bright red. "I'm new in town? Is that what I'm supposed to say?"

"No idea." Customers were backing up behind him. People there to order coffee, not ogle her.

He cleared his throat and dropped his head. "Right then. Sorry. Do you have any herbal teas?"

"Peppermint, ginger, African red bush."

"Peppermint." He dug out his wallet. "Please. Kelly."

"You got it." Now that he wasn't trying to eye hump her, he looked kinda dorky, sweet and shy.

A regular replaced him. "Hey, Kel!" He plopped his travel mug on the counter. "Fill her up."

"Got a long haul today?"

"Nah." Dean adjusted his ball cap. "A load of tires up to Denver. Picking up another trailer there. Someone's household goods."

She filled his mug and made sure the top was secure. "You drive safe now, Dean."

"Will do, Kelly. You stay pretty."

"I always do."

Word of her coffee shop had hit the trucker grapevine, and they often came the three miles off the highway for a decent cup of coffee.

Vince might have had something to do with it.

She kept a steady pep talk going in her head as she served her customers.

Of course, all her careful preparation blew to hell when Vince walked through the door at his normal time.

"Good morning." His big sweet smile encouraged her. "You look pretty today."

"Thank you." She was glad her bit of extra effort this morning was appreciated by its intended target. "The usual?"

He took a seat at the counter, which she took as another good sign. The universe was giving her the great big thumbs-up. Not wanting to leap straight into it, she put his coffee in front of him. "How's your day going?"

"Not bad." Another sweet smile. "All the better for seeing you."

Opportunity had presented itself. It wouldn't get more fortuitous. "So, I was thinking." She leaned her elbows on the counter and got close enough to him that her voice wouldn't carry to the rest of the coffee shop. "About seeing me. Or me seeing you." This was Vince, for the love of God. Vince! She needed to untangle her tongue and speak to the man. "I mean, seeing each other."

Stellar job!

Vince looked at her over his coffee mug, confusion clouding his brown eyes.

She took a deep breath. "I was wondering if you'd like to see more of me." Shit! That had come out all wrong. "I mean not more of me more of me, but more of me."

Vince blinked at her.

Grabbing her courage, she went for it. "I'm asking, and really badly I might add, if you would like to go out with me sometime."

"As friends or like a date?" Vince cocked his head.

Relief surged through her. Stage one complete. "No, not as friends, but on a date. I was thinking it might be time."

"Yes." His grin grew bigger. "Kelly, I would like nothing better than to go on a date with you, and yes, we have both waited long enough."

"Really?" She wanted to tango around her shop.

Vince leaned his elbows on the counter and got closer. "Yes, really."

"Great."

"Great."

They grinned at each other for a long moment. A customer broke the stare down and Kelly filled his order.

Vince stood and dropped some money on the counter. She nearly told him not to bother, but that might be sending the wrong message. Like she could be bought.

For two dollars. Damn! She needed to get a grip.

"I have to get going." Vince jerked his head at the door. "Busy day."

"Sure." She made a flapping motion with her hands that she hoped like hell didn't look as dorky as it felt. "Take care out there."

Nodding, Vince yanked the door open.

At the same time Gabe walked in and they did an awkward directional tussle in the doorway.

Vince stopped suddenly and turned. "When?"

"When?"

"For our...um...date." Vince stepped aside and let Gabe walk in.

Shit. She hadn't thought about that. "Friday?"

"Can we make it Saturday night?" Vince made a face. "I have the kids on Friday."

She could totally do that. "Saturday night it is."

"Seven?"

"Seven." She nodded, almost putting her neck out in her enthusiasm.

Vince grinned back. "I'll pick you up and take care of the rest."

Another thing she hadn't given much thought to. She now had far more empathy for men everywhere.

The bell above the door tinkled on Vince's exit.

Gabe raised an eyebrow at her. "Hot date?"

It gave her great delight to confirm his assumption. "Hot date." And she'd screwed up all the details. "How the hell do guys do this all the time?"

———

Gabe schooled his features as he took a seat at the counter.

In jeans that hugged her dangerous curves and a tight pink sweater that made him want to rub against her like a cat, Kelly looked one hundred percent fuckable this morning. "So, you took my advice and did the asking?"

"I did." She blushed as she nodded and looked so adorable in the process he wanted to…

Back that truck up. Kelly liked Vince, and Vince liked Kelly. Ergo, Kelly and Vince would go out on Saturday night, at seven —because now he had the details in his head to drive him crazy —and they would start where they left off in high school. If memory served, that was a long way down the road to happily ever after. Next time, he should think things through before he tossed advice at people.

Kelly leaned her elbows on the counter and tipped her pretty face toward him. "I asked a man out on a date. I am now a fully actualized, bad ass bitch in charge of her own orgasm."

"You're a praying mantis."

She scrunched her face up at him, which he also found cute AF. "Did you call me a bug?"

"I called you the bad ass bitch bug of the bug kingdom." He needed to keep it light before he started pounding his chest like a silverback or pissing up her leg to mark his territory. Because she was not his. Not his territory. Not his anything other than his friend.

"Aren't they the bugs that rip their man's head off and eat it after mating?" She put a mug of coffee in front of him.

He liked that she didn't need to ask to get it right. Of course, she didn't need to ask. She owned a coffee shop. Of course, she knew what her customers drank. "Yup. Poor dude doesn't stand a chance."

"Seems a lot to pay for a roll in the hay." Her big blues sparkled at him, drawing him into her laughter.

He gave her his best nonchalant shrug. "It depends on the roll in the hay." He sipped his coffee, meeting her gaze square. She needed to get his meaning loud and clear. "Some females are worth it."

"Oh." She blushed and couldn't meet his eye anymore. "Oh."

Counting that as a win, he didn't stay much longer. What had happened between him and Kelly had been mind-blowing and hot as crap, but it was history. The future belonged to Vince and Kelly.

Hands in his pockets, he walked toward home. The weather was turning, growing colder each day. The sharp bite of ice in the air presaged more snow. The weather pundits were warning of a snowy winter. Colorado needed it after the last few dry years.

In Australia, he'd forgotten the joys of a snowy winter. Sure, the ice and the cold sucked, but nothing beat the feeling of lying in bed as the intense silence of a snowy morning blanketed the world. It had been a long time since he'd opened his eyes to a winter wonderland.

Maybe he remembered winter in Twin Elks so fondly because there had been no snow that morning he'd insisted Dad go hiking with him.

Gabe slammed the shutters down on that memory. He'd spent his adulthood not going there, and he was not going to fix what wasn't broken. Some shit hurt too damn much.

He needed to act, do something to get his head in the right place. All this hanging around, stagnating, didn't work for him.

Flipping through his contacts, he found the one he wanted and dialed. "Cara."

"The other veterinarian in town." She chuckled.

This felt better than dwelling on stuff that couldn't be changed. "I'm calling to take you up on that game of pool."

"When?"

He liked that she cut straight to the point. "Saturday night?"

"Meet you at the Elk."

They hung up, and he continued his walk home feeling better. That was what he had needed. The thing with Kelly was circumstantial. They were both at a crossroads in their lives and had crashed into each other.

Granted the crashing made his nether regions throb, but sex didn't mean anything. He was a veterinarian for God's sake. Survival drove the need to procreate.

Ma had left the kitchen door open, so he let himself in and locked the door behind him. Her dog crashed into his knees and lolled his tongue at him.

She really needed to give him a name. He was a great dog, big and untrained, but a great dog nevertheless.

On his way to his bedroom, he passed India's door. Years before, it had been Ben's room. Gabe remembered to this day the intense jealousy he'd felt at Ben getting his own room.

A soft noise, like a sob being stifled, stopped him.

The door was ajar, and he backtracked three steps to see if everything was alright.

India sat crying in the middle of cardboard boxes and pieces of wood.

Gabe had never been able to resist a hurt creature, and he pushed the door open. "India?"

"Gabe." She started and gave her cheeks a hasty swipe. "I thought everyone was out."

He stepped into the room. A piece of paper lay at his feet, and he picked it up. It was the instructions for assembling a crib. He held it out to India. "Is this for Jacob?"

"Ye-e-s." Big tears welled in her eyes and crept down her cheeks. "He can't keep using Poppy's crib. I bought this one."

She threw her hands out. "Only, I can't seem to work out how to assemble it."

Gabe crouched beside her. "Let's see if two heads are better than one."

"No, I can't ask you to do that." India sucked back a big breath and straightened her shoulders. "You've already been so kind to us."

Picking up piece A, Gabe located piece B and slotted them together. "You didn't ask. Bolts?"

She handed him one. "I think these are the right ones."

"Looks like it." Gabe bolted the pieces together, nudged her over and took a seat beside her. "Now we have to find more pieces that look like those two. We have to do the same thing three times."

"Three times?" India gaped at him, her blue eyes wide and startled.

India and Kelly had the same eyes. Physically, at least they did. Except, India looked at him as if he could slay a dragon. Kelly's eyes, on the other hand, yelled that if he took her sword to slay her dragon, she'd nut punch him.

The thought made him laugh as he found the pieces and put the crib together.

"Thank you so much." India blinked at him.

Sure, a look like that made a man feel like he'd done good, but he much preferred the look that he had to work for. "No worries."

CHAPTER
Ten

KELLY OPENED her door that evening and stared at the man standing on her doorstep. "Piers!" Adrenalin prickled through her system. "What the hell are you doing here?"

"Don't slam the door." He held his elegant, long hands up. From his hundred-dollar haircut to his designer shoes, everything about Piers was neat and elegant. "I only want a chance to talk to you."

Kelly gripped the door, not sure what to do. Her gut said to slam the door anyway, but she had some questions for the son of a bitch. "Speak fast."

"Can I come in?" Piers adjusted the pale blue sweater knotted over his shoulders.

"No."

He blinked at her and shoved his hands in the pockets of his pressed chinos. "Fair enough. We can talk out here as well."

"What makes you think I'm interested in hearing anything you have to say?" The preppy exterior was dress up on the bona fide dickhead it concealed. You could slap a dress on a pig, but that didn't make it a beauty queen. "You have a crap ton of nerve showing up here."

"I couldn't get our telephone conversation out of my mind."

Piers grimaced. "We've always gotten along, and I thought I could come here. Explain. Clear things up."

"I'm very clear on things. And as for you and I getting along, that's over." She'd bet her last dollar he had those eyebrows done as well. Definitely took his Brooks Brothers ass down to the salon for streaks and a monthly manicure. "After what you did to India, you're lucky I'm not giving you the same back." She jabbed her finger in his chest. "You." *Jab.* "Took." *Harder jab.* "Your fist." *Thump.* "To my little sister."

"Kelly, stop!" He caught her hand in a strong, but not bruising grip. "Please stop. It's not like that. You don't understand."

She yanked her hand from his toxic touch. "There's not much to understand, you motherfucker. You hit my sister, and then you threatened Jacob."

"No." Piers gaped at her. "What? You can't think I would do that. Any of that. Give me a chance to tell you my side of this."

"You don't have a side." Kelly started closing the door.

Piers caught it. "India hasn't been herself. We had some trouble finding the right balance to the medication. It made her irrational. She makes up stories."

"Like she made up those bruises?" Of course, he would say India was lying. "Let the door go."

"What bruises?" He frowned. "What bruises? Who hurt her? Who the hell hurt her?"

"You did. The bruises are the ones you put on her." Kelly pushed at his arm to loosen his grip on the door.

"I swear, on my mother's life, if India has bruises, they didn't come from me." He let go of the door and ran his hand through his perfectly cut and styled brown hair. "Jesus! No wonder you don't want me near her. I thought it was something she had told you, but..." He turned tormented eyes her way. "She has bruises?" Stepping away from the door, he turned and looked at the sky. "God, this is a nightmare."

If it was a performance, Piers had missed his calling as an actor. He looked distraught.

Kelly struggled to get a bead on him. "Next, you're going to tell me she got those bruises falling down stairs, or walking into a door. With her neck."

"I can't believe this." Piers dropped his head. "Of course, you aren't going to believe me."

"I saw the evidence. You should also know she said it in front of Ben Crowe, which means he has probable cause to arrest you." Kelly took enormous satisfaction telling Piers that.

Piers looked dumbstruck. "I'm going to be arrested? That's insane. I could lose my job, my reputation in our community. Get a criminal record." He swallowed. "I need to call my lawyer."

"You do that." Anything to get him off her doorstep, and he could be damn sure the moment she closed the door, Ben would know Piers was in town. "Because you sure as hell are going to need that lawyer before we're done with you."

"I don't…I can't. I didn't come here for this. For trouble." He dug something out of his pocket. "I came to give you these." He handed her a prescription bottle. "If you know where she is, she really needs these. Now more than ever."

"What are they?" Kelly peered at the bottle.

Piers shoved his hands in his pockets. "Her doctor prescribed those for her condition. It's more serious than I let on before. India is…not well, and if what you say is true, then she's spiraling." He blew out a long breath. "She needs those. I honestly don't know what else she'll do to herself, or Jacob, if she doesn't have them."

"You're making this up."

Piers pointed to the pills. "The doctor's name is on the bottle. I suppose you could call him and see if I'm telling you the truth."

"You're saying India has a mental condition?" Kelly read the label. There was a doctor's name, and she could look up the number. "And this doctor is not going to tell me anything."

"Yeah." Piers shook his head. "I'll call him and tell him what's going on. The bruises could mean she's escalating. At least he'll be able to verify India is a patient of his. Maybe if you know, you can persuade India to drop the charges."

"India didn't lay the charges, and these charges won't be dropped until you see the inside of a courtroom."

"Jesus." He pushed a hand through his hair. "I never thought she would go this far. It isn't true, Kelly. None of this is true."

His distress seemed so genuine. Kelly stared hard at him, trying to find some hint he was lying. "Why would she do any of this?"

"She's not well, Kelly." He shook his head. "She does things, and it's not her fault. But, of course, none of what I'm saying makes any difference. Every abusive bastard out there denies he lifted a hand to the woman. I'm stuck in a double bind here." He straightened his shoulders. "That's not your problem, though. You're protecting India, and I'm glad someone is." He pointed at the prescription bottle. "But whatever you believe or don't believe about me and what happened, could you please make sure she gets those. She needs them."

Turning, he trotted away and disappeared down the stairs to the condo parking lot.

"Damn." Kelly slammed the door shut. Nothing added up. If Piers hadn't put those marks on India, who the hell had? A random attack by some stranger seemed so far left of likely she couldn't even consider it.

She called Ben's number.

"Kelly," he answered. "What's up?"

"Piers was here," she said. "At my condo."

Ben's voice grew harsher. "Are you all right?"

"Yes, I'm fine. He didn't touch me. He said India's mentally unstable, and he didn't do it."

Ben growled. "They all say that. I'm going to swing by and see if I can pick him up."

"Okay." Kelly hung up, headed for the kitchen and poured

herself a glass of red wine. Damn Piers and the chink of doubt he'd opened. Ben was right. Of course, Piers would make up excuses and try to deny the accusation.

But he'd seemed distraught and shocked. Could he be that good of an actor? He hadn't even gotten angry when she'd told him he would end up in jail.

India had always been fragile, prone to mood swings. When they were kids, Kelly had spent most of their lives protecting and sheltering her. India had made up stories when they were younger. But those had been to get their parents' attention. Their parents hadn't bothered with their two children, and she and India had been in desperate need of parental attention. It had been a brief phase, the stories, and it didn't mean India was telling stories now.

Kelly put down her wineglass.

Even this atom of doubt made her the worst sister ever. The walls of her condo closed in on her, and she needed to get out. Most of all, she needed serious chick time.

She jammed the cork back into the bottle, grabbed it and her coat, and headed for the door.

The cold air cleared her brain as she walked.

At Winters House, several of the windows lit the evening and beckoned her. Piers had gotten into her head, and she needed to talk him the hell out of there.

The Victorian mansion was currently full to bursting with Poppy, Ben and their four children, plus Finn and Claire. Horace had moved back into the main house, and Claire's mother, Naomi, now lived in the carriage house with a caregiver.

It was right the old place was finally filled with life and love and family.

Kelly walked around the side to the kitchen door. The kitchen was the heart of the beautiful mansion. Tonight was no exception as she gave a warning knock and walked in.

"Kelly." Poppy stood and gave Kelly her big, sweet smile. "This is a surprise."

Kelly brandished her bottle. "I brought wine."

"Opened wine." Claire Winters raised one of her perfectly fleek eyebrows, but her big green eyes laughed and took the sting out of her comment. "Fortunately, we have more."

"Anybody ever told you that you're a bitch, Claire Winters?" Kelly gave Poppy a hug and bent to kiss the third woman in the kitchen. "Hey, Dot."

Claire snorted and waved her hand. "Oh please, every single day. It gets so old."

"I'm glad you're here." Kelly took a seat next to Dot. She couldn't have handpicked three better women to have this conversation with. "Where are the menfolk?"

"Off doing manly things." Claire got wineglasses off the antique dresser and put them on the table. "They're at Ben and Poppy's house doing stuff behind Ben's back."

"Even Horace?" Claire's father had suffered from a bad hip for years that had restricted his activity.

Claire poured wine. "Oh, yes. We can't stop Dad since he's recovered from his surgery. And that includes spending time with Peg. I'm thinking of breaking the other hip and getting him to slow down."

"You!" Dot slapped her arm. "Your dad has plenty of healthy years left."

Claire raised a brow at Dot. "Have you got your hussy eyes on my father now? Isn't Doc enough man for you?"

"Claire!" Dot shrieked and blushed. "The things you say."

"Get yourself some, Dot." Poppy winked at her and took a seat opposite Kelly. "What's up? You have that wrinkle between your eyes that you get when you're stressing about something."

Kelly took a sip of wine. Coming there had been the right thing to do. "Piers arrived at my condo this evening."

"What!"

All three women reacted as if she'd tossed a hand grenade into the kitchen.

Poppy got her phone out. "I'll call Ben."

"No." Kelly put her hand over Poppy's phone. "I already did."

"Did you kick him in the balls?" Claire—the only woman Kelly knew who looked elegant in leggings and a sweater—moved around doing something with cheese and crackers.

Poppy blinked at her. "Why would she kick Ben in—oh."

Claire and Dot laughed.

Kelly hoped they didn't judge her for what she was going to say. "I wanted to, kick Piers, not Ben, but the thing is…he said some stuff and he's gotten into my head."

"What stuff?" Dot took her hand.

"He brought me some medication for India. For a mental condition. According to him, it started with postpartum depression but it's escalated now." She took a needed slug of her wine. "He says she's been battling with it since shortly after Jacob was born. That her behavior has been getting steadily more erratic."

Claire snorted and put a snack platter on the table. "He would say that. That's how these bastards operate."

"I know that." More for something to do with her hands, Kelly took a cracker and a slice of ham. "But he seemed genuinely shocked when I confronted him about her bruises. He swore he didn't know how they'd gotten there. He gave me the pills and even suggested I call India's doctor."

Dot patted her knee and sipped her wine. "Men who do these things are very clever. They get away with it by manipulating and controlling."

"I know that too." She felt like the worst bitch in the world for even considering the possibility. "India has always been delicate, and the idea of her having postpartum depression is not that farfetched."

Poppy grimaced in sympathy. "I mean, it's possible that both things are true. India is having a tough time, but it could also be that Piers is abusing her."

"That's true." And it made things so much worse for India. To have all that to deal with.

"You know what I would do?" Dot patted her again.

Kelly nodded. Dot should write an advice compendium. She was one of those mature women who seemed to have a slew of good advice.

"Too many times in these situations, we don't give the woman the benefit of the doubt." Dot sipped her wine. "The burden of proof here is not on India, but Piers. If he really didn't abuse her, then he needs to prove that to you."

"Boom!" Claire mimed dropping her mic. "Dot for the win."

And it really was that simple. A weight lifted off Kelly's shoulders. "Who is home with India now?"

"Gabe." Dot sent her a naughty look. "Shall I send your love?"

Claire poked her. "I sense a secret. Have you been a bad girl, Kelly?"

"My lips are sealed." Dot snort laughed into her wine. "But I may have stumbled on someone doing the walk of shame through my kitchen."

"You and Gabe?" Poppy's voice rose on a squeak. "How come I'm the last to find out about this? Holding out on me is a violation of the best friend code." Then she pointed at Dot. "And you should share the gossip with family."

Dot pulled a face at her. "Yes, but I have an evil plan to use Kelly to keep my boy in Twin Elks."

"It's not like that." Kelly's face throbbed with heat. "We're friends."

"Who sneak out of their mother's house and get caught in the kitchen." Dot gave her an angelic look.

"But wait." Claire stuffed cheese and crackers into her mouth. Also, the only woman Kelly knew who could eat what the hell she liked and keep that body. It was hard to keep liking Claire sometimes.

Claire swallowed and turned to her. "What about Vince?"

"Vince is..." Kelly didn't really know what Vince was. "He's taking his time, and I ended up asking him out."

"Oh!" Poppy clapped her hands. "You go, girl!"

"And?" Dot looked at her over the rim of her wineglass.

"He said yes."

A round of high fives followed, even from Dot who didn't seem to mind about her dating Vince.

When things had calmed down, Claire cleared her throat. "Actually, I have something to tell you all."

All focus snapped her way.

Claire gave them a smug smile and giggled. "Speaking of people who said yes…"

CHAPTER
Eleven

SATURDAY FINALLY ARRIVED, and Kelly had her entire closet scattered across her room, or at least ninety percent of it, and she still couldn't decide what to wear.

Vince was on his way to pick her up for their date, and she was still standing there in her bra and panties.

There wasn't a perfect outfit for a first date with the man you've loved for most of your life and lost because you dumped him fifteen years ago. She knew this because she had already wasted precious getting ready time trying to find one.

Vince had never been a fancy restaurant type, and it was Twin Elks after all. At least her makeup and hair were done.

With five minutes to go, she settled on a pair of dark, tight jeans and a soft lavender, off the shoulder sweater. She paired that with heeled boots.

She almost stabbed herself in the eye as she gave her lashes a final touchup. It had to stop. She was nervous as hell.

Was Vince as nervous?

The doorbell rang, so she was about to find out.

Vince smiled as she opened the door. His gaze took her all in and warmed. "You look beautiful."

"So do you." He was similarly dressed in jeans and nice sweater.

Then they both laughed, maybe a tad too enthusiastically for the joke.

Vince pressed a mixed bouquet into her hands. "These are for you."

"They're gorgeous." Kelly took an appreciative sniff. He'd remembered after all these years that she preferred flowers that looked like they'd been gathered in a field. "I'll put these in some water, and we can go."

Nodding, Vince followed her into the condo. He took a long look around him. "This is nice," he said. "Very you."

Kelly hadn't really thought of her condo in those terms. She didn't decorate, so much as find things that appealed to her and put them together. Her few attempts at Pinterest hacks had not ended well. "I bought the place when I got back."

"From Kansas City, wasn't it?" He peered at her photo collection on the coffee table.

Filling a vase with water, she nodded. "Yup. I had a good job there."

"Can I ask why you came back?" He straightened and joined her at the other side of her kitchen counter.

Kelly didn't really have a definitive answer. "A number of reasons." She shrugged. "I had a great life, lots of friends." She hesitated over revealing the next bit, because it was not something she discussed. But they needed to start with a clean slate and no secrets between them. "I was married, for about five minutes."

"You were?" He frowned. "I never heard anything about you're being married."

"It didn't last long." She put the flowers in the water. "We got married in June and were divorced by September."

Vince grimaced. "Damn."

"I know." She tried for a light laugh. Her divorce had been more a relief than anything else. "I think it was a combination of my biological clock ticking away and everyone in our friend group getting married."

He gave that some thought and then motioned the door. "Shall we?"

They did an awkward shuffle over her coat at the front door. He wanted to help her, and she kept trying to put it on herself.

Finally, they got both her arms into the right sleeves, and Vince opened the door and followed her into the night.

Normally she didn't fuss too much about locking things, but since Piers's arrival on her doorstep, she had been more cautious.

Vince led her to a family SUV parked beneath her condo. He had those stick figure family decals in his rear window. A man, a woman, two children with two cats. She supposed it would be churlish to scrape the woman off the window. Maybe take a permanent marker and draw a mustache on her or something.

Where Chelsea was concerned, Kelly's inner bitch came roaring out. Chelsea had managed to get between her and Vince all those years ago, and she had stayed there for all this time. Well, Chelsea wasn't going to win in the end.

"Where are we going?" She settled herself in the SUV and put her seatbelt on.

Vince gave her a shy smile. "It's a surprise."

He plugged his phone into the car.

Fallin' by Alicia Keys filled the car.

"Vince." A breath caught in the back of her throat. "This is our song."

They used to slow dance around her bedroom to it, wrapped around each other, young and in love.

He looked bashful. "Yeah. I made a playlist."

It was such a sweet thing to do and it helped to allay her fears about Vince having had a change of heart. She nudged him. "I bet you put *It Wasn't Me* on there."

"Maybe." He chuckled.

"I hate that song."

His grin widened. "Yeah, I know you do."

Things felt closer to how they used to be than they had in too long. She relaxed into her seat. "You know I'm going to turn it off."

"Yep." He grinned and tucked his phone in his pocket. "I know you're going to try."

Kelly snorted her disdain. "You don't think that's going to stop me, do you?"

As she said it, she wanted to yank the words back. She'd implied that she would go rooting around in his pants pockets.

Her face heated.

Vince shifted and cleared his throat.

She had to clear the air. "I feel like an idiot for saying that."

"That's okay." Vince patted her knee. "A lot of this feels awkward, and we're going to have to wade our way through that."

Relief made her heave a sigh. "You're right. I keep expecting things to go back to how they were, but so much time has passed."

"And both of us have different lives." He took her hand in his and glanced at her. "But I'd still like to explore this, Kelly. I'd like to see if there is anything left."

"Me too." She flipped her hand over and threaded her fingers with his. "But let's try not to overthink this too."

"Overthink?" He grinned. "You, Kelly? Nah."

She couldn't bullshit him. "Yeah. It's my secret weapon."

Vince pulled up in front of Romeo's Pizzeria. He looked at her. "Remember?"

"Our first date." Not a night she was likely to forget.

They'd come for pizza, Vince so nervous he'd spilled soda on the table. Afterwards, he'd walked her home and held her hand. Kelly had stressed about sweaty palms the entire way. At her doorstep, Vince had given her the fastest kiss in history and hurried away.

Months later, he had confessed it had been his first kiss.

She followed him into Romeo's, and the noise clobbered them. A mix of chatter, music, and shouted orders that made Kelly wince.

Threading through tables thrown together, teens spilling over chairs and into the aisles, they found a booth toward the back, away from the jukebox.

"Legit," said a girl whose squeal could peel paint off the walls. She dived into a fevered conversation with two other girls.

The only other adults were an elderly couple who kept their heads down over their meals.

"Sorry." Vince grimaced as he looked around. "I didn't think the pitfalls through."

"No, it's nice." Kelly smiled to reassure him. "Our first date happened here, and now our new first date will happen here."

Wine, however, would have been nice, but Romeo's didn't have a license.

Vince leaned forward. "Were we ever this loud?"

"I'm not sure." A couple took a selfie of her on his lap then launched into an energetic bout of tongue hockey. Kelly grinned at Vince. "I seem to remember us doing a lot of that."

He chuckled. "Yeah."

A teen girl wearing a lot of sparkly eyeshadow and some heavy contouring that looked more like war paint stood by their table with a notepad in her hand. "You know what you want?"

They placed their orders and she sauntered off, stopping to chat with a group of guys on her way.

"I bring my kids here for lunch. It's never this busy during the day," Vince said. "They like it."

It was a great place for kids, and nobody cared if they didn't sit down and quietly eat their meal.

"Kylie, you bitch!" A high-pitched shriek, which made Kelly jump, was followed by a roar of laughter.

"So." Vince leaned his elbows on the table, raising his voice over the noise. "First things first."

Kelly waited for his lead.

"I think we should clear the air," he said. "About what happened when we broke up."

As much as she agreed on principle, Kelly had mixed feelings about that. Part of her needed closure, and another part wanted to pretend it had never happened. But she was a grown up, so closure it was. "Would you like to go first?"

Vince nodded and cleared his throat. "I should have agreed to go to CU with you. By the next morning, I'd already changed my mind."

"But I wouldn't listen to you." Kelly owned up to her part. "I managed to convince myself if you really loved me, I wouldn't have to persuade you to go."

"I did really love you." Vince took her hand across the table. "I would have done anything for you."

"But you didn't want to leave Twin Elks," Kelly said. "I can understand that now. I felt differently back then. I couldn't wait to leave, and I had this great scholarship and a chance to live somewhere else."

"I really didn't want to, but I would have done it for you." His expression grew serious. "I'm still not ready to leave, Kelly. My life is here now, and my kids' lives are here."

"I understand." She put some lightness into her tone. "I've got my itch scratched by now. I came home, didn't I?"

Vince sat back and cocked his head. "Yeah, we didn't really finish that conversation."

"Right."

The waitress thunked their drinks on the table and tossed a couple straws at them.

"Teenage girls." Vince raised his eyebrows. "I have one of those. Hannah is fourteen now."

"Wow." And living proof of why she and Vince had never gotten back together. Kelly would need to get over any resentment if she was going to give her and Vince a chance. None of it was Hannah's fault.

Vince was looking at her expectantly.

"In hindsight, I think my dissatisfaction with my life had been growing for a while." She took a sip of her soda. "I was getting increasingly restless. I hated my job, selling shit to people who didn't need it. One more monkey grinding the consumerism wheel. And I wasn't a fan of the corporate life."

Vince kept his gaze on her.

It was hard because she hadn't really put her thoughts together on this. For once in her life, she hadn't been over-thinking but had gone with her gut. "After my marriage collapsed, I found the same story as a lot of people. Our friends were couple friends and they picked sides."

"Yeah." Vince pulled a face. "That's happened to me now."

"It'll pass." Kelly gave in to the urge to comfort him and took his hand. "The true friends always stay or find their way back to you."

Their pizza hit the table between them, and the waitress added a handful of napkins. "Do you need anything else?"

"We're good." Kelly didn't want that sort of help in her store, but her ad hadn't yielded any applicants yet.

"And opening the coffee shop?" Vince asked.

"I got an email from Dot, telling me the old corner store had closed down, and I remembered people complaining about not being able to get decent coffee." She picked up a slice. "All the pieces clicked into place. I sold my condo, quit my job, and came back home."

"And you like being back?"

That one was easy. "I love it. I love the sense of community and that I know all my customers. And since Poppy arrived, and now Claire, I have a good group of women my own age. What about you? What are your plans now?"

"Obviously, I can't keep driving the long-distance rigs." Vince shrugged. "I have custody of the kids, and Chelsea is making up for her lost youth, spending most of her time with her new man."

"You're okay with the new man?" She knew what she wanted him to answer, but that didn't mean she'd get that.

Vince smiled. "Sure. I mean, I would never have broken up the family, but Chelsea and I both exited our marriage years ago."

Despite what the marriage had meant for her, that she and Vince could never discover if they had a future, she found that sad. It reminded her too much of the cold cohabitation arrangement between her parents. Of course, Vince was a committed father, and would never regard his children as a hindrance, but growing up in a love-lite house was sad. No child deserved that.

The conversation lightened up as they finished their meal and sodas. With the noise around them growing, they didn't linger.

Tension crept into the SUV on the way back to her place. Like knowing what to wear, there really wasn't any precedent. Normal first dates were bad enough. That excruciating moment of whether he was going to go in for the kiss or not, and whether you wanted him to.

Vince parked outside her condo, came around the vehicle and opened her door. "I'll…um…walk you up."

At least she wasn't the only one feeling awkward.

They stopped outside her door and faced each other.

"Thank you for tonight." Kelly smiled at him. "I had a great time."

"Me too." Vince pulled a face. "Although next time we'll go somewhere adult."

He was saying next time. "Will there be a next time?"

"Definitely." Vince shifted closer to her. "And you won't have to do the asking."

"Good." Her heart stuttered as he tucked a tendril of hair behind her ear. Maybe she should ask him in. Or was that too forward? She didn't think they were ready for that stage.

Although she and Gabe had pretty much charged for the

bedroom. Thinking about one man while deciding to kiss another made her the worst kind of trollop.

"Good night, Kelly." Vince leaned down and brushed her lips with his.

Kelly rose to her tiptoes and kissed him back. The sweetness of that time when they were so young and so in love whispered in the air around them. Bunny and Stretch together, forever and ever. Only forever had turned out to be a lot shorter than either of them thought.

Vince lingered for a moment, and then pulled back. "I'll call you soon."

CHAPTER
Twelve

GABE CHALKED the end of his cue. The lay of the table did not auger well for him. Cara Addison was a goddamn hustler. All she had left was the eight ball, and there was no way he could sink his next shot and run the table.

Kelly would be out with Vince. The date he'd set in motion. And he was having his ass kicked at pool by a curvy brunette who looked more like a starlet than a veterinarian.

Cara leaned over the table, her full cleavage straining to wriggle out of her low-cut red shirt. "What you gonna do, Gabe?"

"I tell you what I'm not going to do." He sipped his beer. "I'm not going to stare at your…" He made a motion at the general area of her chest. "Even though they are your secret weapon."

"Secret?" Cara raised a brow and looked at her cleavage. "I think they're more out there."

"Nice strategy, Addison. Dirty, but effective." Gabe grinned at her. Fun, flirty, feisty, and with a mouth on her like a long-shoreman, Cara was good fun.

He shot, missed and stood back to watch the humiliation.

In passing Cara winked at him and bent to take her shot. They might not have chemistry, but Gabe enjoyed the view.

Several bystanders joined him in doing so. Bob Levine nearly swallowed his glass whole when Cara leaned over the table in those painted on jeans. Sky-high, fire-engine-red heels finished the picture. Bob was a dead man. "Watch and learn, big boy," Cara said.

His phone buzzed in his pocket, and he checked the number. Not Kelly, but an international number. It wasn't Belinda or her dad. Those numbers were programmed into his phone.

"Gabe Crowe," he answered.

"Gabe Crowe." Cara strutted around the table, lowering her voice in what she imagined was a good imitation of him. "Gabe Crowe, manly man, stud for hire, and probably the worst male pool player in Colorado."

"Seriously?" He mouthed at her.

She winked back.

"Gabe?" His caller said his name hesitantly, like they weren't sure he'd heard them.

He hadn't because Cara had made him miss the first part. "Sorry. Could you repeat that?" He raised a brow at Cara. "There's a lot of static on the line."

Cara chuckled and racked the balls.

"Gabe! Is that you, man?" A heavy South African accent came down the line. "It's me, Darren Visagie."

Only, the way Darren said his last name sounded like fizz-a-ghee. The last part a growl like a cat clearing a fur ball. "Darren." Gabe's smile came automatically. The huge, blond South African with rugby player shoulders, a booming laugh, and a bottomless capacity for beer had spent time with him in Australia. "Still such an asshole?"

"You know me, man." Darren's guffaw made Gabe take the phone from his ear. "But the ladies love me like that."

"How have you been?"

"No good, man," Darren said. "But I'm not calling to shoot

the shit with you. I heard you left the Moffat project down in Oz."

Word got around apparently, and Gabe's shoulders tightened. "Yeah."

"What happened?" Darren was never one to back off when he wanted to know something. It made him an excellent researcher and a liability in a bar. "You were shacking up with that Belinda chick, making nice with her old man. Life was sweet."

"Yeah, well." He avoided making eye contact with Cara, who wasn't even pretending not to listen to his conversation. "Belinda decided it was time for a wedding ring, and I disagreed."

Pulling a mocking face, Cara gave him huge eyes. As she ordered more beer at the same time, he forgave her.

"Ag." And it sounded like another fur ball expulsion. "That's too bad, man, for you. But it's good news for me."

"How?" His nape prickled. It could be an excellent call.

"I got a project I'm setting up down here in Plett."

Plettenberg Bay, the main town on the Western Cape in South Africa, and one of the most beautiful parts of the world Gabe had been privileged enough to see. They also had a huge population of great whites.

"Looking for a man with your skills to take part. Then I heard you'd left Oz and I thought I'd see if I could get myself the real McCoy."

"How much are you paying?"

Darren's laughter almost broke the phone again. It was an old joke. You didn't get into research for the money. "Well, your salary and a buck twenty will get you a cup of coffee."

"You studying my favorite girls?"

"You know it," Darren said, his voice filled with the same enthusiasm Gabe had for one of nature's most efficient and beautiful predators. "You interested?"

"Of course I'm interested." He nodded his thanks to Cara as

she put another beer in front of him. "Can you email me some details?"

"Consider it done. Same email?"

This was what Gabe had been waiting for. Only better than he could have hoped. He repeated his email address for Darren.

Then he said goodbye the way he and Darren always had. "And Darren? Save some pussy for the rest of us."

He hung up on Darren's thunderous laugh.

"Tell me." Cara pointed her bottle at his phone. It was impossible not to like a girl who didn't blink an eye at the last thing he'd said to Darren.

He pulled a face at the pool table. "Are you really going to cut my balls off again?"

"It's what I do." Cara snipped her fore and middle fingers together. "Neuter males."

Gabe restrained the urge to cup his junk protectively. "That was a guy I met in Australia. He's starting a research study on great whites in South Africa. I don't have the details yet, but he's going to email them to me."

"Pfft!" Cara waved a hand at him. "Great whites! When I have puppies and kitties and Bob over there's schizo parrot."

"You can keep the doggies and kitties." He mimed thinking. "But the schizo parrot, now…"

Cara cocked her head and sipped her beer. "You know, you talk all the time about how a small-town practice is not your thing, but have you ever tried it?"

"No." Gabe shrugged. "Other than school, that is. I knew then it wasn't for me, and it still isn't."

"Hmm." Cara stared at him.

"What?"

"I challenge you to come and spend a day working with me," she said.

Gabe tried not to look at her like she'd lost her mind. "Why would I do that?"

"To appease my curiosity."

"Now there's a good reason." He made sure she caught his eye roll. "And anyway, I don't think I can even remember small animal anatomy."

"It's like riding a bike." Cara smirked. "The ass is under the tail and the other end has teeth."

Then again, he had nothing better to do in Twin Elks. "But I'll take that challenge."

"Call me and we'll set it up." Cara gave him a smug grin.

They played another game of pool, with the inevitable results. Cara got into her car with Gabe's man card tucked in her purse.

The night was cold and clear, and he'd walked to the bar. The opportunity in South Africa was exactly what he wanted. As if to affirm his decision, a few lonely snowflakes danced in the air in front of him. In Plett, he could be out on a boat, under the glorious sun, traveling miles of deep-water ocean in search of great whites.

The sea there was so clear near the headland that you could see into it. In the waters surrounding a promontory called Robberg, literally translated into seal mountain, the great whites came hunting their favorite food source, seals. The locals called the hunting sharks the Robberg Express.

He shoved his cold hands into his pockets. His right hand curled around his phone and he pulled it out. He wanted to share his excitement with someone, and he didn't question his choice.

It was getting late, and she might be in bed. Alone, because his head refused to go to the alternative. He tapped out a text to Kelly. *How did your date go?*

Where are you?

Walking home from the Elk.

Alone?

A lone wolf.

Wanna lope over to my place for a beer, wolf boy?

Why yes, he most certainly would. *On my way.*

It didn't take him long to reach Kelly's condo, not when he put an extra spring in his step.

When she opened the door, face scrubbed clear of makeup, hair in a ponytail, and dressed in pink unicorn pj's—which he found weirdly sexy considering they were flannel—he knew that was exactly where he wanted to be.

"Brrr! It's cold. Come on in." Kelly wrapped her arms over her chest. Not soon enough for him to miss the sharp jut of her nipples.

Gabe shrugged out of his coat and hung it on a hook by the door.

"What can I get you?" Kelly walked into her kitchen. Her pants bagged around her ass, but he had already seen what they hid. A poetic man could write sonnets to the full ripeness of Kelly's ass.

"Coffee?" He'd had enough beer for one night.

"I'll make you hot chocolate." Kelly's look dared him to object. Damn, she was adorable. She looked no older than eighteen.

Which was still too young for his horny thoughts.

"If you have coffee you'll never sleep."

He grabbed a seat at the counter. Her condo reflected the voluptuous way Kelly embraced life. Couches that looked like they would envelop you. Lighting that provided more mood than practicality. And color. Everywhere. Somehow it all worked to frame the vibrant woman making him hot chocolate.

He hated hot chocolate, but he'd choke that crap down. He'd bet his arm she made it extra sweet with stuff floating on the top "How did your date go?"

"Good." She kept her gaze on the pot she was stirring, but that small crinkle started up between her eyes. "It was really nice."

"But?"

She glared at him. "Why would you assume there was a but?"

Gabe leaned over the counter and stroked the wrinkle between her eyes. "Because that tells me you're overthinking something."

"Right." She huffed a laugh. "You're the second man tonight to tell me I overthink shit."

He couldn't say, for sure, that he'd never been the second man before, but he definitely didn't like it. "Give it time, babe. As much as you want it, you and Vince aren't going to erase fifteen years in one night."

"Did you call me babe?" Kelly pinned him with a hard stare. "Again. Don't think I didn't notice the others you've been slipping in here and there."

"You don't like?"

Kelly was nobody's babe but her own. "You bet your sweet ass I don't."

"Sweetie?"

She shook her head.

"Angel?"

She glared.

"Muffin?"

Slapping her hands on the counter, she got nose to nose with him, so close he could easily tilt his head and take that sassy, full mouth. "Try again."

"Kelly."

"Good boy." Unfortunately, she retreated and got busy filling mugs with hot chocolate. And, topping them with whipped cream, and sprinkles. She handed one to him. "How was your night?"

He wrapped his hands around his mug. "Actually, I got a call tonight."

She sipped her drink and left a ring of cream on her top lip. His gaze snapped to her mouth, and he wanted to be the one to lick it off. Her tongue doing his job gave him all sorts of unfortunate ideas.

What the hell was wrong with him? He and Kelly had scratched their itch, and it was time to move on.

In the meantime, she was patiently waiting for him to tell her more. He told her about his call with Darren.

"Gabe," she gasped, almost like she did when he was buried deep inside her. "That's wonderful. That's what you really want."

She walked around the island, slid between his spread thighs and wrapped her arms around him. "I'm so happy for you."

"Thanks." His cock was equally happy she was right where she was, and he pulled her tighter into the hug.

She smelled like vanilla and flowers, and he buried his face in her neck before he did something stupid like taste her.

Her voice sounded raspy as she said, "Are you going to take it?"

"I'm not sure." He splayed his hands over her back, covering as much of her warm, pliant flesh as he could. "I'm certainly going to look at what Darren sends me."

"Okay."

Their chests rose and fell in a matching rhythm. Her breath huffed in his ear, coming harder and faster like his. Heat rose from the light connection of her breasts to his chest.

He could slide his hands down and cup her incredible ass and drag her over his throbbing cock.

Her voice grew huskier. "Gabe?"

"Uh-huh." He had to put some space between them, but it was killing him.

Kelly's hand slid into his hair. "This is only going to complicate both our lives."

"I'm not going to do anything," he said. "And any second I'm going to take my hands off you."

CHAPTER
Thirteen

SUNDAY, Gabe woke with the wrong Ashford sister in his bedroom. Despite wanting to stay with every moving part of him, he had left Kelly's and come home alone.

Face twisted, India stood by his bed ringing her hands. "I need your help."

"Huh?" He tried to get his head working. After he'd left Kelly, he'd not gotten a lot of sleep. Next thing, he'd be humping her leg.

"Gabe?"

And India stood by his bed while a stream of lustful thoughts ran through his brain, and that was plain wrong. He struggled into a sitting position. "What's up?"

Unfortunate choice of words.

But not a problem, given that India's gaze hadn't gotten further than his bare shoulders before she blushed and turned around. "I'm sorry. I didn't think…I'll leave."

"What is it, India?"

Back still to him, she spoke at his door. "It's that dog."

"Ma's puppy?"

India nodded and twisted her fingers. "I know it's silly of me, but I'm...scared of dogs. And I need to get into the kitchen and feed Jacob."

The dog was more of a big dope than a threat, and Ma really needed to give the poor guy a name. "Is Ma out?"

"Yes." India nodded. "She had a breakfast with Doc Cooper."

"Doc?" Ben had mentioned something about the old guy hanging around Ma. Right then, though, he had to rescue a lady from a dog. Not quite a dragon, but you used what you had. "Let me get some pants on, and I'll sort it out."

With a squeak, India scuttled out of his room and shut the door firmly behind her

The Ashford sisters couldn't be more different. India was younger than Kelly, and that might account for some of it. He found jeans on his floor and pulled them on. If it were Kelly, he would have skipped the shirt. Kelly liked his chest, a lot, and it might be interesting to see where the situation led. As India would probably die of embarrassment, he hauled on a T-shirt and jogged down the passage to the kitchen.

Jacob in her arms, India stood by the door frowning and gnawing her bottom lip.

She really was scared of the furry goofball in the kitchen. "Hey!" He softened his tone. "It's okay. He really is friendly and just a puppy."

"I'm not a dog person." India swallowed.

Gabe didn't get how anyone could not be a dog person. Dogs were awesome. How could you not like a creature that lavished unconditional love on you? He opened the door and stepped into the kitchen. He left the door open so India could see she had nothing to fear.

The puppy bounded toward him, writhing and squiggling in his delight at finding a friend. He reared up and tried to put his paws on Gabe's chest.

"Down!" Gabe got hold of his front paws and dropped him to the floor. He turned to India. "You have to be firm with him.

He needs some training, but there isn't an aggressive bone in his body.

The dog tried to jump up again and Gabe pushed him away. "Uh-uh! Down!"

Jacob whined, and India slid past him and the dog to get to the fridge. Her huge gaze didn't leave the dog.

Once again, he tried to jump on Gabe, but less certainly this time.

"Uh-uh, down!" Gabe smiled his encouragement at India. "You see, he's learning already."

But India was still looking at the dog as if he was Cujo. She kept glancing at the dog as she prepared Jacob one of his mushed meals. "He's very big."

"Yeah, but generally big dogs are chill," Gabe said. If India and Jacob were going to stay there, they were going to have to get along with the dog. "I can introduce him to you and show you how to manage him."

"No, thanks." India put Jacob's mush in the microwave for a few seconds. "I won't be staying that long, and it's not like we'll ever be getting our own dog, so Jacob will be fine."

Gabe bit his tongue. A boy and his dog could be the best of friends. Dogs taught children a lot about taking care of another creature, responsibility and affection. A lot of the bad interactions between dogs and kids happened because the kid had never been taught how to approach a dog. Or even when to be wary of a dog. But this was not his business.

"Sit," he said to the dog.

Ma must have been doing something with him, because the dog tucked in his butt and gazed up at Gabe.

His phone rang, and he took the dog with him to answer it.

The big dope leaped onto his bed and made himself comfortable. Of course, he did. He probably slept on Ma's bed at night. He gave the dog a hard stare. "You're about to get a lesson in manners, buddy."

The dog thumped his tail and lolled his tongue at Gabe.

Gabe answered his phone without checking the display. "Yup."

"Gabe?" A laugh he knew well drifted down the line. "What kind of way is that to answer the phone?"

His gut tightened and he had to force himself to keep it light. "Hey, Belinda. How are you?"

"I'm good. You?"

"Same." And he ran out of things to say.

"I suppose you're wondering why I'm calling you."

Yup, he totally was. When he'd left Australia, Belinda had been fuming. She'd told him never to call her and never to try to contact her again. And he'd honored that. He couldn't give her what she wanted, and he needed to step aside and not leave her with the hope that he would change his mind. "What's going on?"

"Listen, Gabe, this is not the sort of conversation I want to have over the phone, but I don't really have a choice. With you being all the way over there." She took a deep breath. "I feel bad about the way things ended. I was gutted when you told me..."

She didn't need to fill those words in. He remembered them well, because even as he had said them, he had known they meant the death knell to not only their relationship, but his work in Australia. "I know you were, Bell, but I'm not in the same place as you."

And he never would be with her, but he couldn't hurt her that much by saying so. He had meant what he said to Kelly. He did believe in the one.

"I know that." Her sigh hitched. "And I understand. As much as it hurts, I do understand."

What he said next came straight from his heart, "I wish I was."

"Ah, Gabe," she whispered. "Why can't you be an asshole, and then I could hate you?"

Tension fisted his gut. He hated making her cry. Even if she hadn't been his one, he had loved her and cared for her. "Please don't cry, Bell."

"I'm sorry." She sucked in a tremulous breath. "I really am sorry. I didn't think I was going to do this, but then I heard your voice…and it all came back to me."

It came back to him as well. They'd had a good life together, him and Belinda. They had so many of the same interests and loved doing things together. Why couldn't he have felt the same? To be honest, until the moment she'd delivered her ultimatum, he hadn't known he didn't consider them getting married as a possibility.

The dog snuck closer to him and pressed against his side, his big head on Gabe's thigh.

"I remember it too." He stroked the dog's neck. "And I wish I could be that man for you, really I do. But I can't, and it's not the way to start a marriage."

"You're right." She sniffed. "I hate it, but you're right. And I honestly didn't call to talk about this." She blew a long breath. "I really called to say that what happened between us shouldn't have affected your position on the project. That wasn't right, and Dad wanted me to see if you would consider coming back."

That made him sit up and blink. "Your dad asked if I wanted to come back?"

"Yeah."

Then why hadn't Steve called and asked himself? Blurred boundaries had sent Gabe back to Twin Elks in the first place. Also, he didn't believe it coincidental that her call came right on the heels of the one from Darren the night before.

"I gotta be straight with you, Bell. I'm considering other offers." Well, one.

She hummed. "Understandable. I'll give you some time to think things over. In the meantime, I'll email you your new offer from Dad. I think you'll like what you see."

"Sure." He'd loved his work in Australia, liked the team he

was a part of. And they'd been making a difference. Slowly but surely, they were making inroads for the sake of the great whites.

"And Gabe?" Her voice strengthened. "Do you think you could promise to call us before you make another choice?"

All his years with that team deserved at least that much. "I will do."

They hung up shortly after.

Gabe petted the dog and tried to shrug off the cloud that hovered above him.

The dog thumped his tail, and Gabe looked up to see his mom in the doorway. "Hey, darling."

"Ma." Dot had that radar that knew when her boys wanted to talk and when to let them sort it out.

Like now, she walked in and sat on the bed beside him. "Was that Belinda?"

"Yeah." He kept his gaze on the dog's fur. "They're offering me my old job back."

"But?"

"I got another call last night from a team in South Africa. They are starting something up and want me to be part of it."

Ma took a careful breath. She didn't want him to leave, he knew that, but he also knew it was not her way to hold any of them back if what they wanted differed from what she wanted. "At least now you have options."

"Yup." But that didn't help him make a decision.

Ma patted his knee. "You'll work it out, Gabriel. You'll look at both offers, weigh the pros and cons, and make a decision."

"Thanks, Ma." Another thing he loved about talking to Ma. She got that he didn't want to pick through it like a crappy salad. "Can I ask you something else?"

"Anything." Ma took his hand in hers. "Shoot."

"Was I an asshole to Belinda? I hurt her, Ma. I really hurt her."

Ma thought that over for a long time. "Do you think you were an asshole?"

"I'm not sure. That's why I'm asking you." He got testy at her answering a question with a question.

Laughing, Ma squeezed his hand. "This is what I think, honestly. It's not our fault when we don't love someone as much as they love us. But…"

There was often a but with Ma.

"But, you and Belinda were together a long time, and you had to know she was harboring hopes in the marriage direction." She stopped his protest with a raised finger. "Even if you ignored the signs, they were there for you to see."

Yeah. She had him there. "I should have got out earlier."

"Maybe." Ma shrugged. "Maybe, like her, some part of you hoped that would change. Or maybe you were avoiding hurting her. And your relationship was tied into your job, and that always makes things tricky."

"By that reasoning, I shouldn't accept the offer to go back there."

"That's your decision." She patted his hand. "But don't be naive about what going back will mean. There's a possibility Belinda is still hoping you'll change your mind, and when she finally realizes that's not going to happen, she can make life uncomfortable."

"I really did love her, Ma."

"I know you did." Ma patted his hand. "Just not enough." She stood and clicked her fingers for the dog. "Also, sitting around here and moping isn't going to do you much good. You think better when you're active."

"What did you have in mind?" Because he knew for damn sure Ma had a plan.

She glanced at him and then away again. "I got a call from Robin—you remember her from school?"

He nodded. Please let this not be another woman tossed at him in the hopes she'd stick.

"She's at the new vet, and she says it's crazy busy." Ma gave him a mischievous look. "She said Cara could use a hand."

Yep, she was matchmaking but in a direction he could handle. He and Cara were friends, but that spark wasn't there. And he could go over and see if he could do something, even if it was hold heads and give injections. "I'll give Cara a call."

"I already did that." Ma grinned at him. "I told her you would be there in twenty minutes." She checked her watch. "And that was ten minutes ago."

"You." Gabe jabbed a finger at her. But he couldn't find the words of resentment over her interfering. Ma was Ma, and you had to love her. And he did. "I love you, Ma, and thanks."

CHAPTER
Fourteen

GABE WALKED into a heaving waiting room. People were milling about. Dogs circled each other, and cats bitched from their carriers. A boy clutching a hamster cage was sobbing into his mother's shoulder in a corner.

It looked like Noah's ark on crack. The first thing Cara needed was a receptionist and some sort of booking system.

A man he didn't know nodded to the empty reception desk. "You have to put your name on the list and the time you arrived."

"I'm the other veterinarian." The words got away from him before he could stop them.

Cara bustled through and stopped and stared at him. "Thank you, Jesus!"

For a horrible moment, he thought she might burst into tears. "I'm licensed for Colorado if you want to point me in the right direction."

"I might take you if you weren't." She picked the list up. "Karen and Trooper?"

A woman with a border collie fought her way past a snarling shih tzu. "That's us."

"Room two." Cara pointed down the corridor. "I'll be two seconds." She jabbed a finger at Gabe. "You, come with me."

Gabe followed her deeper into the building. "I don't suppose you have..."

She shoved a stethoscope at him.

"Never mind."

She looked around, and more talking to herself, she asked, "Anything else?"

"I—"

"Nope the rooms are fully stocked." She gave him a push in the direction of reception. "Take the top name on the list and get started."

It had been years since Gabe dealt with domestic pets. And their owners. He picked up the list and called the top name.

A man wielding the shih tzu followed him into an examination room. Just his luck, there was a high probability of getting bitten with his first patient.

He introduced himself and then said, "What seems to be the problem?"

"Tiger is butt scooching."

Please don't let it be. Please don't let it be.

"I brought him in to have his anal glands expressed." The man flushed.

Fuck you! Whoever the hell you are for letting it be anyway.

Tiger should have been named viper with the speed he could strike. Gabe barely got his hand out of the way in time as he attempted an examination. There was no assistant either, so it was him and Tiger's adoring owner, who was making silly faces at the dog and cooing.

Gabe kept the irritation controlled. "Could you hold his head please?"

"Won't that hurt him?" The owner looked concerned.

Not as much as Gabe tossing the furry little turd out the window. "Get a firm grip and don't let him snap. Okay?"

"Okay." The owner got Tiger's head in a tentative grip. It

wasn't the dog's fault. Tiger thought he ruled the roost and he did, which was not a happy place for a dog to be.

He waited until the man had Tiger under control before he went anywhere near the fiend again. Through much snarling, a few more near misses and a dry heaving owner, he got the anal glands done and Tiger on his way out.

The dog gave him one more menacing stare before he left. Just in case he thought Tiger would forget the indignity done to him today.

Cara called him in to hold another dog that needed stitches.

Next, he dealt with a cat whose teeth needed cleaning and a rabbit who was old and wouldn't last much longer.

And so his day carried on, one thing after another, each of them the tasks that had made him certain he never wanted to do that sort of thing.

By the time they got the waiting room clear, the African sun was shrieking his name.

He sat behind the reception and put his feet up.

Cara brought them both a beer. "Thanks for today."

"I'd say it was my pleasure, but that would be a lie."

"Don't be a dick." Cara shoved his legs off the counter. "You need to let me know what you did today so I can send out invoices."

"Gonna pay me?"

Cara snorted and pointed at his beer. "You're drinking your salary. And think yourself lucky I'm not charging you for losing me patients."

"Hey!" But it was a token protest as he had gotten into it with the owner of an overweight bulldog. "I'm not cut out for this sort of thing."

Glaring, Cara pointed her beer at him. "That's only because you've made up your mind that you aren't. We treat families here, through their pets."

"Thank you, but no."

They finished their beers in silence.

Cara stood and stretched. She had an innate sexiness that was going to do it big time for some man. "Man, am I ever tired. I'm even too tired to play pool."

"Say it isn't so." Which brought up an idea he'd had earlier. "You need a receptionist."

"No shit, Sherlock." Cara rolled her eyes. "But in my defense, I've never been this busy before."

Gabe had to confess, "I may have had a little something to do with that. I asked my mom to get the word out about you on the prayer chain."

"Ah." Cara sipped her beer. "The mighty prayer chain. Thanks, I think, but if today is any indication, I'm going to have to get some help fast."

"Kelly's sister, India is staying with us," he said. Some independence might be great for India. A job, even a temporary one, might show her that there was life after Piers. "I could see if she's interested, and she might have to bring her son with her. Although I'm sure Ma can help with that."

"She anything like Kelly?"

"Nope." The idea made him laugh. "She is nothing like Kelly."

"That's a pity." Cara shrugged. "I like Kelly."

Gabe sipped his beer. Yeah, him too.

———

Kelly was having a weird day, which might account for her weird mood.

Vince sat at her counter drinking coffee. He'd been there for longer than usual and had been talking for most of that time. "So she said she had to have this new nail polish crap, you know?"

Kelly didn't know, because she wasn't really listening. She made a noncommittal noise and smiled. The line in front of her counter was eight people deep, and the bell over the door jangled with another customer.

"But she's fourteen and…"

She turned on the frother and the noise drowned out the rest of his story.

Not that she didn't appreciate him spending time with her, but Vince chattered on, oblivious to the packed coffee shop around him. There was not a seat open, and the orders were piling up. She really needed another body to help with the workload.

"What do you think?" Vince looked at her.

She'd missed something. "Think about what?"

"You're not listening to me." He raised an eyebrow.

She considered lying and then shrugged. "I'm sorry, I'm busy here is all."

"Oh, right. Right." He glanced about him with a look of mild confusion. "It is busy in here."

"You think?"

He looked chagrinned. "Sorry, Kel. I didn't notice."

"That's fine." Although she didn't get how he hadn't noticed with the number of bodies brushing past him. "So, what were you asking?"

"I was talking about Hannah." He leaned his arms on the counter. "She wants to start using makeup, but I think she's too young. She's been using nail polish for a while."

"Hi." A dark-haired guy in his mid-forties edged around Vince at the counter. "Can I get a cappuccino? Extra hot."

"You got it." Kelly gave him her sassy smile.

He grinned back, not bothering to hide his appreciation. "I'm Dave, and I'm new in town."

"Nice to meet you, Dave." Again with the new in town thing. "I'm Kelly."

"I see that." Dave's gaze lingered over the breast under her name badge.

Turning to face Dave, Vince held out his hand. "Vince Greerly. Kelly's…friend."

"Uh...hi." Dave shook Vince's hand, and beat a retreat to the other customers waiting for their orders.

Vince turned back to her. "So, do you think I should let her?"

"What?" Kelly had no idea what he was talking about.

He enunciated slowly and clearly. "Let Hannah wear makeup."

"I don't know, Vince." She burned her hand on the steamer, which made her next words terser. "I'm not her mother. Ask Chelsea what she thinks." Words Kelly never thought would come out of her mouth.

"I did." Vince looked taken aback. "I already told you that."

"Samantha?" Kelly read the name of the next order.

"Here!"

Kelly put the four lattes into a tray and handed them to Samantha.

Vince stood. "Look, I'm in your way."

"I am busy right now." Kelly didn't see the point in prevaricating. "Maybe we can talk later?"

"Sure.' He cleared his throat. "Actually, I was hoping we could have that second date. The adult one."

"Really?" He had promised he would do the asking this time and he had. Kelly's smile was unrestrained. "I'd really like that."

"Friday at seven?" His face flushed and he looked pleased.

"You got it."

Vince leaned over and kissed her briefly on the mouth. "I can't wait."

"Same." An adult date would be great, but her customers were starting to show signs of impatience. "I need to get back to work."

"Sure you do." Vince winked at her and stood. "And Kel?"

"Yup." She waited before she turned the steamer on.

Vince stuck his hands in his pockets. "I'm glad we're doing this." He motioned between them. "Exploring this thing between us."

"Same." And this time she didn't need to fake it. She tugged him back for another quick kiss and let him go. " Now get out of here. People need their coffee."

"Damn right," Dave muttered.

Vince's kiss was nothing like kissing Gabe. With Vince, it was like turning on the switch, but with Gabe it was like shoving a screwdriver straight into the electrical socket.

She couldn't commit to this thing with Vince for as long as she kept almost climbing into Gabe's pants. She wasn't fooling herself about that. If she and Gabe kept carrying on like they were, it was only matter of time before place and opportunity presented themselves.

Vince stepped back and nearly ran right over India. He caught her and steadied her. "India?"

"Vince?" India stared up at Vince.

Vince blinked and stared at India.

"Excuse me." A customer threw him a look and brushed past him with their order.

"Wow! Look at you." Vince stepped out of the way. "All grown up."

India managed a wan smile. "And no more braces."

Kelly kept her eye on India as she completed Dave's order. She didn't like the way her sister flinched around all men.

Dropping his hands from India, Vince studied her. "How are you doing, darlin'?"

"Okay." India responded to his gentle tone. "I have good days and bad days."

"Sure you do." Vince reached for her and dropped his hand before he made contact. "You need to be patient with yourself."

"I will be." India flushed. "Thank you, Vince."

"My pleasure. It's really nice to see you again."

India flushed. "Same."

"Well, I'll see you around." He gave Kelly another wave. "I'll text you."

India slid behind the counter. "Dot is watching Jacob and she suggested I get some fresh air." India had said that as if she expected to be rebuked.

"It's okay, India. All mothers need time to themselves." Kelly forced a cheerful smile. "At least that's what the books tell me."

"I feel...guilty." India scrubbed her hands on her thighs. "Like I should be with him all the time."

Kelly wanted to talk to her sister, but she had customers waiting. "Listen, help me here, and then we can have a cup of coffee and chat some more."

"Oh." India's eyes widened. "I don't think I can work the machine."

"Then why don't you work the cash register? It's really simple."

India gave her a timid smile. "That I can do."

Ten minutes later, Kelly wished she'd put India in a chair with a coffee. Customers made India nervous, and she fumbled their money. Twice she'd rung up the wrong thing, and Kelly had to stop and void the transaction.

A few times a customer had to correct her on the cost of their order.

"India?" India was so fragile, she didn't need Kelly bitching her out when she was only trying to help. "Can you grab some more bags of coffee from the back?"

"Sure." India leaped up with an alacrity that spoke of how much she hated doing the register.

Fortunately, the shop was quieting down, and Kelly managed on her own. But days like that were happening more and more often, and it would start to cost her business if she didn't find help.

Maybe not India, though. Except, it wasn't fair to criticize India for today. Kelly had dropped her in the deep end and expected her to swim. With training, India would be fine.

When India came back with the coffee, Kelly tried again. "Thanks. Do you think you can load those cups into the dishwasher in the back?"

"Sure." India scooped up dirty coffee mugs and headed into the kitchen.

As Kelly was handing over a caramel latte, a crash sounded from the back. Kelly flinched and hoped it wasn't as many cups as it had sounded like.

"Kelly?" Eyes swimming with tears, India stood in the kitchen doorway. "I'm so sorry, I—"

"It's okay, India." Kelly stopped long enough to give her a big hug. "Accidents happen. You wouldn't believe how many cups I've broken."

"Really?"

"Really." It was tragic how India's confidence had disappeared. "Be careful you don't cut yourself."

India nodded. "I'll fix it, Kelly. I promise."

"It's okay, darling." Kelly put as much reassurance as she could into her voice.

Nodding, India slipped back into the kitchen.

India's self-esteem seemed to be rock bottom as well. India had never been an outgoing kid. She was always introverted and quiet, but this whipped look she wore was completely new.

Kelly's anger against Piers hardened. Someone had done this to her little sister, and despite his visit the other night, her money was still on Piers.

India's brokenness hadn't happened overnight. Someone had filled her with fear and anxiety, and that person would pay for that. Kelly would make sure of that.

CHAPTER
Fifteen

GETTING ready for her second date with Vince was easier than the first. Given it was an adult date and the only date-worthy restaurant in town was the Grove, she knew where they were going. Also, Vince had called and asked if they could not go out of town. He didn't want to be too far from his children.

Kelly went all out: hair, makeup, little black dress, and heels that made her legs look miles long. Even if she did say it herself, she had it going on.

Right on time, Vince rang her doorbell.

He looked good in a button-up and dress pants. "Hi."

"Hi, yourself." Kelly leaned in and kissed his cheek.

Vince helped her into her coat. "You look nice."

Nice? *Nice!* Forty minutes on the makeup, thirty for the hair deserved more than nice. "So do you."

He opened the door for her and lying on her seat was a single white rose. And like that she forgave the nice thing. Vince had remembered she didn't like red roses as much as white. On their second date, way back when, he had also brought her a single white rose.

"Thank you." She picked the rose up and smelled it as he climbed in the driver's side.

Vince leaned over and kissed her cheek. "You're welcome. I'm glad we're doing this."

"Me too."

Classical music played over the radio as Vince drove them to the restaurant.

Kelly restrained the urge to fidget. "I assumed we were going to the Grove."

"You assumed right." He smiled as he drove.

Vince drove exactly at the speed limit, signaled before he did anything, and came to a full stop every time. If she had been driving, she might have turned his hair gray by now.

Whistling through his teeth, he tapped one finger on the steering wheel in time to the music.

Not being able to come up with a topic of conversation, she watched the passing scenery.

What was Gabe doing tonight?

When Kelly had called India earlier to check on her, and also to ask for dress advice, India had said that Gabe would be out for the evening and she, Jacob, and Dot were heading over to see Claire and Poppy at Winters House.

Saturday nights with Claire, Dot, and Poppy had become an informal thing since Claire had been there. Kelly was relieved to see India getting out.

"Here we are." Vince broke the silence

The Grove parking lot was nearly full, and they drove down a couple of rows before finding a spot. Vince opened her door for her and took her hand as they crossed the parking lot.

As they walked to the restaurant, delicious cooking smells hit them.

Vince took her coat and handed it to the hovering hostess. "Is this okay?"

"Yes." More than okay. Kelly had no idea the place was so nice.

Vince had made a reservation, and they were taken to a table by the window.

"It's lovely in here, " Kelly said. Beams crossed the high vaulted ceilings. The tables were all set with white tablecloths, gleaming glass and silverware. One perfect lily sat on each table. It was tasteful and elegant and totally worth a great dress and heels. "I've never been here."

"No?" Vince raised a brow. "Why not?"

"No real reason to come." And that sounded a lot more pathetic than she'd meant it to. "I mean, I work long hours, and the Twin Elks dating pool has never been deep."

"Right." Vince laughed.

They looked at each other and smiled. She didn't know if Vince had any hobbies they could talk about. God knew hers were down to Netflix binges and the occasional book, neither of which made for scintillating conversation. She couldn't remember Vince ever reading much.

Tapping his fingers on the tabletop, Vince looked out the window. "The view must be amazing in the daylight."

"Yes." Kelly jumped on the topic. "It's pretty good now. With all the lights and stuff."

"Yeah." Vince nodded.

The waiter arrived for their drink order and Kelly ordered a dirty martini. Vince ordered a sparkling water. "I'm driving." He grimaced. "Can't risk even the smallest infraction on my driving record. Not with what I do."

"That reminds me." She had wanted to know since his divorce. "If you're not doing the long hauls anymore, what are you going to do?"

"I can't be away from home that much anymore." Vince shrugged. "Chelsea is not that keen to keep the kids for days on end, and her new man doesn't have children."

"Ah." The topic of Chelsea always made her want to hit something.

"I'm running trailers between here and Denver. That's keeping me plenty busy." He shrugged. "But I have some money saved. I thought I could see this as a chance to look around, work out what I want to do. As you know, I was a father straight out of high school. I pretty much got the first job I could that paid okay money."

The old stab of resentment didn't come. Maybe because she and Vince were moving on.

All around them, people were chatting and laughing. A couple in the corner had their heads together like they were seconds from jumping each other's bones.

The waiter put her martini in front of her, and she smiled her thanks.

"What about you?" Vince looked over the top of his menu. "Store going well?"

"Very." She glanced at her menu. "In fact, I need to take on some help."

"That's great, Kelly."

"Yeah, it is."

They both ducked behind their menus. There had to be something they could talk about. She tried to remember what they had talked about when they were younger.

She decided on her meal and closed her menu.

Vince was still deciding. Ginger ninja from the coffee shop sat at the bar talking to Robin. That girl was getting more dates in the last week or so than Kelly had gone on in months. A number of faces around the restaurant didn't look familiar.

Was that Horace Winters over there with Peg Hardwhistle? Dear God, Claire must be freaked out by that. No wonder they were doing the wine whine at Winters House.

Vince put his menu down. "Do you know what you want?"

"Yup."

Kelly leaned forward and lowered her voice. "Horace and Peg are over there. Together."

"Horace and Peg?" Vince frowned at her. "Do I know them?"

"Horace Winters. Peg Hardwhistle?"

"Oh." Vince nodded. "I'm sure I've seen them around town."

"Horace is Claire's dad," she said. "And Peg is…" Well, you had to know Peg. "It's a strange combination."

Vince shrugged. "Okay."

Fortunately, the waiter came over and they ordered. With wine off the table, she hesitated over a second martini and then decided against.

Vince smiled at her and nodded. He had the classically handsome features of a matinee idol. "The food's good here."

"It is?" She couldn't remember conversation being quite this hard before. "I've never been here."

"You said. No, the food is great." He smiled. "I've been here a couple of times."

With Chelsea, she was willing to bet.

"Are you still in contact with people from high school?" They couldn't sit there in silence all night.

Vince shook his head. "No. Many of them have moved away. I lost contact with the others. We had different priorities."

"Because you were already a father?"

"Exactly."

The dreaded silence descended again.

"So." Kelly cycled her memory banks for some topic of conversation. Then she hit one. The relief made her almost giddy. She should have ordered that second martini. "Did you decide about Hannah and the makeup?"

"I did." He nodded. "I consulted with some parents with kids Hannah's age and it seems like a lot of girls are allowed to wear some."

"Sounds about right." Kelly drained the last drop from her glass. "Mom never supervised those things, but I remember most of us wore mascara, lip gloss, that sort of thing."

The waiter arrived with their food.

"This looks great," Kelly said.

"Yeah." Vince looked at his plate and then her. "The food here is great."

Vince turned his full attention to his salmon, cutting a careful piece and combining it with an equally careful piece of aspara-gus. She didn't remember him being quite that precise.

Screw it! She motioned the waiter for that second martini.

"I had a thought." Vince looked up from his meal. "This is the first dinner we've had in a fancy restaurant.

"You're right." Kelly was desperate enough to leap at the conversational opening. "We didn't do much of this sort of thing back then." She had to grin at her memories. "Mostly a lot of heavy petting in the back of your mom's car."

Vince blushed and cleared his throat. "There was that."

"Right."

"Fun times."

"Yup."

Vince ate his salmon.

She dug into her meal, and Vince was right, the food was good. "How are the kids?"

"Good." Vince nodded a shade too vigorously. "Doing great. Hannah has a dance recital this weekend, and Chelsea will be there." He looked stricken. "I mean, she is Hannah's mother."

"I know that." Kelly touched his hand across the table. "You can't twist yourself into a tangle every time her name comes up. You and Chelsea were married and have two children together. Anybody who is going to be part of your future is going to need to be fine with that."

Vince let out a relieved chuckle. "I never know how much to talk about her. Given what happened between us."

"That was a long time ago." A lifetime ago. The place in the middle of her solar plexus that used to contract at the thought didn't seem to do that anymore. Chelsea was a bitch, and they would never be besties, but the anger wasn't there anymore. "We were all so young, and we all made mistakes."

"We did." Vince's dark gaze grew serious. "I really am sorry about what happened, Kelly."

That time had been a vortex of hormones and hurt, on both

their parts. "I am too. If I had been older, who knows, I might have handled the whole thing differently."

"I know I never would have jumped into bed with Chelsea." Vince looked pained.

Kelly appreciated the sentiment, but she couldn't be certain. "Who knows what you would have done, Vince. Horace Winters has this thing he says, and it makes sense to me. He says that we all think we can change one part of our past in isolation, and that it wouldn't have a knock-on effect."

"Meaning?"

She sipped her martini. "If you hadn't slept with Chelsea, you would never have had Hannah. I never would have left Twin Elks and discovered that this is really where I wanted to be. It's pointless to speculate about changing that one instance or decision. We are where we are."

"Huh." Vince shrugged. "That makes sense."

"Right." She put her knife and fork down. Killer little black dresses were not best friends with food babies. "We are where we are, and all we can do is decide where to go from here."

Gabe needed to decide where he was going next, and she and Vince needed to decide if there was a next for them. That thought rocked her, and she had to take a huge slug of martini. She had been so busy obsessing about her missed chance with Vince she hadn't given Horace's words too much thought. Time had moved on, and she and Vince were different people. She'd focused so much on their lost opportunity she hadn't really asked herself if she wanted that opportunity back.

Sitting there, over a dinner where they could barely find a subject in common, she questioned that. She and Vince were different people. They were what their lives had molded them into, and those things might no longer be compatible.

"Would you like dessert?" Vince took her hand over the table. "I remember you had a sweet tooth."

"I still do." She laughed. "Do you remem—"

"Well, isn't this cozy?" Chelsea, poured into an electric blue dress and now a blonde, stood by their table.

Vince dropped her hand as if it had the plague and stood. "Chelsea."

"Vince." Chelsea's sneer blasted Kelly. "I should have known you would be hanging around, waiting for my leftovers."

Holy batballs! Kelly knew she had to come up with something, but Chelsea's rudeness completely blanked her mind. And Vince. He stood there and hung his head like her speaking about him like that wasn't hideously insulting.

"Aren't you two the sweetest thing?" Chelsea could have been pretty if she didn't look so bitter all the time. "Young love never dies and all that crap."

"Come on, Chelsea." Vince kept his voice down. Heads had already turned their way. "There's no need for this."

No, there wasn't. Kelly recovered the gift of speech. "What the hell is wrong with you, Chelsea?"

Vince turned to her and made pacifying hand motions. "Kelly—"

"Everybody at this table knows you got pregnant on purpose."

Chelsea gasped.

Her date looked horrified.

Kelly nearly told him to run now, or at least make sure he provided his own condoms. "You wanted Vince in high school, and you got him. You played your hand, and you won."

The diners of the Grove weren't even pretending not to be loving this shit. They even had a couple of smart phones facing their way. Chelsea would be delighted if it went viral.

"Congratulations, Chelsea." Kelly leaned closer to her. "You're the winner. Now, get over yourself, and get on with your life." She gathered her purse and looked at Vince. "And that's a no on dessert."

In the car, Vince turned to speak to her.

"No." Kelly held up her hand. "I'm mad as hell right now, and I can't talk about it."

Vince nodded and drove. They arrived at her condo in a stiff silence, and Kelly stepped out of the car before Vince got around it to open the door.

"Kelly." Vince caught her hand. "I'm sorry our evening ended that way.

"Me too." All her pent-up teenage rage had risen to the fore. As for that feeling like she might finally be over it? Nah, not even a little bit. Chelsea and her spite were the gift that kept giving. She managed to modulate her voice enough to say, "Listen, I'm not mad at you. There is no reason for you to apologize, because none of this is your fault. I need to be alone right now."

Vince dropped his head and nodded. "Okay. But for the record, I really am sorry. This is not the way I saw the evening ending."

Ya think! "I know that. I'll call you tomorrow."

She climbed the stairs to her condo but didn't go inside. Restless anger drove her, and she knew exactly where she wanted to be.

———

The Bugling Elk was still going strong. At this time of night on a Friday, drinks were flowing, and music was pumping. She could have joined Saturday wine and whine, but a girl in a killer black dress and heels needed more.

She hit pay dirt.

Over in the back, Gabe and Cara were playing pool and laughing. Jealousy took a swipe at her. They looked so comfortable together. Well, screw that! Gabe couldn't be kissing the crap out of her one day and the next pulling the friend line with Cara.

She marched over there to set him straight.

"Hey." A tall thirty-something blond man lurched into her path and leered at her. "I'm new in town."

"Good for you." Kelly sidestepped him.

He got in her way again. "You're not very friendly."

"I don't know you." Kelly couldn't believe the nerve of that guy. "And you're in my way."

"It said on Facebook that all we had to do was say we're new in town, and you locals would make us more than welcome." Stepping closer, he ogled her cleavage. "Now, I'm new in town and ready for you to make me feel real welcome."

"You wanna take a step back, pal." Gabe appeared behind the blond, looking ready to throw down.

The guy whirled, looked at Gabe and reconsidered his options. He threw his hands up. "Hey! She didn't say she was taken."

Jeez! Like she was a barstool.

"She shouldn't have to." Gabe stared him down. "But to be clear, she's with me."

With a curt nod, the blond disappeared around the far side of the bar.

Turning back to her, Gabe took her all in and a slow, sexy smile spread over his face. "And hello to you." Looking like sin and smelling like heaven, he leaned down and kissed her cheek. "You look good enough to make me lose my mind."

Kelly smiled back. "Behave yourself."

"With you in that dress?" Gabe stood back and took another slow look from her feet to her face. "Not a chance."

"Ahem." Cara waggled her head. "Standing here."

Laughing, Kelly turned and greeted Cara. "How are you?"

"I'm good." Cara grinned around the neck of her beer bottle. "Kicking his ass at pool always puts me in a good mood."

"Way I hear it, you kick everyone's ass." Kelly threw some sass into her voice. "Of course, you haven't played me yet."

Cara's eyebrows shot up. "That's some fighting talk right there."

"Umm…Kelly." Gabe sidled closer. "She's really good."

Kelly didn't dignify that with a response but selected her favorite cue and chalked it. "Why don't you get the beers?"

With a grin, Gabe strolled over to the bar. He had a damn fine ass on him.

Cara stood next to her. "How did your date go?"

"It was...interesting." She dragged her gaze off Gabe. "This being Twin Elks, you'll hear all about it in about fifteen minutes."

Cara snorted. "That must be some story if you're here instead of there." She also studied Gabe, who stood at the bar with one foot on the rest. "Gabe and I are just friends."

Kelly heaved a sigh. "Same."

"Great ass, though." Cara tilted her head for a better look.

Kelly got her green monster under control. "He has brothers."

"I'm happy to hear it."

In the end, Cara beat her, but Kelly didn't make it easy for her. Being at the Elk helped her forget about Vince, Chelsea, that weird dinner, and her even weirder thoughts about where they went from there. It also helped her not worry about India constantly.

Claiming an early morning the next day, Cara left after their third and decisive game.

"Come." Gabe pulled her on the small dance floor. "I want to dance with the most beautiful woman here."

He wasn't much of a dancer, but he did a really good thigh to thigh, chest to chest slow shuffle to the music. Ignoring the warnings going off in her brain, Kelly pressed her face to his neck.

They fit together like they'd been grafted that way. Even sexually loaded silences with Gabe were more comfortable than the dinner she'd endured with Vince.

Endured? And wasn't that a telling use of vocabulary?

CHAPTER
Sixteen

KELLY STOPPED her car and stared at what had once been a cabin and now looked like a beautiful family home. Ben Crowe, all-around great guy and local police chief, had bought the piece of land after his divorce from Chelsea's bestie, and all-around venomous bitch, Tara.

"Hey." Poppy emerged from the front door, her big beautiful smile already in place. "You made it."

Kelly held up the bags. "And as instructed, I brought provisions."

The plan was for Ben, Poppy, and their four kids to move out of Winters House, where they'd been living with Claire, Finn, and Horace, and into this house when it was ready. From what Kelly could see, that day didn't lay far off.

A deep porch skirted the front of the stone and wood house. Ben had managed to retain the feel of a cabin and add a whole lot more to it.

"Kelly!" Poppy's five-year old son Ryan ran down the porch steps toward her. "Did you come to see my new house?"

"I did." Kelly ruffled his hair. Ryan had more energy than he knew what to do with and had never met a stranger who wasn't his best friend. "It looks beautiful."

"Wait until you see my room," Ryan said. "And I get my own room and don't have to share with Sean." He caught sight of the bags in her hands. "Did you bring food?"

Poppy reached her and kissed her cheek. "India and Jacob are inside with Dot."

Dot had called Kelly and invited Kelly and India to spend Sunday helping Ben at the cabin. Poppy's youngest was a few months older than Jacob, and it would be good for India to be among people, so Kelly had accepted.

"There you are." Gabe strode around the side of the house. "I've been waiting for you."

That should not have made her heart go all dumb and pittery-pattery, but it did. "Me or the food?"

Taking the bags from her, Gabe gave her a naughty grin. "Both. It's an all you can eat buffet."

Oh no, he did not! But he was grinning at her, so he clearly had.

"You're a pig." Kelly shoved his shoulder.

Gabe raised an eyebrow. "And this is news to you?"

Poppy looked from her to Gabe and back again. As Gabe turned away, she gave Kelly a look that promised they would talk later.

Kelly pulled a face. Nothing to say.

Inside the house, Ben had made amazing progress. Of course, most of Twin Elks had lent a hand at some point or the other. Ben was their beloved police chief, and after his disastrous first marriage to Tara, everyone wanted to smooth the way for him and Poppy.

Huge glass windows brought light and the incredible view into the main living area. More wood beams and rock kept it rustic, with dark hardwoods on the floor.

Over by the fireplace, India sat on a blanket with Jacob and Sean as they played with blocks. Sean and Jacob seemed to be steadfastly ignoring each other. India looked more relaxed than Kelly had seen her since the night she'd arrived.

"Hi." Kelly bent and kissed her cheek. "Are you on baby duty?"

"I am." India looked up with a sunny smile.

"India! Hey, India!" Ryan barreled over, and India caught him before he smashed headlong into her shoulder. "I saw a deer outside."

"Did you, now?" India made big eyes at him. "Do you know what type?"

Ryan screwed his face up and shook his head. "Deer type?"

"Ask Gabe." Dot joined them. "He spent his life wandering around those hills with his father." Pausing, Dot kissed Kelly's cheek. "Hello there. Thanks for bringing the food. The troops are getting restless."

"Gabe's dad is dead too, isn't he?" Ryan stared up at Dot. "Like mine."

"Yes, he is." A trace of sadness still lingered in Dot's voice and face, but it was an old sadness grown poignant and wistful. "In a few days, it will be ten years since his death."

Ryan screwed his face up. "I don't remember my dad that well. Sean never even met him." He shrugged. "But we have Ben now."

Dot cupped his cheek. "You have all of us now."

"Ah ha!" Claire strolled in from the back door to the big open-plan kitchen. "I heard a rumor you were here and that you'd brought food." She came over and looped her arm around Kelly. "I'm starving."

"You're always starving." Kelly kind of hated how Claire could eat like a lumberjack and stay so slim.

"Yup." Claire patted her flat belly. "But I have a tapeworm today."

Finn strolled in after Claire and hugged Kelly. "Hey, gorgeous. Looking particularly tasty today."

"Mind yourself, hot stuff, or I might get all carried away." Flirting with Finn was one of the best parts of him settling in Twin Elks.

Finn grinned at her. "I'm not man enough for that."

"You bet your life you're not." Over Finn's shoulder, Gabe winked at her.

"Ugh!" Dot slapped his arm. "Stop it and come and help me get lunch for everyone."

Gabe trailed his mother into the kitchen. "I should be out there doing manly things with hammers and drills."

"No!" Finn, Claire, Dot, and Poppy all yelled at once.

The rest of the party filtered in, consisting of Ben, Claire's father Horace, Doc Cooper, and Peg.

Peg strode into the kitchen. "We should organize lunch stations."

"Woman." Horace looked at her from beneath his unruly gray eyebrows. "You're not organizing anything, and I better not see that bullhorn or that whistle."

Peg's gray permed curls twitched with her desire to take him on, but to Kelly's huge surprise, she settled down again. "I have made lists for the painting crew of who should tackle what."

"That sounds fine." Horace handed her a bottle of water. "After lunch, you can give everyone their assignments."

Doc Cooper made himself a sandwich and then made one for Dot as well. They settled near India and the little ones to eat.

"Did you know about that?" Kelly jerked her head at the couple as she sidled close enough to whisper to Gabe.

He grimaced. "I try not to think too much about it."

"Ma deserves to be happy." Ben sounded annoyed.

Gabe stiffened. "I wasn't saying she doesn't. It takes some time getting used to Ma dating again."

"You had trouble with it in the beginning." Poppy shoved a piece of baguette packed with meat, cheese, and lettuce at Ben. "Gabe is new to all this."

"I'm still not used to it." Claire watched Peg and Horace as they took their lunch and drinks outside and settled in a patch of sun. "But at least Dad refuses to have her whistle in the house."

Kelly took her lunch and a plate over to India.

WALK ON BY   139

"Thanks." India took the plate from her. "I was starting to get really hungry."

Poppy's twins, Brinn and Ciara, had also joined the group of children around India. Her sister had always been good with children. They naturally flocked to her. Whereas with adults, India was shy and cautious, she came into her own around children.

"So, I was thinking." Kelly didn't want to push her, but India looked so much happier now that she wasn't sitting around Dot's house. "I need someone for the coffee shop. Would you be interested?"

India looked stricken and almost dropped her sandwich. "Me?"

"Only if you're ready." Kelly felt compelled to provide the exit clause. "And you're welcome to bring Jacob."

"Or you could leave him with me," Dot said. "I already watch Sean in the mornings."

Putting her sandwich down, India carefully and methodically wiped her hands. "That would be…great."

"India?" Great was not the way Kelly would have described the expression on India's face. "It's only an idea. If you don't want to do it, I can find someone else."

"No, I do want to do it." India's miserable expression told another story altogether. "I really, really do."

India had always been the quieter sister, and the more easygoing one, but this timidity was another rock in the wall Kelly wanted to push over on Piers. "I tell you what." She glanced at Dot. "Why don't you think about it? I did kind of spring this on you."

Dot was watching India with concern. "India, honey." She leaned closer to India. "You need to say if this is really what you want. Kelly won't be mad at you or anything."

Nodding, India kept her gaze on her plate. She mumbled something.

"What?" Kelly had to lean closer to hear her.

"I said, I don't think I'm any good in the coffee shop." Cheeks flushed, India finally met her gaze. "I get so nervous with all those people, and you were really nice about it, but you can't afford to have me breaking all your cups."

India would have been a neat solution for her, but not if it didn't suit both of them. "You're right, I can't. So let's leave things as they are, and I'll get some other help."

"Help where?" Peg strode over to them. "In your store?"

"Yes, I've been getting busier and busier." Kelly had lost some of her appetite. India was like a shell of the sister she'd grown up with. "I need someone for the rush times and also for extended hours."

"Hmm." Peg tapped her cheek. "I'll have to give that some thought."

"Thanks, Peg." Kelly kept it upbeat. "It's important to get the right person."

Kelly waited until India was once more engrossed in the children before she stood up. She needed space. Outside, the wind swept up the valley in an enthusiastic gust that found her on the porch and whipped her hair around her head.

"You okay?" Gabe joined her. He shrugged out of his jacket and put it over her shoulders.

"Yeah." Kelly kept her gaze on the view. "It's not that she doesn't want to work in the coffee shop. It's that she felt like she couldn't tell me."

"I get it." Gabe shoved his hands in his pockets. "She needs time to learn who to trust again. She married a man she loved, and he turned into a douchebag. On some level, she's got to be questioning her own judgment."

He'd surprised her, and she stared at him.

"What?" He glowered.

"That was really insightful."

"I have my moments." He hunched his shoulders. "Although, right now, I'm freezing my balls off. So can we go inside?"

Laughing, Kelly followed him.

"Ah, Kelly!" Peg had her clipboard out. "I have your painting assignment."

Halfway through painting the twins' bedroom blush, Vince called her.

Gabe was working alongside her, and she stood and walked out of earshot. It was a stupid thing to do because she and Gabe weren't even a thing. Not anymore, and not really ever, but she did it anyway.

"Kelly?" Vince always asked as if he hadn't just dialed her number.

"That's my name."

Vince chuckled. "I had a thought for this weekend."

"What was that?" The idea of another date like their awkward dinner sat like curdled milk in her stomach. Her history with Vince was as teens, and they needed to make the transition to adults.

"I have the kids this weekend, and I know they'd like to meet you," Vince said.

Talk about your ball-crunching instant panic attacks! "What?"

"I said, the kids are with me this weekend, and I thought it would be nice if we could all get to know each other."

Kelly didn't think that at all. In fact, Kelly could think of few things she wanted to do less than get familiar with Chelsea's offspring.

And Vince's! She needed to remember that. Fifty percent of those children's DNA came from her old high school sweetheart, now new date. "Great!"

"Awesome." Vince sounded relieved. "This is going to be great. They're going to love you." She wanted to kick herself. She'd oversold this by about, oh say, one hundred thousand percent.

She had to say something that sounded positive. "And you can be sure, I'm going to love them."

"You are?" He sounded delighted.

She had no choice but to double down. "They're your kids, aren't they?"

CHAPTER
Seventeen

KELLY RIPPED off her fourth outfit. She had absolutely no idea what to wear, and with each passing moment, she wanted to get ready less.

"They're only children." India lay on her bed playing with Jacob.

"You say this because children love you." Kelly found her powder blue sweater with buttons up the front. It dipped low enough to show the shadow between her breasts. They were going to think she was a total ho.

"Children like you." But even India couldn't make it sound that convincing. Kelly had no idea what to say to children. Generally, she and children kept a respectful distance. India perked up. "And the oldest is fourteen, so almost an adult."

"She's a teen." Kelly pulled her black jeans back on. They were tight and combined with the sweater's neckline, she might as well be offering twenty bucks for a hand job. What was the going rate anyway? "A person who is almost an adult is a teen, and they are the worst of all."

"Leave the black jeans on. They look great on your butt." India gave her a laughing look. "And even if she's a teen, she's mainly still a child."

"But she's going to think I'm lame. I don't even have Snapchat." The sweater had to go, so she whipped it off. But the jeans really did give her a good butt. "The only reason I'm on Instagram is because of the store."

"Why don't you start with hello?" India chuckled.

The sound stopped Kelly in her tracks. It was the first time India had laughed since she'd arrived in Twin Elks. The last week had been great for India; she had come further and further out of her shell. "Yes, obviously, but then what. I don't even know what music is popular now. Are One Direction still a thing?"

"Ah, no." India shook her head and played with Jacob's feet. Another improvement; India engaging with her son. Before this, she had taken care of the basics but not really done much more. Thank God for Dot. "And don't try to be someone you're not. Be yourself and try to get them to talk about their interests."

"I should have Googled, maybe bought a book. Someone, somewhere must have dealt with meeting a date's kids at some time. " She tugged on a lilac sweater with a V-neck. "Is this trashy? Can you see too much boob?"

"You can definitely see boob, because you got the family allotment of those." India glanced at her own smaller chest. "But you can't see any cleavage, and it's not trashy at all."

Kelly sat down and got on with her makeup. "I'm going to buy a book about dealing with somebody else's kids."

"Is it that serious with you and Vince?" India's face appeared over her shoulder in the mirror. "I thought this was only like a third date or something."

"I'm not sure what this is. None of this is following the normal rules." Vince didn't come out and say stuff. He hinted around it. "All I know is that this is me meeting his children."

India frowned. "That seems like a big step."

"It does, doesn't it?" Kelly turned to talk to her. "That's been on my mind as well. I would have liked a few more getting reacquainted dates before this." She shrugged. "But you know Vince."

"Not really." India blew on Jacob's hands and made him giggle. "I mean, I remember him from when you guys dated. You dated for years."

"Three."

"There you go." India nodded. "But I didn't really know him. I was your kid sister."

Kelly finished her makeup and chose a simple ponytail for her hair. The plan was to go over, have lunch with his kids and maybe watch a movie or something. It definitely didn't call for heels, so she grabbed her Converses. The nice pair that weren't covered in coffee splashes. She held her arms out. "How do I look?"

"Like somebody I'd be glad to have dating my dad." Then India pulled a face. "That sounded better in my head, but you know what I mean."

"I know what you mean."

The doorbell rang, sending Kelly's nerves into overdrive. She made a face at India. "Wish me luck."

"You'll be awesome." India gathered up Jacob and her things.

Kelly answered the door to Vince. "Hi."

"Hi, you." He kissed her cheek. "You get prettier every time I see you."

He used to say that to her way back when and it made her laugh. "I get older every time you see me."

"Hi, Vince." India came up behind her with Jacob in her arms. Her cheeks flushed charmingly pink.

Vince blushed and cleared his throat. "Hey, India. You staying here?"

"No." India smiled back. "We're mooching off Dot at the moment. Jacob and I popped in to visit Auntie Kelly this morning."

"And hello to you." Vince tickled Jacob's tummy with his forefinger. He looked at India with his hands held out. "May I?"

"Sure." India handed him over.

Vince beamed at them over Jacob's head. "I love babies. I could have a football team of them."

"Really?" Kelly had never spoken to Vince about children. She'd assumed he hadn't been delighted to be a young father, and she hadn't been around in those early days of his marriage to Chelsea. He really did look good with Jacob, a natural. Unlike someone else who was still on the edge of a free-fall panic attack. "Shall we?"

Vince kept hold of Jacob as they walked to the parking lot. He turned to India. "Can we drop you?"

"I have my car." India slid past him, careful not to let one part of herself come into contact with Vince. "But thanks anyway."

"No bother." He buckled Jacob into his car seat and stood back and watched as India drove away. "She's incredible."

"Huh?" He caught Kelly in the act of checking out the cleavage situation. India had said there wasn't too much showing, but how much was too much? "India?"

"Yeah." Vince shook his head. "I can't even get my head around what she's been through. What that asshole put her through."

Vince was right. She'd been spending all this time worrying about India not being who she was before instead of seeing her as the strong survivor she was. "That asshole showed up here the other day."

"What?" Vince's face tightened with anger. "Did he try to get to her?"

"No." Kelly walked with Vince to his car. "He's still holding to his story that she is depressed and not acting like herself."

Vince yanked the car door open for her, putting a tad too much heft in it. "Asshole."

"He's very convincing, but I'm going to give India the benefit of the doubt."

Vince stared at her. "Why would you not?"

Again, he was absolutely right. Piers had every reason to lie and India none.

"Has Ben arrested him yet?" Vince checked the traffic before joining the main road outside her condo.

"Not when I spoke to him yesterday," Kelly said. "It seems Piers has not been to work and hasn't been seen at his house either."

Vince's jaw tightened. "There's the proof of his guilt. Right there."

Vince drove them to a new subdivision on the outskirts of town. When she'd last been there, half the houses had been paused, waiting for new buyers. Now they were all full and families were out and about. "When did this happen?"

"It's been steadily growing." Vince pointed to a house on their right. "That was the last one, and the Cranstons moved in about three months ago."

Being friendly with your neighbors was one of those things that still happened in Twin Elks.

As Vince pulled into the driveway of a neat two-story detached home with a small lawn out front, nerves almost got the better of Kelly. She fought the urge to ask Vince if she could stay in the car until he had time to take her home again.

"Come on." He grinned at her. "They're waiting for you."

Like the grim reaper, really. Kelly managed a pathetic smile and climbed out the car.

Vince let her into the house, a neat family home with warm wooden floors and off-white walls. A small pile of books and shoes lay on the bottom stairs waiting for someone to take them up, and backpacks sat under coats in the entrance hall.

"This way." Vince led her down the passage and into a kitchen, which lay open to a dining room and doglegged into a family room.

Two dark heads sat on a navy sofa facing away from them. "Kids," Vince said. "I'd like you to meet Kelly."

Both heads whipped in her direction. Hannah, she recognized from outside of Grover's. She looked exactly like Chelsea, a mirror image with a mouth full of hardware and a look of teenage scorn all over her face.

She found her big girl pants and gave them a tug up. "Hi."

"Hi," the boy said. "When's lunch?"

"Soon." Vince put his car keys on a hook over the telephone. "First come and let me introduce you to Kelly."

While his back was turned, the girl took the opportunity to roll her eyes so far back in her head Kelly wasn't sure they'd ever be able to face forward again.

"That's okay, I can—"

"Daniel, Hannah."

Daniel and Hannah dragged themselves closer.

Vince did the introductions. "Kelly, this is Daniel."

"Nice to meet you."

"And Hannah."

"Nice to meet you. You look so much like your mother."

All three Greerlys stiffened.

"Um...I went to school with your mother. And your father. We all went to school together. When we went to school. I mean we did all go to school. It's not like we could pick and choose when we went." *Shut. Up. Shut up, shut up, shut up.*

"Great," Hannah drawled. Then she looked at Vince. "Now can we eat? You said we were waiting for her. Well, she's here now."

"She has a name." Vince raised a brow at his daughter.

Hannah stuck her hip out and put her head to the side. "Now that Ke-e-elly is here, can we eat?"

"In a moment." Vince turned to her. "Can I get you a drink?"

Thank you, Jesus. "A glass of wine would be lovely."

He flushed. "Umm..."

"We don't drink in this house." Hannah sneered.

"Oh...er...okay." Note to self, next time she was bringing a hip flask. Lots of people didn't drink, and it wasn't like she was a habitual drinker anyway. "Water would be great."

Hannah gave her a scalding look from top to toe. And that was enough of that.

It was super childish, but Kelly gave it right back to her.

With a huff, Hannah turned, slapped her brother's shoulder and they flounced back to the couch.

"I should have warned you about the no drinking thing," Vince said softly as he brought her water. "Chelsea instituted it about five years ago. She didn't like me going to the Elk and coming back smelling of beer."

"But she's not here anymore." Kelly took the glass of water from him. Now she sounded like she was being petulant about a glass of wine.

Vince shrugged. "Yeah, but I try to keep things as constant as I can for those two."

"Understandable." She nodded and sipped her water. "Now, what can I do for lunch?"

"Nothing." Vince grinned and kissed her on the cheek. "I've got this."

Kelly took a seat at the counter. "I see you've learned to cook."

"I won't make *Master Chef* anytime soon, but I know my way around a kitchen." Vince chuckled.

"I'm still as useless as ever," Kelly said.

Daniel dragged out the stool opposite her and climbed onto it. "My mom is a really good cook. She is teaching me and Hannah."

"That's nice." She was the adult. She could be polite and not react, and they could all have a lovely lunch together. With fluffy kitties rolling in balls of wool and unicorns spreading rainbow love sprinkles over them all. "I never learned, and now, I guess, I'm not that interested in learning. I can do a couple of basic things, and I excel at sandwiches and ordering takeout."

Daniel looked like he might laugh but then covered it up with a scowl. "How old are you anyway?"

"Thirty-three. How old are you?"

"Eight."

Hannah joined them at the table. "Don't you own the coffee shop?"

"Yup. It's all mine."

"Huh." Hannah smirked. "My mom said she'd rather choke than get coffee from there."

"Hannah!" Vince scowled at his daughter. "You're being rude."

"I'm not." Hannah looked as innocent as a baby lamb. "That is what Mom says. I heard it. So did Daniel."

Looking uncomfortable, Daniel nodded.

As Kelly would happily choke Chelsea on a cup of coffee before she gave it to her, Hannah's dig missed its mark, and she smiled. "That's okay, Vince. Really. She's repeating what her mother said. Everyone is entitled to their opinion, and there are certainly enough Starbucks around for people who don't like my coffee."

"I like Starbucks," Daniel said.

"There you go." Kelly sipped her water and wished it would magically transform itself into wine. A barrel of wine, with a straw. She didn't entirely blame the kids, although they were doing a great impersonation of little shits. The fault lay with Vince. It was too soon for them, and they saw her as a threat. What had India said she should talk about? "Do you guys have any hobbies? Things you like to do?"

"No."

"No."

"Yes, you do." Vince brought a huge dish of lasagna to the table. "Hannah likes dancing, and she's very good at it, and Daniel plays about everything with a ball in it."

Kelly managed an easy smile for Vince. "Sounds like you."

"Dad doesn't play sports." Hannah scoffed.

Kelly held her ground. "I don't know about now, but he used to. And loved it."

"Well, he doesn't anymore."

"Hannah, can you get the salad out the fridge?" Vince's voice sounded tight and strained. "Daniel, please get the plates."

Conversation stopped while everyone got ready to eat. It didn't flourish much after that either. Despite Vince's attempts to introduce common topics, the moment Kelly entered the conversation, his children exited.

The lasagna was the only high point in the day, and she ate too much. After lunch, she helped them clear away in a tense silence that made her want to giggle hysterically.

"Okay." Vince clapped his hands. "What movie shall we watch?"

A high-pitched panicked giggle got away from Kelly. "No, that's fine. I have to go and...er...check on India and Jacob anyway."

"What kind of name is India?" Hannah whispered to Daniel, loud enough to carry into the kitchen. "That's a country, not a person."

"Hannah." Vince looked thunderous. "India is a lovely name, and it belongs to a lovely lady."

Hannah shrugged and stuck her lip out. "I was just saying."

"I think you should—"

"Now, Vince." Kelly ran out of playing nice. "I want to check on India. Now."

A loaded silence filled the car as Vince drove her to Dot's. "Listen," he said. "I really am sorry about that. They still miss Chelsea and our family."

"I understand." She hoped Gabe was home because a dose of him was exactly what she needed. There was so much wrong with that thought, and even more right with it, and she didn't want to think about it anymore. "But perhaps meeting them so soon was not a good idea."

"You're right." Vince sounded glum. "I forget that they don't have any idea of our history." He stopped the car outside Dot's. "I want us to move forward, Kelly, and maybe I jumped the gun."

"You think?" It was meant to come out light and teasing but it sounded a lot more loaded than she had planned. "Why don't we try this again, another time, when you and I are sure of what's going on between us?"

"Good idea." Vince leaned in for the kiss.

"Not here." Kelly had a sudden vision of Gabe standing in the kitchen window, and she didn't want him watching Vince kiss her. Because she didn't want to upset him. Yeah, bullshit! "I don't want India to see. She's so fragile right now."

Amazingly, Vince bought that load of utter crap and turned the kiss into a light peck on her cheek. "I really am sorry about today, Kelly. I'll call you, and we can make an adult date."

"Great." She scrambled out the car and may have walked a tad too fast toward Dot's kitchen door.

Gabe stood at the sink, one hip propped against it. He raised his brows at her. "That's not a happy face."

"Are we friends?"

A smirk tilted the corner of his mouth. "Amongst other things."

She headed straight for him and dropped her forehead to his chest. "Then get me the biggest glass of wine you can find. Or a beer. Or whisky. Battery acid, if you can't find anything else."

On a deep, soft laugh, Gabe's arms folded around her and brought her closer. "You got it, gorgeous." He kissed her temple. "Anything and everything you want."

CHAPTER
Eighteen

KELLY DIDN'T GET IT. Things with Gabe were so easy. Sitting at Dot's kitchen table, retelling the lunch from hell with Satan's small minions, the funny side poked its head over the cloud.

Even India managed a giggle or two.

Dot joined them for a glass of wine. She immediately took possession of Jacob and cuddled him.

"Chelsea always overindulged those children," Dot said as she made silly faces at Jacob. "I think she was trying to make up for Vince not being around much. And now, of course, she's with her new man."

"Who is that exactly?" Kelly had never mixed in the Chelsea and Tara circle. Up until quite recently, Claire had been part of that coven, but she'd turned away from the dark side, and they'd lost their source of gossip.

Dot made a face. "Some fancy suit from Denver she met through Tara."

"Figures." A niggling sense of dissatisfaction made her petulant. "What is it about Chelsea anyway?"

Gabe looked at her and grinned. "No idea, but she's got nothing on you."

"That's the correct answer." She laughed. "It doesn't help that those kids look exactly like her."

"Kelly." India gave her a reproachful look. "That's not their fault."

Kelly pulled a face at her and felt like a bitch. "I know that, but they were mean to me."

"Poor baby." Dot's eyes danced with mischief. "Did those rotten children pick on you?"

As everyone laughed at her, Kelly found her sense of humor. "Okay, point made. I'm the adult, and they're the children."

"Also, Vince didn't make it easy on any of you by pushing this," Dot said. "But men aren't always that good at thinking through the emotional impact of their actions."

Gabe straightened in his seat. "Hey! On behalf of men everywhere, I object."

"Uh-huh." Dot fixed him with a look. "And as the mother of five of you, I say protest all you want, but men do something and consider the emotional repercussions of their actions after the fact."

Wincing, Gabe said, "True. Mildly insulting, but true."

Kelly was still laughing when she answered her phone.

"Kelly?" Piers on the line killed her smile. "It's Piers."

"Yes, I know." She stood up from the table, not wanting him to hear India. She glanced at Gabe.

He read her look and opened the kitchen door for Kelly to move outside. She had absolute confidence he would manage the situation inside. "What do you want, Piers?"

"The same thing I wanted when we last saw each other. My son and wife are missing and I'm going crazy." He sounded genuinely upset. "The only guarantee I have that they're alright is your word."

"And that's going to have to be good enough until I figure out what's going on," Kelly said.

Piers jumped immediately for the minute gap. "So, you're at least thinking about what I said?"

"I didn't say that." Damn, she needed to be more careful. Piers was no dummy.

"It's okay, Kelly." His tone warmed. "I know how important India is to you. You take care of her, and as frustrated as I am by all of this, I know that as long as they're with you, they're safe."

Like she said, clever and cunning. "She's not with me, Piers." No way was she falling into that trap. "I absolutely know where she is though, and I know that both she and Jacob are fine."

Dot stepped on the porch, her face tight and tense. She raised an eyebrow in question.

Kelly shook her head. No, everything was not all right. Piers was on the hunt now, and he was getting insistent.

"Kelly." There was no mistaking the edge to his voice. "India is my wife, and Jacob is my son; that gives me rights."

"I would say you gave up those rights the first time you lifted a hand to her."

Through the open door to the kitchen, India was freaking out and Gabe had her in his arms. Kelly motioned for Dot to shut the door.

If he heard Jacob or India make a sound, the jig would be up.

Piers's voice was so carefully calm the hair on Kelly's nape stood on end. "I never laid a finger on my wife in anger."

"That's not what she says, and she's my sister. I believe her."

Dot squeezed her shoulder in support.

"Now, I've told you all I'm prepared to tell you. If, and this is a very big if, you're telling the truth, I would suggest you turn yourself in to the police and let them handle it."

"I'm not doing that, Kelly. I've done nothing wrong."

"If that's true, then you have nothing to worry about."

Piers made an impatient noise. "Get India to drop the charges. I've spoken to my lawyer, and he said that would help."

"I wouldn't if I could, Piers. If you've spoken to your lawyer, you should know this is going to court no matter what India does." Kelly's legs shook, and she took a seat on the porch step. Cold seeped through her jeans.

"I'll find her," Piers said. "And once I do, we'll deal with this together."

"You do what you have to do, Piers. India and Jacob are not in Twin Elks, mainly because it's the first place you'd look for them, and I'm not that stupid."

Dot gave her the thumbs up as Kelly hung up. "Well done."

"Hopefully he buys it." If she was wrong about Piers, she would owe her brother-in-law a massive apology. But like she'd said, that was a mighty big if. Dot had set her right. It was a long stretch of the imagination to go from postpartum depression to domestic abuse. "I better see how India is doing."

"Gabe has her." Dot gave her a hug. "Let him sort her out; he's good with fragile."

It took Gabe a while to calm India down.

Her freak-out had exhausted her, so he took Jacob with him to let her rest. She looked so tiny and broken lying on the bed, sleeping fitfully, dried tears on her cheeks.

If the conversation when Piers had visited Kelly had cast any doubts in his mind, they were now put to rest. He spent his life around wild animals who reacted in fight or flight.

India was in full out flight mode, and she was running for her life. He wanted two minutes alone with that fucker to set him right on what happened to boys who put their hands on girls in anger.

When he'd last spoken to Ben, his brother hadn't been able to find Piers. The guy was in the wind and staying that way. Ben wouldn't give up, though. That stubborn streak that pitted him and Ben against each other had benefits.

Ma was sitting in the kitchen with Kelly, and he joined them.

Kelly stood the moment he appeared. "And?"

"She's sleeping." He took the seat beside Ma and took a sip of her wine. "Kelly, you may not want to hear this, but he did it.

I'm as sure as I can be without having seen it with my own eyes."

"Oh, God." She sat down again. "I've become one of those people who victim blame. How could I be such a bitch as to even consider he might be telling the truth?"

Ma opened her arms to hug Kelly, but Gabe got there before her and handed her Jacob. He tucked Kelly under his chin. "Piers is clever, and he preyed on India's weakness to create doubt."

"You weren't even there," she said. Her arms slid around his waist. Like she trusted him and took comfort from him. Yeah, right, because this was all about him and how he felt.

"But I know you," he said. "You're not stupid, and you're loyal to a fault. If he got in your head, it's because he knew what to say to find his way in."

Kelly sniffed. "You give me too much credit."

"Not really." Ma had left them at some point, but he wasn't sure when. "I know, for instance, that you suck at teens."

"Asshole." She squeezed him tighter and then stepped away. "But a truthful one."

She took a deep breath. "I'll go in and see India."

Alone in the night, Gabe strolled out to the porch and looked at the night sky littered with stars. The sky was so different from the southern hemisphere, but no less beautiful. Twin Elks was far enough out that they still got those grand night skies.

Shit was getting complicated fast.

"Gabe." Ma stepped on the porch with his phone. "There's a call for you. Your phone was in the kitchen, and I answered it. It's Steve Moffat."

Speaking of complicated shit, Belinda's father definitely belonged in that category. "Gabe." Steve's voice took him right back to Oz. "How are you?"

"Good, Steve." Not really, but the explanation could get ugly, and he wasn't ready to go there yet. "You?"

"Nah! Good, good." He pictured Steve rubbing his hands

together like he did when conversations got uncomfortable. "Listen, mate, I know you had a chat with Belinda the other day, and she said you'd think about our offer."

"Yeah." With all that had been going on in Twin Elks, he hadn't really thought about it, other than when caught in expressing-anal-glands hell. "I'm still thinking."

"That's fine, fine." Steve's chuckle sounded forced. "Take the time you need. You know we think the world of you down here."

Strange that, because when things had gone tits up with him and Belinda, Steve hadn't hesitated to make his displeasure felt in a thousand different ways. It was the first time Gabe had seen his leaving in that light. "Right," he said. "And I loved my work there."

"Too right." Steve paused. "Listen, Gabe mate, I wanted to say that I don't hold any grudges for what happened between you and my daughter. Really, none of my business and I wanted you to know that. If you did decide to come back to us, we'd bury the hatchet on that and forget about it."

"Good to know." And part of him did feel like that, but this new awareness of perhaps Steve hadn't behaved as he should have wouldn't shut up. Sure Belinda was his daughter, but Gabe had only met her after he'd started working with Steve.

Belinda had joined the project later, and even then, Gabe had done his best to keep their relationship away from the project.

Steve and Belinda had blurred those lines.

"In fairness, Steve," he said. "I am thinking about it, and I know you know about the offer from South Africa. I'm not being a dick about it, but I also have stuff here I need to deal with. It's a long time since I've been home."

"I get that, Gabe, but I also wanted to remind you that you had a good life here. A life that suited you."

"Thanks, Steve." For making this harder than it already was. "I'll call you as soon as I've made a decision."

Damn. Steve had gotten him all stirred up again. His life in

Australia had suited someone like him, with his love for the outdoors and being active. Maybe he should ask Ben if he could join him on his morning runs.

His lack of physical activity was also getting on his nerves.

Their mutual love of hiking, diving, bike riding, skiing—you name it—had drawn him and Belinda together. Come to think of it, they hadn't spent many evenings sitting and chatting. They'd always been too busy climbing some mountain or exploring some reef.

Australians were relaxed and easy. They worked to live, and they lived to the fullest in their incredible climate. He missed that and he missed those times there. Perhaps it was more his lifestyle he missed than the job?

Now that was a thought he didn't want to spend too much time dwelling on.

CHAPTER
Nineteen

GABE'S FEET pounded the asphalt in a steady rhythm that took possession of his brain. Last night's call with Steve had kept at him through the night and into today. Finally, he'd driven himself out of the house for a run after dinner. Running at the higher altitude in Twin Elks created a harsh burn of his breath in his throat and made it difficult to match his breathing with his pace.

Ice rode the air with the sharp scent of ozone and it wouldn't be long before they had snow. Twin Elks under a blanket of snow was a magical memory from his childhood. Ma had never been able to get them back in the house after that first decent snow dump. He and his brothers had built snow forts and had snowball fights that lasted until Ma lost patience and yelled. And even Rafe had kept his head down when Ma lost her cool.

Of course, Mark had to be a pain in the ass and make them all play pond hockey with him. Being that Mark now started regularly for the pros, that had always ended in either him or Luke wanting to pound the hell out of Mark in a mixture of bruised ego and annoyance at their younger brother's cockiness.

Ben had never gotten pissed. The sneaky bastard had always taken his time and picked his moment to get even. Gabe hadn't seen much of his brothers over the past few years, but they had always been close. Well, as close as five boys all with a competitive streak and bullheaded tendency could get. Ma said they got that from Dad.

This from the woman who regularly got her way. He had missed Ma and hadn't realized how much until this visit. There was something comforting about when people knew you well enough you didn't have to start every story with a long explanation.

He took a left into Main Street. Most of the stores were closed for the night. No grilles or alarm systems, because this was Twin Elks. There was a light on in the old bakery. Last he had heard, the bakery had been shut. Looks like someone else had bought the store and was busy fixing it up. It didn't look like a new bakery though.

From across the street, the light in Kelly's place spilled into the night. She was still in there, wiping down counters or something. When he had set out on his run, some part of him must have known what he needed and carried him there.

He crossed the street and tapped on the glass.

With a start, Kelly looked up. Her irritated frown smoothed into a big grin that warmed his chest. Some lucky man would be getting that smile every time he came home to her. Gabe couldn't rid himself of the idea that Vince shouldn't be that guy. Vince was nice and all but letting Kelly go was a bonehead move for anyone.

Kelly grabbed her keys and unlocked the front door. She leaned her shoulder on the doorjamb and gave him a cocky grin. "We're closed."

"Even for me?" Flirting with her came like breathing.

Kelly laughed. "Especially for you. What the hell are you doing anyway?"

"I was out for a run." He looked down at himself. The outfit was a dead giveaway.

She rolled her eyes. "Why?"

"It's good for me."

"At this time of night?"

"At any time."

Snorting, Kelly made way for him to enter. "The only time I run is when something is chasing me."

Belinda loved to run. In fact, they had been one of those couples who ran together, worked out at the gym together, as well as all the outdoors stuff they had in common. He had trouble picturing Kelly hiking.

"You're just in time." Kelly put a plate of pastries on the counter. "I was clearing out today's pastries."

"They don't keep?" The platter looked far more tempting than another five miles and he pulled up a stool.

Kelly poured them both a glass of milk and sat on the stool next to him. "So what bug is wedged so far up your ass you needed to run it out?"

She caught him with a mouthful of milk, and he had to swallow hard before it squirted out his nose.

"Careful there, tiger." She gave him a helpful pound on the back. "Even you can't carry off the milk out the nose thing."

The sense he was exactly where he needed to be settled around him. "This is good."

"Yeah?" Kelly's blue eyes warmed.

"Yeah." Gabe bit into a cherry Danish. "I had a call from Steve Moffat last night after you left."

"Isn't he the guy in Australia? Belinda's dad?"

He liked that she remembered stuff. He might have told her, or Ma had, but Kelly had remembered, like he was important to her. "That's the one. He wanted to assure me that if I came back, he wouldn't hold a grudge against me for Belinda."

"Dufuq?" Kelly looked hostile. "He shouldn't have held a grudge about that in the first place."

Gabe moved on to something with sprinkles. "She's his only child, and he tends to spoil her. I think I might be the first person to tell her she can't have what she wants."

"I suck at resisting temptation." Kelly took a pastry off the plate and bit into it. She moaned around a mouthful as she chewed. A small fleck of chocolate teased him from her top lip.

"Why are you resisting?" Watching her appreciation of food was like his porn.

Kelly pulled a face. "That pesky five pounds too many that I can't seem to get rid of."

"I like those five pounds." The chocolate fleck hovered above her plump lips.

She took another bite. "Enabler!"

He laughed, because being there made him feel lighter.

"There's a reason for sayings like don't shit where you eat," Kelly said.

"I know that." With the chocolate fleck and all the rest, it came out brusquer than he intended. He softened his tone. "It occurred to me at the time Belinda and I first got together, but things were going well both between us and on the project. I got lulled into this false sense of security that it would always be that way."

Kelly still had that chocolate on her lip. "You wouldn't be the first, and you won't be the last. Way I see it, you have two tickets out of Twin Elks and that's a win."

"Hmm. But which one should I take?"

"Only you can answer that." She took another bite, moaned again, much like she did when he was buried balls deep inside her. She licked away a flake of pastry and missed the chocolate. "My gran always used to say that you could never go back, only forward."

"But you did." He couldn't get his gaze to move away from her mouth. Kelly had a great mouth, almost too full for her face, and it made his imagination head south. "You left Twin Elks and came back again."

"I realized what I wanted most." She shrugged. "Now you have to do the same."

He snorted. "Thanks."

"Anytime." She winked at him. That chocolate was super-glued to her top lip. "This is where I want to be, but I had to take my own journey to get here."

"I'm never going to want to be here." It hurt too much, too many memories, too much guilt that he didn't want to think about. He focused on the chocolate instead and the way Kelly could turn anything into a porno. "You have chocolate on your mouth."

"Oh." Her eyes widened. "Where?"

"Right here." Gabe gripped both sides of her face and pulled her closer. He sucked her top lip into his mouth. His voice sounded a lot rougher when he broke their lip lock. "Gone now."

Kelly's breathing had grown labored and color flushed across her cheekbones. The look in her eyes gave him a green light he refused to ignore.

"Gabe." That was all he allowed her before he sealed his mouth to hers. Damn! This woman. The taste of her shot adrenalin through his bloodstream. His libido remembered her and woke with a bellow. Not since he was fifteen and reading a stolen Playboy from the stash under Ben's bed had he gotten hard that fast.

She wrapped her arms around him and opened her mouth to his onslaught. The kiss grew wetter, hungrier, more carnal as Kelly met each thrust of his tongue with hers. Her soft moan into his mouth drove any thought of stopping right out his head.

He tugged her off her stool and between his spread thighs. Full breasts rubbing against his chest felt fucking fantastic. Her nipples were so sensitive. That night between them she had arched into his mouth as he sucked them, moaned and writhed at the slight scrape of his teeth over them.

Kelly was a woman with an appetite matching his and a body built for his.

Gripping her full ass, he pressed his cock against her. That was where he wanted to be, so bad it made him groan.

Kelly rubbed against him, threatening his control, driving him out of his mind.

She dragged her mouth away from his. "Gabe." She panted his name. "We need to stop."

"Is that what you want?"

"No."

He took her mouth again. He didn't want to stop. He wanted to lay her down on the floor and bury his face between her thighs, and then his cock.

"Stop." She got her hands between them and pushed at his chest. Even then her gaze lingered on his mouth. "We need to stop."

He stroked her round ass, committing the shape of it to memory. "Stopping would be a lot easier if this didn't feel so good."

"I know." She stepped away from him. "But this is not a good idea."

It had been a great idea the other night as they tangled together on his old childhood twin bed. "There are good reasons why this is a bad idea," he said. "But right now, I'm having a hard time remembering them."

"Vince, for one." She slipped around the counter and put it between them. "And you're leaving for another."

"Those are both excellent reasons." He took a deep breath to get himself under control. "But I gotta be honest, I still want to say to hell with them."

CHAPTER
Twenty

VINCE CALLED on Saturday night and invited her to spend Sunday with him and his children, this time at the park for some outdoor skating.

Kelly really hoped neutral ground would help, but in case it didn't, she roped India in. When India tried to object, Kelly ruthlessly overrode her protests and may even have added a little guilt. Desperate times!

She pulled up to Dot's house a little after ten. A light flurry of snow danced in the air and promised to get serious later on. Rapping on the door, she let herself into the kitchen.

Gabe looked up and grinned. "Hey!"

"What are you doing?" Kelly had to get closer and make sure she was seeing this right. Talk about desperate times. "Is that a jigsaw puzzle?"

"Maybe." Gabe averted his gaze.

"Gabriel Crowe." She leaned across the table and got almost nose to nose with him. "Are you doing one of Dot's jigsaw puzzles?"

"I like puzzles." His gaze drifted to her mouth and back again. A languorous smile spread his mouth. "But now that you're here I can think of much better ways to relieve my boredom."

Kelly had to move back before she grabbed his face and kissed him. God, this was getting out of hand. She was on her way to meet the man who should be in her life, and all she could think about was rescuing Gabe from his jigsaw puzzle. With kissing and wherever that led. Lots of both. Her voice came out a little breathy. "Is India ready?"

"No idea." By the look on his face, his thoughts echoed hers.

"Kelly." India bustled into the kitchen. "I won't be long. I'm getting Jacob's things together."

Kelly got as far away from temptation as she could and tried to act natural. "No worries. Make sure he's warm enough."

"Where are you going?" Gabe looked between them hopefully.

"Kelly is meeting Vince and his children for skating. Jacob and I are going along to keep her safe." India's eyes gleamed with mischief as she left the kitchen.

Gabe rubbed his nape. "I could also go along. Make sure she's safe."

It really wasn't a good idea. In fact, it was a horrible idea. "Would you like to come?"

"I'll get my coat."

Gabe drove them in Dot's SUV to Winters Park, where an outdoor rink was installed every winter. The powdery dusting of snow had started to cover the grass and benches as they walked over to join Vince and his children.

"Hey." Vince looked handsome with his navy beanie as he leaned down and kissed her cheek. "I see you brought company."

"Yes." Kelly had not imagined Vince's look of relief when he caught sight of her companions. "India and Gabe were hanging around looking pathetic, so I brought them."

"I was looking pathetic." Gabe shook Vince's hand. "India was looking her normal gorgeous self."

India blushed and shook Vince's hand. "I hope you don't mind, but Jacob was getting fretful being cooped up in the house."

Who knew her sister could be such a great liar?

"This is my daughter, Hannah." Vince brought Hannah forward and put his hands on her shoulders. "Hannah, you remember Kelly."

"Hi." Hannah looked like she was having a tooth extracted.

Vince kept the cheerful tone going. "And this is Gabe, Chief Crowe's brother, and Kelly's sister, India, with her baby, Jacob."

Hannah pinkened for Gabe and nodded at India. "Hi."

"Hi." India smiled. "I love your cap."

"Thanks." Hannah flushed. "My mom brought it for me."

"Your mom has great taste." India held her hand out to Daniel. "Hi, I'm India."

They made the introductions again.

Over the fuss of putting skates on, India managed to befriend both of Vince's children. She even had Hannah holding Jacob so she could put her own skates on.

Kelly had no idea how India did it. The warmth extended to India, however, very definitely did not include her.

"I imagine you're a good skater." Kelly was determined to get at least a smile from Hannah. "What with your dancing and all."

Hannah looked at her with teenage loathing. "No."

"Let's skate," Vince yelled and rubbed his hands together.

"Jacob and I will play over here." India waved them all on.

Hannah stepped off the ice. "I'll stay with you."

The struggle played across Daniel's face.

"Nobody sits this out." Vince motioned for India to give him Jacob. "Everybody on the ice."

A laughing India joined Vince on the ice. Hannah and Daniel moved to bracket their dad. Hannah even giving Kelly a death glare to make sure she got that it was deliberate.

Which left Gabe with a pathetically relieved Kelly.

Gabe grimaced as he helped her on to the ice. "They really do not like you."

Vince's group skated off, with India looking like she belonged to them.

"Go figure." Kelly inched along. It had been a while since she had skated, and her balance was iffy. "Not only am I dating their father, their mother hates my guts. So, I'm pretty much o for two."

"Are you dating their dad?" Gabe watched Vince and Daniel horsing around on the far side of the pond. Hannah had taken over Jacob, and she and India chatted away. "Things seem a little…slow."

A fierce defensiveness rose in Kelly. "Not everybody feels the need to charge the gate. Some men have a more subtle and gentle approach."

"Ouch." Gabe raised an eyebrow at her.

Kelly knew she'd been a bitch. "I'm sorry. You're right about Vince and me, and it's driving me crazy. I had no idea this would be so hard."

Gabe shrugged off her bitchiness and smiled. "Don't worry about it. You probably need to spend more time together."

"Probably." But Kelly couldn't muster much enthusiasm for the idea.

Vince was skating circles around a laughing India. He took her hands and spun her with him. India looked happier than she had in weeks.

Hannah and Daniel didn't seem to have a problem with India and their dad. In fact, they looked downright chipper about it.

Vince's children aside, it was getting harder and harder to ignore the growing signs of trouble. She and Vince only had the past in common, and that's all they were able to talk about comfortably. They definitely did not have the sort of flashfire attraction she had with Gabe.

"Those are some heavy thoughts," Gabe said.

"Yeah." Kelly didn't want to think about it anymore. "I'll get over myself."

"Sure?"

"Sure."

They skated twice around the pond, and still Vince and the others stayed over on the far side.

Gabe broke the silence. "I need to ask a favor."

Hopefully of the hot and sweaty variety. Dammit! Kelly really needed to stop that shit. Shut it down. The other evening she'd walked into his arms, and he'd promised her whatever she wanted, whenever she wanted it. Those same words hovered in her mind. "What do you need?"

"Tomorrow is a difficult day for me."

Kelly tried to get a read on his face but failed. "What happens tomorrow?"

"It's what happened tomorrow." The wind blew Gabe's hair back as he skated. "It's the tenth anniversary of my dad's death."

"Oh!" Poppy had mentioned something about that the other day. "I'm sorry."

"Yup." Gabe shrugged, but it looked too nonchalant. "I have this thing I usually do on that date. A kind of ritual."

"Okay."

"I've done it in Australia for the past few years. It's been a long time since I've been able to do it here, and I'd really like it if you came along with me," he said.

"Sure." She'd be there with bells on, but just in case… "What are we doing?"

"We're going hiking." Gabe tightened his hold on her and shuffled her out of another couple's way.

Okay, they needed to get this straight. "You remember what I said about running?"

"Yup." He chuckled.

"That goes for hiking as well."

He tucked her arm through the crook of his. "Are you telling me you're a coach potato?"

"Hey!" She leaned back to look at him. "You don't get curves like mine by being a gym rat or running around like a blue-assed fly."

Gabe laughed, the tension easing out of him. "I can think of one way you like to get sweaty."

"You had to go there, didn't you?" She shook her head.

Gabe shrugged. "I'm a guy."

"Why, yes." She pressed into him. "Why, yes you are."

"Kelly." He grumbled a low warning. "Don't go there unless you want to go there."

She sighed, because wanting wasn't the problem. "What time are we going"—the word damn near choked her—"hiking?"

———

Gabe would never have pegged Kelly as a whiner.

"Are we nearly there yet?" She huffed and puffed in his wake.

"Not long now." Saying Kelly wasn't much of a hiker was like saying a wolverine had a bit of a temper. She sucked at it as much as she hated it, and Gabe was hard pressed not to laugh.

She made a noise suspiciously like a growl. "You said that an hour ago."

"And we would have been there sooner if you didn't keep insisting we stop." As it was, it took them an hour longer to get to where he wanted to go. He could feel her glare boring holes in his back every step of the way.

"You are such an asshole," she yelled at his back.

Gabe turned and waited for her to catch up. She had been a hot, red-faced mess from about twenty minutes in.

She glared at him, her eyes full of vitriol. "I told you I hated hiking."

"Yes, you did." He couldn't quite stop his grin. She was funny as hell, even when she wanted to hand him his balls. "But you came with me anyway."

"I'm only doing this because I feel sorry for you." She simmered down.

Gabe held out the water bottle. "Have some water."

"You should have filled this with chardonnay." She took a giant slug.

Gabe retrieved the bottle and took a sip. "I'll remember that for next time."

"There won't be a next time." She scowled at him.

If she was any other woman, he would have taken her back by now, but this was Kelly, and it felt right that she was there. Besides, putting up with Kelly's tantrums took his mind off the day.

Dad hadn't been perfect, and none of them enshrined his memory, but his death had left a huge hole in all of their lives. Despite having five boys and being semi-Neanderthal in his outlook on marriage and raising children, Dad had always had a special time for each of his boys.

It was Dad who had first put skates on Mark, collected stamps with Luke, driven to Math Olympiad with Rafe, and taught Ben how to read the night skies.

With him and Dad, it had been hiking and exploring the wilderness around Twin Elks. When they could find time, he and Dad had packed a lunch and disappeared for the day. It was Dad who had fostered in him his love of wild things. No rock was too boring to examine, no plant mundane, and no animal too common for them to stop and watch.

The falls were tucked away in the valley one over from Twin Elks, off the beaten path, and buried in a vast tract of preservation land. You had to know they were there to find them.

Even Kelly was impressed as they clambered a huge set of boulders and came out beside the pool the falls disgorged into. "Oh." She lost her murderous rage look for a moment. "This is so pretty."

"This is it." He took pity on her. "And this is where we're going."

"Thank you, Jesus." She dropped her ass on a boulder and wriggled out of her backpack. One arm got stuck, and she flung the backpack away from her.

Not a hiker. Not even a little.

She took her coat off and scooped water into her hands. "Do you think it's drinkable?"

"It comes straight from the source deeper in the mountains. That's about as pure as water gets."

She took a cautious sip from the water in her hand. "It's cold enough."

He took off his backpack and crouched beside her.

Once he'd refilled their water bottles, he took a moment to let the serenity of the place wash over him. "I used to come here with my dad."

Kelly studied the water, but she was listening.

"We found it together one day. He says it was by accident, but I'm not sure it was."

She looked up with a smile. "No?"

"Nah. Dad was a planner, like Ben. He would never have taken me somewhere he didn't first plan how to get to and, most importantly, how to get back from." That view was one of the last things Dad had seen.

Kelly cocked her head and frowned. "Where did your head go?"

"Nowhere." After Dad's death, Gabe had come here to talk to Dad about causing his heart attack and to beg his forgiveness. And he'd done the same thing for the last nine years.

"Right." Kelly gave him a look that said she wasn't buying for a hot minute but kept watching the waterfall.

Gabe spoke his next thought aloud. "He's been gone a long time, but I can always sense him when I come here."

"He died when you were still in veterinary school, right?"

"Yeah. It was during summer break."

Her silence made him keep talking.

"Ma was all excited because we were all home. Ben was on

leave from the Army, and I was on summer break. Even Mark was in the off-season. She had all these plans for a great summer."

Kelly slid her arm through his and rested her head against his shoulder. "I'm sorry, Gabe. I remember he looked a lot like Ben."

"Yup." A memory made him laugh. "Ma has photos of them when Ben was small, and they get that exact same face when something pisses them off."

She cuddled closer to him, and he liked having her there. It made the weight on his chest feel lighter. "Your mom must miss him."

"She does." Even though Dad had not been the most romantic man. "He used to say that he loved her when he married her, and when that changed, he'd tell her."

"Dot once told Poppy that despite his faults, she always knew he had her back."

"Yeah." A knot tightened his throat. "That's for damn sure. If Dad said he would do something, he did it. He used to tell us a man was nothing if he couldn't keep his word."

The memories crowded him, and he needed Kelly's warmth closer. He positioned her in front of him and wrapped his arms around her. The floral scent of her shampoo surrounded him. Her back rested against his chest and kept the pain at bay.

"He also handed out condoms and told us he'd beat the crap out of us if we got a girl pregnant."

Kelly twined her fingers with his. "He sounds a lot like Ben."

"Yeah." But somehow none of them had felt jealous about that. "But he always had a part of himself that he gave to each of us."

"And this was yours?"

"This was mine."

Stellar's jays crashed around in the thinning treetops. A few house sparrows argued noisily in the bushes.

Needing to move, Gabe disentangled them, stood and

walked closer to the water's edge. "We came here the last time I saw him alive."

"Yes?"

"Uh-huh." And the thing he swore he would never say aloud came out. "He didn't want to, and I bugged him into hiking with me."

"I'm sure he enjoyed it."

"Yeah, he did. But he wasn't feeling well, and I should have left him alone." There it was. His guilt. His dirty secret. It hung like a festering wound over the beauty of the day.

"Gabe?" Kelly stood and came to him. "He died of a heart attack, right?"

"Yup. Brought on by overexertion." He couldn't look at her. "He had a heart defect and Doc Cooper had told him to take it easy. Of course, he didn't tell Ma or any of us about that. It was his way. He didn't want to worry us. We only found this out after."

"Gabe." Kelly got her hands on his face and tilted his head down so their gazes met. "Please tell me you aren't taking the blame for your father's heart attack."

He tried to pull away, but she held him and made him look at her. "Not outright. I mean, I wasn't responsible for his heart condition. If he'd told us about it, I never would have forced him to hike that day."

"Oh, Gabe." And she wrapped her arms around him in that way only a woman can. Her embrace brought with it all that was sweet and soft and warm, and it took a man's hard edges and soothed them. And then she said the thing he'd never admitted to himself. "Is this why you don't want to stay in Twin Elks?"

"It's part of it." He should have moved out of her embrace, but he wanted to stay there and sink deep and never come up for air again. "I also like sharks."

She laughed, her silky flesh jiggling in his arms. "The liking sharks thing is weird, Gabe. You can be interested in them, even fascinated by them, but these are not fluffy kittens or cute little puppy dogs."

"Nope, they're merciless predators." He let the mood lighten between them. "The perfect killing machines."

Her face grew serious again as she looked up at him. "Have you ever spoken to Dot about this?"

"Nope." He would hate to see the hurt and condemnation in Ma's eyes. She'd hide it for sure, because that was Ma, and she loved them all, but even the possibility was too much of a risk.

"You should speak to someone," she said, just like a woman to suggest he talk his feelings out. "What about Ben?"

"Ben?" Actually, that wasn't an entirely bad idea. Except what would Ben do?

"Because I think they would be horrified if they knew you were carrying this burden," Kelly said.

"It's not a burden. It happened. I made Dad come for a hike, and then I pushed him the whole way by being a cocky bastard and challenging him. Three hours after we got back, he collapsed." An image that was seared into all of their minds, along with the sound of Ma trying to stay calm, but with an edge of panic in her voice as she had told Ben to call 911.

Kelly patted his chest. "Think about talking to Ben. All right?"

"All right. Are we done with this conversation now?"

"Hmm." Kelly pursed her lips. "We are if you distract me with food."

CHAPTER
Twenty~One

AFTER THEIR HIKE, Kelly followed Gabe to Dot's house. It didn't seem right to leave him, and she needed to check on India anyway. They hadn't spent much time together in the last couple of days, and the guilt nagged at her.

Whatever her romantic crisis, it paled in comparison to what India was dealing with.

When she and Gabe walked into the kitchen—well, Gabe walked and she more staggered—India and Dot were making pies with Jacob sitting in a highchair beside them.

Gabe kissed his Mom's cheek and gave an appreciate sniff. "It smells great in here."

"India has some new recipes she's showing me," Dot said. "I tend to make the same things because that's what I'm comfortable with."

As she smiled at him, Dot studied Gabe's face.

He smiled back and gave a small head shake.

An entire conversation had taken place between them in those few seconds. A twinge of envy pinched. Kelly and India had missed out on that sort of mother. Mom had done a good job of ticking the mommy boxes when other people were around. She never missed a dance recital or a school concert, was first in line with her cookies for the bake sale and was a regular at parent-teacher conferences, but that all ended when the front door closed.

There hadn't been any abuse or neglect, more like a supreme disinterest in her and India as anything other than an extension of the image their parents worked so hard to portray.

It had been a relief when they'd moved to Florida after dad's retirement. They could all stop pretending. But what Gabe and the rest of her boys had with Dot was special.

Dot patted Gabe's cheek. "Why don't you get showered?"

"Are you trying to tell me something?" Gabe grinned at her.

Dot wrinkled her nose. "You stink."

"Thanks, Ma." He turned to Kelly. "You want to use the shower first?"

"Kelly can use my shower." Dot pushed him out the kitchen. Then she turned to Kelly, and it wasn't a question. "You're staying to dinner. Between India and me, we can find you something to wear."

India looked at her with a sweet smile. "Please stay, Kelly. It will be fun."

With India looking so peaceful and content, there was nothing else Kelly could say. It would be fun.

Dot's bathroom was a strictly no-boy zone with pink towels, scented soaps and a clutter of beauty products on the counters.

"I kept my boys out of here." Dot handed her a clean towel and an unopened bar of a floral soap. "Or before you knew it, I would have had underpants on the floor and sweaty socks stinking up the place."

She wanted to say something to Dot about today being the anniversary of her husband's death, but Dot had never spoken to Kelly about her husband's death, and it seemed an intrusion to mention it.

Dot hesitated before she left. "Is he doing okay?"

"He's okay." Kelly didn't pretend not to understand. "He finds today difficult."

"He does." Dot sighed. "None of us love this day, but Gabe takes it harder than the other boys."

Kelly wished she could tell Dot what Gabe had confided in her, but it would betray his trust. If Gabe ever spoke to his family about it, that would have to be his decision. "It's a sad day."

"Yes." Dot's head bowed for a moment. She looked up and met Kelly's gaze. "Thank you for being with him today."

"It was my pleasure." And she meant that.

Dot gave her a quick hug. "You're a good girl, Kelly. Be patient with him. All my sons have their father's pig-headedness, and a woman needs to wait them out."

"It's not like that with Gabe and me." She didn't want Dot getting the wrong impression. "We're more friends than anything else."

"Right." Dot smiled and patted her cheek. "Gabe needs a friend like you."

Dot left and Kelly stood there for a moment, not sure what had happened, but quite sure she and Dot had not reached the same conclusion.

Dot saw her and Gabe as a couple, because that's what she wanted to see. The last time Kelly had been part of a couple had been with Vince. She'd had relationships in the last fifteen years, and she hadn't been a nun, but not like she'd had with Vince.

Not like she and Gabe had been today. Kelly had never been friends with any of the men who had drifted in and then out of her life. None of them had been around long enough, or serious enough to leave a lasting impression.

Kelly took her shower and changed into some yoga pants of India's—thank God they were stretchy—and one of Dot's sweatshirts. This one announced that she shot the sheriff.

"I know that." India's voice from the bedroom she shared with Jacob pulled Kelly that way. She had left India in the kitchen with Dot.

The door was ajar, and India sat on the end of the bed with her phone pressed to her ear.

"Yes," India said to her caller. She dropped her head and picked at the seam of her jeans. "I'm not sure what to believe."

Kelly was about to leave again, but something about the scene stopped her.

Not talking much, India was clearly listening to whoever was on the other side and nodding. There was a strange defeated air hanging over India's slumped shoulders and bowed head.

"I know you are," India said. "But you never mean it."

Kelly's hackles came up. Please God, don't let that be Piers on the phone. But the idea once in her brain refused to go away, so she pushed the bedroom door open.

"Kelly." India started and paled.

"Hey. I heard you in here."

"I'm on the phone." India stood with the phone still pressed to her ear.

Kelly motioned her to continue. "I'll see you in the kitchen."

Feeling like a shit, she stopped out of sight from the bedroom and listened.

"I've got to go," India said. There was a long silence. "I will." And finally. "I do too."

Kelly hurried to the kitchen before India caught her snooping. She wanted to ask her sister who was on the phone, but there didn't seem to be a way to do that without invading India's privacy.

Besides which, it was only a feeling she had to go on. It could have been anyone on the line. There really was no reason to demand an explanation from a grown woman.

Smelling of soap and dressed in sweats and a tight T-shirt, Gabe sauntered into the kitchen. "You beat me to it."

"I'm not as pretty as you." Kelly jabbed him in the arm. "I don't need to spend so much time admiring myself in the mirror."

Dot snorted a laugh. "Don't tell him that. Those boys are vain enough as it is."

"Well, Luke is." Gabe got a bottle of white wine from the fridge and opened it. He poured his mother a glass and put it beside her.

"Thanks." Dot glanced up from her stove. "Speaking of Luke, have you heard from him lately."

"Me?" Gabe held up the wine bottle, offering Kelly a glass. "Nope. Not that Luke contacts me all that often."

Kelly nodded yes to a glass of wine. "He lives in New York, right?"

"Yup. Singlehandedly moving the wheels of commerce forward one day at a time." Gabe snorted. "All pretty suits and handmade shoes."

Dot smacked him with a wooden spoon on the forearm. "Don't be like that. Luke works very hard."

"At being a dick," Gabe said it so softly Dot didn't catch it.

She still glared at him. "I do not want to hear what you said."

Gabe grinned at her and poured Kelly's wine.

"Hi." India wandered into the kitchen.

Gabe offered her a glass of wine. "Everything okay?"

"Oh, yes." India flushed. " Jacob was tired from all the baking, so I put him to bed early." She shook her head to the glass of wine. "And then I had to call a friend. An old friend. I haven't spoken to her in a while."

"That's nice." Dot smiled at her. "Can you put a salad together for me?"

"Sure." India leaped for the fridge.

Behind her back Gabe raised his brow in question.

Kelly shrugged, because she really had no idea what was going on.

"Hey, I've been meaning to speak to you," Gabe said to India. "The other day you and Kelly were talking about you working in the coffee shop?"

"Yes?" India fussed with the salad bowl before settling it in the center of the table. She gave Kelly a guilty glance. "It didn't work out."

"I know the coffee shop didn't suit you." Gabe shrugged. "But if it might work better for you, Cara could do with some administrative support at the veterinary hospital."

India blinked at him and flushed. "Thank you, I'll think about it."

"That could be great." Kelly liked the idea. India needed to establish herself as separate from Piers. She needed to see there was life after Piers, and that she could and would stand on her own feet. "And Cara is really nice."

India ducked her head. "I'm not sure what...I don't think I can make plans yet."

Kelly bit her tongue. Her hesitation could have something to do with India needing time to heal, but her gut told her it was more than that. The veterinarian office was not the same as working in the coffee shop.

India's evasiveness had her skin crawling. "You do that," she said. "It doesn't have to be permanent."

"Let's eat." Dot brought a cast-iron pot to the table. "This is one of Gabe's favorites."

He leaned forward and sniffed. "Tell me that's what I think it is, Ma."

"Beef and ale stew." Dot nodded and grinned. "It's been slow cooking for most of the day."

"With dumplings?" Gabe eyed his mother.

Dot rolled her eyes. "Is there any other way to eat beef and ale stew?"

It smelled like heaven, and Kelly put her plate up for a helping.

"I invited Ben and Poppy and the kids for dinner, but they were all up at the cabin today," Dot said.

"How's the renovation going?" India seemed over eager to turn the conversation away from her.

And now Kelly was being way too suspicious.

"It's going really well," Dot said. "They're expecting to move in soon."

"Claire and Finn must be glad about that too," Gabe said.

"Claire would never say anything." Dot wrinkled her nose "But she and Finn are a new thing, and the house is all full up."

"I'll drive up to the cabin tomorrow and see what he needs me to do," Gabe said. "I'm not the handiest guy, but I can carry wood and bricks around, and I take instruction."

Dot nodded. "Ben would appreciate that. He doesn't always ask for help when he needs it."

"That's an understatement." Gabe snorted.

Kelly sent him a hard look, because that sounded like someone else she knew.

Ducking his head, he had the grace to blush.

After dinner, she and Gabe cleared the table and dealt with the dishes.

India disappeared to check on Jacob, and Dot muttered something about Netflix and *The Great British Baking Show* as she disappeared into her room.

"Everything okay with India?' Gabe glanced up from racking dinner plates in the dishwasher.

Kelly didn't have to be evasive with him. "I'm not sure. She was on a call earlier, when I came out the shower. I can't tell you why, but I get the feeling Piers was on the other side."

"No way." Gabe stood and bristled. "Why would she even speak to him?"

"I can't say for sure that it was him." Kelly shrugged, but the worry persisted. "But why would she look so guilty if it was anyone else?"

Gabe cocked his head. "Could she be seeing someone?"

"India?" The idea had never occurred to her.

"Look, it's unlikely with what she's been through." Gabe dried his hands on a tea towel. "But maybe she needs the affirmation or finds the attention distracting."

She chewed the idea over. "I don't think so, but it's not

impossible. She's always been beautiful, and men are drawn to her."

"Hmm." Gabe leaned his hips against the counter and folded his arms.

That did wonderful things for his biceps and shoulders. The atmosphere in the kitchen did one of those shifts that happened all the time when Gabe was around.

She shook her head at him. "You're looking at me that way again." That way that robbed her of breath.

"I can't help myself." His gaze settled on her mouth for a moment before roaming south, all the way to her toes.

A tangible look that left heat on the parts it touched. "I don't think you're really trying to help yourself."

"You're right." The heat in his eyes intensified. "But I prefer India's older sister to India. I think she's the beautiful one."

"Gabe." What the hell was she supposed to do when he said stuff like that? "We shouldn't—"

"I think we should." He uncurled from the counter.

"Knock, knock!" Vince opened the kitchen door and poked his head around. "I saw you from outside. We were driving past."

Kelly struggled to get her disordered senses from clamoring, but it was like being dunked in frigid water. She put a few steps between her and Gabe.

"Vince." Gabe nodded.

Vince nodded. "Gabe."

"Hi." Kelly squeaked.

Vince glanced from her to Gabe and back again. "Everything okay?"

Not even close. "Perfect." Her voice sounded too loud. "What are you doing here?"

"Looking for you." Vince gave her a boyish grin. He opened the door wider and Hannah and Daniel slunk into the kitchen. "The kids and I were going out for ice cream, and we wanted you to join us."

Hannah crossed her arms and gave Kelly a glare that left her in no doubt as to who was issuing the invitation. "Um, I'm good thanks. We just finished dinner."

"Who's here?" India walked into the kitchen. She stopped when she saw Vince and his kids and gave them a sweet smile. "Hi. This is a lovely surprise."

"India." Vince smiled back. "How are you?"

"Good." India flushed. Then she looked at the kids and lit up from within. "It's so nice to see you guys again."

If she hadn't been standing right there, Kelly would never have believed it.

Daniel stammered and blushed and looked at India like a goddess had walked into the kitchen.

Even more amazing was the instant defrost from Hannah, who blushed and giggled.

"I had so much fun with you the other day." India drew them deeper under her spell. "I've told your father I want Jacob to grow up to be like you two."

Vince beamed.

Hannah and Daniel adored.

Gabe smirked and Kelly wanted to puke.

"Would you like to come for ice cream with us?" Daniel blinked at India.

Vince nodded. "You're welcome to come. Kelly has turned us down."

"Oh, well—"

"Go right ahead." If they liked India, Kelly felt no compunction tossing her sister to the lions. Besides—and it was a totally weak justification—India needed to get out of the house. "I can stay and watch Jacob. I'm tired anyway from my hike today."

Vince looked taken aback. "You went hiking? You hate hiking."

"Not all the time." Gabe smirked.

"Right." Vince looked confused. "Are you sure you won't

come for ice cream?" He remembered his manners. "Of course, you're welcome to join us too, Gabe."

"I'm sure." Kelly flapped a hand at them. "Take India with you and don't let her come back until you make her laugh."

It took a few more minutes to get everyone out of the kitchen, minutes in which India effortlessly enslaved Vince's kids to the point where Hannah volunteered her babysitting services.

Dot joined them in the kitchen to tell India she'd leave the door open for her. She stood beside Kelly and watched Vince open the door for India.

India looked up and smiled at Vince.

Vince smiled back at her.

Ducking her head, India climbed into the car.

"Well now," Dot said. "Isn't that interesting?"

CHAPTER
Twenty-Two

GABE WOKE FEELING different the next day. His conversation with Kelly at the falls had shaken something loose that had been stuck in him for too long. He had been like a dog walking around with a thorn embedded in its paw.

Speaking to Kelly had gotten rid of the thorn. His paw might still be sore, but the source of the pain had gone. She was one hell of a girl. Other than the insane sexual chemistry, he really liked her.

Tucking his hands behind his head, he chuckled at the memory of her playing pool with Cara. Both women trash-talked better than Mark mouthing off to an opposing team.

Kelly had suggested he talk to Ben, and despite his initial resistance it made a lot of sense to him. He rolled out of bed and headed for the shower.

He bumped into India in the hallway. As per usual, she averted her gaze from his bare chest, but he had put on boxers, so he smiled. "Good morning."

"Morning." She tried to duck past him.

Some devil in him had asking, "How was going for ice cream?"

"Fine." And she smiled. "Vince has the nicest children. I'm not sure what happened with Kelly and them."

He was glad India was having a good time, but Ma wasn't the only one finding the current dynamics interesting.

In the bathroom, he locked the door and turned on the shower. The pipes creaked the same way they had since his childhood. He had tried to talk to Ma about moving somewhere smaller, but there was where she wanted to be. She held high hopes for filling the house with grandchildren one day.

Ben's four were a good start, but instead of appeasing her, they had made the grandma light in Ma's eyes even more feral. Not for one second did the lack of blood connection occur to her. Those kids were now hers, and Gabe suspected they had been Ma's grands since the moment Ben had brought them after trying to arrest Poppy.

The story still made him chuckle. He checked the shower temperature and stepped inside.

Poppy, so the story went, had been transporting all four kids right across the country from Philly to San Diego. She'd hit Twin Elks burning up with fever, with a carload of sick and bored kids. Ben had pulled her over for shooting a light. Poppy had passed out, and Ben had been left to deal with the diarrhea, vomit, and panic. Of course, he had roped Ma in. Gabe would have done the same.

Ben had found his happy ending, and he deserved it.

Which brought Gabe's thoughts full circle. He didn't begrudge anyone their happily ever after, but he wasn't going to stand aside and let Kelly get hurt. If Vince was Kelly's one, Gabe wouldn't stand in their way. Sure, he thought Kelly could do a whole lot better. Vince was a helluva nice guy, and Gabe had nothing against him. It beat him how any man faced with Kelly and India could be giving India the sort of glances that he should have been giving Kelly.

Ma was in the kitchen when he got there. He kissed her cheek. "Morning."

"Morning, sweetie." She gave him the same smile he'd been getting since his earliest memory. Ma had a way of making you feel like the most important being in her orbit.

He was such a Momma's boy. Then again, he had a great mother, so who gave a shit.

"Have you had breakfast?" He poured himself a cup of coffee.

Ma brought him the creamer and set it down beside him. "Not yet. I thought I'd make us some eggs."

"How about you take a load off and I make us some eggs?"

"Oh." Ma looked taken aback, and then her eyes twinkled. "That would be lovely, Gabriel."

He took a pan and a bowl out and got cracking eggs. "I wanted to ask you something." Ma was the most perceptive person he knew. He poured her a cup of coffee, doctored it like she liked and set it in front of her. "Vince and India?"

"Ah." Ma sipped her coffee and sighed. "That's perfect. The coffee." She blinked at him. "Not the Vince and India situation."

"But you do think there is a situation?" He whisked the eggs and seasoned them. Ma had taught her boys well.

Ma grimaced. "I think India is in too vulnerable a position for there to be any sort of situation with anyone." She held up her hand. "However, I definitely think Vince is interested."

"Dammit!" Gabe slammed the pan on the stove and added oil. "He can't do that to Kelly again. Last time it was Chelsea, and now it's India."

"Whoa there, kiddo." Ma glared at him. "That's my pan you're manhandling, and I'm not sure Kelly will care any more this time than she did last."

Gabe turned and stared at her. Ma didn't look cracked in the head. "He broke her heart. She's never gotten over him."

"Really?" Ma sipped her coffee. "It seems like she broke his heart more than he broke hers. She walked away first. It was only after she left he couldn't keep it in his pants when Chelsea provided her shoulder for him to cry on."

Eggs hissed as he dropped them in the heated pan. Kelly had walked away first, that much was true. "I don't get what you're saying."

"Here's what I think," Ma said. "For a couple so in love, they managed to toss it all away really fast. You know Kelly, better than most of us." Ma smirked. "Do you think if she really cared about something she would walk away so easily?"

"That's not how Kelly sees it."

"Right." Ma nodded. "And the more interesting question is why."

Gabe had no answer for that, also no response, because he wasn't exactly sure what Ma was getting at. Some truth about what Ma had said hovered outside his perception as they ate breakfast together.

Ma trotted off with Peg soon after, and he drove out to see Ben.

When he pulled up to the cabin a little way out of town, Ben was already there, hard at work.

"Hey!" The house looked ready to him. "You've made more progress."

Ben climbed down a ladder where he'd been drilling holes for light fittings. "Yeah, one final push and we're done."

"That's why I thought you might need a hand." He opened his arms wide. "In the interest of complete honesty, I need instruction and strict supervision."

"Can you sweep?" Ben handed him a broom.

"That I can do."

He helped clear away some of the site debris, and then managed not to screw up putting in some pot lights. Mostly because Ben had already meticulously marked their placement. He stepped back and surveyed the large open-plan kitchen and living area. "The place looks great. Did you do it all yourself?"

"As much as I could, and with a lot of secret help that I'm not supposed to know about." Ben stood beside him and looked at his work. "Raising four kids is not cheap."

The way Ben had shouldered his new family impressed the hell out of Gabe. "Did you ever doubt? I mean about taking on some other guy's kids and raising them?"

Ben gave it some thought.

One of the things he liked about Ben, that he didn't answer flippantly. Of course, it could also drive Gabe batshit crazy on occasion.

"I suppose so," Ben said. "In as much as I didn't feel I was up to the task. But I don't see them as some other guy's kids. They're Poppy's, and because of that, they're mine."

Gabe got that. "That's what Dad would have said."

"Yeah." Ben gave a fond smile and shook his head. "Dad was rock solid."

Opportunity hovered, and okay, he and Ben got into it sometimes, but they were brothers, and nobody knew him and Dad like Ben. Other than Ma, and Gabe didn't want to take his guilt to her. "I've been thinking about him a lot lately."

"Dad?" Ben looked at him. "What got you thinking about Dad?"

"Yesterday." Gabe tried to keep it light, but after that clumsy beginning, it might be a lost cause. "I always think of him on that day."

Nodding, Ben clapped him on the shoulder. "Same. I spent the day with the kids. I like to think Dad would have liked that."

"I'm not sure what he would have made of Ryan." Gabe laughed. Dad had been a great guy but more disciplinarian than buddy.

Ben smiled. "Yeah. He probably would have left him to Mom."

"True that."

Ben slapped his hands together. "Feel like helping me install electrical plates?"

"I live for it."

He followed a chuckling Ben into the kitchen. "Listen, I wanted to talk to you about something."

Ben grunted, which meant he was listening, and Gabe had his permission to proceed.

"I brought up Dad for a reason."

Looking up, Ben waited for him to continue.

"I got to thinking about him yesterday and how he died." He was dancing around the issue, and that was a waste of both their times. "Actually, that's not it. There's something that's been bugging me since he died."

"Seriously?" Ben looked up from where he was crouched in front of Gabe and put his screwdriver aside. "That's a long time for something to bug you."

"It more like eats at me." Fuck! Now he wanted to bawl, and he refused to do that in front of Ben. The wound felt fresh, as if Dad had died yesterday.

Ben waited.

Gabe looked away from the compassion on Ben's face. It would shatter his control for sure. "That day Dad died, do you think you could have done anything differently?"

Ben cocked his head. "Like something to prevent his death?"

"Maybe." He cleared his throat and stopped wimping out. "Yes."

"No. Gabe, I don't." Ben stood and came to a stop in front of him. He cupped the back of Gabe's neck, and it was a touch that comforted, forged a bond between them and not a challenge. "There was nothing anyone could do." Ben gave him another long moment. "Gabe?"

"That day. He didn't want to hike with me." Jesus, he couldn't cry. Would not. *Man, the fuck up!* "I made him, and then, like the little fucker I was, I pushed him."

"You been carrying this shit all this time?"

All he could manage was a nod. He couldn't make eye contact with Ben. That would strip him raw.

Ben brought his other hand up and held him still. It was a thing Dad used to do as well. Ben took care of those he loved.

Simple. "Listen to me, Gabe. Dad was sick for a long time, and he chose not to tell anyone. Not even Ma. He made Doc Cooper swear never to tell her a damn thing."

He knew all this, but something about Ben telling him it in that no-nonsense way he had made it feel more real.

"That's screwed up, Gabe, and Ma was mad at him for that for a long time after he died." Ben tightened his grip. "After I found that out, I was mad at him as well. If he'd told us, maybe we could have done something. Maybe he wouldn't have had to die. But that's on him, brother."

Gabe nodded and stepped away. He needed space to think. "Why do you think he never told anyone?"

"Dad was a stubborn bastard." Ben shook his head and gave a wry laugh. "Maybe he thought it couldn't beat him. Or maybe he didn't want to worry Ma and have her fussing over him. He hated that."

"Yeah." Dad had hated that. All of them had made a point to leave the house when Dad had contracted a cold. He could be worse than a grizzly coming out of hibernation. "I always wondered, if I hadn't taken him hiking that day, if he might have lived longer."

"Honestly?" Ben shrugged. "I can't say for sure the hike didn't impact him. But would you have acted the same if you had known about his heart condition?"

"No."

"There you go," Ben said. "It wasn't your fault, Gabe."

"Maybe."

"Definitely. You loved him, and he loved you. He would hate you carrying this shit." Ben watched Gabe for a long moment, and then dragged him into a rough, back-slapping hug.

Gabe slapped back and then separated.

They both looked anywhere but at each other. Enough.

"So." Ben crouched down again. "You and Kelly?"

Shit! He should have remembered how the town gossiped.

"Me and Kelly nothing. Kelly likes Vince." Then as they were in a sharing mood, he opened up further. "I've got this nasty feeling that Vince is getting a thing for India."

"Damn, that's the last thing either Kelly or India need right now."

Gabe nodded his agreement and joined Ben on the floor. He tried to pick up what Ben was doing and stay out of the way. "Should I say something to Kelly?"

Ben looked at him in stark horror.

Gabe had to laugh. "I'll take that as a no."

"How is India doing?" Ben lined up a plate and screwed it in place.

"She's okay. I take it you haven't found Piers yet?"

Ben looked grim as he reached for another tile. "Nope. That son of a bitch sure is slippery."

"Listen, I'm sure Kelly won't mind that I tell you she got the feeling India was talking to Piers on the phone last night."

Ben scowled. "Dammit! If she's talking to him, she might be thinking of going back to him."

"Why would she do that?" Gabe handed Ben another plate. "Why would anyone go back to some asshole who smacked her around?"

Ben lined the plate up. "It's not that simple. These fuckers get these women to thinking they're not worth anything more. The women keep thinking if they did something different, they could change him."

"Kelly is not sure. Just a feeling."

"One thing I've learned as a cop is not to discount people's feelings about shit. Kelly knows India best." He sat back on his heels. "But Gabe, there is nothing anyone can do."

Kelly was going to hate that. Gabe wasn't all that fond of the idea either. "I'll keep an eye out."

"Call if you need me."

"Will do."

"Now." Ben raised an eyebrow. "Are you going to sit there looking useless, or are you going to actually help?"

"I was thinking useless worked."

Ben chuckled. "Get to work."

CHAPTER
Twenty-Three

KELLY HAD NO IDEA WHY, but Mondays always felt busier than any other day of the week and seemed to drag on later into the evening. She was bone tired and looking forward to a hot soak and a glass of wine as she finally reached home and climbed out of her car.

A dark form loomed in the darkness. "Kelly."

"Shit." Her heart hammered loudly in her ears. "What are you doing here, Piers? You scared the crap out of me."

"Didn't mean to startle you." Piers pushed his hands into the pockets of his pressed chinos. "I thought you'd be home earlier."

"Mondays are busier." Piers had no business being there, and no way was she going to stand there and chat with him. Ben needed to be told he was in town, and she needed to let Gabe know at Dot's house. "I have nothing to say to you."

Piers stepped in front of her. "You're angry with me."

"No shit." She stepped around him, but Piers was there again. "Get out of my way."

"If I do, you'll go into your condo." Piers looked regretful. "And as soon as you get there, you'll tell everyone you can that I'm in town."

Piers didn't look nearly so harmless anymore. The feverish

gleam in his eyes bothered her, and she was hyperaware that Piers was bigger than her. "You shouldn't have come here."

Kelly tried to get around him.

"Where else would I go?" Once more he cut off her escape. "You know where my wife is, and you're going to tell me."

The whole bullying her in the parking lot thing got old, right then, and Kelly lost her temper. "Get out of my way. I'm not telling you where India is."

"Don't raise your voice to me." Piers grabbed her by both shoulders. His fingers bit into muscle. "Where is my wife?"

"Screw you." Kelly tried to wriggle free, but he really was strong.

"Now, Kelly." He shook her, hard enough for her head to snap back on her neck. "You're going to tell me."

"Fuck you." Kelly kicked him. Her toes crunched against his shins.

Piers backhanded her. "Bitch!" He fastened a hand around her neck. "Nothing would make me happier than to break your bitch neck." His fingers tightened. "I've wanted to do this since I first met you."

She couldn't break his hold. She scratched at his hand, trying to hit him or kick him but he kept her out of reach.

"Somebody needs to teach you a lesson. Someone needs to teach you to mind your place, Kelly."

Her lungs screamed for breath. His face loomed large, wavering around the edges.

"Where is India?"

Lightheaded as she was, she managed two words. "Fuck you." She would never give him India.

Car headlights arced over the building and caught them, burning into her eyes. Brakes squealed and tires screeched on the asphalt.

Piers released her so fast she stumbled.

Footsteps pounded behind her.

Piers was getting away.

No.

Kelly lunged for him. She caught the preppy jersey around his throat and almost brought him to a stop.

Piers ducked out of the sweater and ran. He bolted into the ally and vanished over the wall.

A dark form flew past her and chased after Piers.

Her legs were shaking so badly they couldn't hold her anymore. Kelly dropped to her knees, not caring about the stones digging into her knees. Piers had tried to choke her, and as her brain processed the information, shock set in. Her entire body shook, and her teeth chattered. She was so cold.

"Kelly." Vince knelt in front of her. "Shit, Kelly. Are you okay?"

"Did he get away?"

Vince nodded. His face a grim mask. "What did he want?"

"India." Her throat hurt, and her chattering teeth made it hard to talk.

"Jesus!" Vince surged to his feet. "He can't get her. I have to —" He whirled back to her, conflict creasing his face. "Do you need a doctor?"

His expression made her laugh. It was all so oddly funny, and she couldn't stop the laughter. "Go." She waved him away and staggered to her feet. "I'm fine. Go and make sure India's safe."

"You aren't fine, Kelly." Vince steadied her.

Kelly stumbled around him and picked up her purse. She had to grip her purse tightly to hide how hard her hands were trembling. "If he finds India, he'll kill her. Go."

And Vince vanished.

There you had it. Nothing like near death to bring clarity. Sobbing, she stood there while Vince roared off to save her sister. And not one of those tears was for Vince.

———

Gabe finished putting the last of the dinner dishes away and wiped the counters. Ma had been tired and gone to bed early.

India had offered to help him, but he liked the alone time. Ma would say he was brooding, but he wasn't. He was the opposite of brooding, whatever that was. For once, his mind was not twisting itself around something and was just hanging out.

A minivan screeched to a halt outside the house, the front wheel ramping the sidewalk. Vince jumped out and ran toward the house.

Adrenalin surging, Gabe met him at the back door. "What is it?"

"Is India here?" Vince looked strung out.

"Yes. Why?" Gabe didn't like how freaked out the man looked. "What's going on, Vince?"

"Piers is here." Vince lowered his voice.

"Shit." India would freak out if she heard, so Gabe closed the door to the house. "Tell me."

"Piers arrived at Kelly's and demanded she tell him where India was."

Everything in Gabe stilled. "What do you mean demanded?"

"I got there before he could do any real damage." Vince ran a shaking hand through his hair. "He ran off when he saw me."

It took everything in Gabe not to shake the details out of Vince. "Real damage? As in some damage was done to Kelly?"

Vince nodded. "He roughed her up, but he let go of her as soon as he saw me." He glanced toward the door. "We have to make sure India is kept safe."

"Where. The fuck. Is Kelly?" His skin felt too tight to contain him. He wanted to rip something apart with his bare hands. Vince would do for a start. "Tell me you didn't leave her there."

"India's in danger." Vince must have read the murder in his expression. "I checked, and she said she was fine. She said I should get to India before Piers did."

Gabe had never wanted to hit a man more. "You left her."

"She was fine." Vince speared his fingers through his hair. "I checked, and you know Kelly. She's tough."

Before he broke the man, Gabe left.

Kelly had been left alone after having been attacked. Any lingering guilt he had felt about Vince and her evaporated. Yes, Kelly was tough, but nobody was that tough. The entire drive to Kelly's place his heart stuck in his throat. He had no idea what he'd find when he got there.

Outside her condo, he parked next to her car. Lying on the ground a few feet away from the car was a tube of lip balm he'd seen Kelly apply a hundred times, a hair tie, and some loose change. Gabe pocketed them and took the stairs to her unit two at a time.

"Kelly," he called out as he knocked. "Kelly, sweetheart, it's Gabe. Can you let me in?"

Movement sounded from the other side of the door. "Gabe?"

"Yeah, sweetheart. Vince told me what happened. Open the door, sweetheart, please?"

The chain latch scraped and then the lock tumblers rolled. She opened the door with her chin thrust out and defiance in her gaze. "I'm fine."

"You going to let me in?" It took him a moment to get himself under control. A red mark stained the pale peach of her cheek. He got to her neck and he had to breathe deep to fight back the primal beast in him that surged to the surface. Piers had put his fucking hands around her neck and squeezed hard enough to bruise.

"I'm fine," she said, but her voice shook, and tears gleamed in her eyes. "I'm fine."

Gabe needed to touch her, forge that connection with her. "Kelly." He moved slowly so as not to frighten her and wrapped his arms around her. Drawing her gently against him, he enfolded her. "You're not all right."

"I am." She was so tense in his arms she almost vibrated. "I am."

"No." He drew her as close as he could.

She collapsed against him. "No, I'm not." Her hands fisted in the back of his shirt and she clung to him. "I'm not all right." A sob shuddered through her. "I was so scared, Gabe. He had his hands around my neck, and I thought he would kill me."

She broke like water over a dam. Sobs wracked her body so hard he had to support her. Scooping her up, he kicked the door shut then carried her to the big sofa.

There he sat with her in his arms while she wept. Every sob ripped right through him, and he added it to the growing tally of what he owed Piers. The man would pay for every mark on her, and every fearful moment she had. From Piers's hide, Gabe would exact any bad dreams she suffered or any moments of uncertainty.

All he could do now, though, was hold her and rock her until the storm passed. He lost track of time as he handed her tissues and held her against him. Eventually the sobs grew further apart, and the tears lessened to a trickle.

She blew her nose noisily and took a deep breath. "I'm sorry. I don't usually cry."

And Vince had left her in this state and gone running for India. Gabe had some payback for him as well. "Wanna tell me what happened?"

She shook her head. "But I will anyway."

Gabe let her take her time, pick her words.

"Piers must have been waiting for me," she said. "When I parked, he was already there. He wanted to know where India was and when I wouldn't tell him, he...he hit me. I mouthed off at him and that's when he shook me, then he put his hands around my neck." She shuddered. "I don't know what would have happened if Vince hadn't shown up."

A loud knock at the door startled Kelly into tightening her grip on him.

"It's okay." Gabe rubbed her back. "Nobody is getting in here, and nobody is getting near you."

"Gabe?" Ben said from the other side of the door. "Ma called me and told me."

Kelly relaxed a little.

"Can I let him in?" Brother or no brother, police chief or not, nobody came in who Kelly didn't feel one hundred percent comfortable with. Dammit! He should have guessed Piers would escalate his search for India.

"Yes." Kelly nodded and swiped at her tear-stained cheeks. "Let me go and wash my face."

Gabe opened the door to a grim-faced Ben. "Ma called me."

"You said." Gabe stood aside so he could walk in. "I was going to call you, but Kelly was in shock."

Ben shook his head. "This prick is pissing me off big time."

"Ben." Kelly walked back into her lounge. "I'm sorry, I—"

"Hey, sweetheart." And Ben wrapped Kelly in a hug. "Why don't we have a cup of tea, and you can tell me what happened?"

Gabe needed to do something. "I'll make the tea."

Ben sat beside Kelly on the sofa and listened to her story. None of the anger he had shown to Gabe appeared in his voice or expression. His brother was really good at his job. With his calm and capable manner, he invited people to trust him and instilled in them the confidence he would do what needed doing.

Gabe made tea and put the mugs on a tray with milk and sugar.

"I want you to come down to the station tomorrow and make a statement," Ben said. "I'd also like you to press charges. For the attack on you."

"Oh." Kelly picked up her tea, but her hand shook and she had to cup it between her palms. "I can do that."

"He's adding more to the heap of trouble he's already in." Ben added sugar to his tea. Lots of sugar to his tea, like he always had. "Even some fancy talking lawyer is going to have trouble explaining this one away, on top of the existing charges."

Kelly nodded. "Then I'll do it."

"Good." Ben sipped his tea. "Now, have you seen a doctor?"

"I don't need to doctor."

"Kelly." Ben and Gabe spoke at once.

She pulled a face at them. "Honestly, I'm okay. I'm shaken up and bruised, but I'm okay."

"We should take some pictures," Ben said.

Kelly nodded.

"I'll get a few with my phone now." He stood and retrieved his phone. "And then, in the morning, we can get some more at the station."

By the time Ben left, Kelly was drooping.

There was no question of Gabe leaving, so he helped her get ready for bed. She didn't protest when he put her in her cotton pj's and disinfected the scrapes on her knees she'd gotten when she'd fallen on the asphalt. She sat like an obedient child as he washed her face and handed her toothbrush to her.

After he'd put her to bed, he locked up then showered and found a spare toothbrush beneath her sink. He put his boxers back on and slid into bed beside her.

Kelly lay on her side, her eyes half open. "I'm so tired," she whispered. "But I'm scared to close my eyes."

"I'm here." He kissed her forehead and arranged her with her head on his chest. "You go to sleep. I'm here."

CHAPTER
Twenty-Four

KELLY DID SLEEP, and undisturbed by bad dreams. She woke to Gabe making coffee.

"Poppy put a sign on your store that you're closed for the day," he said as he handed her a cup of coffee. "We need to see Ben, and then you can come back here and rest."

"I need to check on India." Gabe made good coffee.

"Ben has already been by this morning, and he's put a man on her. In case Piers shows up, but he still doesn't know where she is, right?"

"I didn't tell him anything." Her throat felt sore and raw, as well as other bumps and bruises. It all seemed surreal in the bright light of day, but the marks on her body were evidence it had happened.

After a light breakfast, they met with Ben at the station, where Kelly had to go through it all again and get photographed by one of Ben's men.

Gabe stayed by her side throughout, a quiet, dependable presence that kept her grounded and helped her not lose her shit.

By the time they parked outside her condo, all Kelly wanted

was to crawl back into bed and watch something mindless on television.

"What the hell?" Gabe scowled through the windshield.

Vince sat on the steps leading up to her condo. He stood as Kelly got out of Gabe's car.

"I came to see how you were." Vince could barely look her in the eye.

Gabe growled. "You sure didn't give a fuck last night."

"Look, last night—"

"You left her alone." Gabe grabbed Vince by the sweatshirt and hauled him closer.

"Gabe!" Kelly stepped between them. "I think Vince and I need to talk this out."

Gabe didn't look happy about it, but he dropped Vince and stepped back. "You screwed up, man."

"You'd better come in." Tired as she was, she and Vince needed to talk. In light of last night, pretense was pointless. "Gabe?"

"I'll pick up some stuff from Ma's." Gabe still looked murderous. "For when I'm back."

"Okay." He wasn't going to hear any argument from her. Being alone was not what she wanted. "I'll see you shortly."

Vince followed her into her condo and stood inside the door, shifting from one foot to the other. "Are you okay?"

She nodded. "Gabe and I just got back from the police station. I'm pressing charges."

"Good." He shoved his hands in his pockets and looked at his feet.

"How's India?" She needed to call her sister later.

Vince grimaced. "The news really freaked her out. She also wanted to rush over and see that you were okay."

Well, that made one of them, as Vince clearly hadn't felt the same need last night. "Vince?" This needed saying. "Please look at me."

"I'm so sorry about last night, Kelly." He looked truly

remorseful. "Gabe is right. I should have stayed with you and made sure you were all right before I took off."

"Yes, you should have. If I meant anything to you, you would have. Instead you checked that India was okay."

Vince flushed. "India has nothing to do with this."

"Really?" Kelly knew India had a lot to do with it. "But even before last night, Vince, something has been missing. I think you've felt it too."

"I...kept hoping maybe it would grow." He rubbed the back of his head. "I kept thinking if we got to know each other again, we could rediscover what we had."

"Me too." Kelly stopped in front of him and took his hand. "But I think we've had our time, Vince. Whatever there was between us didn't survive into adulthood."

Vince shook his head. "There were so many times through my marriage that I thought about you. Wondered what would have happened if things had turned out differently. This doesn't make sense."

"I did the same." Kelly looked into his handsome face, but she didn't feel what she thought she would. She would always be fond of him, and he would always be her first love, but he wasn't the one for her. "I clung to this belief that if it hadn't been for Chelsea, we would have been together." She took one of his hands. "Who can tell if we would have been happily married now or fizzled out by the time we were twenty-one."

"For the record, I always thought it was the happily married option."

She managed a smile for him. "Same."

"Friends?" He kissed her cheek.

Kelly hugged him. "Always."

He hugged her back, and then they both stepped away. "I really am sorry about last night."

"It really is okay." Kelly couldn't resist a little meddling. "But have you considered that you might be dating the wrong sister?"

"No." Vince flushed. "And I'm not going to consider that either. India is in no position to start anything like that."

She noticed he didn't comment on himself.

Gabe let himself back into her condo, but the look he threw Vince was anything but friendly. One of them was still holding grudges from last night. On some level, she was pissed with Vince, but his actions had clarified so much for her. At least the confusion had cleared in that area of her life.

"You okay?" Gabe came to her side. His gaze searched her face.

She managed a weak smile. "I am."

"Something keeping you?" He turned to Vince.

Vince flushed. "Look, you're pissed with me about leaving Kelly alone, but—"

"I'm gonna stop you right there." Gabe got into Vince's face. "You had choices last night, and none of them should have been leaving a woman who had been attacked on her own." Vince backed up a step, but Gabe crowded him. "You left her in the parking lot and ran off to see if India was okay." Gabe looked like he was getting madder. "That fucker could have come back. She could have been more seriously hurt than you knew."

"I was worried he was going to get to India." Vince looked ashamed of himself.

Clearly, Gabe was not in the mood to be forgiving. "Then use your phone and call me or Ben and tell us what's going on. What you never do is leave a vulnerable, hurt, frightened woman to fend for herself."

"Kelly." Vince looked over Gabe's shoulder at her.

"It's fine, Vince." She stepped closer to them. Angry as he was, Gabe didn't frighten her at all, and she put her hand in the small of his back. "What's done is done. Maybe you should go home, Vince."

Vince tried to sidestep Gabe. "Are we okay?"

"You heard her." Gabe got in his way again. "If this was up to me, you wouldn't come near her again. You wouldn't even get close enough to her to see the color of her eyes."

"Gabe." She stroked his back. "This isn't fixing anything."

"Maybe not." He folded his arms. His biceps tried to escape the sleeves of his T-shirt. "But it's making me feel a helluva lot better. The only person I'd like to take apart more is that fucker from last night."

"I won't stop you if you do try." Trusting her instinct, she pressed her cheek against his shoulder. "I'm tired."

He turned from Vince and put an arm around her. "Let's get you comfortable, and I can get us something for dinner."

Vince lingered a moment, watching them with a small frown, and then he nodded and left. The door clicked behind him.

Gabe helped her to the sofa and came down beside her. He put an arm around her shoulders. "Kelly." He sounded hesitant. "I don't want to add to your already crappy twenty-four hours, but…Vince." He took a deep breath and tucked her under his chin. "A guy doesn't behave like he did to the girl he cares about."

"You're right." She appreciated Gabe was picking his words carefully and trying not to hurt her, but it wasn't necessary. "I think I knew that even before last night. The thing between Vince and me was something we had as teens. It didn't make it into adulthood."

Gabe kissed her head. "And you're okay with that?"

"Yeah." It surprised the hell out of her too. "I am. Actually, it's a relief, to be honest. I kept having these dates with Vince and wondering what the hell was missing."

"What was missing?"

"That spark." The one she had with Gabe that needed only them in the same room to burst into flame. "Also, we didn't seem to have much in common. And his children really didn't like me."

He chuckled. "Yeah. They really didn't like you. What did you do to them?"

"Hey!" She poked his stomach and came away with a bent finger. But it was nice to have him teasing her again. It made her feel more normal. "I need to check on India."

Standing, he handed her phone over. "I'll get us something to eat."

"Kelly." India answered on the first ring. "I've been so worried. Dot told me what happened. Are you all right?"

"I am." She didn't want India burdened with the details. "But, sweetie, how did you manage to live with that monster as long as you did? You're so much braver than me."

India sniffed. "No, Kelly. He didn't start out that bad. A little controlling here and there, slowly taking over aspects of my life." She gave a humorless chuckle. "I actually used to think it proved how much he loved me that he wanted to be part of every tiny detail of my life."

Guilt swelled in Kelly for not seeing it before. "I'm so sorry you went through that. I should have known."

"No, Kelly." India sounded sad. "I kept it from you and over time I got very good at hiding it." She took a deep breath. "Ben came around and said you were pressing charges?"

"Yes."

"Good," India said. "When he attacked you, it felt worse than it happening to me. It made me see how sick and twisted Piers is."

If that was the only good to come of this, Kelly would be thrilled. "The surest way to make sure he doesn't touch either of us again, or Jacob, is to put Piers behind bars."

"Yeah." Weariness replaced the sadness in India's tone. A sort of marrow-deep weary that had infected every part of her body. "Ben thinks it's better if I don't come and see you or you come here. In case Piers is watching you."

As much as Kelly wanted to see India and make sure with her own eyes that she was all right, Ben made too much sense. Piers of last night would not be deterred easily. He'd been prepared to strangle the truth out of her if he had to. "I think

Ben's right," she said. "You stay safe and out of sight. I'll call you tomorrow and check on you."

"Or I'll call and check on you." A wisp of mischief crept into India's voice. "Although I hear Gabe is taking excellent care of you."

"Too soon." But Kelly laughed anyway. "Take care of yourself. I love you."

"I love you too." India hung up.

Kelly wandered into the kitchen, where Gabe was doing something with chicken breasts that smelled fantastic. She eased on one of her island stools. "And he cooks as well."

"There really is no end of my talents." Gabe flashed a grin. "India okay?"

"Yup. Ben says we should stay clear of each other for a day or two, in case Piers is watching."

Gabe nodded. "Makes sense. I spoke to him when that dickhead was here. He said Piers hasn't been spotted anywhere. He might have gone home."

As much as she hoped so, Kelly would never forget the look in Piers's eyes. He would do whatever he must to get to India and feel no remorse about it. "That's highly doubtful."

CHAPTER
Twenty-Five

GABE STAYED THE NIGHT AGAIN. He lay awake a long time listening to Kelly's soft breathing. He kept her tight to him, like he could physically keep anyone from getting near enough to hurt her again.

His blood still simmered at what Piers had done. He hoped he got to Piers before Ben did, because Ben would never allow him to beat the fuck out of that piece of shit.

Kelly's bruises had darkened and looked worse as the discoloration came to the surface. Every time he looked at her neck, he wanted to rip Piers apart.

She sighed in her sleep and settled closer to him.

He relaxed into the warmth and softness of her nestled into him.

When he woke in the morning, his cock was well aware of being in bed next to Kelly. He edged his hips back.

With a murmur, she cradled her ass back against him.

Gabe hissed out a breath and counted to ten. Then he counted again. His dick didn't give a crap about sensitivity or being a good guy. It remembered how good things with Kelly had been that one night and it wanted more.

He disentangled himself and rolled out of bed. His dick

would get over it. No way he was going to hit on Kelly in this state. He reached the kitchen and got the coffee going.

Then because he didn't trust himself to get back into the bedroom with a warm, silky Kelly in bed, he got working on breakfast.

He was putting the eggs and bacon on the plate when Kelly padded out of the bedroom.

She wore a pair of pajama bottoms with penguins all over them and a shapeless T-shirt. Absolutely nothing about the outfit was sexy or revealing, yet his libido woke to the fact that she wasn't wearing any underwear under her pj's.

"Hi." She gave him a sexy, sleepy smile. "Something smells good."

"Bacon and eggs." He smiled at her, keeping it platonic. "But first…coffee." He put a cup in front of her.

As she cupped the mug between her palms, Kelly hummed her appreciation.

The sound ran velvety fingers down his spine and his mind conjured images of what else made her sound like that.

"I thought I would open the shop today."

That did it. His libido retreated and outrage rushed in. "Say what now?"

"Gabe." She gave him that smile she used when she was trying to wriggle her way around him. He steeled himself. It wouldn't work this time. "I run a business; I can't afford not to open the store."

"This is Twin Elks, and I'm betting everyone knows what happened to you." The thought of letting her out of the condo made his blood run cold.

She eased off her stool and walked toward him.

Dammit. That smile snuck around his guard and made him want to give her whatever she wanted.

Then she did the worst thing she could have done. If she'd argued with him, he could have fought her. But no, that wasn't Kelly's way.

She slid her arms around his waist and put her cheek against his chest. "You've been wonderful, Gabe. I can never thank you enough for being here and keeping the bad dreams and the horrible replays away."

"I didn't do anything." His backbone was melting faster than a spring thaw and he tried to firm it up. "I don't think you're ready."

"And you're probably right." She dropped her head back and looked at him. "But I can't hide away in this condo. If I do, he wins. That monster robbed my sister of her will and her right to feel safe, and I refuse to let him do the same to me."

Fuck it! Her argument made so much sense, but the primal protector in him wasn't done yet. "Just one more day."

"Don't you think he's taken enough from us?"

Double fuck it and damn. He couldn't argue with that, and especially not with those beautiful blue eyes beseeching him to understand. He pressed his forehead to hers. "I'm going to worry about you all day."

"And that makes me feel better already." She kissed his cheek and looped her arms around his neck. "And if you wouldn't mind, I would really appreciate it if you took me to the store and waited while I open up."

As if she could stop him. "Done."

"Thank you." Her face softened, and something weird happened in his chest, in the region of his heart. He was probably hungry. "Thank you for everything, Gabe. Having you here made everything feel better."

He forced himself to reply past his thick throat. "It was my pleasure."

———

Kelly took her time getting ready. Brave words aside, she felt nervous and exposed leaving the condo. Walking to the car she couldn't get rid of the being-watched feeling. Like Piers was out there, waiting for her to slip up.

As if sensing her thoughts, Gabe stayed close to her as they walked to his car. "I'll drop you off at work and hang around for as long as you need me."

"You don't have to do that." But her objection lacked any starch.

The look Gabe leveled at her assured her he wasn't asking her permission. "I'll be there to bring you home as well."

"Okay." Because she really wasn't going to fight him about that.

They arrived at the store, and Kelly unlocked and turned on the lights. Her early morning crowd would be gone already, but opening the store was more of a moral victory.

The bell over the door tinkled.

Kelly jumped and nearly dropped her handful of mugs.

"Ah, Kelly!" Peg strode right up to her. She took in all Kelly's bruises and shook her head. "That pig!"

"Thanks, Peg." Peg wasn't part of her early crowd. "Can I get you something?"

"One of those frappy things you make for me would be lovely." Peg shrugged out of her coat, came around the counter and moved through to the back.

Kelly looked at her, then at Gabe. She had no idea what Peg was doing.

Shrugging, Gabe followed her. "Are you looking for something, Peg?"

"Goodness me, no." Peg emerged wearing an enveloping blush colored apron with Keep Calm and Drink Coffee emblazoned on it. "I'm here to help."

Kelly almost sprayed milk across the store. Her voice sounded weak as she managed, "Help?"

"In the store." Peg got busy stacking cups atop the coffee machine. "You didn't think we were going to let you do this alone today, did you?"

"No?" Kelly stood frozen as Peg rolled right over her. "But I really don't—"

"Of course, you do." Peg finished the coffee cups and opened the baked goods boxes. "You were saying the other day at the cabin that you needed help anyway, and you need it today more than any other day."

Gabe shrugged and looked at her. "She makes a good point."

"Exactly." Peg arranged muffins on a tray, studied her creation and made a couple of adjustments. She fanned slices of banana bread on the next tray. "I am yours to command."

Did anyone command Peg? Did anyone dare command Peg?

"Okay." Kelly didn't have the fight in her for that.

The doorbell tinkled and Randy, a trucker who came by every morning for a hazelnut skinny latte, stopped in. "You all right, sweetie?" He handed his payment and reward card to Peg. "You want me to hang around?"

"I'm okay." His concern touched her.

Peg punched his reward card and handed it back to him. "We appreciate your kindness, Randy. We all look out for each other in this town."

"That's the truth." Randy's beard bristled as he scowled. "You see that dickhead anywhere around, you tell me. Me and a couple of the boys will take care of him for you."

Kelly handed him his drink. "Thanks, Randy."

Another couple of customers wandered in.

"What can we get you?" Peg bellied up to the counter.

"That's Walker." Kelly smiled a greeting. "The usual?"

"Missed you yesterday, girlie." Walker shook his bald head. "Hated to hear about your troubles." He looked at Peg for agreement. "Shouldn't happen to anyone. Let alone a nice girl like our Kelly."

"Speak it, Walker. Speak it." Peg swiped his card and handed it back to him. "We'll have that coffee ready for you in a moment."

As if word had gotten out, the trickle opened into a flow of customers. Everyone had a kind word for her, until it was almost overwhelming. By the time the flow had turned into a deluge, it was overwhelming, and Kelly wished they would find something else to talk about.

Even Pete the realtor revealed a dark side that would be hard to forget.

"Disembowelment would be too good for that kind," Pete said. "What we should do is have these abusive types hanged, drawn and quartered."

He then took a long ten minutes to tell her the details. Turns out Pete also spent his weekends reenacting medieval times.

"Oh dear." Peg looked pale.

Feeling slightly nauseous, Kelly turned away from Pete and into the full-frontal pity-fest from the mothers who looked after the daycare center.

Again, Peg proved invaluable. "You're very kind, girls, but Kelly would like to put it behind her," she said. "Have a little something sweet with that coffee. I always say coffee and a nice cupcake or piece of walnut cake change my outlook on the day."

She never thought she'd say it, but having Peg there was a godsend. Not only was Peg efficient and friendly, she managed to sell more baked goods than Kelly normally did.

By the end of her day, Kelly understood what being killed with kindness really meant. The bell over the door tinkled again, and Gabe strode in. He had changed since he'd dropped her off, and his smile made all the bad things slink away.

"Hey." He kissed her cheek. "You look tired."

"Nice! Is that the polite way of telling me I look like crap? " She rolled her eyes and made sure he saw it. She was done with being treated like a victim for the day. What she needed was a dose of normal.

Gabe watched her, assessing, and then grinned. "I was going for talking you into bed."

Kelly welcomed the distraction. Flirting with Gabe felt closer to her normal self. "Is that all you got?"

"You know the answer to that." He took a stool at the counter. "How did it go today?"

"Well." She gathered the used cups from the tables. "Randy offered himself and some trucker buddies for protection or payback, Hank Styles offered me the use of his chain saw, Robin left me a pocket pepper spray, and Donna gave me this." Kelly pulled out a wickedly curved hunting knife.

Gabe's eyes widened. "Remind me not to piss Donna off."

"I'll start packing up." She took the cups through to the back and loaded the dishwasher.

Peg took the cups out of her hands. "I've got this. You go on home and rest."

"Are you sure?" After a day of working with Peg, Kelly was happy to let her take over.

Peg emptied the trash and recycling cans. "I'm sure.

"Okay then." Kelly gathered her coat and purse. "Thanks for everything today, Peg."

"You're welcome, sugar." Peg attacked the countertops with antibacterial spray. "And I'll see you in the morning."

Kelly thought about arguing. For less than a second then nodded. "See you in the morning."

"I'll open up." Peg's entire body jiggled with the force of her wiping. "I got the hang of the machine now, and you look like the sleep will do you good."

"Okay."

Gabe tucked her arm in his as they left the store. "Did you just hire Peg?"

"I think she might have hired herself."

On the way to her place, they stopped to pick up a pizza and a bottle of wine. Did it mean Gabe would be spending the night again? Maybe he intended to eat and leave.

His expression gave nothing away as he kept his eyes on the road.

At her condo, he got out first and checked the parking lot before opening her door.

Her condo felt small and intimate with both of them in it. Last night she hadn't given it a thought past comfort when Gabe climbed into her bed. Tonight, the small space between them was loaded with unspoken thoughts.

"I'll get changed," she said and scurried into her bedroom. To delay dealing with the ambiguity, she had a quick shower. She hesitated over her yoga pants and a comfy sweater or something a little more alluring. Then she got pissed at herself for being so silly. This was Gabe and pizza.

Gabe had lit her small fireplace and set the pizza and wine on her kitchen counter.

He looked up and smiled. "Better?"

"Yup. I don't smell like Colombian roast anymore."

He handed her a glass of red. "Colombian roast is one of my favorite smells."

There it was again, the innuendo that wasn't quite anything. And dammit, she was hungry. She grabbed a piece of pizza, folded it and took a big bite.

He wasn't a folder, but he made short work of his first piece.

"Gabe? What are we doing here?"

He stopped with his piece halfway to his mouth. "Huh?"

"I'm confused and too tired to dance around the subject." She gestured between them. "Is this pizza and wine between buddies, or is it something else?"

Raising an eyebrow, he put his pizza down. "Considering you were attacked a couple of nights ago, it's whatever you say it is, Kelly. I'm here, and I can sleep on the couch if you want."

"Or?"

He bit into his pizza. "You tell me."

"I'll give it some thought." The power surged to her head and her smile dared him to challenge her.

Gabe rounded the island and stopped in front of her. "While you're mulling, let me present the options."

"Sure." She knew that tone. It stroked over her senses and

ignited the slow burn that was always present when Gabe was near her.

He parted her thighs and stepped between them. "Option one, and this is not my favorite, is that we finish our wine and pizza and I tuck you into bed and sleep on the couch."

"Hmm." She tapped her chin. "The advantage being that we both get a good night's sleep."

"One of us at least." He pushed her hair away from her neck, his fingers trailing over her skin and leaving shivers behind. His mouth replaced his fingers. "Option two is we finish our wine and pizza." He kissed a trail to her earlobe and sucked it into his mouth. His breath rasped in her ear causing shivers to cascade down one side of her body. "We put the TV on and snuggle on the couch until it's time for bed."

"What happens then?" Her breathing was getting hard to control as he worked his way along her jaw toward her mouth.

"Then we both go to your bed and talk about the first thing that comes up." He kissed her laughter from her lips and drifted toward her other earlobe.

She grabbed his hips to anchor herself as he made the other side of her neck so sensitive it almost hurt to touch. "Is there an option three?"

Gabe stopped and brought his mouth to hers. He stopped within a breath of kissing her. "Option three is my favorite."

"What is it?"

"We forget about pizza and wine."

"Option three. I choose option three." Kelly closed distance and kissed him.

Gabe groaned and gripped the back of her head. He slid his tongue between her lips. "Thank you, Jesus."

"I need…" She didn't have the words, so she slid her hands under his shirt and found hot, silky skin. She needed all of him. The way he made her feel. The way he took her out of herself. The way they moved together like they were designed for each other.

"Wrap your legs around me," Gabe rasped against her ear.

Kelly wrapped her legs and arms around him.

He picked her up and carried her into the bedroom. His hot gaze bored into hers, promising her all the pleasure they'd shared that one night. Since that first night, they'd only ever been one moment away from being back in bed.

Gabe lowered her to the bed on her back. He stood above her and fisted the back of his sweater. His T-shirt came off with it.

"Stop!" Kelly had waited too long to see this again, and the last time had been blurred by secrecy and alcohol. She sat up and spread her hands over the flat, muscular plane of his belly.

He sucked in a breath as she caressed his abs.

It was too much temptation, so Kelly kissed those beautiful ridges of muscle.

Gabe's hands tightened in her hair.

His skin was salty on her tongue. Men like him weren't supposed to exist in real life. Somehow, she'd thought she had exaggerated his body in her imagination.

Wrong.

He even had those lateral lines disappearing into his jeans. It was a goddamn crime to forget those.

She undid his belt and jeans and slid his zipper down as her mouth paid tribute to those gorgeous lines. The backs of her fingers rubbed against his rock-hard erection.

Gabe Crowe was enough beautiful male to make a girl's thinking power fly out the window. There would be no drunken fumbling this time.

She slid his boxers down and his erection sprung free.

"Kelly." Her name sounded like a plea.

A plea she was more than happy to answer, so Kelly fisted his cock and slipped him into her mouth. She sucked him deep.

"Fuck." His muscles tensed, and he threw his head back.

Kelly took her time, learning the shape of him on her tongue, finding out what he liked in a nonverbal language of gasps and soft groans, muscles tightening and hands tangling in her hair.

"Babe." Gabe pulled back. "Not like this."

He kicked out of his pants and pulled his socks off.

Kelly wriggled out of her yoga pants and her sweater.

Gabe watched her with an intense burning gaze as she took her bra off.

"Kelly," he whispered her name like a prayer as he lowered himself over her. He braced above her and cupped her breast. He cupped the other breast and lowered his mouth to her. "I dream about these."

She cried out as the wet heat of his mouth engulfed her nipple. He sucked her into his mouth, his hand exploring the fullness of her other breast.

"You're so sexy." He sucked her other nipple and slid his hands down her ribcage to her belly. It rested there with the very tops of his fingers slipping under her panties.

That hand nearly drove her mad, waiting there as he continued to suck and lick her breasts. She tilted her hips in silent invitation.

An invitation he ignored as he concentrated on her breasts.

She couldn't stand it anymore. "Gabe."

He hummed against her breast.

"Touch me. Please."

"Here?" He slid his hands deeper, over her mound.

She pushed into his hand. "Yes."

Gabe slid his fingers down, parting her wet folds.

It felt so good she panted something incoherent. She wanted him to keep doing what he was doing.

"You're so wet." Gabe eased a finger inside her. "Is this where you want me?"

"Yes." She was panting and straining against those fingers.

He withdrew and slid his fingers over her clit. "Or do you need me here?"

"Dammit, Gabe. All of it."

Lowering his head, he dropped hot, wet kisses on her belly. "Greedy." He slipped two fingers inside her. His thumb strummed her clit. He sucked the skin inside her hip. "But there's a problem."

"What?" Kelly opened her legs wider.

Gabe looked at her spread open for him. "I'm just as greedy. I want to taste all of you."

His mouth on her made her cry out. Hot and wet, his tongue parted and licked through her.

Kelly writhed against him, so close already.

He swirled his tongue around her clit and then sucked her.

"Gabe." She jackknifed up.

He planted a hand on her belly and pushed her down, then got serious about driving her out of her mind with his lips and his tongue. He ate her out with a single-minded purpose that had her writhing and whispering incoherent pleas for more.

Her orgasm hit her fast and hard and she bucked against him.

Gabe stayed with her through it, until she fell back limp on the bed, and then he crawled up her body. He ran his tongue over his lips. "You taste so good."

Kelly wrapped her legs around his hips and brought his hard cock close to her center. "And you do that so well."

"I believe in doing a thorough job." He flexed against her and her satisfied body responded in a languorous wave of sensation.

"Me too." She ground herself against him. "But you didn't let me finish the job."

"Next time." He kissed her. "Be right back."

Kelly rolled on her side and enjoyed the sight of a naked, fully aroused Gabe finding a condom in his wallet and returning to the bed.

He stood by the bed and fisted his cock.

Watching him roll the condom on did delicious things to her libido, and she was ready for more as he eased onto the bed beside her.

"Get to work, woman." He rolled to his back, a big beautiful animal and all hers.

Kelly straddled him and braced her arms on either side of his head. She hovered with the tip of him just inside her. "Is this where you want me?"

"Fuck yes." Gabe gripped her hips and pulled her onto him.

Kelly gasped as he filled her completely.

Beneath her, his back arched. "You're so hot and tight."

Having him under her appealed to her, and Kelly took control. She ground down, bringing him deeper inside, and then rose on him. There she waited, before impaling herself on him again.

Gabe let her set the pace for a while, happy to let her experiment.

Slowly, another climax began deep in her belly, and she tightened around him.

As if this was what he'd been waiting for, Gabe grabbed her hips and surged into her, bringing her hard down on him. Again and again, he thrust up, driving them both relentlessly forward.

Kelly gave herself over to the hot rush of sensation and hurtled over the edge in a burst of sensation that zipped all the way to the end of her toes.

Beneath her, Gabe tensed, slammed her down and emptied inside her.

They rode the aftershocks together in a slow slide until Kelly collapsed on his heaving chest.

Gabe stroked her back.

Kelly matched her breathing to his until sweat cooling on her body made her reach for the covers.

Gabe got rid of the condom in the bathroom and joined her in bed.

Curling around her, he tucked her into him. "For the record, option three was the best choice."

CHAPTER

Twenty-Six

GABE STOOD in Kelly's kitchen eating cold pizza for breakfast while he waited for her to get ready for work. He hadn't felt this good since the last time he'd tangled with Kelly.

Kelly hadn't minded being woken up in the night for a replay, and she didn't get prissy about morning sex. If he were a cat, he'd have been purring.

"Ugh." Kelly strolled in wearing jeans and a sweater, her wet hair scraped back in a ponytail and no makeup. "Cold pizza?"

He liked that she felt okay being natural in front of him. He shrugged and took a big bite of his pizza. "It's the breakfast of champions."

"Not this champion." Kelly shuddered and poured herself a mug of coffee. She added cream and sugar.

Coming up behind her, Gabe nuzzled her neck and drew in the fresh smell of a newly showered Kelly. He hummed his approval against her neck. "Not a morning person?"

"You with your cold pizza breath." She wrinkled her nose but giggled anyway and didn't move away.

He checked the time. Too late to lure Kelly back into bed. "I'll drop you off when you're ready."

"Actually, I was thinking." Her tension telegraphed through

her muscles before she spoke. "I was thinking I could take myself to work today."

He didn't like that, but coming at Kelly head on was like waving a red rag at a bull. "You ready for that?"

"I'm not sure." She turned and faced him, hips pressed to the counter. "But I've got to be a brave little soldier at some point."

Keeping it light and easy, he shrugged. "Sure, but that doesn't have to be today."

"I think I'd like to try." She squared her shoulders, ready for his argument.

Gabe stepped away and poured himself a cup of coffee. He needed that space to get his primal side under control. The chest-thumping, keeping her safe in his lair side that wanted its say. "Okay."

"Okay?" She choked on a mouthful of coffee. "That's all you have to say?"

"Um…no." He could write her a novel on how much he didn't want her out there and vulnerable without him, but you didn't pull that crap on Kelly and get away with your scalp intact. More importantly, she'd charge in the opposite direction. "Call me if you get unsure at any point. I'll be around."

She cocked her head and grinned at him. "That almost cost you a molar didn't it?"

"Damn straight." He sipped his coffee.

Kelly crossed the kitchen and slid her arms around his waist. "I won't take any chances, and I'll call you when I get home."

"Can I come by?"

"Tonight?" She frowned and stepped away. "I think we should talk."

"Probably." He sensed where she was going before she spoke. "I think we're past pretending what happened between us was a one-off."

Kelly snort laughed. "That's for sure."

"I really like you, Kelly." The next bit would take some

nimble footwork because he didn't want to piss her off or be an asshole. "But I won't be staying in Twin Elks."

"I know that." Kelly nodded, but her expression gave nothing away, and she took another sip of her coffee. "The thing I need to decide is if that's enough for me."

———

Gabe arrived home, his conversation with Kelly still playing in his mind. In fairness, the decision was hers. He couldn't offer her more than a friends with benefits, good for as long as it lasts type of set up.

Staying in Twin Elks had never been in his game plan. He still had to make a decision between Australia and South Africa and get his life back on track. His time with Kelly had been special, but it had to end at some point.

India and Ma were in the kitchen when he let himself in. Jacob sat in a highchair, crushing cheerios and burbling.

Ma's dog zeroed on him, tongue lolling, body wiggling and tail whipping from side to side. "Hey, big guy."

The dog buried his nose in Gabe's crotch. "Have you given him a name yet?"

"Morning." Ma greeted him with a smile. "How's Kelly doing?"

India's gaze locked on him. "Is she okay?"

"She decided to take herself to work today," he said.

Ma frowned. "Is that wise?"

"I don't like it." He sat at the table. "But Kelly's not a child, and she does what she thinks she needs to."

India nodded. "That's true. I wish I could see her."

"That's not a good idea, sweetie." Dot patted her shoulder. "We need to make sure that ex of yours doesn't find out where you are."

India ducked her head and fed Jacob some porridge.

"Speaking of, has Ben said anything about finding Piers?"

Ma shook her head. "He's disappeared, but if he's around, Ben will find him."

Something was off with India, and Gabe watched her before he asked, "India, do you have any idea where Piers would be?"

"No." She started and glanced at him. "Why would I know where he is?"

Scalpel sharp, Ma's gaze focused on him.

He would speak to her later. "You know him better than anyone."

"Oh." India blushed. "I see what you mean, but no. He never lived in Twin Elks, and when we came here together, we stayed at the hotel."

He nodded and stood. "I need to change. I thought I might hang out with Finn and see if he needs anything painted." Looking at Ma, he said, "Give the dog a name and take him to training."

She grinned. "Yes, darling."

Gabe went to his room. His old *National Geographic* magazines were still in the bookshelf, neatly arranged by date order. He'd loved those things as a kid and spent hours poring over them.

Firing up his computer, he sat down to check his email.

Ma's dog was in the front garden, barking up a tree. Some squirrel must have been laughing its ass off at the poor canine.

An email from Belinda had come in two days earlier, and he hovered over it. He and Belinda had pretty much said all that needed saying.

The dog leaped on the tree trunk.

A squirrel dashed from the tree to the telephone wire and shot across it.

With a yip, the dog followed.

The squirrel took the wire across the road. Dog chased it, right under the wheels of a black pickup.

Tires screeched followed by a sickening yelp.

The dog's body flew through the air.

Gabe ran through the kitchen yelling. "Ma! Call Cara; tell her I'm on my way."

Fuck! Fuck! Fuck! That pickup had been coming too fast to stop, and it had hit the dog too fucking hard.

"I didn't see him." The driver was out his truck, nearly weeping. "I didn't see him."

Dog lay too still in the road, panting hard, blood running out of his nose.

"Here." Ma thrust a blanket at him. She was sobbing and trying to keep it together. "Is he—"

"No." Gabe wouldn't speak that word. He checked the dog's airways. Still breathing, thank God, and his gums were still pink. They had a chance, but the poor creature labored for each new breath, his eyes glazed with pain.

Gabe took the blanket from Ma. "He's probably in a whole world of pain. Ma, can you hold his head for me?" He covered the dog with the blanket and spoke to the dog. "I know, buddy, and this is going to fucking hurt, but it's got to happen." As Ma held his head, Gabe slid his arms under the body. The dog whined and wriggled. Gabe tightened his hold. "Come on, big guy. Let me get you somewhere, and then I can help you. I can make it go away."

The dog's eyes had gone glassy, and he was breathing too hard. "Come on, big guy. You hang in there for me."

The trust in those big brown eyes nearly killed him.

"Gabe." Ma choked on his name. "Please?"

"I'll do what I can." Gabe lifted him. "I'm so sorry big guy, this is going to hurt like hell."

The dog yelped and tried to struggle. Gabe tightened his grip and prayed like hell he wasn't doing more damage.

"I can drive." The pickup driver ran ahead and opened doors.

The dog was heavy, and Gabe held him tight to his chest as he eased into the passenger seat.

Gabe didn't like how inert he was. "Get us to the vet. Quickly."

The pickup driver took off. Every minute that passed seemed like an eternity. Both Gabe and the driver kept talking to the dog, both of them willing the creature to keep fighting. A few more breaths, a few more beats of his heart, and they could get him help.

Cara was waiting for him outside with a stretcher. "Breathing."

"Just."

"Heartbeat."

"Intermittent."

Gabe lowered him to the stretcher.

Cara took the other side, and they got him on the operating table. She handed Gabe the oxygen mask and Gabe put it over his muzzle. The dog didn't fight him, and as easy as it made the job, it set off warnings in Gabe's head.

Cara jabbed the pain relief into the dog's back leg.

Gabe prayed for a good vein and growled his relief as he managed to locate the cephalic vein in his foreleg and get the drip running.

Those big eyes drooped, and Gabe stroked his head. "There you go, big guy. Gabe and Cara are going to take the best care of you."

Cara checked his vitals again. "Okay, let's get him into x-ray. See what's happening."

———

They'd done it. Gabe leaned his back against the cold, sterile wall and looked at the dog, sleeping in a recovery cage. They weren't out of the woods yet. They'd opened the dog up to find the bladder damaged.

Cara with a needle was a joy to watch as she stitched up the damage. It had taken two hours, and Gabe had flushed the dog's abdomen as thoroughly as he could and got a drain in.

The rest was up to the big guy's will to live and how the antibiotics worked their magic to prevent any further infection.

God knew how, but the dog hadn't sustained any fractures. He'd be bruised and sore when he woke up. The whiteboard above the cage remained blank. This guy really needed a name.

Gabe picked up the marker and wrote.

"Bruce?" Crouched by the cage, Cara frowned up at him. "Like the shark from *Finding Nemo*?"

He dug that she got it straight away. "All those teeth. The way he smiles. Big guy who wants to be friends."

"I like it." Cara smiled. She placed the Elizabethan collar around Bruce's neck. "Come on, Bruce. We're rooting for you, big guy." Her shoulders slumped suddenly, and she turned her head away. Silent sobs shook her.

Closing the distance between them, Gabe tugged her to her feet and yanked her into a hug.

Tears may have been shed by him too. There may also have been a lot of snot involved. But what happened behind the scenes in a veterinary's office, stayed behind the scenes.

———

In the waiting room, Ma held hands with the pickup driver. The place was full, and Gabe only recognized Donna and Robin from the Twin Elks prayer chain, but he'd bet his life they were all there. Ma stood as he came in, a silent question on her face.

"He made it through surgery." Damn, his voice shook again, and he was shit scared he might start bawling in front of the goddamn prayer chain. "He's still not out of the woods, but it's up to him now."

The waiting room broke into cheers and whistles, which got louder when Cara came in after him.

Gabe looped an arm around her neck. "You're a helluva

surgeon, Dr. Addison."

"Likewise, Dr. Crowe." She beamed up at him. "We did a good thing today."

"Yes, we did." Without questioning himself, Gabe grabbed his phone and dialed Kelly.

"Hey," she answered immediately. "How is the dog?"

That was Twin Elks for you. "We think he's going to make it."

More cheers broke out in the waiting room.

"That's great news." Kelly warmed his chest with her delight. Cheering came down the line from her side. "We should celebrate."

"Tonight?" He couldn't think of anyone he'd rather celebrate with.

Kelly laughed. "Tonight."

"We can discuss our options."

"Excuse me." Belinda's Australian accent rang like a bell. It was so out of place it took him a moment to register it came from the waiting room.

Kelly may have said something else, but Gabe's hackles came up.

"Excuse me," Belinda said. "But I'm looking for Gabe Crowe. Someone at the hotel said he was here."

"Gabe?" Kelly must have been waiting for a reply.

Trying to see past the crowd, he said to Kelly, "Give me second here."

"Gabe." Tall, blond, toned, and tanned Belinda stood in front of him with her big sunny smile and threw her arms wide. "Surprise."

"Belinda?" His brain still couldn't make sense of it. The phone was still pressed to his ear and Kelly must have heard. "Kelly?"

"Yeah." She sounded guarded.

"I need to call you back."

"Sure." And she hung up.

Belinda dropped her arms and shoved her hands into the

pockets of her puffy jacket.

All eyes were on him and Belinda, and he looked at Ma for a maternal interception.

Ma stepped forward with an easy smile. "Hello." She held out her hand. "I'm Dot, Gabe's mother. We never had the chance to meet."

"Belinda." Belinda took Ma's hand and shook it, giving a breathy laugh. "Belinda Moffat. I've heard a lot about you."

"Likewise." Ma threw him a glance that promised they would talk later. "Did you just get into town?"

Belinda shrugged and looked around at all the people eyeballing her. "Yeah. Flew into Denver and drove here. I wanted to surprise Gabe."

"And Gabe is certainly surprised." Ma laughed. "Why don't I take you to the hotel, and we can let Gabe get settled here?" She tucked her arm through Belinda's and walked her to the door. "We've had some excitement this morning."

Belinda glanced over her shoulder at him.

God, he knew that determined look on Belinda's face and he didn't like what it implied. Arriving unannounced was so like her, he should have expected something like it. Outside, Belinda climbed into Ma's car, looking bewildered by Ma's constant stream of chatter.

"Damn. I hope I'm wrong about what she's doing here."

"Best you find out then." Donna drew in a deep breath and pinned him with a hard stare. "I love your mother, Gabriel Crowe, and I wouldn't do a thing to hurt her, but if you play fast and loose with our Kelly, then you'll have me to answer to."

The rest of the prayer chain followed her out, each with a special glance promising future retribution. Robin jabbed her middle and index finger at her eyes and then him.

"I take it that was an unexpected complication?" Cara nudged him with a shoulder.

Talk about your understatements.

"For the record, I'm on Kelly's team as well."

CHAPTER
Twenty-Seven

GABE WANTED TO HIDE AWAY. More specifically, he really wanted to hide from Belinda. But she was sitting in Ma's kitchen, waiting for him when he came home.

"Hi." She stood and wiped her hands on her jeans. "I hope you don't mind, but I didn't have a reservation at the hotel, and your mother said I could stay here."

That was so like Ma. His gaze stuck on the suitcases by Belinda's feet. "Ma didn't give you a room to sleep in?"

"No." Belinda grimaced. "I mean, yes, she did, but I was waiting for you. I wanted to see..." She turned big, pleading eyes his way.

Ah, hell no. A hundred reasons sharing a bed with Belinda was a horrible idea flooded through Gabe. In the weeks since he'd been in Twin Elks, this side of Belinda had slipped his mind. She was an expert at bending things to her will with her big brown eyes and slightly helpless air. He was willing to bet she'd worked her magic on Ma.

"Your mother was fine with me staying here. She didn't mind where I slept."

There you had it. "You can stay in one of my brothers' old rooms."

"Thanks." If she had any emotions about where she was sleeping, she kept them to herself. The silence in the kitchen stretched into awkward. "So, I never thought I'd see the day you were saving Fido."

"He's my mother's dog." Her flippant remark irritated him. He was proud of the work he and Cara had done today. He didn't always have to fly to exotic destinations and haul on scuba kit to do his job.

And yes, the irony of that last thought was not lost on him.

Belinda laughed "Yeah, but it's not exactly your thing, is it? Rushing to the aid of the family pet."

God, he hoped he didn't sound as pretentious and up himself as that when he spoke about his work with great whites.

Ben's truck pulled up outside the house, and he joined them in the kitchen. "Ma told me about her dog." He clapped Gabe on the shoulder. "You did a good thing."

Gabe had never been gladder to see his brother and have a body between himself and what he suspected was going to be a very awkward conversation.

"Ben Crowe." Ben held his hand out to Belinda. "Gabe's older brother."

Belinda shook his hand. "Nice to meet you. Gabe speaks about you a lot."

"I can imagine." Ben rolled his eyes. Behind Belinda's back, he gave Gabe a hard stare, silently demanding, *What's she doing here?*

Gabe met it and tossed back, *No clue.*

"It's nice to meet you, Belinda. It is Belinda, right?" Ben tucked his thumbs into his utility belt, playing up the aw-shucks county police chief thing. He should come with a matching set of dueling banjoes. "Ma says you're staying here. Both of you."

"Yeah." Gabe didn't even try to look happy about it.

After a moment, Ben nodded. "Actually, Ryan heard about the accident and is having a hard time with it. I promised him I would come over and get the news straight from you."

"Gabe did a great job." Belinda beamed at Ben. "He saved that dog."

Belinda hadn't even seen Bruce, so he had no idea how she'd come to that conclusion. "I had some help."

Ben gave Gabe one of his rare smiles. "You always were good at saving things and putting them back together again."

"Yeah." And the good feeling came back. It was so stupid that Ben's approval meant as much as it did, but it lit a warm glow in Gabe. "I also gave the poor animal a damn name at last."

Ben grunted. "About time."

"What did you name him?" Belinda swung around to look at him.

"Bruce."

Her eyes lit up.

Damn! He should have thought of another name, because Belinda was an expert at reading into things.

Ma came through the door from the house. "Gabe." She pulled him into a hug. "How's the dog?"

"Bruce." Belinda grinned at her. "Gabe named him after Bruce. The Australian shark in *Finding Nemo*." She giggled. "Two things Gabe loves; Australia and sharks.

"Oh." Ma looked taken aback. "Well, the poor dear did need a name. Is he doing okay?"

"He should be." Gabe grabbed Belinda's stuff. "We flushed out his abdomen as well as we could before we closed him back up, and Cara has him on some strong antibiotics to prevent infection."

"Thank you so much for having me here." Belinda hugged Ma.

Ma looked over Belinda's shoulder at him. A look that promised she would be getting answers in the near future. "That's fine. Why don't we get you settled?"

"Gabe." Poppy poked her head around the kitchen door.

The grin Ben gave her was as large and goofy as ever. He leaned down and kissed her. "Babe. How's Ryan?"

"He's doing okay." Poppy glanced at Belinda and then came back to him. "Ryan's worried about the dog."

"Bruce." Belinda thrust her hand at Poppy. "Hi. I'm Belinda. Gabe's…" she gave him a coy look.

"Ex," Gabe said.

"Ex-girlfriend." Belinda kept on smiling, but she threw him a look of reproach.

Poppy glanced between them and then at Ben.

Ben raised an eyebrow.

Dot cleared her throat.

"Nice to meet you." Poppy gave Belinda a warm smile. "I'm Poppy, and I'm married to Ben."

Belinda clicked her fingers. "You have all those children, right?"

"Four." Gabe wanted out of the kitchen and away from that scene. "Poppy and Ben have four children."

"Yeah, but they're Poppy's children, aren't they?" Belinda frowned. "I'm sure you told me that."

Ben's face looked carved from stone. "They're our children."

"But first, they were mine." Poppy took pity on Belinda. "Ben has gotten a crash course in fatherhood."

"Tea," Ma yelled. She flapped a hand at him. "Let's clear those suitcases. Belinda can have Mark's old room, and then we can have tea." She turned an over-bright smile on Belinda. "Unless you prefer coffee to tea?"

"Tea is fine." Belinda followed Ma out of the kitchen.

Ben grabbed his arm. "What the hell, Gabe?"

"I have no fucking idea." Gabe yanked his arm away, but he had a very good idea of what Belinda was doing there, and he didn't like it.

In the house, he followed the sound of chatter to Mark's room.

Belinda was looking around her. "This must be the brother who plays ice hockey."

"That's my Mark." Ma did some more hand flapping. "Put the cases near the wardrobe."

Gabe did as he was told. "Bathroom's across the hall." He pointed in the right direction. "Take your time and settle in."

"I'll get on that tea." Ma dogged his heels into the kitchen.

Poppy and Ben had left already.

Ma checked the hallway before turning on him. "What is she doing here, Gabe?"

"I didn't invite her," he whispered. "She just showed up."

"What do you want—"

Belinda reappeared, and Ma grabbed the kettle and put it on. The three of them limped through tea and then dinner. A dinner Belinda picked at, and rejected most of, because she was on Keto. Now Gabe had no issue with Keto, but before Keto, Belinda had been Paleo, and before that gluten free, and before that Vegan. It had made grocery shopping with her a living hell.

Ma escaped to her bedroom as soon as she could, and Belinda helped him clear up the kitchen. Afterward, he got himself a beer and they sat in the lounge together.

"You told me you came from a small town, but this is tiny." Belinda laughed. "I'm expecting a tumbleweed to roll down the street any minute."

Gabe laughed along with her, but the criticism of Twin Elks bugged him. He got the hypocrisy, and that he'd said worse about Twin Elks. "It has its appeal."

"Does it?" Belinda stopped laughing. "And what would those appeals be?"

"My mother." Gabe kept his gaze on the street. He didn't want her looking too deeply into his face. Belinda had been with him long enough to read his expressions. "Childhood memories. People." He waved his beer at the view. "The mountains. There's a lot of good hiking around here."

"The mountains are pretty. Maybe we could go hiking sometime." Belinda was still staring at him. "You know why I'm here."

Gabe barely kept the grimace off his face. "Can we not do this?"

Belinda drew in a careful breath. "I traveled a long way to do this, Gabe."

"I'm not sure why you did." Gabe really hated to be cruel, but she'd surprised the shit out of him. "Things haven't changed for me."

Belinda got to her feet and gave him a tight smile that didn't reach her eyes. "I'm tired, and you've had an emotional day. You're right; let's not do this now."

Gabe let her go, because his answer would stay the same. He stayed where he was as she closed Mark's bedroom door. But there was somewhere he wanted to be and Ma's wasn't it. After putting his beer in the kitchen, he grabbed his coat.

It was late, but Gabe still had the key from when he'd been looking after her. He let himself into Kelly's condo and called softly so as not to startle her if she was still awake, "Kelly."

All the lights in the condo were off. He toed off his shoes and hung up his coat before sneaking through to the bedroom.

Tucked up in bed, her hands under her pillow, Kelly was fast asleep. She got up early for the store and went to bed early most nights.

Calm crept over him. That was exactly where he wanted to be.

He shucked his clothes and slid into bed beside her. Her warmth beckoned him, and he pulled her close.

She stirred and turned her head. "Gabe?"

"Yeah." He kissed her cheek. "Go back to sleep."

"Did you creep into my place in the middle of the night?"

He pushed his nose into her neck and inhaled her scent. "Yeah, I'm a creepy asshole."

Kelly sighed and closed her eyes. "Okay then."

CHAPTER
Twenty-Eight

KELLY CARRIED on her day with her smile frozen on her face. What were the chances some random Australian woman had walked into the veterinarian's and knew Gabe?

"I don't know what she's doing here," Peg said for about the hundredth time. "And neither does Dot." She discarded coffee grounds with aggressive banging.

Amazingly enough, she and Peg worked well together. Peg didn't chatter too much—other than right then when she wanted to dissect the arrival of the Australian. She didn't break stuff, and she stayed cool when the rushes hit them. She also seemed to be loving the hell out of being in the coffee shop.

"Here you go." Peg handed off two coffees to customers. "Dot said they broke up months ago."

Kelly took a careful breath in. It dragged a grappling hook down her windpipe. Nope, denial wasn't really helping her. Gabe's ex had arrived in Twin Elks.

And what made a woman travel halfway around the world to see a man?

Ding! Ding! Ding! If you guessed because she wanted that man back and was there to get him, then Kelly had a prize to give away.

"Kelly?" Vince still popped in for his regular coffee, and she was glad of it. "You okay?"

She slapped a smile on her face. "I'm fine. Indigestion." That started in the heart region.

This wasn't like her. She didn't get jealous or anxious over men.

"The usual?" She kept her smile in place.

Vince nodded. "You know me."

But the tightness in her chest was a reality, which meant Gabe had come to mean way, way more than she had ever planned. Could she have been more damn stupid? She'd gotten attached to a man who was only passing through.

Kelly got on with making Vince's regular coffee.

That couldn't be right. She knew better than to get attached. All those years when she had been waiting for another chance with Vince, she had managed to keep her relationships light and noncommittal.

Perhaps it was because the sex was so great.

"There you go." She put Vince's coffee in front of him.

"Thanks," he said.

That was it. Relief almost made her dizzy. The raging attraction between them, followed by the off-the-charts sex had confused the issue. After all, she'd been celibate for months before Gabe's arrival. It was so easy to get lust mixed up with love. Having made sense of her emotions, she felt much better, as if a weight had been lifted.

The ache in her heart would disappear soon. She turned her attention to Vince. "So, how've you been?"

"Good. I went over to see India last night," Vince said. "She's incredibly courageous."

Kelly welcomed the distraction. It beat the hell out of thinking she might have fallen in love with Gabe Crowe. Which was so ridiculous she wouldn't even give it another second of mental energy. "She really is. I hate what she suffered through with that asshole."

"Ben still hasn't seen any sign of him?"

She shook her head. "None."

Surely, she was being overdramatic. She couldn't have fallen in love with Gabe. They'd gone to school together for years and years, and she'd barely noticed he was there. Except, he'd always been hot, and girls had always looked at him. Kelly had looked along with the rest of them, but then she'd had Vince.

"I don't like it." Vince looked grim. "I don't think he's going to give up and go away."

"Me neither." Some of her frustration about Gabe crept into her tone. "I wish I felt more certain she was done with him."

Vince reared back as if she'd struck him. "Why wouldn't she be done with him?"

"What?"

"India has been through so much. She needs time to process what's happened." He stood and put money on the counter. "Plus, Jacob has really not been feeling well, and he's been really tiring to look after."

"I wasn't criticizing." She'd never seen Vince buckle into his armor so fast. "I'm frustrated Piers is still out there and could influence her."

Vince gave her a tight nod, his expression still annoyed. "I understand that, Kelly. But maybe it's a good thing that you and India can't spend too much time together right now. She needs to be surrounded by total support."

"Right." And ouch! Vince was really letting her have it. In the world according to Vince, India was always the victim, and Kelly was always the girl who took care of herself.

Gabe didn't see her like that.

And the grappling hook scraped down her chest again.

Vince passed Poppy at the door. They stopped a moment and said their hellos before Poppy walked into the store and climbed on the stool. "Hey, you."

"Hey yourself," Kelly said.

Poppy stood on the footrest and peered over the counter. "What are you making me?"

"Whatever it is, you'll like it." Kelly got busy making Poppy a drink. She wanted to bring up the subject of Gabe, but she didn't want to be obvious. "What are you doing here anyway?"

"Nice!" Poppy pretended to be upset. "Actually, I'm hiding."

"From the house?"

"There are a lot of us crammed into that house," Poppy said. "And sometimes we tread on each other's toes."

"Only natural," Kelly said.

Poppy wrinkled her nose. "Especially since Claire is in full bitch mode today."

"What's up with her?"

"I have my suspicions." After checking behind her, Poppy leaned forward with her face alight. "If I tell you, you have to promise not to tell anyone."

Kelly mimed locking her lips and throwing away the key.

"We-e-ell," Poppy said. "Based on the evidence of her not drinking wine with dinner, and I heard her tossing her cookies the other day…"

"Oh my God!" That was the best distraction. Kelly lowered her voice to a whisper. A thing like that could go viral in minutes in Twin Elks. "You think she's pregnant."

Poppy nodded, glowing like a little girl. "Only you know what a control freak that girl is." She giggled. "She's taking some time to get her head around the idea."

Kelly put a drink in front of Poppy. She hoped Poppy didn't ask what it was because she honestly couldn't remember what ingredients she'd tossed together.

"What do you think Finn will say?"

Rolling her eyes, Poppy waved a hand. "Oh, he'll be thrilled. That man has been waiting to be a father for years."

"That's so lovely." Kelly was horrified when tears prickled behind her eyelids. She was delighted for her friend.

Poppy looked at her. "Kelly?"

"I'm thrilled for Claire. That's all." She ducked her head.

"Really?" Poppy's gaze called bullshit. "And this has nothing to do with a certain Australian who arrived in town?"

"No." But the lie was less than convincing.

Poppy looked around the quiet coffee shop. "Can you close up early?"

"I suppose I could." It would also mean she didn't have to risk Gabe coming to fetch her with the Australian in tow. He still hovered around at closing time. "I definitely could."

"Good," Poppy said. "Because I want to go up to the cabin and take some measurements, and I want company while I do."

Kelly was good with that, so they packed up the coffee shop. She also sent a text to Gabe explaining to him that she was with Poppy.

The text was delivered but not read. She forced herself to stop staring at her texts and allowed Poppy to drag her out of the shop.

Down the street, piles of building debris littered the sidewalk outside the old bakery.

"What's that about?" Poppy jerked her chin.

It was funny how quickly Poppy had become part of the Twin Elks community. "Somebody bought the old bakery and is busy turning it into a health store and yoga center."

"Oooh!" Poppy looked excited. "That will be nice."

Kelly grimaced. "As long as you don't picture Peg doing down dog."

A tall man passed them and smiled. "Ladies."

She and Poppy nodded a greeting.

Kelly had never seen him before.

"I'm new in town," he said.

As they walked away Poppy glanced at her and shrugged. "What was that about?"

"No idea." Kelly should ask Peg. She always knew what was going down in Twin Elks.

They reached Poppy's car and climbed in. Poppy mostly

drove Horace's old 1966 Chrysler Imperial LeBaron. Poppy had a thing for the old car, and Horace didn't drive it much anymore.

"I also escaped because Gabe and Belinda were at the house and you could cut the tension with a knife," Poppy said.

Way to bury the lead. "What were they doing there?"

"Gabe said he brought her around to meet everyone, but I think he was avoiding being alone with her." Poppy handled the old boat of a car like she was born to it.

Kelly tried not to be too delighted by that news. "Well, it's probably the shock."

Poppy's hard stare called bullshit. "Plus, Dot is doing that thing she does when she doesn't like someone and she's trying her best to hide it."

"The squeaky voice?"

"Yup." Poppy flapped her hands about. "With hand waving."

Kelly made an impressed face. "With hand waving? I thought hand waving was reserved for Tara."

"Speaking of Tara, has anyone seen her around?" Poppy didn't have much time for Ben's ex. Then again, Tara still went out of her way to make life difficult for Poppy.

She shook her head. "Nope. Her broomstick hasn't been spotted recently."

They cackled together.

Poppy took the road out of town toward the cabin.

Large and rambling, the house bore no resemblance to Ben's rough cabin, but it still held that cottage air about it with its stone and wooden features.

Poppy parked and sat forward, staring at the house. "It's beautiful, isn't it?"

"It is." Kelly squeezed her hand. "And built with love by that man of yours."

"That's the best part." Poppy gave a misty smile and climbed out. "Let's go get those measurements."

Kelly followed her into the house.

The house looked ready for its family and Poppy took her

through the tour, pride and love shining through with each step. They stopped in the master bedroom and looked out at the view. The last of the sun caressed the mountaintops but left deep gray shadows in the valleys.

"When I first got in my car and headed for California, this was not what I saw for my future," Poppy said.

Kelly leaned her tired head against a wooden pillar. "I know."

"I had pretty much given up on life and decided I had only one direction to go."

She knew that too, so Kelly let Poppy talk.

"In the space of a few weeks, I met Ben and Dot and then you." Poppy opened her arms wide. "Suddenly my life was filled with possibilities."

Kelly nodded. She'd been there at the time.

Slipping an arm around her waist, Poppy tugged her closer. "My point is this, don't give up on anything. Stay open to possibilities."

"You're creepy." Kelly couldn't believe Poppy had gotten all of that from walking into the coffee shop earlier.

Pointing at her, Poppy smiled. "And you're hiding how you really feel about Gabe."

"Not so much hiding as not really knowing." The ache in her chest started again, and Kelly crossed her arms over it. "I didn't see this coming."

"Ah, Kelly." Poppy side-hugged her. "Neither did I, and then one day it hit me that Ben was standing right in front of me. Do you think Claire planned on Finn happening, or being pregnant now?"

"If she is pregnant."

Poppy smirked. "She's pregnant. I'd bet my right arm on it. Anyway, none of us saw love coming, yet here it is."

Love? They couldn't be at that point already. These things took time. "Anyway, Belinda is not the point."

"What is?"

"Gabe isn't staying." Kelly had to wrap her arms tighter around herself. "He wants nothing more than to get the hell out of this town."

"Maybe." Poppy shrugged. "Maybe not. If it helps, you have Dot on your side about making him stay."

That wasn't right either. Kelly shook her head. "I wouldn't want him to stay if it wasn't right for him."

"Damn." Poppy stared at her. "You really do have it bad."

"Could we not talk about this anymore?" She'd been in emotional freefall for the last few days, and she needed to find a hole and crawl into it for the rest of the night.

Poppy nodded. "Sure. As long as you'll remember to do what's right for you here."

Kelly nodded, but the promise was a hollow one. How could she do what was good for her, when inside, a battle raged as to what that should be?

CHAPTER
Twenty~Nine

HER CONVERSATION with Poppy didn't stop Kelly from letting Gabe crawl into her bed again that night.

Kelly woke up before her alarm, very conscious of the warm man spooning her. Not wanting to wake him, she lay there and let the sweetness of the moment surround her.

She didn't delve into what had brought him to her, but he was there, and it might be the last time she had him like that. They were playing Russian roulette with their emotions, and it needed to end before one of them ended up with the wrong barrel spin.

Turning in his arms, she tried to memorize the lines of his beautiful face. In honesty, she couldn't say she was okay with Belinda showing up and staying with Dot, but the problem was larger.

The longer this thing carried on with Gabe, the harder she risked falling. She traced the lines of his face.

His eyelids fluttered open. "Hi."

"Hi."

His dark eyes filled with humor. "I suppose I owe you an explanation."

"No." Kelly didn't want to talk. Moving her body against his, she kissed him.

Gabe responded immediately, rolling her to her back as he deepened the kiss. He raised his head and looked down at her with his tar-dark eyes full of the same need taking her over. "Kelly?"

"Yes." She took his mouth again.

Gabe groaned, and the kiss grew hungrier, deeper.

Twining his fingers through hers, he raised her hands over her head and pinned them to the bed.

His erection pressed against her hip.

His desire for her fanned the flames inside Kelly. Robbed of her hands, she couldn't do much more than move against him. His warmth crept past her skin to the hidden places inside her and made them glow. One more time, she could risk it.

Holding her hands in one of his, he lowered his mouth to her breasts and gave them all the attention they craved.

Thinking became impossible as her body took over. She arched into the heat of his mouth. A moan came from the deepest part of her, the part that demanded fulfillment from him.

He pushed her thighs apart and slid his hips between them. "You have no idea what you do to me."

She would say she had a really good idea, because he did the same to her.

"Gabe." She tilted her hips up. "I need you."

He sucked her nipple deep and released it. "And you'll get me. All of me."

His fingers slid over her wet folds and worked their magic, but she wanted more than that. The need raged through her. If she had only this of him, she wanted all of him. She wanted him inside her, making her feel like only he could.

"Now." She wrapped her thighs around his hips. "I don't want to wait."

"Babe." He pressed his cock against her. "You're impatient."

"Yes."

He studied her for a moment, then let her go and grabbed a condom from her bedside table.

Once he was sheathed, he pushed inside her.

The sense of completeness rushed through Kelly, and she moved with him. Already they fell into a rhythm as if perfectly designed that way.

He knew how she liked to be touched, and he knew how to wring gasps of pleasure out of her.

Kelly let the sensation carry her over the edge.

Gabe joined her and rode the aftermath with her, his forehead pressed to hers.

Their breathing found a matching rhythm and sweat dried on their skin.

Gabe dropped to his back and they lay side by side. He entwined their fingers. Bringing her hand to his mouth, he kissed her knuckles. "I should creep into bed with you more often."

Reality cast its harsh light into their intimate bubble. For both their sakes, Kelly couldn't keep ignoring the obvious. Like a Band-Aid removal, it was best done fast. "Gabe?"

He shifted beside her. "Yes."

"We need to talk."

"Uh-oh." Propping himself up on his elbow, he looked down at her. "No good conversation ever followed that phrase."

Theirs would be no exception, and she couldn't even muster a slight smile for him. "First off, please understand that I don't regret anything that's happened between us."

"Yup. Already this is starting to suck." He cupped her face and locked his gaze on hers. "What are you doing, Kelly?"

"I'm putting an end to this thing between us."

His eyes darkened. "Gonna give me a reason, because from my point of view, we're good together?"

"We are." She felt too vulnerable on her back, so she sat up and tucked the sheet under her arms. "That's part of the problem. We're too good together."

Sitting up, he frowned at her. "Still not seeing the problem."

"If we let us go any further, things could get complicated." Kelly took a deep breath and came as clean as she could. "You taking care of me after Piers, coming here to get away from your ex, that is starting to feel like a lot more than casual."

"Kelly." His expression softened, and he ran his fingers over her cheek. "I'm leaving."

"Exactly! This thing has a shelf life, and for both our sakes, I don't think we can pretend like that's not the reality." She motioned her bed. "If I thought it was just sex, I wouldn't be doing this. But I like the other stuff as much. I like hanging out with you, drinking beer and playing pool. I love how you make me laugh. I'd even go hiking with you again."

"No." He blinked at her. "You don't mean that."

She grimaced. "Okay, maybe not the hiking thing. But the rest of it is true. I think of you as my friend, Gabe, and not only my lover. And that reeks of trouble."

Gabe sighed and scrubbed his hands over his face. "But we said we weren't going to do this again before and look how well that turned out."

"I remember." If anything, the prohibition had made her want him more. "But this time, we need to stick to it." She kissed his cheek. Already his face was imprinted on her mind. Hoarded in her memory were the different expressions he used. "I don't want this to end badly between us. I want to be able to see you when you next drift into town and know that we're friends."

"I have to go. Please say you understand that." His expression begged her.

And she did. She might not like it, but she did. "I absolutely understand, and I wish you all the best for yourself. I want you to have those things that make you happy."

He gazed into her eyes. So many emotions flit between them —fondness, friendship, sadness, and even a little frustration— before he finally nodded. "Okay, Kelly. But I really don't want you to cut me out of your life."

She couldn't if she tried. "You'll see." Leaning over, Kelly kissed him. "This is for the best."

―――――

At the door, Gabe hesitated. Shaking hands seemed ridiculous, and Kelly was standing there sex tousled. By him.

Screw it.

He reached for her and kissed her.

She opened her mouth for him, and he slid his tongue home. If it was the last kiss he'd get from Kelly, then he wanted to make it one to remember. The taste of her was all things good, like coming home and new adventures all at once. Too soon, she separated and stood back. "Bye, Gabe. See you around."

"Bye, Kelly." He didn't bother with a smile but turned and left.

The cold morning air nipped at him as he walked home. He dragged his feet, not really wanting to deal with Belinda and all the decisions her arrival demanded from him.

Around his relationship with Belinda, however, he wasn't at all conflicted. If anything, her showing up had made his position even clearer. What they'd had was dead. Especially when he compared it to what he'd almost had with Kelly. What they could have if he stayed in Twin Elks.

Kelly was warm and generous and passionate. She made love with her entire being, and she threw herself into life as if she had one day left to live.

He loved the way she could make him belly laugh. He treasured those times they'd spent hanging out watching television or downing beer at the Elk. He'd never had a female friend before, and if he and Kelly couldn't be more than friends, he was going to make sure he didn't lose her.

CHAPTER
Thirty

THANK GOD IT WAS SATURDAY, and she didn't have to deal with the morning rush, because Kelly was not doing well.

Peg had offered to come in this morning, but Saturdays were quieter, and Kelly had told her she'd do fine on her own. She should have let Peg take over and stayed at home herself.

"Kelly, hon." Ronnie Falkirk held up her cup. "Is this nonfat milk because I hate that shit?"

It might have been. Kelly took the cup. "I'll remake it for you."

"Awesome," Ronnie said in her quart and pack of twenty a day rasp.

"Sorry about that."

Ronnie hoisted herself onto a stool while she waited. "You doing okay today, hon?"

"Sure." Kelly slapped a smile on her face. "Just tired. I didn't sleep well last night."

Kelly had never thought she'd miss Peg so much.

Ronnie patted her eye-searing copper hair. "Must be mercury in retrograde."

"What does that even mean?" Kelly put whole milk in a stainless-steel jug.

"Not sure." Ronnie cackled. "But it makes me sound smart and mysterious when I say it."

"Hey, Kel." Kathy peered at her and blinked rapidly. "Did you put caramel in this?"

"Probably not." Kelly took the cup from her. "Sorry, Kathy. I'm having one of those days." She pumped caramel into Kathy's cup. "It's probably mercury in retrograde."

Kathy looked uncertain. "Oh, right. Sorry about that."

"What are you gonna do?" Kelly shrugged and frothed Ronnie's milk, ending all conversation.

She replaced Ronnie's coffee and handed it to her. Maybe Peg would consider working there permanently. Peg had a knack for it and certainly seemed to enjoy it.

Ronnie winked at her. "Any chance you can drop a shot of whisky in here?"

"That's illegal, Ronnie." Kelly kept her face straight. "As you know because you've been dispatch for our police department forever."

Sighing, Ronnie winked at her. "A girl can try."

She needed to get it together or she'd be giving away all her day's profits in fixing her mistakes.

It didn't make any sense. She'd ended relationships before and after a good cry, she was back to her normal self. Besides, the thing with Gabe had ended before anyone could get hurt. It was probably that she'd gotten too used to Peg being there and having four hands instead of two.

After work, she was calling Peg and making her an offer. Nothing ventured and all that.

The door opened and Vince walked in, a frown creasing his face.

"Kelly." He tapped his fingers on the counter. "Is India with you?"

That chased all thoughts of Gabe out of her mind. "No. We haven't seen each other since Piers attacked me."

"Would you have any idea where she would go if she wasn't at Dot's?"

Kelly's belly tightened. "She isn't at Dot's?"

"No." Vince pushed his hand through his hair. "I dropped by there earlier, and Dot says she hasn't seen her since early this morning."

"Jacob." Kelly grasped at the straw. "Where is Jacob?"

"Dot said he was with India."

She couldn't think where India would have gone, especially without telling anyone. She knew Piers was still out there somewhere, and it wasn't like India to take such a risk.

Kelly dug her phone out of her purse and dialed India.

It went to voicemail.

"Damn."

Vince frowned. "She didn't answer when I called earlier either."

"Hon?" Ronnie came closer. "Is everything all right?"

"Do you know where Ben is?"

Ronnie nodded. "Sure, I do. He's up at the cabin. He said he would be working up there with his brother today."

Gabe was there as well. It couldn't be helped. "I need to speak to him."

"Want me to holler him up?" Ronnie raised her eyebrows.

She didn't want to go through official channels yet. India might have gotten itchy feet and taken herself and Jacob shopping or something. It seemed a strange time to, but India had been cooped up in Dot's house for a few weeks. "No thanks. I'll give him a call."

Kelly dialed Ben's number, and then Poppy's, but both went to voicemail. She was probably overreacting but that uneasy feeling in her belly wouldn't go away.

Before she could talk herself out of it, she dialed Peg.

Peg answered immediately. "Kelly."

"Hey, Peg. Listen, I'm at the store and—"

"Do you need me to come in?" Peg sounded breathless in her eagerness.

"Yes. I want to run up to the cabin and speak to Ben." She glanced at Vince's concerned expression. "It's about India."

"On my way." Peg hung up.

It took Peg less than ten minutes to get there. She stormed through the door already shedding her coat. "Off you go. I got this. I'll lock up tonight as well."

"Thank you." Kelly pulled her apron off. "I can get the keys from you later."

"Or I could open on Monday," Peg said, picking at the counter edge with a nail. "Like a regular thing. Like all the time."

"I can't pay you much." Kelly shrugged into her coat.

"That doesn't matter." Peg beamed at her. "I don't need the money, but I sure love having something to keep me busy." She jammed her fists on her hips. "I have big plans for this place."

Whatever that meant, but Kelly didn't have time to get into it then.

Vince walked outside with her. "What do you want me to do?"

"Could you see if you can find her around town? I'll go and talk to Ben. If anything is wrong, I need him to know." She opened her car door and jumped inside.

Leaning down, Vince tapped on her window.

Kelly rolled it down. "Yes?"

"I'll text you if I find anything. I'll also ask some truckers who travel through here if they've seen her car."

He really was a good guy, just not the guy for her. "Thanks, Vince. I'll keep you updated."

Tapping her car roof, he nodded, and then trotted back to his SUV.

Driving to the cabin, Kelly couldn't decide between speeding up the mountain and going slow enough to spot India. Anyone following her must have thought her car had a personality disorder. But she made it to the cabin and parked next to Ben's truck.

She walked through the open front door and followed the sound of men's laughter. Let that be a lesson to her. Gabe was moving on with his life, and she should quit being a whiner and do the same.

The brothers were in the kitchen installing hardware on cabinet doors.

"Hold it straight." Ben scowled at Gabe.

"I'm trying."

"You really suck at this."

"How's that?" Gabe chuckled and adjusted his hold on the cabinet door.

Ben spotted her and straightened. "Kelly?"

Gabe whirled around and gave her a smile that looked like he was pleased to see her. See, he was doing great at the being friends thing. "Hey."

"What's up?" Ben put his screwdriver down and walked toward her.

"I'm not sure." She felt stupid suddenly. "Maybe nothing."

Ben put a hand on her shoulder. "Why don't you tell me anyway?"

"It's India." She didn't want to sound alarmist. "Vince came around to the store a little bit ago and said she wasn't at your mom's place. Dot said she hasn't seen India since earlier this morning."

"Did you try calling her?" Ben frowned.

Kelly nodded. "Her phone goes to voicemail."

"Where's Jacob?" Ben's intense focus helped calm her worst fears.

"Dot told Vince he was with India."

"Do me a favor, Kelly." Ben rubbed his nape. "Do you have Piers's number?"

"Yes."

"Call it." Ben looked grim.

Kelly didn't like what Ben was implying. "Why would I call him?"

Ben grimaced. "Call it, Kelly."

She found the contact and called Piers.

"Hello, Kelly," Piers answered.

It took Kelly a moment to respond. She had been sure he wouldn't answer.

Ben looked even grimmer.

"Piers."

"I'm surprised to hear from you after that unpleasantness between us," Piers said.

Is that what he was calling trying to strangle her?

"Ask him," Ben said.

Kelly's heart thundered in her ears. *Please don't let Ben be right.*

Gabe slipped his arm around her waist and tucked her closer. "It's all right."

She took the strength he offered. "Have you seen India, Piers?"

"My wife, India?" Piers chuckled. "Why, of course, I have. I've seen her every day since we got married, bar recent unfortunate events."

Kelly refused the bait. "I mean today."

"Ah." Piers chuckled. "Yes, I have. She's sitting in the car next to me. And before you send your pet cop after me, let me assure you that we are already out of his jurisdiction."

"Where are you taking her?" Her knees felt iffy, so Kelly leaned into Gabe. She didn't understand what was going on.

Piers chuckled. "Remember when I asked you where India was? Well, now you know how it feels. And I won't be standing trial in Colorado."

"You kidnapped her." Kelly's anger almost choked her.

"Really, Kelly." Piers clicked his tongue. "So melodramatic. But we both know you won't believe a word I say." The phone crackled, and he said, "India, darling. Speak to your sister. She's worried about you."

"Kelly." India came on the line.

Ben swore and turned away. He jammed his hands on his hips and muttered.

"India." Kelly nearly choked trying to wrap her head around India being in the car with Piers. "What's going on? Can you speak?"

"Yes. I can speak." India sighed. "Piers didn't force me to go with him. I made the decision on my own and then called him to pick us up."

Her head whirled and she breathed deep, trying to center herself. Gabe's calm presence provided a needed life raft. "I don't understand."

"Piers and I have been talking for a week or so now," India said.

India had spoken to Piers since he attacked her. That was beyond unbelievable.

India filled the silence. "He's really sorry about what happened to you. He didn't mean to hurt you."

"Yes, he did, India. He tried to strangle me."

India huffed. "He has a temper, Kelly. I told you that. It's best not to argue with him when he's in one of his states, but you argued with him." India paused. "Didn't you?"

"Are you victim blaming me?" Kelly stared at Gabe.

"No." India's voice softened. "I'm sorry. That was uncalled for. I don't know what happened with you and Piers. I wasn't there, but he was really worried about me, and that made him behave in a way he's ashamed of now. He's really sorry though, and he's promised me to make it up to you."

It would be frosty in the real down under before that happened. "And what about what he did to you? The way he threatened Jacob?"

"He's changed, Kelly." India sounded heartbreakingly sincere. "Since I left him, he's been seeing a family therapist to understand why he does these things. He's making good progress too."

Again with the cold nether regions. "How do you know he's not lying to you?"

"You're not married, Kelly. You don't understand how marriage works. There has to be trust, and if Piers tells me he's changed, I have to believe him."

"No, you don't." Her raised voice echoed through the empty house. "What you have to do is get out of that car and come back to Twin Elks. If Piers has really changed, then he won't mind you staying with Dot until he's proven himself."

"We're a family." India sighed. "Jacob needs his father, and I need my husband. Try to understand. Please, Kelly."

She couldn't do it. Couldn't give India the approval she wanted. It was so wrong and none of the crap India was spewing made any sense.

India sighed. "You're angry with me. You've always protected me, and I'm so grateful for that. But I'm all grown up now, and I can make my own decisions. I can't lose my family."

It was on the tip of Kelly's tongue to tell India not to come crying at her door when everything exploded in her face, but she bit it back. If—when—Piers decided to use India as stress relief again, she wanted to make sure she was there for her sister.

"I don't agree with this decision," she finally managed to say. "I think you're making a mistake. But I love you, India, and if you need me, I'll be here."

"I love you, too." India's tone brightened. "And you don't have to worry about me. I won't need you like that again. Piers promised."

Kelly hung up and stared at her phone. "Tell me I'm wrong about this." She looked at Ben. "Tell me I'm full of shit and the odds are really that Piers has changed and will never so much as yell at her for the rest of their lives?"

"Babe." Gabe kissed her temple. "I'm so sorry about this."

Ben winced. "I really wish I could, Kelly."

"How did you know?" She stayed close to Gabe, needing him too much to worry about her future heartbreak.

Ben shoved his hands into his pockets. "When Gabe told me you thought she was in contact with him, I guessed it was only a matter of time. I hoped like hell I was wrong, but the possibility was always there."

Helplessness welled up and choked her. "I don't believe this."

"It happens more than anybody would like it to," Ben said.

"Why?"

Ben shrugged. "Assholes like Piers are masters at playing on vulnerabilities. Somehow, he convinced India she would be better off with him than without him.

Kelly's head hurt and her chest felt tight. "Just this once, can we all please be wrong? Can Piers please have changed?"

CHAPTER
Thirty-One

GABE COULDN'T STAY AWAY. He'd restrained himself from going to Kelly's the night before, but that morning he couldn't fight it.

He was at her door earlier than was strictly polite.

She answered it looking like hell. Deep shadows underscored her eyes, and her hair was a tangled mess.

"Did you sleep?"

Kelly shrugged and walked away from the door. "Not really." She trudged into the kitchen. "Want some coffee?"

"Sure." He guided her to the couch and pressed her to sit. "Why don't I make it?"

The smile she gave him was teeth in a stricken face. "That would be great."

Gabe made the coffee and kept an eye on Kelly.

Her attention was locked on the phone in her hand.

"What are you doing?"

She glanced over her shoulder. "I've been trying India all morning, but she's not answering."

"She could still be asleep." He kept it gentle. "It isn't even eight yet."

Kelly shook her head. "Not India, she gets up early and makes that bastard breakfast. She hasn't even texted me back."

And probably wouldn't, but he kept a lid on that. Piers was cunning, and there was no way he was going to let India have free contact with Kelly, today or any day for that matter. Kelly was India's salvation, and Piers needed to cut that cord. Damn this situation sucked.

"Babe." He eased on the sofa next to her. "I think you're going to have to wait for India to contact you."

Kelly gaped at him. "He could be beating the shit out of her right this minute."

"But you can't do anything about that." He hated having to say it.

"Of course, I can." Kelly glared at him. "I can keep reminding her that I'm here, and she doesn't have to take this."

"She chose this, Kelly." He took her hand. "And until she makes a different choice, you are powerless."

Kelly snatched her hand back. "So, she made her bed and now she has to lie on it?"

"That's not what I meant." And now he really regretted opening his mouth. If Kelly wanted to sit there and stare at her phone, that was her choice. After a few days that had to get tiring, and maybe she would stop. "Forget I said anything."

He returned to the kitchen to finish the coffee.

"It's so easy for you, isn't it?" Kelly stood by the sofa, trembling in her anger. "It's easy for you to walk away from your family. Put them in a box and shove it way back on the shelf until you feel like taking them out again."

The attack left him guessing, and he couldn't fight back. And ouch! "That's not fair, Kelly."

"I think it is." She thrust her chin out, pleading for a fight. "You put thousands of miles between you and them, because God forbid, they should need you for anything." She dragged in a ragged breath. "If they need you, you might fail them. Fail them like you did your dad. And so you stay away. In your head, you even convince yourself they're better off without you."

"Shit." He couldn't stay there or he'd fight back and say stuff he didn't want to. Kelly was upset, and he cut her some slack for that, but it only went so far.

He stalked to the door and yanked it open.

"Oh look." Kelly's voice chased him out the door. "It's Gabe Crowe doing what he does best. Getting the hell out of Dodge."

Gabe resisted the urge to slam the crap out of the door. He got that she was upset, but damn, when Kelly got mad, she tossed the gloves away.

He stormed home, breathing deep the entire way.

Ma and Belinda looked up when he stalked into the kitchen.

He couldn't deal with their questions. "I'm going for a hike."

It took him a few minutes to grab some water and his hiking boots. His backpack was still in the truck from his hike with Kelly.

Damn woman had steam coming out of his ears. Granted, he had put distance between him and his family. He'd also left Ben shouldering the majority of the burden with Ma. Not that Ma needed much, but she did need the connection with her sons, and Ben played proxy for all five of them.

He parked at the trailhead and climbed out of the truck. Crisp, chilly air laden with the musty smell of scrub oak and dried plains grass met him. Gabe breathed it deep. It was one of his childhood smells. It brought back those happy days playing with his brothers outside after school. His long hikes with Dad. Walking into the kitchen and finding Ma there. He saluted Ma, trying to keep all of them in line and losing the battle to sweaty socks and wet towels on the floor.

Ma was due for a sainthood. No doubt about that. Maybe it had something to do with being older, but coming home this time had made him realize how much he missed that sense of family. Having all of them together for Ben's wedding had been great. Even putting up with Luke's prissiness, and Mark's galloping ego. Even tolerating Rafe's asking him about not being a proper doctor.

Small creatures rustled in the brush framing the trail. Icy mud cracked beneath each step he took. Like it always did, the sense of space around him eased his anger and calmed his mind.

"Gabe?" Belinda called from behind him.

Biting back a curse, he turned. Couldn't she understand he wanted to be alone?

Also dressed in hiking gear, Belinda headed down the trail toward him. "Hi." She looked uncertain. "I hoped you wouldn't mind some company."

He did mind. "I'm not in a talking mood."

"Gabe." A dimple appeared in her right cheek, and her brown eyes lit with amusement. "I lived with you for three years; I can tell when you need to disappear into your cave."

Yet, here she was.

"I wanted to get out of the house and ease some of the cricks from that bloody plane ride." She smiled. "I'll be back here not saying a word."

Gabe nodded, because he'd already gone twelve rounds with one woman today and didn't have another twelve in him.

Belinda stayed true to her word, and she kept pace with him easily. Unlike someone who had caused the steam coming out his ears. That woman could get him to steam up in other ways too. Except they'd agreed to cool that off. More like turn it right off.

Jays crashed through the bushes around him. Soaring above them, a red-tailed hawk whistled to its mate. He'd forgotten how big the skies were here. They arced from horizon to horizon in one unbroken, azure curve.

Belinda tapped his shoulder and pointed. "Look."

"Elk." Gabe identified the small herd. "We don't see them that often. Lots of mule deer but less elk."

She breathed deep and took a slow turn. "It really is beautiful. I see what you love so much."

"Yeah." Because wherever he traveled, he always took a bit of Twin Elks with him. He turned and carried on. The magic of being out there in nature soothed him and his mood started to improve.

They reached his place much sooner than he had with Kelly. A slight breeze ruffled the water and sent a light spray from the falls their way.

"Oh, wow." Belinda crouched to cup the water. "Is this where you used to come with your dad?"

He must have told her about that. "Yeah. We loved coming here."

"I can see why." She stood and gave him a misty smile. "Thanks for sharing it with me."

He shrugged, because he hadn't started there with the intention of sharing it with her, but she'd followed him, and he needed the peace being there brought too much to change his direction.

Belinda dropped her backpack on the rocks. "Do you remember that trip we took in Algonquin?"

They'd done a lot of that sort of thing together. "Canoeing and camping?"

"And skinny dipping." Belinda dropped her jacket and whipped her shirt over her head and bent to untie her boots.

"Are you nuts?" He couldn't believe what he was seeing. "You'll get hypothermia."

"Chicken," Belinda tossed over her shoulder. She was long, lithe and tanned and her body had been the first thing he had noticed about her. Then her big easy smile.

The same one she was giving him now as she wriggled out of her leggings.

"You not up for this?" She took off her socks.

Gabe took a seat on a big rock. "Nah. You go ahead. But that water is going to be bitching cold."

"You sure?" She reached behind her and unhooked her bra.

Belinda had great breasts and he was a normal guy with a

healthy libido. He looked, and then she stepped out of her panties and he looked some more.

Shoulders back Belinda stood for a moment, happy to show him what she had. Algonquin had been one of the first trips they'd taken together, back at the time when they had crawled all over each other at any opportunity.

When he still didn't move, Belinda turned and picked her way to the water's edge. She shrieked as she stepped into the pool. "That is freezing."

"Go ahead." He laughed at her shocked expression, but he couldn't leave her alone in frigid water. "I'll sit here and wait for you."

Belinda gave him a coy look. "You sure I can't persuade you to join me?"

"I'm good."

"Yes, you are." She peered from beneath her lashes. "I miss the way we were together. I miss making love with you."

Up until recently, he might have said the same, but now he saw how their relationship had become habit and convenience over the last year or so. They had been good together, shared so many of the same interests and values. They had never even argued about what to watch on television. There hadn't been any reason to change things, until she'd asked for more. That's when it had become crystal clear to him that it wasn't what he had wanted. "Belinda, don't."

She threw up a hand in defeat. "I get it. You don't want to do this. I'll have my swim on my own then."

If he went to Australia, she would see it as an invitation. He'd never spoken about marriage to her, or even hinted at anything beyond what they had, but she'd still thought that's where they were heading. If he'd been less of an ass, he would have left sooner. But he was working for her father, and she'd fit him so well that he'd taken the path of least resistance. For that, he owed her an apology.

The only part of Belinda still visible was her head, which she kept out of the water.

She swam back to the edge and climbed out. Goose bumps covered her skin and she shivered.

"Here." Gabe handed her his sweatshirt to dry off.

"Th-thanks." She rubbed the cotton vigorously all over and then pulled her clothes back on.

Taking a seat beside him, she wrapped the sweatshirt over her shoulders. "Want to talk about what's got you in such a bad mood?"

"Something a friend said." Belinda really wouldn't want to hear about his relationship with Kelly.

She bumped his shoulder with hers. "What did this friend say?"

"They said I walk away from my family all the time. In fact, they said all I do is walk away from people and things."

Belinda wrung water out the bottom of her ponytail. "No, you don't."

"Really?" His lacerated ego needed to hear it wasn't true. But an irritating voice in his head insisted that another person he'd walked away from was the one helping him delude himself. "I walked away from us."

"I changed the rules." Belinda shrugged. "Honestly, you never once said you saw marriage for us. I suppose a lot of my friends were getting married. Some of them having babies, and I wanted that too."

Gabe really looked at her. "Are you saying you've changed your mind about getting married?"

"Yes." But she couldn't meet his gaze, and three years of living with her also gave him an insight into her tells. "I would be happy with what we had."

"Belinda." He needed to be one hundred percent upfront with her. Letting her harbor hope was as unfair as staying when he knew he wasn't in it for the long run. "There is no more you and me. Not like that. You were right to break up with me."

She flinched. "I don't understand. Why can't we go back to what we had?"

"Because that's not what you really want." He put his arm around her. "Not really, Bell. You want the trip down the aisle and the ankle biters. And that's a beautiful dream, but it's not going to happen with me."

"I came all this way hoping you'd had enough time to miss what we had." Her voice wobbled. "And also, to say that you working with my dad is not connected to us. I think he might miss you even more than I do."

It would be so easy to open his mouth and say yes. He'd loved his time in Australia. Going to work every day had never been a hardship. But the words refused to come. Instead he said, "I'm not being a prick. I'll let you know as soon as I do."

Her soft sigh rebuked him. "Is there someone else?"

Again, he opened his mouth to say no, but that wouldn't come out either. He totally copped out. "This is about me, and what I want out of life."

CHAPTER
Thirty-Two

KELLY SCRUBBED her condo from top to bottom. She even attacked the grout between her shower tiles with an old toothbrush, but she still didn't feel any better.

India hadn't called, and she was even starting to think a call from Piers might beat the maddening silence.

She had been a total bitch to Gabe as well, and she owed him an apology. Especially since she suspected he might have been right. There was nothing she could do. India was an adult and she had the right to make her own decisions.

It was torturous to watch her walk right into the fire and ignore everyone screaming at her to get the hell out.

The doorbell rang, and she ran to answer it.

"Hey, Kelly." Ben stood on her doorstep. "I came to see how you were doing."

She motioned him inside. "I'm okay. I keep waiting for her to call."

"I don't think that's going to happen." Ben looked regretful. "If Piers follows a pattern, he'll be trying to regain lost ground with her."

Kelly hated even saying it aloud. "But it won't last."

"Probably not," Ben said.

Her doorbell rang again, and hope reared its head, again. Either India or Gabe would both be a welcome sight.

Instead, Vince stood on her doorstep. "Have you heard from her?"

"No." She held the door open wider. "Ben and I were talking about it."

"I can't stand this." Vince tugged his hair. "I can't stand not knowing what he's doing to her." He glared at Ben. "Can't you do something?"

"Not if I can't find them. I put a call into DPD, and they're not at their house, or anywhere else Piers frequented." Ben shook his head. "I think he's taken her out of state."

"He could be doing anything." Vince balled his fists.

He was not helping at all, and Kelly needed him to stop. "Vince! We need to keep it together here."

"He must have threatened her to make her come back to him. There is no other explanation." Vince paced to her window and stared out.

Kelly exchanged a speaking glance with Ben.

Funny, she didn't think that at all. And God, did she want to think that was the truth. "Vince, I spoke to her, and she said she went willingly."

"She would say that." Vince turned and glared at her. "Because he must have made her say that."

"Vince." Ben got right into Vince's space. "I need you to listen up and listen up good."

Vince glared at him and then looked away. "Yeah?"

"There will be no trying to find them and confronting Piers." Ben's voice was steel hard. "There will be no amateur heroics happening. Not one of us like it, but India has to call this play."

"I can't believe she would go back to him." Vince looked at Ben, beseeching him to tell him it wasn't true.

Kelly empathized, but that didn't make her blind to the truth.

Ben clasped his shoulder. "One of the hardest things to understand is how often the abused partner goes back. The best thing we can do is get on with our lives and accept her decision."

Vince's face tightened. "I can't do that, Ben. I can't accept that anyone would choose this for themselves."

"Me either." Kelly stepped closer to the two men. "But I know my sister, she meant what she said to me on the phone. I made it clear to her that I thought it was the wrong decision, but that I was still here for her if she ever needed me."

Ben gave her a nod of approval. "Good." He gave Vince's shoulder a small shake. "There is nothing else we can do anyway."

Vince glared over his shoulder.

"Okay." Ben's tone changed to pragmatic. "Say you find them. Who do you think is going to pay for that?"

Kelly caught the direction he was headed. "Piers is a bully. He's not going to take you on. Remember he ran away from you the minute he saw you, but he will take his anger out on someone."

"If he touches her, I'll kill him."

Apparently, they weren't even pretending Vince didn't have a thing for India anymore.

"I never heard that," Ben said. "Because if you find them, tempers are going to flare. Shit is going to go down that could land your ass in jail." Ben stared Vince down. "You're a father. You don't get to storm around like a hormonal teenager and do what the hell you like."

Vince's shoulders drooped. "I feel so helpless."

"I get it." Ben clapped his shoulder. "If that was Poppy, I'd be going insane about now."

Somehow Kelly couldn't picture Ben not doing something. For all his advice to Vince, she didn't think it would wash with Ben if Poppy was in danger.

Ben looked at both of them before he said, "If it helps, I've got everybody I can get keeping an eye out for them. If Piers sticks his head up, we'll find him."

That did help, and Kelly impulsively hugged him. "Thank you."

"S'okay." Ben cleared his throat and patted her shoulder. "I also came by because Ma asked you to dinner."

She almost refused, but then stopped. She had an apology to give at the Crowe house, and also a dose of Dot sounded right about perfect.

Ben turned to Vince. "You'd be welcome, too."

"Nah." He shook his head. "The kids are waiting at home for me."

———

Being around Dot soothed Kelly. The way she calmly managed dinner preparations as they talked helped Kelly find her feet again.

Dot shook her head and sighed. "That poor girl. He has her so turned about she's confused about what's good for her."

"I keep thinking I should have seen something in him." Kelly chomped a peeled carrot. Dot had refused her offer of help, which meant she had probably heard what a disaster Kelly was in the kitchen.

Dot gave her a gentle smile. "It would be a much easier life if the bad guys wore black hats and the good ones wore white." She put a salad in front of Kelly. "Toss, please. And darling girl, the reason men like Piers get away with all they do is because they're very good at keeping their evil hidden."

Evil was a good word, and it fit. Piers's handsome, country club exterior concealed a monster.

The carrot turned to chalk in her mouth, so she put it down and tossed the salad. "I've been looking after India since we were little girls."

"I remember." Dot opened the oven, and the most delicious

aroma of roasting pork filled the kitchen. "You were such a ferocious little thing, always standing between India and anything that wanted to hurt her."

"But I failed." More tears threatened, and she gnawed on her carrot before she started bawling again.

Voices from outside drew Dot to the window. "Gabe's home," she said, and her smile faded. "I guess Belinda found him."

Great, and fuck you too, Universe.

Gabe breached the kitchen door and stopped when he saw her. "Kelly." His manner stiffened. "Everything okay?"

"Oh, hey!" Belinda slid her arms around his waist from behind and peered over his shoulder. "This is a nice surprise."

Damn they made a beautiful couple. Standing there in their hiking gear, they looked like one of those gorgeous Pinterest fitness couples.

"Gabe." She managed not to choke on her carrot. She and Gabe were not a thing anymore, because she'd made it like that. "Hi, Belinda. Been for a hike?"

"Yes." Belinda giggled and pressed her nose into Gabe's neck. "We hiked to Gabe's special place. I'm afraid we were naughty."

"Great." Kelly forced the word through gritted teeth. Gabe's special place was clearly his party place as well. Which didn't matter to her because she had ended things.

"We went skinny dipping." Belinda winked at Kelly.

Gabe moved away from her. "Belinda went skinny dipping." He kissed Dot's cheek. "Something smells great, Ma."

"I've got a pork roast going." Dot patted his arm. "Go and get cleaned up, and we'll eat shortly."

He gave Kelly a nod. "See you soon."

Still grinning—and why wouldn't she be if she'd been naughty with Gabe—Belinda perched on the kitchen table. "How you doing, Kelly?"

"Fine." No way she was getting into the India situation with a virtual stranger. A virtual stranger boning the man she was in—

The man she had recently had an arrangement with, of a purely sexual nature.

"Kelly is staying to dinner." Dot filled the loaded silence.

Belinda bared her teeth. "Great." She stood and stretched, giving them all a peek at her taut, tanned tummy and long toned legs. "I better go and jump in the shower." She grinned at Kelly. "Gabe's big on conserving water."

Kelly sat there and absorbed the blow. Another blow to her bruised and battered self. She shoved images of a naked, gorgeous Belinda climbing into the shower with Gabe, their beautiful bodies twining around each other.

Dot tutted and put her hands on her hips. She glared after Belinda. "That one is here to make trouble."

"Gabe seems to like her."

"Gabe broke up with her." Dot leaned over the table and got in her face. "And don't you forget that. Just because Belinda wants a thing a certain way, does not mean she's going to get it."

Kelly nodded, but why wouldn't Belinda get everything she wanted? She was gorgeous, funny, clever. She and Gabe had so much in common and a long and familiar shared history. "Sure."

And suddenly she needed to be by herself and safe in her own home. There was no way she could sit across a table from them at dinner, not when she felt like an exposed nerve ending. "I'm sorry, Dot, but would you be mad at me if I went home?"

"Sweetie." Dot pulled her into a hug. "Of course, I won't. I'm madder that you're leaving me here with that bottom feeder."

Kelly choked back a laugh and managed a smile for Dot before she left.

———

Gabe got a towel around his hips and put some distance between himself and Belinda. The woman had more arms than an octopus, and she'd busted in on him as he was getting out of the shower. "Belinda." He backed away to the bathroom door. "We've had this conversation." Trying to protect her feelings wasn't working. "This is over, and it's not going to happen."

"But Gabe, I saw you at the waterfall today. You wanted me."

Biology was a real bastard sometimes. "What you saw was a natural response."

"Gabe!" Ma pounding on the door was a welcome respite. "Kelly just left." Her footsteps faded down the hall. "She looked upset."

Dammit! Before he could talk himself out of it, he ran out of the bathroom. In his room, he grabbed a pair of sweats and got moving.

"Gabe." Ma followed him out the door. "You're not wearing a shirt."

He waved over his head. "I know."

"Or shoes."

He stepped on a rough stone. "Shit!"

Kelly walked fast for someone who had bitched him out through their entire hike. Her head was bowed and her shoulders hunched, and he despised himself for being even the slightest contributing factor. He hated that they weren't speaking to each other. "Kelly!"

She stopped and turned, then took him in and gaped. "You're half naked."

"You left." He hobbled up to her.

"I'm not good company tonight." She eyed his bare chest with a look that drove the cold out. "And you're going to get sick."

"Listen, I don't want to fight with you." He had to bend his knees to get her to look at him. "I'm sorry about what happened earlier. You're going through hell right now, and you don't need my sanctimonious lectures."

"Oh, Gabe." Her beautiful blue eyes filled with tears. "You're not the one who should be apologizing. I was a total bitch to you."

"I should have backed off." He wanted to touch her, comfort her. Friends hugged friends, so he pulled her against him.

Her warmth sank bone deep into him. His body responded to her curves pressed against him.

She raised her arms and slid her hands up his back. "You must be freezing."

"It's somewhat chilly."

Her laughter warmed him from the inside out. "I really am sorry, Gabe. I don't want to fight either."

"Babe." He kissed her cheek and stamped on the urge to trail his lips across her silky skin and find her full mouth. "We're good. All fixed."

Not really, but as fixed as they could be.

"Gabriel Crowe," Peg bawled from her front porch. "What are you doing out there with no clothes on?"

Damn the old biddy. He called back, "Trying to have my wicked way with Kelly."

"Just like your father." Peg shook her head. "That man had no concept of right time and place."

He could have lived his entire life without knowing that morsel about his father. Before he let her go, he gave Kelly one more squeeze and stepped back before he surrendered to the need to kiss her. "Come and have dinner with us, Kelly."

"No." She managed a smile, but he never wanted to see that haunted look in her eyes again. "I really would rather be on my own."

And what could he do? He wanted to protest and argue, but he had no right to keep her there. "Okay. Call if you need me."

She nodded but she wasn't looking at him.

"Kelly?" He waited until she looked at him. "Call me if you need me."

And some part of him hoped like hell she needed him sometime soon.

He watched her walk away and disappear around the corner before he turned for home.

Arms crossed, Peg scowled at him. "You're an idiot."

Arguing wouldn't do him any good, because Peg was Peg, and he also suspected she might be right.

CHAPTER
Thirty-Three

GABE DIDN'T SLEEP WELL and woke the next morning in a crappy mood. His mood wasn't improved by finding Belinda already up and sitting in the kitchen with Ma.

Ma looked up when he came in. "You look tired."

"Yeah." He helped himself to coffee. "I didn't get a great night's sleep."

"Must have been that fight you had with Kelly last night." Looking annoyingly smug, Belinda drank her tea.

Gabe bit back his irritation. He didn't want to give her the satisfaction of getting a rise out of him. "I didn't have a fight with Kelly last night."

"Really?" She raised her eyebrows. "Because we missed both of you at dinner."

He'd come home, grabbed a sweatshirt and some shoes and gone to the Elk for a beer and a burger and an ass kicking at pool, courtesy of Cara.

Ma gave Belinda a sharp look. "I told you that last night."

"I must have forgotten."

Yeah like hell she had, which brought up a question. "Kelly was upset last night. Did you say something to upset her?"

"What could I have said?" Belinda spread her arms.

He didn't buy that either, but his phone rang, and he checked caller id.

"Hey, Cara. What's up?"

Cara chuckled. "I've got something for you Dr. Wildlife Whisperer. Interested?"

Let's examine his choices. Spend the day with his toxic ex or go and wrangle a critter. "Is it a skunk?"

Cara laughed harder. "Nope. You coming?"

"On my way."

Gabe threw on some clothes and shoes, brushed his teeth and kissed Ma goodbye. "Cara needs a hand."

"I can come with you." Belinda popped up from the table. "Help you. Like I always do."

Ma got her by the arm. "You don't want to do that, dear."

Belinda cast him a beseeching look. "But—"

"No." Ma had raised five big and active boys, and if she didn't want you to get out of her grip, you stayed put. "You're going to stay with me. We'll have some breakfast, do your laundry so you can start packing, and discuss the differences between reality and fantasy." She waved him off. "You go ahead. Say hi to Cara for me."

———

Cara's critter was a fawn, and it was being clutched to the chest of a sandy-haired boy of about ten or eleven. "I found him."

"Where?" Damn this wasn't good. Does would often leave their fawns alone while they foraged. People often mistook them for being abandoned.

The boy's mother looked anxious. "We think it might be sick."

"Let me have a look." Damn Cara for putting this on him. He sent her a look that told her so. Still, it beat the at home alternative, and he examined the fawn thoroughly. It was very young, but there was nothing wrong with it. But he also needed to impart some wisdom.

Colton was looking at the fawn. "Can I keep him?"

"Listen, Colton." He crouched to get eye level with the guy. "When I was your age, I used to rescue all sorts of things. Once even a deer, like you did."

"Did you keep him?"

"No, I put him back where I found him." He glanced at the mother, and she nodded for him to go ahead. "Because often their mothers need to leave them alone so they can feed. They leave them somewhere hidden from predators. Do you remember where you found him?"

"Under a bush." Colton frowned. "Mom and I were out for a walk. I only saw him because my water bottle rolled under his bush. He was lying so still."

"And his mother will remember where she left him." He stood and looked at Colton's mother. "We need to put him back and hope she hasn't returned for him yet. I would put him back and keep an eye on him from a distance."

"Why can't he live with us?" Colton was not giving up without a fight.

"Because he's a wild animal," his mother said, relieving Gabe of the necessity. She scooped up the fawn and cradled it next to her chest. "Now say thank you to doctor Gabe."

"Thank you." Colton didn't look at all thankful as he followed his mother out.

Cara leaned against the doorjamb. "Look at you doing the people thing."

"Shuddup." He joined her in the corridor. "How's Bruce doing?"

"Come and see." She opened the door to the holding area.

Bruce thumped his tail when he saw Gabe. He pointed to the cone. "Has he been at his stitches?"

"He tried." Cara pulled a face. "And now it's the cone of shame for him."

"Poor guy." Gabe crouched and stuck his fingers through the mesh. "Any sign of infection?"

"Nothing." Cara grinned. "I'm going to get him on some gentle exercise tomorrow before the poor guy goes out of his mind."

"Do you hear that, Bruce?" He really was a good-looking dog and Gabe suspected a Great Dane must have been involved in his conception. "Cara is going to take you walking."

Cara chuckled and then shook her head. "I've been even busier lately. I really do need to get on that assistant thing."

"And a receptionist."

Cara made a face at him. "Yeah, but I'm battling to find the right person." She wore a mulish expression. "Apparently I'm not easy to work with."

"No." Gabe faked shock and stood. A Maltese poodle wagged its tail at him. "What's up with him? Neuter?"

"Yup." She motioned the room next door. "I have something interesting on the other side if you want to take a look."

Did he ever. "Let's do this."

They worked late into the evening, and Gabe couldn't say he'd been bored once.

Some people might find Cara difficult to work with, but he liked her attention to detail and how exacting she was when it came to her patients. Twin Elks was lucky to have a vet like her.

He also really liked the way she kept a six-pack of beer in the vaccines fridge.

It was full dark outside by the time they shut the front doors and grabbed a cold one.

Cara took a swig and sighed. "Thanks for your help today." She took another sip. "And I don't think I ever thanked you for getting the prayer chain involved in my business."

He chuckled. "Never underestimate the power of the prayer chain."

"They're scary." Cara snorted.

He pointed his beer bottle at her. "And best you remember that, missy."

Gabe was tired but he felt great. It felt like a long time since he'd had a good time at work and shared a beer with his coworkers afterwards. He wanted to call Kelly and share with her, but that option was no longer open to him.

Rapping on the front door made Cara swear as she got to her feet. "I'm hoping this is pizza and not an emergency."

"Great idea," Gabe called after her. "Did you order pizza?"

"Gabe."

The urgency in Cara's voice got him moving to the front.

The woman standing with Cara looked familiar. As he drew closer, he put the pieces together. It was the mother of the boy who had brought him the deer. "Mrs. Clark. Everything okay with Colton?"

"No. I don't know." Mrs. Clark wrung her hands. "I was hoping to find him here."

"No." Gabe glanced at Cara and she shook her head. "It's just the two of us here. And the animals."

Mrs. Clark paled and squeezed her eyes shut. "I don't know where he is. I don't know where to look."

"I'll call Ben." Gabe grabbed his phone. In Twin Elks they didn't have to wait to report a kid missing. Ben would get right on it. "When did you last see him?"

Mrs. Clark's hands shook as she tried to push a tendril of hair back. "I can't remember. Let me think."

"Here." Cara handed her a paper cup of water and guided her into a seat. "Breathe and think this through."

"It must have been shortly after we left here." She sipped the water and gathered herself with a huge breath. "Yes, that was it. We took the fawn to where we found him. Like Dr. Crowe told us to, and then we came home for lunch. Colton was really worried about the little thing and I said we would check later."

"Did you?" Gabe waited for Ben to answer his phone.

Mrs. Clark shook her head. "No. I got busy, and then I had to pick my daughters up from dancing."

"Hey, Ben," Gabe said as his brother answered. "Can you meet us at the veterinarian's? We need a hand finding Colton Clark." He hung up. Ben would be on his way as soon as he could. "What was he wearing?"

"Umm…" Mrs. Clark pressed a hand to her head. "Jeans, blue jeans and a Titan's sweatshirt."

"Don't tell my brother Mark that." Gabe tried to ease her worry. "He plays for the Strikers."

"Right." Mrs. Clark swallowed and gave him a wan smile. "I knew that."

He crouched at her feet. "Can you tell me where you released the animal?"

"Do you think he might have gone back there?" Hope dawned on Mrs. Clark's face. "I drove past but I didn't see anything."

"It's what I would have done," Gabe said. "When I was Colton's age, I was animal mad."

"So is he." She grabbed his hands in an iron grip. "We should go and look."

"Good idea." Gabe stood and grabbed his coat. He turned to Cara. "Can you talk to Ben when he gets here?"

She nodded.

"Also, get hold of my mom and get the prayer chain working."

Mrs. Clark swayed on her feet. "You don't think he's—the prayers."

"No, it's not that." Gabe put his hand under her elbow. "But in this town, nothing happens that the prayer chain doesn't know about."

CHAPTER
Thirty-Four

GABE DROVE with Mrs. Clark sitting beside him, her knuckles white from clasping them together. "It's getting cold," she said.

"Yup." Gabe drove through town and took the road leading up to the hiking trails. "But we have a blanket."

She shook her head. "I can't believe he would do this."

"Maybe he hasn't." Gabe squeezed her ice-cold hand. "Let's eliminate this possibility and get the prayer chain and Ben working on the alternatives."

They didn't speak much as he drove. A sharp wind tossed bare tree branches around as a new weather pattern moved in. They would probably have snow sometime tomorrow. By which time, they would have Colton safely with his mother.

Shit! If he'd only watched his mouth, Colton wouldn't be out here on his own.

His phone rang and it was Ben. "Hey there. I've got Mrs. Clark with me and we're heading up to Overhang pass."

"I'll meet you there." Ben hung up.

Mrs. Clark guided him close to the trailhead for the hike where she and Colton had left the fawn. Gabe parked and grabbed his flashlight out of the trunk with a blanket.

"I want you to stay here and wait for Ben." He didn't fancy

her chances in her present shoes. "I'm going to take the trail and see what I can find."

"I feel so useless standing here." She was holding it together amazingly well. At least on the outside.

"You're waiting for help, and also in case Colton is closer by than we think." He held up his phone. "Tell my brother I have it on me."

Gabe took the trail at a quick pace, the flashlight lighting his way. He'd hiked the area as a kid all the time and knew it well.

Coyotes chuckled in the distance, but not close enough to be trouble.

He found the area Mrs. Clark had described and crouched to peer beneath the bushes. The ground had been flattened and some branches snapped where Colton had put the fawn back.

The fawn was long gone and larger hoof prints in the old snow on either side of the bush suggested the doe had been back at some point. At least, Gabe could see no sign of a predator having gotten the little creature. But there was also no sign of Colton.

Gabe walked slowly further down the trail, scanning his flashlight over the floor. A boy-sized shoe print had cracked the thin ice layer on the side of the trail.

Colton must have come to check on the fawn without his mother. Gabe owed his own mother an apology for the number of times he'd done this sort of thing to her.

Senses straining in the dark for any sign of the boy, he moved down the trail.

The ring of his phone jarred the silence and made him jump.

"Gabe," Ben said. "I'm coming up behind you."

"Great." Searching through vast black emptiness could take too long. "Maybe we need to get search and rescue out here. It's dark and the temperature is dropping."

Then Ben said, "Any sign of him?"

"Yup. He was here, and it looked like he might have gotten

turned around and gone further down the trail rather than back to the trailhead."

"Damn." Ben drew a deep breath. "I'll call the mountain rescue boys."

They would need them if Colton had gotten himself turned around in the dark. Easy enough in the daytime, the trails looked very different at night. Noises in the dark could all carry threats for one small boy and disorient him.

Gabe remembered that feeling well.

His phone rang again, loud and discordant in the dark. "Ben?"

"They're on their way. I'm almost with you."

"Good." Gabe shone his flashlight around him to orient himself. "Tell them I'm about—"

"Doctor Gabe?" A small querulous voice came out of the dark.

Heart pounding, Gabe stopped. "Gimme a second, Ben." He strained his vision against the dark. "Colton?"

"Doctor Gabe." His name came out on a sob. "Is that you?"

"It's me, Colton." He knew Ben could hear them. "I'm going to turn and wave my flashlight; can you see it?" He spoke to Ben as he waved. "I think I have him."

"Thank Christ." Ben breathed hard. "Is he okay?"

"I'll let you know." Gabe hung up. "Colton, can you walk."

"Y-yes." The voice came from Gabe's left and he moved in that direction.

"Did you hurt yourself?"

"N-no." Colton sounded like he was crying now.

Poor little guy. He must be scared shitless. "Can you tell me what hurts?"

"Nothing hurts." Colton hiccupped. "But I got scared and I had an...accident."

"What sort of accident?"

"The bathroom kind."

Gabe's heart ached for the kid. "I'm sure you did," he said. "I would have too."

"Really?"

"For sure."

The bush crashed and a short form coalesced out of the dark.

Gabe reached for him and picked him up. He didn't give a crap about Colton's wet pants. "There you are."

"Doctor Gabe." Colton's entire body shook with tears. "I was so scared, and then I peed and my pants were wet. Mom is going to be mad because of me going away, and only babies pee themselves."

Ben emerged from the dark and breathed a huge sigh of relief. He kept his voice easy and soft. "Hey, Colton."

"Chief Crowe." Colton's eyes grew huge. "Did you come and find me?"

"Yes, Colton. Your mother is really worried about you," Ben said. "You shouldn't have gone off in the dark like that."

"It wasn't dark when I got here."

Ben clenched his lips together as he tried not to laugh. "You still shouldn't have been here on your own."

"I know."

Gabe wrapped the blanket around Colton and got moving. "Let's get you back to your mother."

"She's gonna yell." Colton sighed.

"Yup." Gabe had no doubt. "And you understand why, don't you?"

"Yeah," he whispered. "I'm not allowed on the trails without an adult."

"But that's where you were." Ben had his dad voice on. "What were you doing there?"

"I went back to check on the deer." Colton smashed his face into Gabe's shoulder and Gabe strongly suspected he was now wearing snot and tears as well as the wet patch on his belly from where Colton clung to him.

The three of them walked in silence until they rounded the trail to the trailhead. Several more vehicles had joined them, and headlights lit the parking lot. As they walked, Ben had called off search and rescue, but it looked like Twin Elks had turned out in full force.

Mrs. Clark ran for him and grabbed Colton. The reunion made his eyes sting. He turned his head away and caught Ben doing the same.

"Gabe?" Ma separated from the knot of bodies. She grabbed him and hugged him. Holding him at arm's length, she checked him out. "You used to do that to me all the time."

"I remember." He gave her another hug. "And I can't tell you how sorry I am."

"Here you go." A woman shoved a cup of coffee into his hand. "You did good."

Somebody else handed him another blanket to wrap around his shoulders.

"You reminded me so much of your father just then." Tears rode Ma's voice. "You looked so like him carrying that little boy out. He would have been so proud of you."

Then Gabe had to hide his face.

After a moment, Ma wriggled clear. "But you don't smell like your dad. You stink."

Ben remained in the center of all the activity, answering questions and moving people in the right direction. Ben belonged there, an integral and valued member of the community. Ben fit.

A weird sensation crept over Gabe, and it took him a moment to put a name to it.

Cal Rogers from search and rescue walked past him and slapped his shoulder. "Give me a call. We could use you."

"Will do." He didn't even have to think about his response, and the weird sensation grew stronger.

Ben crossed his arms. "Ma was right. You looked like Dad out there. And the way you handled Colton was exactly like him."

"Dad would have had me on yard work for the next three months if I'd pulled a stunt like Colton did."

Ben snickered. "True that, but first he would have made sure you were safe."

"I didn't do much." It wasn't like his life had ever been in any danger, and Colton hadn't gone too far. In fact, it could be construed as his fault that Colton had gone out there in the first place.

"No." Ben jabbed a finger at him. "I know that face. What's going on in your screwed-up head?"

Brothers! Always there with a kind and encouraging word. "I told Colton to put the deer back."

"In the middle of the night?"

"No, but—"

"Without his mother?"

"Well, no—"

"Then stop that crap." Ben slashed the air with his hand. "And this crap is really not what Dad had in mind when he told us a man takes responsibility for his actions."

"Maybe."

"What's with maybe?" Ben rounded on him, frowning. "Do you think he would want this for you?"

"What?"

"You aren't responsible for Colton being out here. And you aren't now, and nor were you ever, responsible for Dad's death."

Dave Mills passed them and nodded. "Night, boys."

"Night, Dave."

Peg shouldered her way through the crowd. "Well done, Gabe." She squeezed his shoulder. "We're proud of you."

Shortly after, the area cleared, and he and Ben got into their cars.

His phone was in his hand to call Kelly before he'd even thought about it, but he stopped. Kelly had called it right. The way they were heading could only lead to heartbreak.

If he left.

If.

As his headlights played over the familiar landmarks of Twin Elks, the if grew stronger.

That night, he'd been part of something he hadn't felt in a long time. Community. And not just the search for Colton, but before that when he'd been working with Cara and then drinking a beer after work with her.

For all his grand talk about not enjoying domestic practice, he'd spent his day happily working with everyone's family pets. He finally got what Cara had tried to show him, why she loved her job as much as he had loved his sharks. The thing about being a small-town vet that made it special was that it wasn't only about the animals. It was about the people he touched through their pets.

He liked that sense of connectedness and he wanted more of it. First, though, he had something to do.

———

After a much-needed shower and putting his clothes in the washer, Gabe sat Belinda down in the lounge and asked Ma to give them ten minutes.

"I've got two seasons of *Love Island* to binge watch." Dot kissed his cheek. "Do the right thing, darling."

"Trust me."

She patted his cheek and gave him a misty smile. "Always."

Belinda looked at him and winced. "That's not my favorite expression of yours."

"I'm sure." Because she sure as shit wasn't going to like what came next. But it was time to make some decisions. "Belinda, it's time for you to go home."

"But I just got here." She gave him her quirky smile. The same one he used to tell her he liked when they were together.

It didn't work this time and hadn't worked for a long time. "First off, what you did to Kelly was immature and bitchy."

She gaped at him.

"Kelly is…" So many things and none of them he wanted to share with Belinda. "She's a good friend and a really great girl. You were way out of line to suggest that there was something between you and me."

With a nonchalant shrug, Belinda managed an almost convincing innocent act. "I'm not responsible for what someone infers."

"Yeah, you are." He shut that bullshit right down. "Especially when that's what you're trying to get her to do." Sitting forward, he snagged her gaze. "There is no us, Belinda. Not anymore. And there won't be in the future."

"Gabe." Her eyes filled with tears.

He hardened himself against them. When he'd left Australia, he had been absolutely clear about where they stood. She wanted marriage, he didn't, and they had ended things. Her decision to come was on her. "It's time to go home. Your being here won't change my mind."

She thrust her chin out. "It did the other day at the waterfall."

"Belinda, I got wood when a naked body appeared in front of me. It's biological, and it doesn't mean anything," he said. "Go home. I'll be calling your dad to tell him, but you can give him the message as well. I won't be returning to Australia."

She gasped. "Gabe! Don't be stupid. You love your job. Don't let what happened between us take that from you."

"It's funny you say that." And not in a hardy har har way. "Because that's exactly what you and Steve did to me. I'm good at what I do, and I was a big part of that team, but when things between you and me collapsed, Steve made it as uncomfortable for me to stay as he could."

"He didn't mean to." Belinda couldn't meet his gaze

Yeah, she'd always been Daddy's girl, and if Daddy's girl got mad at someone, then Daddy acted as her henchman. "Yes, he did. He pushed me out and didn't do it subtly either. I'm worth more than that." He held her gaze. "My loyalty to that project was worth more. I won't be going back because you and your father showed me exactly how much I meant to the project, and I can't forget that. I would be stupid to forget that."

She blinked at him. "You're making the wrong decision."

"No, I'm not." He stood. "I've never been more certain of anything in my life."

As she stood, a bitter expression twisted her face. "I suppose this means you're going to South Africa?"

"It doesn't matter." And he wasn't obligated to tell her anything, but he was done with lies and half truths. "I haven't made that decision yet. For now, I'm making the best of being here."

CHAPTER
Thirty-Five

KELLY DRAGGED herself out of bed and got dressed. Only Poppy could and did get her out of bed that Sunday morning. The alternative was to stay in, eat ice cream and binge watch Netflix, and it was putting up quite a fight.

Today was a big day for Poppy, and Kelly needed to stop being a selfish ass. Poppy and Ben were finally moving into their new house, and it was a day for celebration.

Gabe would be there. And she really needed to put that in perspective because in Twin Elks, she'd lay money on most of the town being there as well.

When she arrived at Winters House, her prediction was proven true by the sheer number of vehicles clogging the road.

"Kelly." Peg waved to her and brandished her megaphone. "We need to get this lot organized."

"You're the best person for that, Peg." She ducked past Robin and Donna with a smile and a wave. "I'll go and find Poppy."

"Tell her we're all out here." Peg blew the whistle around her neck. "I'll get this parking snarl sorted."

Kelly quickened her pace, and Peg let fly on her whistle.

"Kelly." Hank Styles leaned against his pickup, an old ball

cap shading his eyes. "You tell Poppy not to let anyone else take her wood items."

"Will do, Hank." She made it to the front porch.

The door opened, and Claire beckoned her inside. "Get in here."

"Hi."

Claire shut the door behind her and leaned on it. "They're out there. Waiting."

"They're here to help." Kelly couldn't quite stop her laughter.

"They're circling." Claire peered through the window. "I'm not sure what to do with them."

"Ignore them?" She herded Claire to the kitchen. Claire always looked fantastic, but it was supercharged today. She had that glow thing pregnant women were supposed to get. Maybe Poppy had called it right after all.

"Brinn, please sit down and eat," Poppy said as she opened the kitchen door.

"I can't." Brinn popped up on her chair. "My stomach wants to get moving."

Poppy caught sight of her and rolled her eyes. "Not even Uncle Finn can get them to eat."

"I'll make some snack boxes." Kelly moved to the fridge. She refused to ask if Gabe was there yet. "Maybe Dot can help."

Poppy and Claire gave her a look loaded with skepticism. "Dot and Gabe are upstairs packing a few last things."

Ben walked into the kitchen and gave her a big smile. "Thanks for coming to help."

"It doesn't look like you'll need me. You have the whole town out there."

Poppy teared up. "Everyone is so sweet."

"Babe." Ben kissed her forehead. "Don't go all weepy on me now. I need you."

With a laugh, Poppy dried her eyes and pushed him away. "Okay, you get out there and get them all organized. Kelly and

WALK ON BY   295

Claire are in charge of supervising the children, and Dot can run with the prayer chain."

Finn walked into the kitchen and winked at Kelly. "Hey, gorgeous."

"Hey, hot stuff. Ready to leave Claire for me yet?"

He put his arms around Claire's waist. "I'm not man enough."

And the man who was man enough but couldn't be, walked into the room.

Kelly got a stronger than usual jolt from seeing him. He didn't look any less delicious than ever with a form fitting long-sleeved T-shirt and jeans. She felt differently about him now. Or had finally admitted to some kind of feelings.

Whatever.

"Don't get tired." Finn kissed Claire's forehead. "And you shouldn't lift anything too heavy."

Poppy looked at Ben, Ben looked at Gabe, Gabe looked at her and they all looked at Finn and Claire.

"What?" Claire bristled.

Finn gave his slow, sexy smile. "So, not quite a secret?"

"I've had four babies." Poppy grinned at him. "I recognize all the signs."

"And I've had five." Dot strolled in. "And you didn't fool me for a minute."

Claire pulled a face. "Maybe a minute?"

"Half a minute." Dot winked at her and pulled her into a hug. "Congratulations, sweetheart. Does Horace know?"

"Know what?" Horace strolled into the kitchen. Finally having had his hip done made him look years younger and a couple of inches taller.

Dot smirked at him, but she would never tell Claire's news. "Mind your own business."

"I'm pregnant," Claire blurted out and then paled. "God, I never thought those words would come out of my mouth."

Horace froze and gaped at her, and then he grinned. "Well, hot damn!"

As if him Horace's reaction had given them all permission to celebrate, the next few minutes blurred into a confusion of hugs and tears, and more hugs.

Kelly did her share of hugging. She ended up in Gabe's arms. The familiar tingles swept through her and she averted her gaze and wriggled out of his hold. There couldn't be any more of that, not for all the wanting and needing in the world.

Finn whistled and brought them all to a stop. "We'll celebrate later. For now, let's get all these people out of our house, so Claire and I can fill it up again."

They all followed Ben to the porch.

He stood there and silence spread over the assembled folk. Even Peg dropped her bullhorn and looked at him.

"Right." Ben pulled a notebook out of his back pocket. "This is how we're gonna do it."

Next time she moved, Kelly was so getting Ben involved. He got people all moving in clear and defined directions, accomplishing the tasks he set them.

Claire had opened the attics of Winters House and given Poppy and Ben a number of beautiful pieces. The rest of the town had chipped in as well with all manner of stuff. They loved their police chief, and they loved his new family, and they wanted to help.

The kids kept Kelly busy and away from Gabe. Not that she caught more than the occasional glimpse of him anyway. He was busy hauling stuff and driving trucks and offloading other stuff.

By seven that evening, the last of the trucks drove away from Poppy and Ben's new house. She, Claire, Finn, Dot, and Horace were the last to leave.

Kelly fed the exhausted children burgers and bathed them and put them to bed. Little Sean was well past it by that point, and it took Dot and Finn to get him settled.

In the kitchen, Finn had opened a couple of bottles of wine, and Claire and Poppy were opening pizza boxes.

The house looked beautiful. High ceilings with large exposed beams crisscrossed the space above their heads. Hardwood floors gleamed beneath their feet, and huge sheets of glass let light in when it was daylight. Now they revealed a quiet, star-studded night and reflected a room lit with a warm, mellow light, and filled with people who cared for each other.

Ben lit a fire in the huge hearth and then held up his glass. "To new beginnings."

"To new beginnings," Horace said and raised his glass to Claire. "Of every sort."

Everyone was tired but happy as they ate pizza and finished off the wine.

Dot yawned first. "I'm sorry to break the party up, but I'm beat." She hugged Poppy first and then Ben. "I'm very happy for you."

"Thanks, Ma." Ben gave his mother the sweetest smile.

Kelly's eyes pricked. The love between mother and son was palpable.

"I need to get Claire home." Finn tugged Claire to her feet.

Horace stood. "And that's my ride."

Dot took Kelly by the arm. "Gabe and I will drive you home."

A few more hugs and they were all on their way into the cold and calm night. Kelly sat behind Gabe as he drove Dot's SUV home. They dropped her off first, and Kelly let herself into her condo.

Today had been such a happy day. Poppy had been through so much to get her happily ever after. And Claire with a new baby on the way, more happy news.

Kelly was thrilled for them, core deep thrilled, but it did highlight where she was in her life. Or wasn't. She'd spent so many years waiting for Vince, convinced that her happiness lay in that direction. In a few weeks, all that had been turned on its ass.

Having Gabe around had kept all those thoughts at bay. And then the disaster around India and Piers had deferred thinking about it again. But tonight, seeing her close friends so happy had made her take a long look at where she was.

It wasn't like she felt she had accomplished nothing. She loved her coffee shop, and she'd built it into a successful business. With Peg onboard, she could grow it further.

She poured herself a glass of wine and flipped on her gas fire. Sitting on the rug in front of it, she had to admit that a small part of her was jealous of her friends. They had found their fairytale and were living it. The same part wanted to whine about her lack of a fairytale ending.

A knock at the door startled her. It was late for visitors.

Gabe stood on her doorstep. "Hi."

"Hi." Looking at him affirmed her decision around Vince. Even if she and Gabe had no future, Vince had never made her heart pound like Gabe did.

He shoved his hands in his pockets. "Can I come in?"

"Sure." She stepped out of the way and opened the door wider. "I'm having a glass of wine. Want one?"

"Sure." In the kitchen, he helped himself, looking so natural and right in her space it made her chest hurt. He shouldn't have been there. This wasn't helping her to stick to her decision. She didn't want him to go either.

Gabe brought his wine over to the sofa and sat.

She joined him there. "Quite a day."

"Yup." He put his glass on the coffee table. "I never thought I'd see Ben get married again after that crapshoot of a marriage to Tara. Today he's got an amazing wife, four great kids, and they moved into a house he built."

"Yeah." It was a happy story. "And Claire is having a baby."

Gabe laughed. "Finn says she's struggling with it. She's scared as hell she won't be a good mother."

"She'll be great." Kelly had no doubts. "Have you seen her with Poppy's kids?"

"Yeah." Gabe turned and took her glass from her. "Which brings me to us."

"Bad segue."

He cupped her face. "What do you say we add our own happy ending to today?"

CHAPTER
Thirty-Six

KELLY FEIGNED sleep as Gabe left her early the next morning. Last night shouldn't have happened. It was a direct result of getting swept up in the happily ever after surrounding her friends.

Last night had, however, confirmed her instinct around keeping her distance from Gabe. The danger to her heart grew with every encounter.

Gabe had left a sticky note on her fridge. *Gone to see a woman about a dog. We need to talk.*

Wasn't that supposed to be her line?

See you later.

Fortunately, the coffee needs of Twin Elks waited for no woman's naval gazing and she got ready for work and out the door at her usual time.

Peg sensed her mood and kept the chatter to a minimum.

She carried on with her day feeling scratchy beneath her skin. Something was very off, and she couldn't put her finger on it. Gabe had been different last night. There had been an unguarded look in his eyes that made her heart beat faster. It also made it hard for her to breathe.

He texted her twice during the day, but she didn't answer

him. She needed to walk her talk and put distance between them.

Still nothing from India. Like she did every day, Kelly sent her an innocuous message. If Piers read the text it would look like nothing more than a quick hello, how are you. But Kelly extended that contact so India would remember she was still there for her.

Vince came in near closing time. They'd dropped all pretense of small talk. "Any word?"

"Nope." Kelly shook her head. She made Vince his regular coffee and sat down at the counter opposite him while Peg closed.

Vince was a good-looking guy and certainly a nice enough one. Any woman in his life would be treated like a princess. Even Chelsea, who he'd never loved, had always gotten the best of Vince.

"Vince?"

He looked up at her, and then he flinched. "Uh-oh."

"Uh-oh what?" She hadn't said anything yet.

Vince jabbed his forefinger at her. "That's the face you get when you're going to ask some sort of penetrating question."

"Really?" She checked her reflection in the stainless steel of the coffee maker. "I have a face for that?"

"Most women do." Vince nodded. "Hit me with it."

She intended to anyway. "Do you think we were ever in love? Like really in love?"

"I was." He looked affronted. "You were my entire world, and I was devastated when you broke up with me."

"But you're not anymore?"

He gave her a sweet smile. "No. Not anymore, but I was for a long time." Then he frowned. "Are you saying you weren't really in love with me?"

"I thought I was." She tried to sort her swirling thoughts. Her head had been doing a vortex impersonation all day. "But if we were really that in love, don't you think we would have tried harder to be together?"

Vince looked struck by that. "I had a baby on the way. I needed to step up and do the right thing."

"But that didn't necessarily mean marriage." Kelly had no idea where she was going with that, but she couldn't make sense of her confusion.

"Not for me," Vince said. "I was raised that way."

That made sense. "Do you think we would have lasted?"

"I can't say for sure." Vince shrugged. "But I would have given anything to try."

"Oh, Vince." He was such a good, honest man and she gave him a hug. "You really are a good guy. I hope my sister is smarter than I was."

"I don't—"

"Please, Vince." She pinned him with a look. "Let's not pretend on this one. You have feelings for India. Strong ones." She kissed his cheek. "And I'm glad you do. If she ever gets her shit together, she's going to need someone like you."

Still blushing, Vince nodded.

"What about you and Gabe?" He turned the tables on her. "What's happening with you guys?"

Kelly breathed through the chest constriction. "He's leaving. We can never be any more than we are."

"That's not what I heard." Vince frowned. "I heard from Ronnie who had it from Cara that she and Gabe are going into partnership together."

The blood drained from her head and she stared at Vince. "What?"

"Ronnie took her poodle to Cara this morning, and Gabe was there. When Ronnie asked Cara about it, she said Gabe had decided to buy into the business." Vince frowned at her. "You didn't know this?"

"We haven't really spoken in the last day or so." Gabe was staying in Twin Elks? And he hadn't told her? She could drive herself mad trying to decipher the whys and wherefores of that.

His note had said he was going to see a woman about a dog. That must have been Cara. She checked her last text.

I'll be around at 7:30. And then another text. *Kelly?!*

They needed to talk, they really did, but she was struggling to pull air into her lungs. She was on the verge of what felt like a panic attack with no idea why.

"Kelly?" Vince hovered over her. "Are you going to faint?"

"No." But she held on to the counter anyway because her legs were like jelly. Gabe was staying in Twin Elks. What the hell did that mean?

Shit! That's where her future dreams stopped. It had been bundled under the general heading of "and they lived happily ever after." There was no detail to that hazy future dream.

She needed to think, so she sent back a text. *Really tired. Rain check?*

He came back immediately. *Sure.*

———

A night's sleep brought no more clarity, but the day following did bring more texts from Gabe. He was getting pissed at her, and she didn't blame him. She couldn't avoid him forever, especially not in a town the size of Twin Elks. A town he was now staying in.

She didn't even really understand why she was avoiding him. But every time she thought of seeing him, her chest tightened, and she struggled to breathe.

Her reprieve ended that evening as she got home from her store.

Gabe sat on the top step outside her condo, his long legs stretched out in front of him.

"Hey." She tried to keep it light as she smiled up at him. "Are you my new garden gnome?"

Face carved from stone, Gabe stood. "Let's take this inside."

"Okay." So, not laughing today. Not even cracking a glimmer of a smile. Her hands shook as she opened her front door and stepped inside. "Can I get you something to drink?"

"No." Gabe crossed his arms. "But you can tell me why you've been avoiding me."

She couldn't answer that. "You didn't tell me you'd decided to stay in Twin Elks."

"You didn't give me the chance." He pointed to his sticky note still on the front of her fridge. "But it does say on there that we need to talk." He held out his phone. "As it does in the barrage of texts I've been sending you."

"So, let's talk." She hung up her coat and dropped her purse. Hiding from him was beyond juvenile. "You go first."

Needing fortification, she put the kitchen counter between them and poured them both a glass of wine. It seemed like the sort of conversation that would need it.

"I realized that I wanted to be here." He shrugged. "As much as I loved what I used to do, I want something different now. My priorities have changed."

"So, you turned down both job offers?"

"I turned the one down in Australia." He shoved his hands in his pockets. "And I sent Belinda back to Australia."

"What about South Africa?"

Gabe stared at her before he answered, "Really?"

"What?"

"We're going to play this that way." Gabe clenched his jaw. "You're going to keep firing questions at me and avoid answering my initial question."

Busted, she sipped her wine and tried to find something to say. Then she got as close to the truth as she could. "I'm scared."

"I get that." He took the other glass of wine and sipped. "What I don't get is why."

"I don't either." And tears pricked the back of her eyelids. "I don't understand why this is happening to me."

He stared at her.

Kelly fidgeted with her glass, caught herself and met his gaze. "What?"

"Correct me if I'm wrong, but I thought you had feelings for me." This new formal Gabe was intimidating. "The entire reason you ended things was to protect yourself."

"Both of us. I was protecting both of us." That was not the problem. Or maybe it was. "You changed the rules, Gabe. You were never going to stay, and I never let myself entertain the notion that you might. I'm battling to switch gears."

"Uh-huh." He didn't look like he was buying a word of it. "Bullshit."

Clearly, not buying. "It's not bullshit."

"Yeah, it is." His eyes had gone onyx hard as he finished his wine. "I have a different theory on Kelly Ashford."

"I'm not interested." He clearly had her confused with someone who would put up with crap.

He came around the island toward her. "You were closest to the truth when you said you were scared." He closed the distance between them until their toes bumped. "But you didn't go far enough. You're terrified."

Kelly held her ground. "That's not true."

"Sure it is." He shrugged. "You're feeling trapped, and you're chewing your leg off to get free."

"I'm not trapped." But that breathing difficulty was recurring. "This. Us. We aren't…" She didn't know what they were.

"And that's how you like it. Isn't it, Kelly?" His gaze bored through to her soul. "You specialize in relationships where there isn't a chance in hell of them growing into anything bigger."

He'd crossed a line now. "What the hell is that supposed to mean?"

"The only other serious relationship you've ever had has been with Vince. A man married to another woman." He shook his head. "It's so much easier for you to be the girl that got left behind than to actually step into the scary world of putting your heart on the line."

"I loved Vince." But had she really? Hadn't she asked Vince that very question yesterday? Vince had come back with a positive yes. He had loved her. But she hadn't been able to say the same. Gabe had cut far too close to the raw truth, and she bit back. "We aren't even in a relationship. So far, we've not been anything more than fuck buddies, and you were more than happy with that."

"Fuck buddies." He stepped away from her. "You really fight dirty, Kelly."

"I fight dirty?" She couldn't believe the nerve of him. "You accused me of being too chickenshit to have a real relationship."

He gave her hard stare. "You choose unavailable men, Kelly, and you do it because you're the one who's not available. It's easier to be the victim though, isn't it?"

She was so angry she wanted to pick up the wine bottle and hit him with it. "Get out!"

"I'm going." Anger darkened his expression. "But let me send that panic attack you're having into a tailspin. Those feelings you have for me, Kelly. I have them for you too. Big time." As a declaration, it lacked a lot in the delivery, but the unflinching truth was right in front of her. "In fact, I've got them so bad that I want to see where they lead. I want to see if this is the real thing because I suspect that for me, it is."

She had to force air into her starved lungs. It sounded a lot like he was telling her he was in love with her. But she was too chickenshit to ask and confirm it.

She wasn't scared of getting involved. She knew how to love. He couldn't be right.

Could he?

Gabe turned and stalked for the door. He yanked it open and looked over his shoulder. "Get your shit together, Kelly. We could have something special here, if you are ever brave enough to reach out and grab it."

CHAPTER
Thirty-Seven

KELLY WOKE the next morning with a heavy head and sticky eyes from crying herself to sleep the night before. She wanted to march up to Gabe and tell him he didn't know anything about her. Demand that he take back his stupid accusations.

She'd had plenty of committed relationships. Except, she couldn't think of one example.

But, what had happened in high school hadn't been her fault. Vince hadn't been to blame either. They both wanted different things, and he hadn't wanted to leave Twin Elks.

Then he'd tried to make it up with her, and she'd been too young and stupid to hear him. And too frightened of getting hurt. Too afraid what Vince wanted from her was a commitment about the future. Young as they had been at the time, Vince had been talking about their future together. Down the road he had been thinking marriage and children.

Her chest tightened and she had to suck in a deep breath. Her heart beat erratically and sweat broke out.

She forced herself out of bed and got ready for her day. As she stepped into the shower, her breathing eased. Gabe's point might apply to her and Vince. She might have chewed her leg off to get out of that. But she'd been eighteen. Who wanted to get tied down at eighteen?

Vince had.

He'd said when she had asked him that he had wanted to take their relationship all the way.

Okay, so Vince was one relationship and a first love. It didn't really count. What about the other men?

She did a mental inventory as she got dressed. One depressing conclusion kept coming back to her. All those relationships had ended because they hadn't been Vince. But if she hadn't, deep down, really wanted Vince and her to grow into a forever thing, did that prove Gabe's thesis?

It seemed unthinkable now, but she might have used Vince as an excuse to get out of all her previous relationships.

Gabe had snuck up on her. She hadn't seen him coming. Not when they had gotten drunk and fell into bed that first night, nor any of the nights following. Not even when he took such tender care of her after Piers's attack.

He'd snuck under her guard. She'd allowed herself to feel for him because he was going away, and it wouldn't cost her anything. By the time she'd pulled back, it had already been too late.

Staring at her reflection, Kelly had to sit down. Gabe had called it.

Now what?

The doorbell rang, and her heart knocked against her ribs. She couldn't decide if she was more hopeful or dread filled that she would open her door and Gabe would be standing on the other side.

With a deep breath, she yanked the door open.

India stood there with Jacob in her arms. A new black eye said it all. Opening her arms, Kelly pulled her sister and her nephew into a hug. She let her senses absorb the reality of them being there. She let all of her take them in.

"Can I come in?" India whispered against her shoulder.

Kelly stepped aside. "Of course, you can."

"I didn't know…" India flinched. "After going back to Piers, I didn't know if I was welcome."

Kelly didn't hesitate. "You're always welcome here."

"He did it again." India pointed at her eye. "And you told me so."

"That doesn't matter. I really didn't want to be right about this." Kelly hesitated. She was relieved India was there, but this time, she was going to wait and hear where India's head was. "You have my support, India, but you can't ask me to accept you going back to Piers again."

India nodded. "I get that. I suppose I wanted too much for things to be right between Piers and me. I didn't want to accept that our marriage was over."

"Is it?"

"Yes. While I was here with you and Dot, seeing how other people were…How Vince treated me. How Gabe treated you. It changed something in me. Even when I was with Piers this time, I couldn't shut the door on the doubts."

"Did you tell Vince you were here?" Kelly took Jacob from her sister and led her to the sofa. "He's been really worried about you. He's contacted me daily."

Taking a seat, India shook her head. She looked sad. "I haven't. I want to call him. It's not that I don't want to see him, but this is all…too much. I need time."

"Fair enough. But I am going to tell him you're safe and here." Kelly wouldn't push her. It wouldn't be fair to Vince to pretend India was anywhere near ready to jump into something new. "What are you going to do about Piers?"

India squared her shoulders. "I want a divorce."

"Do you know a lawyer?" India was a grown woman, and she needed to own this or the worst might happen, and she would turn back around again.

India shook her head. "I thought I could ask around town and see if anyone can help."

"Dot or Peg would be the best people to ask." Kelly took Jacob into the kitchen. "Has he had breakfast?"

"Not yet." India handed him over. "I waited for Piers to go for his run yesterday evening." She giggled. "I stole his car."

Kelly blinked at India. This was a side to India she'd never seen. "You did?"

"How else was I going to get out of there?" India shrugged. "I didn't stop until I crossed the state line into Colorado. He can't press charges here without risking arrest. And it made it a lot more difficult for him to come after me without a car."

"I like it." Finding her first smile of the day, Kelly put Jacob on the floor and fetched a set of blocks India had left behind and put them in front of him. In her kitchen, she put juice into a sippy cup for him. "Are you hungry too?"

"I am." India nodded. "But I can take care of that. You need to open your store."

"I'll call Peg, and she can open." Piers knew exactly where her condo was and this time he wouldn't hesitate to come straight there. Despite India having his car, Kelly had no doubt Piers would find his way back. He regarded India and Jacob as his property, and he would want to get it back.

India blinked at her. "Peg is working for you?"

"Peg doesn't work for anyone." Kelly shook her head. "She works with me, and she's really good at it."

"I'm glad." India pressed her hands to her eyes. "I'm tired. We were in Phoenix. Piers has a house there. I drove through the night, only stopping when I had to. I need to call Ben, so when Piers comes after me, we'll be ready for him."

———

Things moved swiftly from that point. Ben met them at Dot's place.

"We'll keep an eye on you," he said. "I don't mean to scare you, but wherever you are is our best bet of finding him."

"I know that." India blanched but seemed resolved. "But I'm not going to sit here and wait for him to find me. I've given enough of my life to him already."

Kelly glanced at Dot. This was not the same India who had arrived broken and fragile the last time. "Do you have a plan?"

"Not so much a plan, as a list of things I need to organize." Her hand shook as she lifted her coffee cup. She wrapped both hands around it. "Jacob and I need somewhere to stay."

"You're welcome here," Dot said.

"Thank you. And it's really kind," India said. "But Jacob and I need somewhere more permanent. I'm going to need a job of some sort as well. But first, I need a lawyer and a good one."

"Right." Dot clapped her hands, startling Jacob. "I'll activate the prayer chain."

Those words chilled Kelly to the bone. The prayer chain had unfathomable powers. "Okay."

Dot hit the phone lines. Two minutes later, Karen came back with the name of a divorce lawyer in Denver. Another ten minutes later, the lawyer called India and agreed to meet with her.

The phone rang again, and Dot picked it up. "Yes, Darla." She made listening noises for a few minutes and then hung up. "That was Darla," she said. "She has a very nice three-bedroom bungalow on Cedar available for rent. It has a reasonable back yard for Jacob. The rent is manageable, and it's close to St. Stephens daycare." She glanced at India.

India was looking a little overwhelmed, so Kelly answered. "Tell Darla we'll be happy to take a look."

"Next. A job." Dot tapped a pencil on her notepad. "Does India have any skills I can work with?"

"Umm…she worked as an executive assistant before she got married."

"Perfect." Dot beamed. "Cara and Gabe are in desperate need of someone to run the admin over at the veterinary hospital."

It was like standing in the middle of a five-lane highway as rush hour descended on you.

"Darla will show the property to you tomorrow morning." Dot stood up. "India and Jacob can stay here until they find something. All right?"

"Um...yes." India nodded. "That's wonderful. Thank you."

Dot leaned over and patted her hand. "You Ashford girls are always part of Twin Elks. You were born here and raised here and that makes you ours to look after."

Kelly was so grateful she could cry, but India was drooping in her seat. "Why don't you go and rest?"

"I think I will." India stifled a yawn and stood. Her phone rang, and she checked caller display.

By her pallor, Kelly guessed it was Piers, and she stood and motioned for the phone. "I can take it."

"Or me." Ben held his hand out.

India shook her head. "I've been ignoring his calls all night. I need to do this." She left the room as she answered the call.

Kelly toyed with the idea of following her, but Dot was right, India needed to lead the way. They could all help and support her, but India would make the decisions that needed making.

It being Twin Elks, Vince's arrival on Dot's doorstep wasn't exactly a surprise. He looked at Kelly. "Is she okay?"

"She seems...stronger." Despite her black eye. "I haven't gotten the details yet, but she arrived a couple of hours ago and said he'd done it again."

"Fucker." Vince glanced at Dot and paled. "Sorry."

"Not at all." Dot bustled around bringing coffee and her famous coffee cake to the table. "Fucker about covers it."

"She's spoken to a divorce lawyer." Kelly dared not look at Dot, or she would start laughing hysterically, and given the last forty-eight hours, it might take a straitjacket to shut her up again.

"Good." Vince took a seat at the table. His shoulders slumped. "Thank God."

Kelly really hoped his relief and optimism were signs of what was to come.

Ashen and shaking, India came back into the room. She saw Vince and stopped. "Hi."

"Hi." Vince stood and cupped her face gently. He examined her eye. "You doing okay?"

"Mostly." Her hands shook as India pushed her hair back off her face. "I told him I wasn't coming back. And that I wanted a divorce."

"That must have been very hard to do." The tender way Vince looked at her sister brought a lump to Kelly's throat. Vince looked at India as if she was his entire world. Kelly had always dreamed of someone looking at her like that.

Someone does, whispered a tiny voice inside her. *You're just too scared to see.*

India let Vince pull her into a hug. "He was furious. He threatened me."

"It's the way with cowards like that." Vince held her close to him. "But you don't have to be scared. We've all got you."

"Amen," murmured Dot. "We're all here for you, girl."

———

Gabe heard the news about India's return with his face in snapping distance of a pissed off German shepherd.

"That poor little mite of a girl." Kathy shook her head. "To think of that happening to such a gentle soul."

The dog with the fishhook embedded in her gum was not a gentle soul, and she rumbled a deep warning for Gabe to get the hell out of her mouth. "Kathy, I'm going to have to sedate her to get this out. How did it happen again?"

"Chris's bait box." Kathy looked at her dog with concern. "Baby likes to get in there and eat the old bread."

Baby had her eyes fixed on his jugular. "Right. Well, Cara and I will get that out and give you a call when you can pick her up."

After Kathy left, he walked Baby through to the work area.

Bruce got up from his bed beside Gabe's desk and wagged his tail.

Gabe motioned him back. Bruce was always up for playing, but with Baby in pain and scared, he didn't think it was a good time for a meet and greet. He got Baby's shot ready as he waited for Cara. They also really needed some help behind the scenes.

"You heard?" Cara bustled through. "About India?"

"Yeah." He motioned at Baby. "Give me a hand?"

Cara picked up the syringe. "You hold her; I'll give her the shot."

"Ah, no." Gabe took the syringe back. "You hold. I jab."

"Chivalry really is dead." Cara approached Baby and caught her head against her shoulder.

Moving quickly, Gabe got the shot done. "You're okay, girl." He rubbed Baby's ruff. "We'll get that out for you, and you'll feel much better."

Baby slumped against Cara and Gabe picked her up and put her on the nearest examination table.

"Are you going to call Kelly and see if she's coping?" Cara hovered as he examined the hook. "Damn! That thing is jammed in good."

"Really, Captain Obvious." He glanced over his shoulder. "And nope."

Cara leaned closer. "Good thing she didn't swallow it."

"Thank you, God." Gabe got a pair of cutters and cut one side of the hook. He pulled the barbed end out and fresh blood flowed from the wound. "That should put her in a much better mood."

"I'll get a cage ready for her." Cara moved to the recovery room. "Wanna give her some antibiotics?"

Gabe nodded. "To be safe, we'll keep an eye on her overnight. Take a couple of X-rays. She got into a bait box, and I want to make sure she didn't swallow anything else."

"Is there a reason you're not calling Kelly?" Cara propped her shoulder against the doorjamb.

Gabe carried Baby to her cage and lowered her to the blanket. He gave her a shot of antibiotics. The rest Kathy could give orally for a couple of days. But that wound should clear up quickly. "Don't you have patients?"

"Nope." Cara shrugged. "I have this hot as shit new partner, and we get through double the patients in half the time."

He gave her a mock bow. "Things with Kelly and me are—"

"Don't say complicated." Cara held up her hand. "Or I'll jab you with what's left of Baby's shot."

"So vicious." He faked a shudder. He might not have worked with Cara for long, but long enough to understand she wouldn't back off when she wanted to know something. "She's not ready for what I want."

"Uh-huh." Cara nodded Yoda-like. "Which would explain why you're wimping out and staying away from her."

Now that was pushing it too far. "How am I wimping out? She's got a thing about serious commitment."

"Dude." Cara made a face at him. "I have commitment issues; Kelly has a case of the jitters."

Gabe returned her hard stare with one of his own. "Why don't we discuss your commitment issues instead?"

"Nope." Cara shook her head. "You only get to have an opinion on my love life when you sort out your own. And as mine is currently nonexistent…" She shrugged.

What the hell, he was fresh out of ideas. "What do you think I should do?"

Cara's look was scathing. "That's up to you to decide, but if a girl is scared, it's because she's scared of getting hurt. So, it seems to me, the best thing a guy can do is convince her he's got her back, and he's there to stay." She shook her head. "And I don't see keeping your distance as a good strategy to convince her of that."

CHAPTER
Thirty-Eight

KELLY WENT STRAIGHT to Dot's house once she'd closed the store for the day. Dot had set up the appointment for them to see Darla's house and India was keen.

Unlike the last time, India didn't seem paralyzed by fear. She had an air of determined resolve that despite the last time, made Kelly hope that India was done with Piers.

They met Darla at the property, and she handed them the key. "Take a look around, and I'll be back."

Darla left, and they walked up the paved walkway through a large grassy yard, brown, but it would be a lovely green swathe in summer. Deep flowerbeds bordered the front of the house, ready for spring color.

A shaded front porch, which would look great with a few hanging pots and a couple of rocking chairs, guarded the wooden front door. The inside was charming with a lot of the original trim. A central entrance hall led to a living room on the left, which then opened up into a dining space and open-plan kitchen.

On the right, a passageway led to an office, then two bedrooms and a shared bathroom, plus a master suite. Large windows let in lots of light that made the hardwood floors gleam throughout.

There was plenty of space for India and Jacob, and a dog for Jacob. Except, India was scared of dogs, so no dog. Which was a pity, because the yard was custom made for a couple of kids and a big, playful dog.

Kelly could see it now. A fresh coat of paint would freshen everything. The kitchen appliances looked to be in good condition and the quartz countertops and light cabinets gave the kitchen a light and airy contemporary feel.

She could picture India on the other side of that island, getting Jacob a snack. A male figure entered Kelly's picture and it wasn't Vince, because when she really examined the picture in her head, that wasn't India in the kitchen.

She could picture herself there. The kids, the dog in the yard, all hers. Kelly needed to sit down, so she plopped onto one of the counter stools.

"Are you okay?" India looked at her. "You look faint."

Kelly couldn't talk about it. "What do you think of the house?"

"It's okay." India wrinkled her nose. "It's not really my thing. I much prefer something newer and more modern."

"Like my condo?"

India smiled. "Exactly."

It didn't take a massive mental leap to arrive at it being her house and not India's. Further possibilities unfurled, like perhaps Darla would be interested in selling and not renting the house. Maybe India could take over her condo.

And Kelly couldn't believe she was even thinking that way. She had walked into the house less than ten minutes before. To put that in perspective was to remember that three days before, she'd been having a panic attack about commitment.

Since she'd entertained the idea, it wouldn't go away.

"Kelly?" India gave her a searching stare. "What are you thinking about?"

"I'm thinking if you don't like this house it would be perfect for me."

India wrinkled her nose. "Really?"

"Really. And then you and Jacob could stay at the condo."

India gave it some thought. "That sounds really workable. Of course, I'm not sure how I'm going to be financially. I could take that job at the veterinary hospital."

"Fortunately, you're on good terms with the current owner and we can work out a deal." The more she spoke, the more excited Kelly grew. In her imagination, she filled the house with furniture.

She needed to stop and not get ahead of herself. Darla hadn't even said the house was for sale. "Let's go chat with Darla."

"Are we doing this?" India looked half scared and half excited.

Kelly pulled her into a hug. "We're doing this."

Darla was waiting outside when they got there.

"Would you consider selling?" Kelly turned and looked at the house. She really did love it.

Darla frowned. "I hadn't." She raised her eyebrows. "I mean, I suppose I could. Pete was telling me the other day I should consider it. Apparently, we have more people looking for houses in the area."

"Let me know." Kelly tried to keep her excitement contained. "Either way, I'll take it."

"For India?" Darla glanced at India.

"Nope." Kelly couldn't stop her grin. "For me."

The next day she brought Poppy around to see the house. The children came with them and immediately started chasing each other around the yard.

"It's a great house," Poppy said. "But isn't it rather large for one person?"

Kelly needed to talk things through with someone. "I've been thinking lately that it might not always be me."

"What?" Poppy gaped at her. "Are you and Gabe—"

"No." She could stop Poppy's question but not the stab of pain that followed it. "Gabe and I are not a thing anymore."

"Why not?" Poppy wore that expression that meant she wouldn't stop until she got answers. "Ben was saying the other day how awesome you guys are together, and now that he's staying, I don't see the problem."

"Well." She wished she understood. "It seems I have issues around getting into relationships. Specifically, around trusting other people enough to let them all the way in."

Poppy frowned and looked thoughtful. "Did Gabe say that?"

"Amongst other things." Things that still echoed in her mind and pounded into her bruised heart. "He says that's the reason I've been so hung up on Vince all these years. Because it's less risky to love someone who isn't attainable."

"Wow." Poppy looked impressed. "I wouldn't have thought Gabe could put that together."

"You think he's right?" As much as she might not want to hear it, Poppy would give her the truth.

Poppy linked her arm through Kelly's. "I think your parents did a number on you. You protected India from the worst of it, but they taught you it wasn't safe to love."

"I suppose so." She hated talking about her parents. Nothing she'd ever done had been good enough. "But since Gabe said that, I can't get it out of my mind." She gave up on her brave face and let the hurt come. "I can't get Gabe out of my mind."

Poppy hugged her arm. "Are you going to do anything about that?"

"I'm not sure I can do anything." She stomped on the inner voice calling her a coward. "He's really angry with me."

"I would guess he's more hurt than angry," Poppy said. "Dot says he fell hard for you."

Kelly stared at her friend. "How much gossiping are you all doing about me and Gabe?"

"Enough." Poppy grinned. "And in case you were

wondering if we're the only ones, we're not. In fact, Ronnie has a pool going."

"On whether we get together or not?"

Poppy snorted. "Nah! On how long it takes."

———

After Poppy had taken the children home, Kelly locked up the house and went to see the bank. The news there was very positive, and she hurried around to tell India.

India and Jacob were taking advantage of the mild day and sitting in the garden on a blanket. It was a huge difference from the India of a few weeks before who had cowered inside Dot's house.

"So, it looks like I'm getting a house." She couldn't contain her good news.

India grinned and got up and hugged her. "That's awesome. Does that house come with a man?"

"You too." Kelly rolled her eyes. "I didn't peg you as being a big fan of marriage."

India shook her head. "What do you mean? I've already placed my bet with Ronnie."

God, that hurt more than it should.

"Kelly?" India looked at her. "I'm sorry. I didn't mean to upset you."

"You didn't." It wasn't India's fault. "It's more the situation."

Sitting down on the blanket again, India motioned Kelly to join them. "Trusting someone enough to love them can be terrifying."

India was a survivor of that. "Do you think you will again?"

"I'm fairly sure I will." India took the grass Jacob was gnawing out of his mouth and replaced it with an apple slice. "Vince came around last night, and we talked."

"And?" If Vince was pushing India, he'd have her to deal with.

"It was nice." India shrugged. "We both got honest about how we felt, but it's also too soon for me. He said he was happy to wait."

Staring at her sister, Kelly knew she didn't have that sort of courage. "How do you do it? How can you be brave enough to take another chance?"

"It was easier for me." India took her hand. "I had you to hide behind. Mom and Dad didn't matter so much to me, Kelly, because you made sure I had all the love and attention I needed."

"I don't think I know how to love like that," Kelly whispered her greatest fear. What if she was not only unlovable, but also lacked the ability to love?

"I don't think you have to worry about that." India looked so certain. "Because everything I know about love, I learned from you."

Car brakes screeching made Kelly look toward the road. Piers jumped out of the car and Kelly leaped to her feet. "India! Get inside."

India scooped up Jacob and ran for the kitchen.

"You." Piers rounded the hood and stormed toward her.

Kelly got between him and the kitchen door. "Get away from her."

Piers made a grab for her. "Get out of my way."

"No." Kelly pushed in front of him.

"Bitch." Piers raised his hand.

Something flashed in her peripheral vision and a broom came down on Piers's head. "Don't you touch my sister!"

Piers gaped at India for a second and then anger darkened his face. "You'll pay for that."

"No, I won't." India swung the broom and caught him across the shoulder.

Piers lunged for her, and Kelly slammed her shoulder into him. It hurt like hell but stopped him long enough for India to hit him twice more.

Snarling, Piers caught the broom. With a yank he ripped it out of India's grip and tossed it away.

"Run." Kelly grabbed the back of Piers's shirt. "Run inside and lock the door."

"No." Pale and shaking, India stood her ground. "I'm not running anymore."

"Get your stupid fucking ass in the car." Piers grabbed India's arm.

India flinched and tried to tug away. "No, I'm not going with you. I'm staying here."

"Like hell you are." Piers tried to yank her, but Kelly hung on to him for dear life, and he tried to shake her off.

An enraged bellow stopped them, and they turned toward it. Peg ran down the road and vaulted Dot's wooden fence. She came at Piers like a juggernaut and slammed her fist into his solar plexus. "You son of a bitch!"

Eyes boggling, Piers bent over and retched.

Peg exploded into full on karate kid, punctuating each word with a punch or a kick. "Don't. You. Ever. Touch. Another. Woman."

Piers's knees hit the ground, and he toppled over, his arms shielding his head. "Get her off me."

But Peg wasn't done. She grabbed a handful of his hair and yanked his head back.

Piers screamed.

"Men like you make me sick." Peg bared her teeth. "You're cowards and you're bullies and you get your kicks hurting people who are weaker than you." She shook his head like a terrier with a rat. "But remember this, you little bitch, some of us fight back."

Peg hauled back and kicked him in the ribs.

"Ah...Peg." Ben was there, calm and in charge. "Can I take it from here?"

In all the action, Kelly hadn't seen him arrive, but he was standing between Piers and Peg.

"You're lucky." Peg sneered at Piers. "Ben saved you."

Kelly was sure of it. She put her arm around a convulsively shaking India. "Are you all right?"

India's teeth chattered as she nodded. "I s-stood up to him."

"Yes, you did." Sudden laughter rushed through Kelly—a reaction to everything that had happened—and once she started, she couldn't seem to stop.

It was infectious, and India and then Peg joined in.

Shaking his head, but smiling anyway, Ben hauled Piers to his feet and cuffed him. "Your luck ran out."

"India? Baby?" Piers turned pleading eyes at her. "It won't happen again. I promise you. On Jacob's life."

"No, it won't." India stopped laughing long enough to say, "Because I'm divorcing you. And I've hired a lawyer, and she's going to make sure Jacob and I live comfortably for the rest of our lives."

"That's our girl!" Peg hugged her and then dragged Kelly into a group hug. "We did it. We got that piece of shit good."

Well, Peg had done the biggest part. And India.

India had slayed her demons, and now it was up to Kelly to do the same.

CHAPTER
Thirty~Nine

AS MUCH AS she wanted to rush right over and throw herself on Gabe's mercy, Kelly had a few things to take care of first. Also, she was stalling because she was scared, but she wasn't admitting that to anyone.

"What if he says it's too late, or that he's changed his mind?" She had asked herself that question so many times she was ready to scream. She gave herself the same answer India had given her when she asked. "But what if it's not too late, and he feels the same?"

It took her only five minutes at the rescue center to pick out the dog she wanted. A retriever mix with awkwardly long legs and a way of scrunching up her face in a doggy smile.

Darla had named her price for the house, and Kelly had agreed without haggling. Whatever happened with Gabe, she was going to get on with that part of her life.

She named her dog Cricket and took her place in the waiting room beside Doug and his yowling cat.

Cara walked into the waiting room and stopped. "Kelly? What are you doing here?"

"I have a dog." Kelly pointed at Cricket. "I brought her for a checkup."

"Right." Cara gave her an assessing smile. "Did you have anyone particular you wanted to do that checkup?"

"I thought Gabe." She tried to keep it casual.

Grinning, Cara pointed. "Second door on the right."

"Hey?" Doug sat up straight. "We were here first."

"Doug, sweetie." Cara could go one hundred percent Hollywood starlet when she wanted to. "I'll take care of your kitty for you."

Doug blinked at her, opened his mouth and snapped it shut again.

While Kelly waited in the room with Cricket, she tried to work on her speech. It was probably the most important conversation of her life so far, and she couldn't think of one thing to say.

Her plan had been to get a dog and a house and show Gabe that she wasn't scared of commitment or settling down. The rest of it remained under a hazy notion he would take it from there.

The door opened and she jumped.

"Kelly?" Gabe stood in the doorway, frowning. "What are you doing here?"

"I got a dog." She pointed at Cricket. "Her name is Cricket, and the pound said I should bring her for a checkup."

He looked better than ever. How could he be even better looking in person than in her mind? The white coat was giving her all sorts of ideas that were hindering her ability to speak even more.

He took a careful breath and closed the door. "Do you have any information on her?"

"The shelter gave me this file." She handed it to him.

Gabe took the file and opened it. He stared at the top sheet for a long time and then growled. "What are you really doing here, Kelly? And what's with the dog?"

"She's mine, and I'm going to take care of her." Kelly stroked Cricket's silky black head. "She's going to live with me in my new house."

"You got a house as well?" His brows rose to his hairline. "Why?"

"Because I'm getting my shit together."

Gabe gaped at her. He leaned against the examining table. "You're gonna have to spell it out for me, because right now, I feel like a dumbass."

"You said if I got my shit together, we would have something special." Her mouth was so dry she needed to stop and swallow. "You said all I needed to do was reach out and grab it. So I am."

"Am what?"

"Reaching out and grabbing it."

He stilled, his gaze boring into her. "All the way in?"

"All the way." If India could stand up to Piers, she could be brave. "I'm in love with you."

Gabe blinked at her. "What?"

"I said I'm in love with you." It came out easier the second time, and she squared her shoulders. "I'm in love with you, and I love you."

"Are you sure?"

He was pissing her off. "Yes, I'm goddamn sure."

"Why are you yelling at me?"

"Because you're not telling me you love me back."

"Well. I do. A lot. A whole helluva lot. So much that it scares the crap out of me."

They were both so loud that they must have been easily heard from the waiting room. "Then why aren't you kissing me?"

Gabe grabbed her. "Damned if I know."

Epilogue

THE WIND WHIPPED the snow against the fifties cement block of the Twin Elks Public Library and sent fat flakes pattering against the windows.

Secretary stared at the empty place and sighed. "I never would have thought this, but I actually miss her."

"She stays close to Claire these days," Treasurer said. Then a smug grin spread over this face. "Now that she's having a baby."

Social Media looked confused. "Do ghosts have babies? I didn't think—"

"Claire is having the baby, dear." Chairperson leaned forward and patted her hand. She turned to Treasurer. "How is Claire doing?"

"Glowing and growing." Treasurer crossed his hands over his chest and smirked. "Any time now. Which reminds me, we need to wrap this up."

Counter Intelligence snorted over her knitting. "If it's a boy, gonna call it Horace?"

"God, no." Treasurer responded instantly. Then thought about it for a moment. "Maybe as a second name. Tradition and all that."

Catering sighed. "I like babies. Never had one of my own, but I like them anyway."

"It's not too late." Chairperson gave her a smile of encouragement.

"Yeah it is." Catering folded her arms. "Besides which, haven't got the patience to put up with any man long enough to get myself one."

"Right." Secretary tapped her gavel. "I call this meeting to order."

Treasurer looked over and winked. "I love when you get all bossy."

Secretary blushed.

Chairperson giggled and said, "If you like bossy, you're dating the right person."

As much as she wanted to object, Secretary was honest enough not to. "Reports?"

"Operation High School Sweethearts was a fail." Communications looked forlorn. "And I was sure it would work out. There were frissons."

"There still are, dear," said Chairperson. "They're just frissons in another direction. We could change direction and call it Operation High School Sweethearts' Sister."

Secretary shuddered. "That sounds all kinds of wrong."

"You're right." Chairperson chuckled. "But they're so sweet together. He's so loving and patient with her."

Communications sighed. "But the operation was still a failure, and because High School Sweethearts failed, we also have to admit Operation Veterinarian failed."

"But he's back, and he's staying." Chairperson got misty eyed. "And I couldn't be happier."

"Indeed." Secretary beamed. "So, what's next in our commitment to revitalize Twin Elks by actively growing the community?"

"There's that new yoga teacher." Communications looked around at the table. "The one who renovated the old bakery."

"Hmm." Chairperson tapped the table in front of her. "Counter Intelligence? I think we need more information before we act."

Counter Intelligence finished casting off her stitch before she said, "On it."

"Next item on the agenda." Secretary consulted her clipboard. "The ongoing social media campaign."

Everyone looked to Social Media, who preened a little. "Well, I did try to report last time."

"But it wasn't on the agenda." Secretary tapped her clipboard. "And if we don't stick to the agenda, what's left?"

Everyone waited.

"Anarchy." Secretary smacked the table with her clipboard. "Utter and total anarchy."

"Sounds like fun." Chairperson giggled.

"I have established our town on most social media platforms," Social Media said. "I have stressed the family values and also…" She cleared her throat and looked coy. "The number of available persons."

The committee stared at her.

Chairperson asked the question on most minds. "What does that mean, dear?"

"I mean that I have created the impression that Twin Elks is a town with many people who are aching to find that special someone." Social Media blushed. "I have encouraged newcomers to say they're new in town. That way people can try them out."

Secretary's eyes started out of her head. "Like a real life Tindr?"

"What's Tindr?" Treasurer looked to Chairperson, who averted her gaze.

"Nothing quite so distasteful." Social Media looked affronted. "Merely the suggestion that we are a town of single people who would be amenable to other single people."

"No wonder we've got all these horny men running around the town." Secretary gaped at her.

"What horny men?" Counter Intelligence put her knitting down. "I haven't seen any. Where are they?"

"I'm sure you meant well." It was clear by Chairperson's expression that she was struggling to find something more encouraging to say. "But why did you not discuss this with us first?"

"I tried." Social Media puffed up indignantly. "I tried, but you said I couldn't talk about it because it wasn't on the agenda. And it's been ages since our last meeting, so I kept on doing what I had been doing."

"Oh, dear." Chairperson glanced at Secretary, who shrugged. "She's not wrong."

Chairperson's phone rang.

All gazes swung her way.

"No cell phones." Secretary rapped the table.

"I think your rules have caused enough mischief," Chairperson snapped back and checked caller ID. She frowned. "It's my son."

"Which one?" Communications tried to peer at her screen.

"Something must be wrong. It's after midnight in New York." Chairperson answered the call. "Luke?"

"Mom?" Luke's raspy, deep voice sounded strained. "I'm in trouble, Mom. I need to come home."

There are currently four books in the Passing Through series. If you want more of Twin Elks, Colorado—the town where love comes to stay—check out book #4 in the series, Running On

Empty. The series order is Drove All Night, Ticket To Ride, Walk On By, and Running On Empty. They are all standalone novels, but you always get a little extra if you read them in order.

————

————

Ten little fingers and ten perfect toes mean Luke Crowe's in trouble.

Luke Crowe has everything a man could want—looks, a great job, a healthy bank account, and near-legendary luck with women—until an ex-girlfriend drops a surprise package on his door in the form of his six-week-old daughter, Daisy.

Always a man with a plan, Luke goes home to sleepy Twin Elks, Colorado, and his mother. However, his mother, Dot, is not that eager to put her life on hold and raise Luke's daughter so he can keep his life on its current course. Suddenly, Luke must devise a new plan and one that shouldn't involve the town veterinarian and pin-up gorgeous Cara Addison.

Cara is a Twin Elks enigma. Any attempt to date Cara lands the male residents of Twin Elks in the friend zone. Until smooth-talking, smoking-hot Luke Crowe comes to town and challenges her man moratorium. But Cara has a good reason for swearing off men—her controlling and abusive ex-husband.

Reeling from her previous marriage, Cara is unable to trust her judgment when it comes to men. With a new daughter and his life spinning out of control, Luke has no room for once-bitten-twice-shy Cara. As their attraction tugs the couple closer together, both of their pasts keep pulling them apart.

It's that time again—when the charming residents of Twin Elks must prod, pester, and persuade these two strangers to give up their ideas of passing through and take a chance on love.

Chapter One

Luke Crowe's legendary luck with women ran out 35,000 feet above New York as his flight to Denver reached cruising altitude.

Daisy screwed up her eyes, went puce in the face, and screamed. Luke huddled in seat 2B, caught like a rabbit in headlights as the new most important female he'd ever know screeched her displeasure.

The buttoned-up suit sitting in 2A slid him the horrified side eye and valiantly kept his gaze on his laptop, pretending for all he was worth that there wasn't a thoroughly pissed-off six-week-old yelling her objections directly into the ears of God.

In return, Luke managed a constipated smile, the sort of I'm-sorry-but-there-is-precisely-nothing-I-can-do-and-babies-are-babies more grimace than a grin that he'd seen mothers in crowded and public spaces flash. That just two days ago, he'd been 2A offered no consolation.

Putting Daisy against his shoulder, he patted her tiny back, his palm covering her from diaper to neck and a tangible reminder of her fragility. Fuck, she was tiny and so vulnerable, and his to keep safe for the rest of her life. Terror tiptoed up his spine.

———

For first dibs on news, deals, and giveaways, and so much more, join the @Home Collective

Or if Facebook is more your thing, join the Sarah Hegger Collective

Anything and everything you need to know on my website http://sarahhegger.com

About the Author

Born British and raised in South Africa, Sarah Hegger suffers from an incurable case of wanderlust. Her match? A hot Canadian engineer, whose marriage proposal she accepted six short weeks after they first met. Together they've made homes in seven different cities across three different continents (and back again once or twice). If only it made her multilingual, but the best she can manage is idiosyncratic English, fluent Afrikaans, conversant Russian, pigeon Portuguese, even worse Zulu and enough French to get herself into trouble.

Mimicking her globe trotting adventures, Sarah's career path began as a gainfully employed actress, drifted into public relations, settled a moment in advertising, and eventually took root in the fertile soil of her first love, writing. She also moonlights as a wife and mother. She currently lives in Ottawa, Canada, filling her empty nest with fur babies. Part footloose buccaneer, part quixotic observer of life, Sarah's restless heart is most content when reading or writing books.

Praise for Sarah Hegger

Drove All Night
"The classic romance plot is elevated to a modern-day, wholly accessible real-life fairy tale with an excellent mix of romantic elements and spicy sensuality."
Booklife Prize, Critic's Report

Positively Pippa
"This is the type of romance that makes readers fall in love not just with characters, but with authors as well."
Kirkus Review (Starred Review)

"What begins as a simple second-chance romance quickly transforms into a beautiful, frank examination of love, family dynamics, and following one's dreams. Hegger's unflinching, candid portrayal of interpersonal and generational communication elevates the story to the sublime. Shunning clichés and contrived circumstances, she uses realistic, relatable situations to create a world that readers will want to visit time and again."
Publisher's Weekly, Starred Review

Hegger's utterly delightful first Ghost Falls contemporary is what other romance novels want to grow up to be." – Publisher's Weekly, Best Books of 2017

"The very talented Hegger kicks off an enjoyable new series set in the small Utah town of Ghost Falls. This charming and fun-filled book has everything from passion and humor to betrayal and revenge." – Jill M Smith, RT Books Reviews 2017 – Contemporary Love and Laughter Nominee

Becoming Bella
"Hegger excels at depicting familial relationships and friendships of all kinds, including purely platonic friendships between women and men. Tears, laughter, and a dollop of suspense make a memorable story that readers will want to revisit time and again." Publisher's Weekly, Starred Review

"...you have a terrific new romance that Hegger fans are going to love. Don't miss out!" Jill M. Smith – RT Book Reviews

Blatantly Blythe
"Ms. Hegger has delivered another captivating read for this series in this book that was packed with emotion..." Bec, Bookmagic Review, Harlequin Junkie, HJ Recommends.

Nobody's Fool
"Hegger offers a breath of fresh air in the romance genre." – Terri Dukes, RT Book Reviews

Nobody's Princess
"Hegger continues to live up to her rapidly growing reputation

for breathing fresh air into the romance genre." – Terri Dukes, RT Book Reviews

"I have read the entire Willow Park Series. I have loved each of the books … Nobody's Princess is my favorite of all time." Harlequin Junkie, Top Pick

Also by Sarah Hegger

www.ingramcontent.com/pod-product-compliance
Lightning Source LLC
Chambersburg PA
CBHW071153100726
47908CB00002B/365